THE WITHERED ROOTS

BOOK TWO OF THE MALICE OF LIGHT

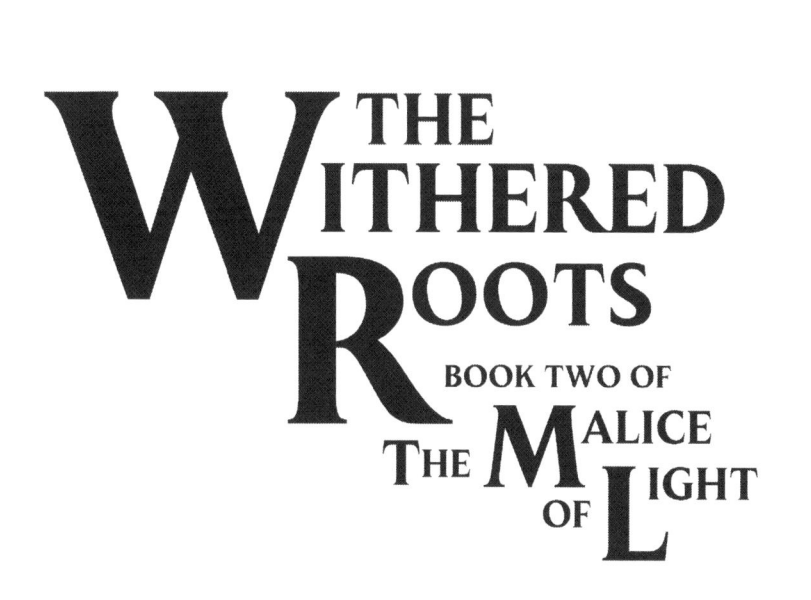

BRADY J. SADLER

This is a work of fiction. Names, characters, business, events and incidents are the products of the author's imagination. Any resemblance to actual persons, living or dead, or actual events is purely coincidental.

Copyright © 2024 by Brady J. Sadler

www.bradyjsadler.com

Cover art by Evan Simonet

All rights reserved.

No portion of this book may be reproduced in any form without written permission from the publisher or author, except as permitted by U.S. copyright law.

ISBN: 978-0-9853679-5-4 (eBook)
ISBN: 978-0-9853679-6-1 (Hardcover)
ISBN: 978-0-9853679-7-8 (Paperback)

Also by Brady J. Sadler
www.bradyjsadler.com

The Days of Astasia
Eve of Corruption (2012)

The Malice of Light
The Acrid Sky (2023)
The Withered Roots (2024)
The Smoldering Vein (Forthcoming)

Relic Meyers
Relic Meyers & The Rhythms of Ruin (2024)

AETHA

VAINA

COPERA
VALE
NOVETH
EASTLUND
GUYEN
WESTERRA
KARRANE

THE VALK SEA

LAUSTREAL

NOVETH

For my son, Oliver.

I love you, man.

Thank you for everything you've taught me.

PROLOGUE
The Sixth Scion

Six years before Desmond Everton would have the skin flayed from his body, he sat comfortably in the shade of a giant oak tree. There was no ash around his eyes, but they were still distant, looking for something far away from his life in Sathford.

He had thought Raventhal Spire would be enough for him, but his first eight months in the academy had shown him that he was too good for the place. He excelled at every area of lore and had begun to even outperform his professors.

Restlessness was settling in again.

Yes, Desmond was bound for amazing things. The memories of Verenshire—the seat of House Everton in Eastlund—seemed so far away, but as he stared up at a pristine sky framing the avian statues decorating each tier of Raventhal Spire, his mind started to drift to home, and to the brothers who drove him away.

Gryphin, Warrik, and Jaimy Everton were largely responsible for Desmond's flight from his family home, so he should perhaps be grateful for the cruelties they had inflicted upon him since birth. Without their constant disparagement, he may not have accomplished so much at such a young age. But he harbored nothing but resentment and disdain for his kin. His mother alone taught him about love, but her passing left him with hard men who had no patience for his peculiarities.

Desmond closed his eyes and breathed in the autumn air, appreciating how far he had come from those cold days in the iron lands.

"Well, if it isn't the next Archmage, in the flesh!"

Desmond clenched his eyes even tighter against the sun, trying not to give the ridiculer the satisfaction of any visible reaction. The inevitable laughter came regardless. Without risking a glance, Desmond knew who had joined him in the solitude of the courtyard.

He pictured with perfect clarity the weaselly gnome Kolm Rofly chewing on a stalkweed, staying a few bouncy steps ahead of the others—the others being the beautiful elf, Layla Abrigale, and the human twin brothers from Westerra, Owen and Oakley Harver. The group was as inseparable as they were insufferable, especially when it came to tormenting their betters.

Kolm was the main antagonist, seeming to love nothing more than to invent new ways to shame or embarrass Desmond, but his company only ever fueled the harassment. Each of them even reminded Desmond of his brothers—with the exception of Layla. The gnome had a rodent face like Jaimy, his youngest brother, while the twins were broad-faced like Gryphin and Warrick, a pair that also just happened to look like twin brothers.

"My lord of Everton," the high-pitched mocking voice continued, "I don't suppose you would mind if we crossed your royal lands here."

Owen's southern drawl was punctuated by his dumb chuckles as he added, "Don't you want a front-row seat for the Archmage's arrival? Maybe you can impress him enough to be whisked away to the Arcania to serve as his apprentice."

Failing to maintain his composure, Desmond's eyes opened at the mention of Fainly Lopke, the Archmage of the Arcania in Andelor. *The Archmage here?* He got to his feet, adjusting his gray robes so that the green stole hanging around his shoulders was prominent—his peers still wore their white ones to mark the lack of progress in their studies.

"Look at him," came a soft voice that was cruel poison to Desmond's ears, "just can't wait to be the first one to kiss the teacher's ass."

Desmond raised his eyes only slightly toward Layla—he was never able to resist her—and instantly regretted it. While he had never seen someone as beautiful, he had also never known anyone to be more cruel.

Layla Abrigale was soft and round while most elves Desmond had seen near the borders between Eastlund and Lohkrest Woods were hard and sinewy. She wore her hair short, just long enough to tuck behind her elegant elven ears. It seemed the most vile form of punishment for Desmond to be tormented by someone who was everything he could ever imagine wanting in a mate.

She gave him another mocking look as her group passed by, making their way toward the southern vestibule. Desmond waited, not wanting to accompany them to the gathering. While he had not been at Raventhal long enough to know how these surprise visits would go, there were whispers around the spire that the Archmage was known to visit the various academies across the Joined Realms unannounced to seek out pupils who might be worthy to join the Arcania in Andelor.

Desmond impatiently ran his thumbs over his twitching fingertips as he tried to maintain an uncaring posture—at least until the others had left him. He desperately wanted to sprint ahead of them, to possibly be seen by Fainly Lopke. While Raventhal had been a good escape for him—better than Eastlund, at least—he aspired to better things, and the Arcania was the gateway.

Finally, Layla and her companions slipped through the great onyx doors that marked the passage to Blackwing Hall. It wasn't until just then—alone—that Desmond finally realized why he had the courtyard to himself. Clearly, rumor had quickly spread of the Archmage's appearance, and no one told Desmond.

Desmond the pariah. Desmond the gifted. Desmond the recluse.

He took a moment in that solitude to remind himself of his destiny, the greatness that awaited him. *Every truly great person has had to endure this*, he told himself. *How is greatness earned if not alone, forged in the deepest misery?*

One of the thousands of ravens drawn to the school's towers cawed above as it took wing, breaking Desmond's reverie. He pushed his hair back and made his way toward the dark doors.

The southern vestibule matched each of the other three inner passages that connected the courtyard to the three towers that encircled the spire. Though "towers" was a generous term. Blackwing Hall, much like Harrow Hall and Shreath Hall, was less a tower and more a decorative turret to provide access to Raventhal's vast undercroft.

As Desmond quickly crossed the vestibule, he could hear rising voices from across the common room. When he entered, he saw not a single person sitting in any of the room's lavish furnishings; instead, there was a press of students clogging up the decorative arch that led to the stairs. Kolm was pushing his way through the legs of the taller students, while the Harver twins forcefully shoved other gray-robed peers out of the way. Layla was on her tiptoes trying to see.

"Come now," High Mage Konrath's voice bellowed, "make a path for the Archmage. He didn't travel all this way to be accosted by the entire academy." There was a jovialness to his tone that sent a wave of chuckles through the gathered students as the crowd began to part.

Desmond froze, standing in the center of the common room and feeling altogether on display as the sea of gray, green, yellow, and blue robes moved to reveal three figures approaching him.

High Mage Konrath Hoon was a tall human in his fifth decade, powerfully built with long graying hair falling to his shoulders. He had a youthfulness to his chiseled face, despite its aged crevices and the salt-and-pepper stubble that adorned his broad jaw. He offered warm smiles to those who had come to witness the Archmage's arrival.

Master Audreese Groaves was the palest elf Desmond had ever seen. There were few Masters at Raventhal, but Audreese was simultaneously the most renowned and the most reclusive, choosing to stay underground where she could continue studying the twisting passages of the Old Ways. Now, she stalked behind the short Archmage and his Chosen, her eyes lowered in a way that reminded Desmond of the strange kinship he felt with her.

Desmond's eyes moved from Master Audreese to the Archmage himself, Fainly Lopke. The gnome was a living legend, and despite his own cynical ways, Desmond found himself awestruck. While the man was the height of a human child, his presence was overwhelming. Like most gnomes, he had slightly protruding round ears, a bulbous nose, and cunning eyes that could see something beyond Desmond's human sight.

Those eyes bore through Desmond now, and his mouth went dry.

"This is him?" Fainly stopped mid-step, eyes fixed on Desmond. He had his arms behind his back, his head tilted slightly.

Konrath was turned around speaking to another student when he noticed the Archmage had stopped. He turned toward Desmond and gave a knowing smile. "Ah, you've found our Desmond Everton. Came to us from Eastlund—Verenshire, no less. Quite an unremarkable place to produce such potential. Desmond here earned his first green mark within his first week of joining the academy."

Fainly's face was stone. "Impressive. Tell me, Desmond, what brought you to the Spire?"

The question caught Desmond entirely off guard. He had not expected to be questioned by the Archmage immediately upon meeting him. While he had imagined this encounter many times since joining the academy, he felt completely unprepared now to even open his mouth.

There was a long uncomfortable silence while the gnome locked eyes with Desmond. Whispers began to blossom, which quickly erupted into chatter amongst the gathered students, until finally Kolm offered a suggestion.

"He came to take your job!"

The jab came with a wave of laughter and Desmond could feel his face redden. He clenched his fists and felt heat rising behind his eyes. But before that flood of emotions could break the dam and force him to cry in front of his peers and idols, Fainly turned from Desmond to address the rest of the students.

"And should he take my job, what do you suppose he would have done with you all?"

Kolm's arrogant smile withered and his face sagged in sudden shame. The younger gnome's abashed look cooled the angry flames threatening to break Desmond. But that relief was short-lived; Fainly returned his gaze to Desmond, waiting for a reply.

He opened his mouth, shifting his sight from the Archmage to High Mage Konrath, then finally to Master Audreese. The elf was looking straight at Desmond, uncharacteristically holding his gaze. Something about the look in those dark eyes emboldened Desmond, and his own gaze returned to Archmage Lopke, cold and knowing.

"Greatness," Desmond said.

Fainly seemed pleased with that answer, the corner of his mouth curling slightly. "I look forward to seeing your demonstration."

"Yes," High Mage Konrath stepped toward the gnome, "I believe we have enough here—everyone, listen! I have an announcement!" The Chosen's powerful voice stopped all murmuring. "Tomorrow there will be a demonstration in the atrium. Initiates, you are to bring your assigned keyshards to perform a single focus spell or conjuration. Accepted, you are to..."

The High Mage's voice faded as Desmond's mind wrestled with news. *A demonstration!* This was his chance. He had always secretly believed he would have the opportunity to prove himself to the Arcania, so he may someday be accepted in those prestigious halls. But he never would have imagined the chance would come before he even earned his third green mark.

He surveyed the other students in the hall who were visibly panicked and shocked by this revelation. The Harver twins were looking to each other for reassurance that they hadn't misheard. Layla was nervously biting her nails. Kolm cursed through clenched teeth.

Their collective misery delighted Desmond. Newfound inspiration and determination flowed through him, carrying him from the common hall as if in a trance. He didn't remember passing by any of his nervous peers, they were nothing to him right now. His thoughts were purely on the demonstration and how he could properly show his mastery of focus magic.

As he walked back to his quarters, he wondered which of his keyshards he would use for the demonstration. Initiates were allowed a single minor keyshard for each trial they passed—Desmond had one of each already, but favored his blue shard of Eyen. While minor keyshards held significantly less arcane power than lesser keyshards, they were still a challenge for mages unaccustomed to working with foci.

Focus magic was the primary type of magic practiced in the world, and it involved drawing trapped arcane power out of an attuned object—called a focus—and maintaining control over it, which was the primary challenge. Desmond had seen many of his peers injure themselves and others while trying to control whatever they unleashed from their keyshards. But to Desmond, control had always felt natural. He credited that to his powerful mind, which his father had always said was "aimlessly wandering."

"What was that all about?"

Desmond recoiled, but let out an annoyed sigh when he saw an elf girl's scowling face peering out of one of the dormitory's many doors. Fallon Shaw was a child, but the closest thing Desmond had to a friend. Yet, he rarely had patience for someone so untalented and undisciplined. She couldn't even be bothered to attend the Archmage's arrival!

Stopping briefly at her door, Desmond told her about the demonstration tomorrow. "It should be fairly entertaining."

The girl did not share his enthusiasm, her face displaying the same horror that the other students offered in response to the news. "Master Blane took my keyshard—said I would have to earn it all over again."

"Yes," Desmond said with annoyance, "well that is what happens when you conjure up roots that nearly strangle a halfling—not that Brynt wasn't partially to blame for that. You shouldn't have taken him on the challenge."

Fallon twisted her mouth, biting off any response. "I bet you're excited. Getting to show off in front of the Archmage—that should land you in the Arcania soon enough." She gave him a sad look, as if expecting something in response.

"Yes," he offered as he turned toward his door across the hall from her quarters. "The sooner I'm in Andelor, the better."

As he opened the door to his quaint sleeping cell, Desmond was greeted by a kitten's meek cry. On the bed, Cinder popped up to stretch as his master entered the dismal room. He was a bright orange cat with ratty fur. Desmond had found the little thing on one of his rare excursions outside Raventhal's walls. Cinder had been huddled in a corner, wet and hungry. Desmond brought the cat back to his room, even though students technically weren't supposed to keep pets.

Desmond sat down so Cinder could hop onto his lap, where the kitten curled up in his gray robes to sleep some more. As he sat there petting the only thing he had ever truly loved, Desmond began to ponder. He had never known a creature so pathetic and dependent as his sweet Cinder, and it gave him an idea.

He reached over to a wooden box that rested under the small table behind him. As he dragged it across the floor, Cinder jerked, but curled back up when he saw that it wasn't a predator. Desmond opened the box to reveal his keyshards, small and colorful jagged gems. Reaching in, he plucked an amber colored shard and held it up to his pet, surprised to see how similar in color they were.

Syrina, he thought. *Now that would impress.* Of all the magic locked in those shards, it was said beast magic was by far the wildest and hardest to master—probably because not many tried. Many aspiring wizards care only about calling up flames or summoning winds; few sought to command creatures of the wild.

Desmond began to smile wickedly. "How would you like to be part of a demonstration, Cinder?" The cat continued to purr in absolute contentment.

The next day, Desmond waited in the atrium's side hall as Oakley Harver embarrassed himself in front of the entire academy while trying to empty the contents of a water pitcher with his aquamarine keyshard. As usual, he couldn't even make the water ripple.

"How long they going to let him do this?" his brother asked under his breath. "He looks like an idiot!"

Desmond was alone with Layla, Owen, and Kolm, the last demonstrators of the day. It had been a long line of embarrassments. Only two other students managed to properly display their aptitude for focus thus far, and Desmond was certain his display would put theirs to shame. He couldn't help smiling.

"What's so entertaining?" Kolm asked, squaring up to Desmond as if his presence would somehow threaten the taller boy.

"All of you," Desmond said without pause, staring down at Kolm's weasel face. "You all amuse me with your colossal ineptitude. Can't even conjure a spark between the lot of you."

Kolm seethed, his legs seemed to buckle under the unexpected retort. "That so, Lord Everton? You're just so great, aren't you—above us all!"

"That's right," Desmond said, again without flinching. "I am better," he punctuated the words as he looked from Kolm to Layla, "than each and every," to Owen, and finally back to Kolm, "one of you."

"Owen Harver!"

"Damn," Owen said under his breath, then turned to offer Desmond a disgusted glare. "Be great all you want, Everton, just do it alone." He spun around to face his fate in the atrium.

Kolm turned away as well, skulking back to the shadows. Only Desmond and Layla remained, and the elf was looking at him strangely now.

"I think you're right, Desmond," Layla said, stepping toward him, her mouth hanging open almost...lustily.

But that can't be, Desmond assured himself. Surely this was another means to mock him. His logical thoughts fell away though as she reached out and rested a hand on his chest, over his suddenly racing heart. She stepped even closer, pushing her body against him now. Desmond had no choice but to step back against the wall, but she stepped with him. *What's happening?* His thoughts raced—he'd never been in such a position.

Before he could rationalize it more, his eyes became locked on Layla's. She was so beautiful, that everything—the demonstration, his aspirations, the Archmage—fell away as he became lost in her mesmerizing eyes. He wanted nothing more than her, he now realized with perfect clarity; her presence was the source of his misery because he couldn't have her.

But now he did.

Breathless, he licked his lips. "What are you doing?" he whispered.

She only smiled, her tongue brushing her upper lip. Desmond felt her hands suddenly, working their way into his robes. His body reacted accordingly, and he felt himself stiffen. One of Layla's hands found what it was looking for, and Desmond gasped, closing his eyes against whatever these overpowering sensations were.

He thought he wanted her to stop, but his body certainly never wanted her to. *Don't ever let this stop*, he thought miserably.

"You are great, Desmond," she whispered. "You are destined for great things." She stood on her toes to whisper even softer, her lips nearly touching his, "And I cannot wait to see you fuck it all up."

The world grew cold then, despite the heat now overtaking his body. He opened his eyes to see that cruel grin spread across Layla's perfect lips. "Good luck out there," she nodded down to his robes. "Don't break anything."

Desmond looked down to see what she—and now Kolm, stepping back into view—found so amusing. His robes now protruded awkwardly, displaying the results of Layla's natural charms.

"Desmond Everton!"

Oh no. Desmond's mind raced, unsure how to proceed. Of all the things he had mastered at the spire, this was certainly not something he had been prepared for. How could he possibly focus on the demonstration? He glared vilely at Layla and Kolm, who were now beside themselves, covering their mouths so the entire assembly did not hear their mocking.

Despite it all, he could not shake the thought of Layla's touch. It was a poison to his mind now, and it crept into his every racing thought. His body would not relax. He adjusted himself as much as he could and walked carefully to the atrium.

As he stepped in front of the gathered peers, he saw a sea of blank faces staring at him. Up front, seated at a long table were the High Mage, Master Audreese, and the Archmage himself. "We understand you needed an assistant for your demonstration," Konrath said, motioning toward the other wall. Fallon Shaw stood up with Cinder tucked carefully against her chest. The young elf made her way to Desmond, giving him a confused look.

"You alright?" she whispered as she handed over the kitten.

Desmond just stared at her, trying not to move too much. He was partially hunched over, awkwardly taking Cinder as the cat gave a weak yowl. Reaching his other hand into his robes, he felt his keyshard and tightened his fist around it. While certain parts of his body would not obey his command, he was determined to appropriately control the magic within.

Fallon hurried back to her seat, and Desmond just stood there holding the cat. Someone coughed in the distance and someone else chuckled.

"What do you have for us?" Archmage Fainly Lopke asked with a level voice.

Something about the way the gnome addressed him emboldened Desmond, and despite the stiffness that would not yield, the rest of his body relaxed slightly. Taking a knee, Desmond set Cinder carefully on the carpeted ground. The cat let out a weak meow again and found a seat on one of the carpet's floral patterns.

"I have chosen to demonstrate how to focus command a creature to do my bidding," he said, his voice thick with restrained anger and unrequited passion. Drawing the keyshard out of his robes, he kept it clenched in his fist. He closed his eyes and tried to focus, but all he could see in his mind was Layla licking her lips and grabbing his—

Cinder yowled in response. Desmond opened his eyes and saw that cat stretching and digging its claws into the carpet. *I'll be careful*, Desmond thought, closing his eyes again to try focusing once more. He pictured Cinder standing on his front legs, picking his back legs up to a wave of gasps and applause from his peers.

But instead he heard snickering from the hallway behind him where Layla and Kolm still gloated over their wicked deception. A burning rage kindled within Desmond, stoked hotter by the blood that flowed to his midsection, churning his stomach.

Cinder let out another weak meow, followed by a strange whining sound from his throat. Desmond wouldn't let himself get distracted. He clenched his eyes tighter and focused on the bestial power within the keyshard, channeling it into his desire for Cinder to prop himself up on his damned front legs and finish this miserable episode.

Fires raged behind Desmond's eyes, and he grit his teeth against the tears that began to well. Cinder's whining took on a more desperate tone, and gradually became more painful. The smell of burning hair preceded the chaos.

It started with a distant "Desmond..." that was on the edge of his hearing, drowned out by the blood pumping in his ears. His intense focus meant for the demonstration's spell instead coiled within his stomach, threatening to erupt. Layla's face still danced in his vision, and he imagined a white-hot blade gathering from his twisted guts, driving it into the elf.

In his mind Layla gasped in pain and ecstasy, and the atrium exploded into screams. Desmond jerked his eyes open, finally free of the spell that was consuming him and he saw Cinder thrashing about on the carpet as flames devoured the poor creature.

Desmond froze in terror as Master Audreese threw her red robes over the fiery remains and High Mage Konrath knelt down to inspect the ruin. Feeling a burning in his hand, Desmond opened his clenched fist to see a bright and shiny ruby where he expected to see his amber keyshard. Sudden laughter drew his attention back to the hall, and he saw Kolm howling and falling to his knees, pointing at the horrific scene. Layla stood wide-eyed with her hands over her mouth.

Slowly the realization set in, and Desmond played the events from just moments ago back through his mind. While Layla distracted him, Kolm reached his mischievous hand into Desmond's robes and swapped his keyshard of Syrina for one of Wick's—and fire was the easiest of the focus magics. Most mages could summon a spark without even meaning to, especially in the throes of battle.

Or of passion.

As Desmond's stomach roiled, ready to empty itself onto the burned carpet, his hateful eyes glared at Layla who played the fool, acting shocked by the misery she had orchestrated. Now that all the passion she had instilled within him had finally died away, Desmond scrambled to his feet, letting the keyshard fall to the floor as he fled the atrium.

Even in his haste, Desmond couldn't help but notice the Archmage—still calmly seated—watching with concentrated interest.

Later that evening outside the High Mage's study on the highest floor of the spire, the two initiates awaited their punishment. While Kolm seemed unbothered, lounging on the stiff sofa as if he were awaiting a meal, Layla was on the verge of tears.

She turned to the gnome. "How could you?!"

"Oh, you know he had it coming," Kolm said. "He's a pompous noble who thinks he's above us all. He needs to be brought down a bit. It'll do him good."

Layla just stared at him, feeling a growing revulsion just sitting this near to such a wicked boy. "That poor cat...how can you laugh? That was horrible!"

Kolm scoffed. "We'll get him a new cat, there are dozens down by the docks. I didn't know he'd immolate the thing. I just thought maybe he'd singe its whiskers or something. Honestly, I could never get that shard to even toast my bread—thought it had been drained."

"It was drained."

They turned to see High Mage Konrath standing before the doors to his study, which had been opened without their noticing. The Archmage stood beside Konrath, his hands behind his back and his face devoid of emotion.

Konrath's face, however, was full of fury. He held out an open hand and in his palm rested a small, dull red keyshard. "I am not sure how you failed to notice or report, Rofly, that your keyshard was dead, but your little trick did not work."

Confused, Layla looked to the keyshard and then to Kolm, who just frowned.

"What do you mean?" Kolm asked. "He burned that thing up."

This time Fainly spoke. "Yes, he did. But he did so without the aid of a focus. Whether or not he knew what you had done—switching out an initiate's keyshard is a dangerous and tired prank, if you ask me—you apparently angered him so much that you allowed him to ascend two ranks with a single stroke."

"Yes," Konrath said, closing his fist. "He should be thanking you two. Without your encouragement, he may not have mastered the skills to pass an Accepted's trial, but now he is on that path." As he crossed his arms across his broad chest, he added, "However, I do not think it likely he will thank you, as you will be confined to custodial duties below the spire, under Master Audreese's watch."

"For how long?" Kolm asked in a whiny voice.

Fainly stepped forward. "Be glad it is not worse. My Chosen has a soft spot for his students, but if you pulled such reckless and foolish pranks while under my watch at the Arcania, expulsion would be the only option."

Kolm swallowed and averted his eyes to the floor.

"And you," Fainly said, switching his focus to Layla. "Do not attach yourself to such wretched company. The High Mage tells me you show promise. Do not piss it away by playing such stupid games."

Layla hung her head. The High Mage added his own thoughts to Fainly's, but Layla could hardly comprehend the words. She was drowning in shame by the time she got to her feet and walked to the stairs. They were not allowed to take the Chosen's Gate, which led directly to the first floor. Instead, they were forced to spend the rest of their evening descending the tall tower.

Kolm prattled on about how no one had a sense of humor anymore, but Layla fell back to walk in solitude. Her thoughts were on Desmond. She wondered how it had come to this—what had made her so set on embarrassing him? Was it the approval of Kolm or the Harvers? She doubted it.

Perhaps she did resent Desmond's talent, much like she knew Kolm did. But could that truly be it? She had a lot to figure out and was suddenly glad for the long descent that lay ahead of her.

Desmond ignored the soft tap at his door. Night had fallen, and he hoped whoever it was would assume he was asleep and leave him be. But it came again, almost softer this time.

"Desmond." Fallon's voice was normally meek, but it was barely even audible beyond the door. "I thought you might want...well, I'll just leave it here outside your door."

There was a long pause before she added, "I'm so sorry."

Desmond barely heard her as he sunk deeper into his misery, not sure if it was rage or sadness that was consuming him. He couldn't stop hearing the final wails of Cinder—whose name now felt like some cruel jape at his expense.

There was no real telling how much time had passed before the knock came again.

"Go away," he snapped this time, wanting only solitude.

But the knock came again, soft but followed quickly by another, and then another, until there was a consistent tapping. Desmond sat up in his bed as the sound became a rapid stream of impossibly fast taps. He felt he had no choice but to investigate. As he threw the door open, he was shocked to see the Archmage standing before him.

The gnome regarded him kindly, his hands cradling a decorative container which he now presented up to Desmond. "This was left at your door."

Desmond regarded him with confusion, wondering how he had knocked. But he remembered this was the Archmage and reached to take the object. It was an elegant wooden bowl with a lid, sealed with hempen rope and decorated with imagery of trees and vines—clearly a vessel of Oakus.

Fainly must have seen the confusion on Desmond's face. "I suspect it is the remains of your...familiar."

The realization sent another stab of pain through him, but he was grateful for Fallon. A sudden wave of guilt crashed over him as he reflected on how dismissively he had treated her. But he didn't have the time to dwell on it.

"I have something else for you," Fainly said. "May I perhaps come in?"

Desmond stepped back and motioned for him to come in, embarrassed by his meager quarters. His cell was devoid of decoration—a basic mattress on the floor, a simple desk against the wall, and stacks of books occupying the rest of the space.

"This reminds me of my own room in the Xoatian Academy on Caim," Fainly said as he stepped into the room. "Sometimes I miss those days."

Desmond wasn't sure what to say. He stood awkwardly, holding the remains of his cat, waiting to hear what the Archmage had to say about the demonstration.

Once again, as if sensing Desmond's thoughts, Fainly turned, his arms behind his back. "I sense something in you, Desmond—something your peers will always lack. You have...an affinity."

Desmond just stared, completely unsure of what was expected of him.

Fainly reached into his robes and produced a small black book. "You do not strike me as one who fears knowledge. And if I were to assume—I would say you also do not have patience for those who do not understand your capabilities?"

Desmond's eyes became fixed on that book. He was unsure of what it was, but something told him that it held the answers he sought. His desire to read it was sudden and palpable.

Fainly held it out to him. "I ask that you read this and study it. Do not fear its contents. I believe it holds the power that was meant for you and you alone."

Those words echoed in his head—"for you and you alone"—and he reached out to take the book without asking any questions.

"Embrace it, Desmond," Fainly said, holding his gaze as he kept his grip on the book. Both mages held the book, feeling its ancient power. "Do not shy from its promises."

Desmond nodded, and Fainly released it.

"You have a gift, Desmond," Fainly said with a crooked grin. "I look forward to seeing you at the Arcania once you tire of this place."

The rest of Fainly's visit was lost to Desmond. He was reeling as the worst day of his life suddenly transformed into the greatest night of his life. He was honored by the Archmage, who almost personally invited him to the Arcania. And the gifts—

After Fainly had left the room, Desmond stared at the vessel that held Cinder's remains and the strange black book. He set them both on his desk, each one representing distinctively different emotions that warred within him. The bowl that Fallon had gifted him marked his grievous past while the black book whispered of a glorious destiny.

He was drawn to the book—its cover was a deep, absorbing black—and he opened it carefully. Inside, its pages were crammed with intricate writing—arcane instructions, he could tell. These were incantations—old ritualist magic that he had read about from the Ghultan empire.

As he read the words frantically, he felt something rising within him. Mindlessly, as his eyes rapidly followed the flowing scripts, his hands opened the container that Fallon had left him. He felt tears welling in his eyes as he read the ancient spell that would give him the validation he knew he deserved.

The tears streamed down his face as he read on, and he coated his hands in the ashes of his only true friend in this world. He began to mouth the words over and over that would give him dominion over those who did not deserve to question him. As his reached up to wipe away the tears with Cinder's ashes, he left ghoulish black smears down his face.

Another knock at the door threatened to interrupt the ritual, but Desmond kept chanting the words that he already memorized as he stood up to answer. Opening the door, he saw the subject of his curse, her head hanging in shame.

"Desmond," Layla said weakly, unable to face him, "I just wanted to…"

She trailed off as she looked up to him, seeing the black streaks running from his ashen eyes and his mouth inhumanly reciting words at impossible speeds.

The sight of his eyes rolled back in his head must have terrified her, because she opened her mouth to scream.

But she couldn't; she couldn't do anything now unless Desmond commanded it. The spell was done, and Desmond's face relaxed. His sight was now set on Layla, whose terror had fled. She looked at him seductively. As she stepped into his room, she began removing her robes.

Fainly watched from the end of the hall as the door to Desmond's chamber slowly shut,

"There's your sixth scion, Ruke," he said defeatedly. "I hope you know what you're doing."

The Archmage faded into the dark of night as Desmond gave himself completely to the Shadow.

Chapter One

Homecoming

In the cold cell, Anika dreamed of Matty. Her shackles wouldn't allow her to move much, so she remained curled up on a meager pile of hay and chose to be elsewhere.

The dreams were vivid, for which she was thankful. Matty was alive, and he held her in powerful arms that kept her true memories far away. They spent an entire night laying under the stars along the banks of the Bracing River, just outside of Blakehurst. Eating Ransil's rabbit stew and sharing a cask of ale from The Early Mule, it was a perfect evening.

But there was no wind.

It was a dead world she dreamed of, as much as she wished it were real. Even as she slept, she knew it was folly to wish it all were true.

"You're dead," she told Matty in the dream.

He smiled. "I know. But we lived." He reached up and brushed a tear off her face. "I'm not a greedy man, and I'm grateful for what you gave me."

"Anika," a voice called.

She turned away from Matty in the dream, looking for the source. But darkness surrounded her. When she turned back to Matty, it was her brother Gage next to her, with blood splattered all over his face.

"I'm grateful for what you took from me," Gage said coldly. "You chased my mother away, Anika. It was you—the Light within you. You drove her away, and I'm grateful. Because you made me."

Gage suddenly produced a blade and drove it into Anika's heart.

She woke with a gasp, greeted by consuming darkness. The only shapes she could make out were framed by a distant torch that burned around the corner of the dungeon's long hall. There were nearly twenty vacant cells, with only herself and two thieves occupying this particular wing of the majest's prisons.

Anika had lost track of the days, but she couldn't have been here longer than a week. The shackles had been placed on her four—*or was it five?*—days ago when she had risked summoning Stormender back from the jailor's hands. The effort exhausted her, and she could barely even catch the knife as it spun back toward her. She had been backhanded for that stunt and put into irons. The jailor no longer carried the weapon in his belt.

Fortunately, that slap and the irons were truly the extent of the abuse she endured in that dark place. She counted herself fortunate, as the hulking jailor seemed to ignore her in favor of occasionally fondling the two prisoners—handsome, young Karranese men—in the other cells. It seemed an exchange of sorts, as those men seemed much better fed than Anika and were provided with long, flat pillows to sleep on. But she ate her hard bread and cold fish and slept in her rough bed of hay without complaint.

Time was elusive as she drifted from dreams to nightmares, finding no energy or desire to even move from the dirty hay except to occasionally relieve herself in the foul pan left for her in the corner of the cell. She quickly became accustomed to the rancid smells, which sadly reminded her of happier days in the tanning shed at home.

Thinking of Blakehurst was becoming too painful for her though, so she tried to direct her thoughts to the present. Since the events in Oakworth, it felt like she had been caught up in a storm—quite literally, in a sense. She remembered walking out of The Harvest Breeze in a haze, leaving her mother's body where she had found it. Part of her knew it had been Gage that killed her, but something else inside of her refused to accept that.

She remembered letting her head fall back and looking up to the sky, wanting nothing more than to escape the world that had started crumbling around her. She vaguely recalled drawing Stormender, feeling the winds gathering around her. But after that, she fell into a strange dream of soaring through the sky like a bird, seeing all of Noveth from a great height.

In that dream, she had felt an inexplicable sense of freedom and bliss, but also sadness and dread. She had never felt as small as she did when she saw the world through the eyes of a bird. So many places to go, but no direction or home. Every path was open to her up there, but where could she go?

Anika had eventually awakened in Cassith, a small nome on the outskirts of Pyram in Karrane. While Cassith was much larger than her home of Blakehurst, Anika would eventually find it to be dwarfed by Pyram, the nearby capital named for the great pyramid erected in Xe'danni fashion. It was on that remarkable monument that the first chamberlords built their premiere merchant city, and it was under its shadow that Anika had finally opened her eyes to see a kind old woman with skin a shade darker than her own sat near an open window.

"The child awakens," the old woman had said, without taking her attention away from the colored beads that she threaded onto what looked like a decorative shawl. "Falling from the sky would seem to be such a tiring affair."

Groggy as she was, Anika noted the soothing Karranese accent carrying the old woman's words. *No*, Anika thought, *that was a dream*. The flight must have been imagined; she could not fly. But her mouth was so raw she couldn't even produce a sound of argument.

"There's water there on the table," the woman had said, concentrating on her craft. "Drink slowly. Small sips."

Anika obeyed, difficult as it was. The moment the water touched her tongue, her instinct was to tip the cup back and swallow all she could. She remembered hearing some story from her youth about a mother wandering the deserts of Xe'dann only to discover an oasis. After nearly dying of thirst, the woman drank too much at once and died instead from the water itself. Anika always wondered if there was truth to the tale, but she sipped nonetheless.

With her thirst quenched, Anika began to examine her surroundings. She seemed to be in a normal quaint home, clearly far from Vale.

"I won't ask where you come from," the woman said, as if sensing Anika's thoughts. "However, if a nomarch asks, I must confess all I know. Those who do not confess face a month in the majest's prisons." The woman finally looked at Anika. "You may look Karranese, but your fashion and sudden arrival tells me this is not the home you're looking for."

As Anika struggled to think of a response, she watched the woman work. She was hunched and slightly crooked but had youthful eyes and nimble fingers. Once she may have been a beautiful woman, but now she was a relic. Whoever she was, Anika found her presence comforting, and sunk deeper in the cozy bed.

It was then that Anika realized that her body had a dull ache; it wasn't true pain, but the pleasant numbness that came after a much-needed rest. She sipped slowly again and asked, "How did I get here?"

The woman finally set her beadwork down in her lap, looking at Anika as if for the first time, her face soft with empathy. "No, I don't suppose you would remember. You fell from—"

"You," the jailor said, disturbing her memory, "up."

Anika opened her eyes to see the brawny jailor staring down at her. He held an ornamental lantern, producing more light than Anika had seen since her imprisonment. It took her eyes a moment to adjust, but when they did, she was surprised to see the jailor jamming a key into her cell's lock. With a twist of his wrist, the door's latch released, its hinges squealing in protest as her cell slowly opened.

As she struggled to sit up, she asked, "Where am I going?"

"Nowhere," a voice came from the darkness beyond the lantern's light. Metallic footsteps clicked against the stone floor in the shadows, and a figure stepped into view. The nomarch was clad in studded leather armor affixed with steel plates inlaid with precious stones. "Not until you answer my questions."

The woman stepped into the cell, now bathed in the lantern's soft glow. Anika could see the nomarch was maybe ten years her elder, but well-muscled and armed with two elegant sabers at her hips. The steel plates of her armor were decorated with swirling patterns, formed from flowing Karranese glyphs that Anika could not decipher.

"Shall we begin with your name, prisoner?"

The jailor hung the lantern and left the keys in the cell door before turning to leave them. Anika futilely adjusted what remained of her clothes, knowing full well she would not be able to make herself any more presentable. "My name is Anika."

The nomarch kept a level gaze, her eyes boring into Anika as if she could see the validity of her words. "That's no Karranese name—and your house's name?"

Anika sat up a little prouder. "Lawson."

The nomarch's brows tightened slightly. She had a similar complexion as Anika, but her hair was much coarser, tied into tight braids and falling to her shoulder like thin ropes. "You come from the iron lands, then? Were you a tallybride?"

If Anika remembered correctly, a tallybride was a woman who married to pay out a family debt. It was not a flattering thing to be called as she understood, but she was not overly concerned with propriety. "No, I was raised in Vale. My father was an Eastlund ranger."

The nomarch's expression remained hard. "Why were you found robbing a chamberlord? Do you know the punishment for such a crime?"

Anika weighed her words carefully. "I wasn't robbing her. I was looking for...someone."

"Who?"

Biting her lip, Anika looked at the stone floor, considering her current situation. If she lied, she may be able to bide her time and continue her search; if she told the truth, perhaps someone in Pyram would even help her find the answer she sought.

The nomarch spun on her heels. "Perhaps you need more time alone." She collected the lantern and began locking the cell.

Anika opened her mouth to protest, but her thoughts were spiraling out of her control, and she did not know what to say. Maybe she did need more time alone.

"I'll return only once more," the nomarch said, not unkindly. "Consider your responses well, as they could mean the difference between your freedom and a lifetime in the mines of Suthek. The majest has extended you as much patience as I'll allow." She turned the key, locking the cell. "You were found in my nome, and ultimately your fate is in my hands; you should be grateful they are just."

With that, she turned and the golden cloak she wore swirled elegantly and followed, leaving Anika in the darkness alone.

As she laid back down on the rough straw, Anika thought back to the old woman who had been so kind to her.

"—from the sky," the old woman finished. "My son, Halim, found you in the ruins of a pavilion outside his home. You were lucky he came upon you, as a girl such as yourself laying alone in the markets at that time of night...I thank the Light it was Halim—always my most noble son—who found you and not Makar...that one would have sold you to the pillowhouse for an ale and a copper. But no, Halim brought you here to recover, which I did not expect you to do. But you children are so defiant these days..."

Anika smiled at the memory, wishing she had trusted Zenese to begin with. If she had listened to the old woman, she would never have risked going into that chamberlord's manse. It was certainly foolish to think her mother had been a chamberlord.

It was even more foolish to think her mother was still alive.

Perhaps it was most foolish to think that there was a mother out there who wanted her at all. She curled up as that thought took hold, bringing fresh tears. Anika convinced herself that those tears were for the only mother she truly knew, Renay Lawson, whose body she left to rot alone in an empty room.

For Matty, who she let die on a desperate gambit to save her brother from some dark prophecy she wasn't even sure she believed in.

For Zenese, who gave her shelter and kindness, which Anika repaid with deceit.

But in truth, she cried for her father. In her consuming grief, she'd abandoned him and failed him. Wherever Bennik Lawson was, Anika could have flown there and rescued him. Together, they could have figured out what to do about Gage. Instead, she came here, and whatever power she may have had faded when Stormender was taken from her.

As sleep began to take her, she called out to the blade, but there was no answer. She was alone, and she had failed everyone she had ever loved. As darkness consumed her thoughts, the tears that came flooded her dreams with grief.

The knife spun suddenly, causing the majest to recoil from the table. His vizier held up a gnarled, shaking hand, motioning the majest to remain calm. The chamber was silent for a long moment, the only sound coming from the seabirds that bickered outside the large open doors facing the sea.

"Whatever power possesses it," the vizier advised, "is too weakened to take hold. We are seeing echoes of a craft, untrained and unguided."

Lekan Nafir cautiously sat back down in the golden seat at the head of the long table. His trusted councilors were convened, occupying the two seats nearest the majest, across from one another. Lekan was a young boy just crossing into manhood, and he watched the enchanted knife with nervous but spellbound eyes.

The ruler of Pyram was the picture of Karranese royalty. He wore a gem-encrusted vest and a thin crown of rose gold banded in silken decorative sashes of yellow, orange, and crimson. His skin was darker than many of his people, which commonly marked his birth as more closely traced back to the founders of Karrane.

To Lekan's left sat his vizier, a pale-skinned elderly elf who the majest now turned to face. "Elrin, have you ever seen a keyshard like this?"

He motioned to the gleaming sapphire that was affixed to the knife where the blade met the guard. The stone was polished smooth, not jagged like most keyshards the majest had seen. He had heard that polishing a keyshard would affect its potency, even drain it completely of its magic.

But this was something else.

"No," Elrin said, his dark almond-shaped eyes fixed on the weapon. "But there are others of my kin who may have. As I've admitted before, I have abstained from the feysleep, and my own life does not date back to the Unthroning when the Keys of Transience were shattered. But I believe there are those on Caim—in Fehir'whin and Xoatia—who would swear on their lives that this is a Key reforged."

Silence fell between Lekan and the two councilors, who both looked at the other for some additional explanation. The Keys of Transience were objects of legend, lost to time.

Finally Lekan spoke, "That would be a bold claim, would it not?"

Elrin raised his eyes. "Yes, your eminence. Bold and possibly blasphemous."

"Blasphemous?" Lightmother Taliah leaned across the table to motion to the blade. "How would a Key be blasphemous? Would it not be a miracle for such power to fall into our great city just as the chamberlords begin the usurpation of our dear majest?"

"The power would be a boon, yes," Elrin offered tightly, "but do you not consider the debt that comes with such power?"

Silence once more.

"Allow me to enlighten," Elrin said, pushing away from the table to slowly get to his feet. "At the behest of Stane, the Purveyors shattered the Keys to give birth to the Light. Which means the Light exists because the Keys were shattered." He paced behind the majest's high seat, stepping toward Taliah. "What sort of power do you think would have any interest in reforging the Keys?"

"Shadow?" Lekan whispered, as if afraid to speak the word in the Lightmother's presence.

Elrin raised a finger. "Astute, your eminence. Though I might say, any power that seeks to defy the Light."

"Or the Light itself," Taliah offered in response. "There is nothing in your books or mine, Elrin, that implies the Keys hold some sort of power over the Light, only that their existence restrained us from its blessed embrace."

The vizier stopped his pacing, his eyes locked on the Lightmother's in consideration.

Emboldened, Taliah reached toward the blade and tightened her dark hand around its grip. She held it up as the majest leaned away from her—but the vizier held his ground, watching for some sort of reaction from the blade.

"What if this is a weapon of the Light, delivered to us in our greatest hour of need?" she asked with a rising fervor.

"Then, I would ask," Elrin said calmly, "who would deliver us such a thing?"

Chapter Two

Runaways

They had kept a hurried pace since leaving Oakworth, hoping to stay ahead of the news. Given their connections, Ransil and Grip both knew how urgent it would be to get the most accurate report to the queen before she did anything rash based on hearsay. And there would be plenty of hearsay flowing out of Oakworth.

Aside from the accursed storm and the incarnate that nearly laid waste to the baron's keep, there was Anika's disappearance, her mother's murder, and her brother a primary suspect. Ransil wouldn't be surprised if Gage and Robin both had wanted posters with their likenesses in every inn and winesink along the Bracing River by now.

But he couldn't help them now. They had vanished just like Anika. There were reports of a woman taking to the sky with huge wings, shrieking or howling, depending on who you asked. But with the recent harpy attack, Ransil wasn't sure how much weight those claims carried. Regardless, his logical mind didn't prevent him from imagining the Anika he knew transforming into a monster like Corvanna.

Practicality had kept Ransil's thoughts in line during all the chaos. He focused on what he could accomplish now, so he might help Anika when the time came.

After parting with Anika that fateful morning, Ransil had immediately followed Grip back into the baron's secret library. They both knew they wouldn't have much time before the place was raided by the Cafferys' guards, eager to hide whatever schemes their lord had been brewing in the dark. The underground library had been filled with archaic tomes and ponderous ledgers, but Ransil and Grip procured a few important-looking documents and Shrouded paraphernalia that the Guild might be able to use and took their leave as chaos swept the town.

Wanting to avoid the main roads, Grip led them south so they could eventually cut through the Hollowood and cross the rural lands leading to Stelmont.

"It's safest if we get to the Wane Coast and take a ship up to Andelor," Grip explained during their flight. "I can find us a mount or two on the other side of Hollowood. There's a roadside inn run by Crane."

"She's still alive?" Ransil asked, huffing as he tried to keep up with the swift elf.

"Hopefully," Grip said, looking to the dark woods between them and Crane's establishment. "Goblins are one thing, but there are darker things I'd rather not face in those woods."

Regardless, they pressed on to put Oakworth well behind them.

Ransil had never felt so old. His legs were cramping miserably as he tried to keep up with Grip's long strides, but he didn't complain. If anything could be said about Ransil Osbury, it was that he could endure in silence.

"Do you want to perhaps ride on my shoulders?" Grip asked with a wicked grin. "I promise I won't fondle you much."

"This isn't Guyen," Ransil said flatly, breathing a sigh of relief as Grip slowed her pace. "And I don't see any dire serpents that could swallow me whole, so I'll make do on my own legs." The setting sun now lit their way along the borders of the Hollowood, but they would have to stop to rest—there was no way he would allow them to trek through that foul place in the dead of night.

Grip fell to a knee as she reached a fallen tree, her face now almost serious for a change. "This may not be a swamp, dear, but it doesn't mean these grasses are safe for halflings. It's fairly common for other foul beasts to lurk in the tall weeds, snatching up children who wander too far from the Valeway."

"We should rest while we can," Ransil said, catching his breath as he leaned against the fallen tree. "This isn't the most ideal place to camp, but it will have to do."

They both surveyed around, and aside from birds soaring across the sky and a deer grazing on a hill in the distance, they were alone between the Horin Hills and the foreboding trees to the west. Ransil unslung the small pack from his back, his iron pan clanging against the metal cups that dangled from it. He ran a hand through his hair to push it out of his eyes and scratched his scruffy jaw.

Sitting down, Grip reached a gloved hand to softly touch Ransil's furry cheek. "You don't shave these days, I see."

While his instinct was to smack her hand away, he resisted. They may have had their troubles in the past, but Grip had helped him and his friends when he needed her most. She had earned something from him—he wasn't sure what that was yet, but it certainly wasn't his disdain.

"I never shaved," he confessed. "Some halflings just can't grow beards until they become tired old grouches that chase after foolish young half-elves."

Grip chuckled at that, her lavender lips parting to reveal straight, white teeth. She was always the most beautiful person Ransil had ever known.

Ransil looked into her glass eye, suddenly feeling uncomfortable in a way he hadn't felt since they had first met in Caim, where she had lost her original eye. *So many years ago*, he thought. Turning away from her, he drew out his two daggers and tossed them in the grass next to his pack.

"I can get us something to eat," he said, kneeling down to inspect their rations.

"Where do you think she went?"

Ransil paused; he had hoped he wouldn't have to think about that yet. "I don't know. I can't begin to imagine what Anika's going through. She's lost everything," he turned to face Grip. "And if she's to believe the voices that are doubtless ringing in her head—it's all been taken from her by her brother."

Grip shook her head in disbelief. "What are the odds—the Child of Light and the Child of Shadow in the same village. Brother and sister, no less!"

"We don't know that," Ransil offered, but his words were hollow. Deep down, somehow, he knew the truth. Bennik never shared the entire story, but there was an incident with Gage and his mother that drove her from Blakehurst. Ransil played along with the story that she had died, but he knew something much darker lurked in the Lawsons' closet.

"I think you do," Grip said, reading his mind. "Regardless, there's something more at work here than just old prophecies. There are many of my kin that believed these Children were merely gifted wizard, able to work spells that others couldn't. While I share that opinion, ultimately, it doesn't matter." She crossed her legs and faced Ransil eye-to-eye. "These are pawns, my love. Pawns on a game board, and the players are going to pit them against one another."

Ransil felt the truth of that. Whatever Anika's destiny might be, she was still the kind-hearted girl that Ransil had seen grow up from a babe—raised by one of the finest men he had ever known.

"We have to find her," Ransil said, staring into Grip's enchanting, mismatched eyes. "I need your help, Grip. I can't let her fall into the wrong hands."

Grip reached out a gloved hand to take hold of Ransil's. The halfling grasped it with both of his. "We won't," she said. "We're both gamblers, and the odds are that she will eventually be drawn to Andelor—and that's where we'll go to wait for her. Where else would she go?"

Where else? Ransil wondered, having not a single clue. He hoped she might still hold out hope for her father, but there's no telling where Bennik would have been taken. Perhaps up north? Maybe Sathford, where it was said the harpies had ransacked Raventhal Spire looking for keyshards.

The world was enormous, and if Anika truly wielded the raw power of Eyen, controlling winds and storms, she could go anywhere. *Maybe the rumors of a flying, howling woman were true,* he thought miserably.

Grip moved a hand once more to his scruffy face, pulling his eyes back to hers. She leaned in and kissed him—not forcefully as before, during their unpleasant reunion, but softly. Ransil's hardened exterior melted away, and he felt like a boy again.

He let her tongue find his as she pulled him forward atop her. Grip reclined back in the long grass and Ransil felt helpless in her embrace. Thoughts of Anika, Gage, the incarnates, and the world crumbling around them seemed distant memories at that moment. His years of solitude in Blakehurst had suppressed his desire for love, but it threatened to drown him now. And he welcomed it.

In the distance, a wolf howled in the depths of the Hollowood, but the thieves ignored the gathering dark, making up for the lost years between them.

"Why would he take it?!" Fallon asked frantically, pacing across the earthen hall. They had been resting in the strange underworld while Naya recovered her strength, and they were to leave on the morrow. But Quinn had disappeared and her keyshard with him.

"Fear," Naya groaned, her energy still not entirely returned. She secretly cursed herself for not killing the boy herself when she saw the uncertainty in his eyes. The druid was hers entirely, she could sense it. But the boy had no conviction within him, only logic. All her life she had known men of logic—weak scholars who only believed what they could learn in a book. The boy was bound to thwart her plans one way or another.

She showed Quinn more mercy than anyone had ever shown her. Perhaps it was the loss of her hand, and the unpredictable sorrow that overcame her when she saw the ruin of Mosby in the Oakhold. In normal circumstances, she would not have hesitated murdering the boy if she believed he threatened the Shrouded. The thought of getting soft strengthened her own conviction, and she swore to herself that she wouldn't hesitate again.

"He fears what's to come," Naya added, getting to her feet. "He is a boy who thinks he can run and hide from the difficulties ahead. He is not like you, Fallon. You have seen why the Light must be stopped."

The druid didn't seem to hear her, lost in her own thoughts. "He knew that it was a gift from my father—he knew what it meant to me."

Anger found its way into Fallon's ranting, and Naya let herself smile as she cradled her aching stump. Despite the small setback, Quinn's folly may serve to further strengthen the young elf to her cause. The druids were already looked upon with suspicion by the Luminaura, so they should make likely allies for the Shrouded, if given the proper motivation. Naya knew she had to tread carefully.

While Fallon continued to pace angrily, Naya moved slowly toward her creation. The golems all stood lifeless around it, awaiting command, but Naya still lacked the strength to coordinate them. After the events in the baron's chambers, she was afraid to even touch the Shadow until she was sure Gage was far away and her mind was able to focus.

She reached out a hand to lay on its massive bulk. A mix of tree, mud, and roots, her champion was glorious to behold. When the Highshroud first explained the nature of the incarnates, Naya imagined gods made flesh—giant humanoid representations of the aspects they governed. In those imaginations, an incarnate of Oakus was a massive green giant, swollen with muscles which were corded with green vines and patched with moss.

But as she ran her hand over the rough flesh of her child, she now knew that a true incarnate had to be monstrous and inhuman—it needed to incite fear and reverence, not wonder and affection. To that end, Naya was proud of what she had managed to piece together in such a short time. It may be unfinished, but as she turned to Fallon, she was certain the time was drawing near.

"I have to go find him," Fallon said, finally acknowledging Naya's presence, her eyes seeking assurance. "Before he gets too far." She grabbed her twisted oaken staff, as if the foolish girl thought to navigate the Old Ways herself.

Naya raised a hand, attempting to calm both herself and the druid. Her patience was nearing its limit with the elf, but she could not deny her power—it was radiating from the druid in waves. She was delivered to Naya by the Shadow, of that much the priestess was certain. In a time of such desperate need, how could she doubt it?

"We will find him," Naya said with as much softness as she could muster. "I assure you, we will. Even now, I can feel him through the shard he carries." A lie came to her then, and she stepped closer, assuming the meekest presence she could so that she might appeal to the druid's sympathetic nature. "We know where he's bound to go."

Fallon looked up, surprised. "We do?"

"Of course," Naya said, forcing a kind smile. "He is a scared child. And where do scared children run to?"

Realization slowly washed over Fallon's face. She turned to look back down the dark tunnels of the Old Ways. "He can't get back into the spire. It's warded. Not even Master Audreese can enter from here without performing the proper rites from the undercroft."

Naya nodded, assuming that would be the case. But, she maintained her composure. "Yes, but he'll find a way home. He'll take your father's keyshard and give it to his masters to lock up in their shardvaults."

Fallon's expression twisted between concern and confusion as she considered that possibility. But as the druid's brow furrowed in anger, Naya felt that she could have hugged that pesky boy Quinn—he had laid out the path that Naya needed. She didn't have the innate power to awaken the incarnate, but she believed Fallon did.

Anyone who studied magic knew how tied it was to emotion. An impassioned mage could conjure more power, for better or worse. And Naya needed a surge of Oakus' power if she hoped to control a golem the size of the incarnate. She knew that Fallon was sent to her by the Shadow—a devotee of Oakus wronged by the Light—but until now she wasn't sure how to quickly turn the girl to the Shrouded's cause.

It was almost too perfect.

"We only have one choice, Fallon," Naya said, putting her good arm around the elf's waist and directing her toward the incarnate. It stood overlooking the great hall, watching them with dull green keyshards for eyes, waiting for the spark that would turn the Shadow's simmering rage loose on the world above. It wore plates of oaken armor like some great earthen knight, protecting the moss-like flesh beneath. He was a masterpiece.

But he needed a name.

As they regarded the massive golem in silence, the darkness of the halls beyond became oppressive, as if the Shadow had felt Naya's need. Sudden visions of blood and darkness came to her, a great dread swallowing the world in a mass of black, smoking roots. And the words came.

"Mawsurath is our only chance to stand against the Light," Naya gently pushed Fallon toward the incarnate, "and he awaits your command."

As the elf stood before the creature, its dull eyes began to flicker.

Ransil awoke with a start, feeling as if he had slept for days. He could tell it was early, the sun only barely peeking through dawn's hazy clouds. He was naked, curled up in the grass, hugging up with his pack as if it were his truest love. It took him a long moment to remember where he even was, but as the realization hit him like a kick from a mule, he sat up and jerked his head in every direction.

Grip was gone.

He wanted to scream, and then scream some more before slapping his stupid, fat face. How could he have let himself be played by her again? Would he never learn? As much as he wanted to rage and pound something with his fists, he settled for cursing under his breath as he scrambled to find his clothes. Maybe he could still catch up to her.

His mind was racing, struggling to rationalize why Grip would sneak away after what they had done last night. The last time they had engaged in such an affair, it was Ransil who had left her in the middle of the night. Back then, he had not wanted to explain to her that they couldn't be together since he was leaving the Guild.

Was this her revenge? Would she be so petty when the stakes were so high?

As he shrugged on his green woolen tunic, cinching it with his leather belt, Ransil noticed his pack's contents had been spilled out onto the grass. Knives of various sizes, wrapped foodstuffs, candles, lockpicks—most of his belongings looked accounted for.

Except for the documents they had procured from the baron's secret library.

Fresh anger surged through Ransil and he shoved his big feet into his boots and sheathed his daggers. He quickly repacked his bag, threw it over his shoulders, and covered it with his cloak before racing toward the Hollowood.

Whatever Grip planned to do with the information in those documents, Ransil knew he had to stay in the loop. It may be his only chance to help Anika against whatever the baron's Shadow priestess was plotting—those plans certainly involved the Lawsons, and with Bennik missing, Ransil was the closest thing to a father those two had.

Despite knowing what deadly threats awaited him in the Hollowood, Ransil ran toward the trees as fast as his short legs could possibly carry him. He tried desperately not to let his anger with Grip cloud his better judgment, but that fury pushed his legs harder, and soon he had to embrace it just to keep himself moving. He crossed the plains before the sun could properly greet him, and soon the eerie chill of the Hollowood made him silently curse Grip for making him return here.

It had been years since Ransil had dared to trek through these trees; there was never a good reason to journey through the Hollowood. It was a forest that was rightly avoided by any travelers, full of goblins, gargantuan spiders, and even darker things that were drawn to its harrowing depths. It was said that there was a deep ravine in the center of the forest that the Shadow itself had used to escape from the Abyss below the earth.

Ransil had never seen such a crevice, but if it existed, he hoped it did not lie in his path.

He slowed his pace slightly as a tangle of growth threatened to trip him, but he quickly came upon a game trail with clear footprints that had to be Grip's. Following the trail was easy—he was no expert hunter, but he knew a thing or two about stalking prey—but he became so focused on Grip's prints that his foot caught a reaching root and he fell hard, rolling into a heap.

Hissing in pain, he grabbed his right ankle to ensure it wasn't broken. Fortunately, it moved just fine, though he just wasn't sure how well he'd be able to run on it. Looking down the path, Ransil didn't see the root that tripped him. It was as if it had emerged from the ground just to grab his foot. But he didn't have time to dwell on it.

A goblin screamed nearby, behind a wall of dark leaves and spiderwebs. There was a loud burst, as if a barrel of rocks had been smashed against a stone wall. Another goblin screamed.

Ransil got to his feet, favoring his uninjured leg.

Just as he was about to limp in the direction opposite the goblins, a boy's voice stopped him short.

"Help!"

It sounded like a desperate child, scared for their life. There was another eruption, followed by another goblin hollering. Ransil cursed and made his way toward the child's plea. He pushed aside a curtain of leaves and shoved himself through several layers of spider webs. For a moment he was afraid he'd become stuck, but he finally fell forward and landed in a small glade.

His nose caught a savory smell, making his stomach rumble in hunger. He looked up and nearly retched. He saw a smoldering corpse on the ground in front of him, blackened flesh in the shape of a goblin reaching its bony arms up to prevent whatever flames had consumed him from doing so. He had clearly failed.

Ransil looked beyond the smoking creature and saw a boy in a dirty yellow mage's robe. One of the boy's arms was caught in a tree branch, which had somehow coiled around his limb, locking it in place. His other arm was flailing, a stream of flames lashing about in its wake. A goblin with a blackened spear danced away from the fire, trying to bury its weapon into the boy.

Ransil rolled to his side and reached for one of his knives, swiftly letting it fly toward the foe. His aim was true and the goblin fell over with the small handle of Ransil's blade protruding from its eye.

Another goblin slashed at the boy with a wicked sword, but the young mage spoke a word and the fire trailing his arm burst in a cone that hit the attacking goblin full in the face. It fell to the ground, rolling and thrashing, trying to put the flames out. But, like its companion, it failed and its body was consumed by the inferno.

Ransil got to his feet to attend to the boy.

"Please," the boy said, holding his arm out now in Ransil's direction. "Don't kill me!"

Ransil stopped and held his hands up. He had never seen a mage so young, but he didn't care to see how advanced in his learning the boy was. "I'm no goblin."

The boy's face relaxed for a moment, but then there was a horrific creaking sound, followed by the branch around his arm beginning to tighten. Fresh fear washed over the boy's face as he reached a hand up to tug at the branch.

"Help!" His voice was shrill and frantic. "It's going to pull my arm off!"

Ransil rushed over and took hold of the tree. It's bark felt alive, quivering under his touch. Regardless, the halfling pulled as hard as he could while the branch seemed to take on a serpentine quality, wrapping tighter around the boy's arm. The mage screamed in pain now, and Ransil feared the tree was about to shatter the child's bones.

Desperate to save the boy's arm, Ransil pulled out his dagger and buried it into the tree where the branch met the trunk. The entire tree stiffened as the blade sunk deep, and the branch loosened enough for the boy to slip free. Ransil was barely able to pull his dagger back out before the branch lashed out at him. He managed to roll with the blow, landing on the ground in a heap but avoiding any significant injury.

Ignoring the pain, Ransil got to his knee to see the boy scrambling away from him, clawing at the forest floor to save himself.

"I won't hurt you," Ransil said with annoyance. "I just saved your arm from being eaten by a tree."

But the boy's mouth just flapped uselessly as he raised an arm to point over Ransil's head. The halfling turned to see what the boy was gawking at, and he saw the tree that had pinned his arm was moving toward him. It no longer looked like a tree—it looked like an ogre wearing tree bark. The earth below it was pushed aside in heaps as slithering roots dug their way up through the dirt to pull the monstrosity forward.

Momentarily frozen in fear, Ransil merely watched as the tree raised itself up, stretching its branches like stiff tentacles, reaching for its prey. When one of those limbs reached out for Ransil, the halfling finally rolled away, back toward the scampering boy. Together they ran out of the glade away from the attacking tree.

"Did you do that?" Ransil asked, grabbing the boy's robes to keep him from stumbling over the brush.

"I—I don't know," the boy replied, finally finding his footing and joining Ransil as they ran for the nearest way out of the forest, following the game trail.

Even as he ran for his life from a living tree, Ransil couldn't help sparing a miserable thought for the love of his life that had nearly gotten him killed yet again. *Damn you, Grip*, he thought with annoyance as he burst out of the woods into the sunlight. The boy fell into the grass, gasping for breath.

Ransil turned to face the Hollowood, wondering if somehow Grip had set this elaborate trap so he couldn't follow her. He knelt down next to the boy, catching his own breath. He knew that if Grip had encountered the boy during her own trek through the woods, she would have let him die rather than let a rescue threaten her own agendas.

"It's better off this way," Ransil said aloud.

The boy sat up, looking around. "Which way?"

Ransil couldn't help but laugh and shake his head. "I don't know."

Chapter Three

Too High a Toll

Robin peered down the alley, seeing no sign of activity. Night had fallen, and the streets of Sathford were as tightly guarded as he remembered—meaning the thieves had done their skulking about in broad daylight, concealed within the mill of bodies that shuffled through the busy streets, pilfering merchants and sailors of their coin.

Night had once belonged only to the Lord Mayor's personal enforcers, commonly referred to as the Collectors—short for the clever moniker, the Tolle Collectors. The Collectors were originally formed to gather up the Guild agents that once ruled the dark streets of Sathford long before Robin's time. But their effectiveness secured them long-standing employment, much to the Guild's chagrin.

Now it seemed the Collectors had to share the dark streets with the paladins, clerics, and chaplains. The Luminaura was a new presence for Robin, another set of watchful eyes that he had to elude. Fortunately, he was raised in the shadows, skulking before he could even walk, forced to steal if he wanted to eat.

Despite the circumstance, he felt more at home than he ever had in Blakehurst, crawling through the grime on a mission of subterfuge.

Satisfied that the patrols had passed, Robin slithered out from the hole, further soiling the only set of clothing that remained to him. But the weight of the pouch in his hand comforted him. He would now be able to buy himself and Gage proper disguises so they might finally leave their room.

It had been three days of sitting idly in their small room as Gage recovered from his wound. Robin was relieved enough that the injury was not fatal, but he found himself more than unsettled that Gage had recovered as he had. Without the attention from a cleric or healer, a stomach wound was more often than not a death sentence, and yet Gage had acted as if it were no more than a scratch.

Whatever was healing Gage had simultaneously been taking a toll on him. Since leaving Oakworth, he had become more sullen and occasionally even short with Robin. He laid in their shared bed, sleeping or brooding. Whatever scraps of food Robin managed to secure—crusty bread, partially molded cheese, bones with a few pieces of meat remaining—were left mostly uneaten on the floor near the bed.

Robin could only hope that the night's earnings might lift his companion's spirits. While he had not yet managed to contact Master Audreese in Raventhal, the coins he plucked from the distracted butcher would get them one step closer. The church was guarding the spire, and Robin heard whispers of something making the High Mage nervous. Whether it was the church itself, or just the recent battle between the goblins or harpies, Robin wasn't sure. All he knew was that he would need some queens to find a way into Raventhal.

As he got to his feet and brushed some of the grime off his blue shirt—nearly black now from filth—Robin began to wonder if tonight might be the right time to broach the subject of Gage's mother. He had been careful not to speak of the incident, but each day that passed in which they did not discuss everything that had happened in Oakworth felt like another wedge that was driving them apart.

His mind wandered back to that dreadful morning—when he had become a murderer.

"We need to get to a chapel—a healer," Robin had told Gage as he helped him to his feet in The Harvest Breeze. "There's too much blood."

"No," Gage had said, in a dark voice that chilled Robin. He put a firm hand on Robin's shoulder and pushed him away. It wasn't a violent shove, but it still pained Robin. "I'm fine."

Robin had watched in disbelief as Gage stepped toward his mother's body, as if the ruin of his stomach did not bother him in the least. He stood tall, his shoulders only slightly hunched.

"I need to see."

Robin didn't move. "See what?"

When he turned to Robin, his eyes were full of loathing, without a shred of sadness. "I need to see her die."

Together they watched as the blood pooled around Renay's lifeless body. Robin could hear the voices of their companions through one of the open windows. They couldn't stay.

"She's gone," Robin said, finally taking a step toward Gage. He wanted to reach out to him, but touching him felt wrong at that moment. *I just killed his mother*, Robin had thought, as if the realization was just sinking in. *How will he ever love me now?*

But as if in response, Gage turned toward Robin and embraced him. Time fell away as they held each other, and Gage's body softened as sadness finally replaced whatever hate Robin had seen in his dark eyes.

The memory pained Robin in a strange and soothing way. They hadn't spoken of Renay since fleeing The Harvest Breeze and then sneaking onto a covered tinkerer's wagon bound for Sathford. The two barely spoke at all during that long ride, but they found comfort in each other's arms and lips, letting their bodies say the things they could not find words for.

It wasn't until they arrived in Sathford that Gage had become truly withdrawn. Baron Caffery had wasted no time in sending out riders with news of the murder, and the first poster that the pair had seen hanging on one of the parapets of the Sathler Bridge had crude drawings of them.

According to the artist, Gage looked like some evil wizard that might have been painted in a book of fables, his dark hair wild and his eyes narrowed in a look of malevolence. Meanwhile, Robin's visage was much too accurate for his liking, and he had immediately drawn his hood when seeing it.

"Come on," Robin had said, drawing Gage away from the thoroughfare. Another guard was actively hanging a copy of the wanted poster on the opposite parapet. Robin guided Gage away from the main road leading toward Castle Tolle's market square, weaving through side alleys where young boys and women were dragging wagons loaded with various goods bound for the docks.

At the time, Robin had thought it was a miracle they hadn't been noticed. But soon they had heard various city folk discussing the recent assault, and how the Luminaurian army had thrown the monster and its horde back to save Sathford; Robin nearly blew their cover.

He found himself needing to bite his tongue to fight the strange desire to regale them all with the tale of how Gage's sister had been the one to defeat the monster. Despite the current circumstances, he still found it thrilling to be caught up in such an adventure, and he always seemed to struggle with keeping secrets or letting mistruths go uncorrected.

But he only had to look to Gage to remind himself that they were not on some heroic quest—they would be hanged for murder if they were found. No Collector would care about Gage's mother being driven mad by her faith; it didn't matter that she had tried to kill him.

There was no doubt in Robin's heart: they were fleeing for their lives. And the only place he knew where to go was back to the Guild in Andelor.

"What are you doing here?"

Robin froze, his wandering mind snapping back to the present. He couldn't move, as much as he needed to turn to see where the voice had come from.

"I said, what are you doing here?"

"Nothing, m'lord," came a woman's voice in response. Robin jerked his head in that direction to see two dancing shadows on the cobbled street beyond the alley.

"Just returning from a bit of tumbling," the woman's familiar voice said teasingly. "Did you want to buy me a room at The Riverstone and let me collect your toll, love?"

Robin heard a soft chuckle. "Off with ya, then. No loitering, and keep your business off the streets." The patrol moved on, their footsteps fading into distance by the time Mirim shuffled into the alley.

"What was that?" Robin hissed.

Mirim gave him a raised eyebrow and her signature knowing smirk. "Subterfuge, love. I didn't want him asking any—wait, what happened to you?" She motioned to Robin's ruined shirt and filthy pants. "Were you hoping the guards might confuse you for a pile of garbage?" She chuckled softly.

"Shhh!" Robin warned, motioning her closer. "Why would you try to bring him back to the inn?! Gage is still there and our faces are posted all over town!"

Mirim gave him a look of disbelief, as if he were speaking a foreign language. She was Jathi, with tanned skin and dark silken hair, and an accent that intoxicated most Vale-folk. But Robin was far from intoxicated at the moment, and Mirim seemed to know it.

"Love," she said, laying a delicate hand on his shoulder, careful to avoid touching his filth. "Even a Collector would not be caught dipping his wick while on patrol—there's no quicker way to be sent down the river than to defy our Lord Mayor's decree." She looked at the coin purse Robin gripped in his hand. "You have your tricks, and I have mine. With how loudly I propositioned him, he won't step foot in The Riverstone for at least a fortnight."

Robin relaxed, understanding the ploy.

"Did you get it all?" Mirim asked, motioning Robin to follow her. "I certainly hope so—that brute was so excited for a complimentary ride that he nearly thrust me through that headboard of his."

Opening the purse for the first time, Robin counted the contents. Three queens and nearly four times as many kings. Certainly enough to buy them some more time and clean clothes. "Looks like nearly a month's wages," Robin answered with a hint of sadness. Thieving was in his blood, but he couldn't always shake those feelings of shame that crept up on him when he took another's livelihood.

At least that butcher isn't wanted, he told himself, searching for some way to absolve himself of the guilt. *He can keep working to earn this back and then some, but we won't have that chance.* He tied the purse strings and locked step with Mirim whose long legs glided silently toward their destination.

"Who do you serve from the spire?" Robin asked in a low whisper. Now that they had some time to breathe, he needed to get back to the task at hand. "The professors? Any of the masters?"

Mirim considered that, smoothing her hair out as they walked through the tightening alley. The sounds of distant merriment this close to the "five casks"—the collection of five popular alehouses in close proximity near the Bridge Quarter—now gave them much better protection against unwanted ears.

"That Chosen could ring my bell whenever he chooses, or his pet elf," she said in a husky voice. "But no, I don't linger around those parts much. It's not like those stuffy mages carry any real coin." She turned to give Robin another raised eyebrow. "Is that your mark?"

As much help as Mirim had provided thus far, he was not yet sure he wanted to trust her with his plans. He hadn't even fully revealed them to Gage yet, but that was mostly because he was still working out the details himself.

"Never mind," Robin said, nodding toward the end of the alley that opened up to The Riverstone's very doors. They stopped before stepping into the street, looking for any signs of patrols. Then, Robin reached into the purse and drew out a queen, holding it up for Mirim to see. "Get the room for three more nights, just in case. You can keep the rest for yourself."

She reached for the coin, but Robin slipped it into his fist, motioning for her to look him in the eyes. "You're to come back in three nights and knock once and then thrice. Hopefully we'll be gone, but just in case, make Hogan think you're getting ready for another set of sailors to work through."

"Understood, love." She cast a quick glance at the rest of the coins. "You two want some company tonight?" Grinning, she motioned to his filthy pants. "I can show you where things go? Plenty of sailors want a lady around, despite their appetites."

Robin tucked the purse into his pants and gave her a condescending smile. "We'll be fine. Go make a show of going up to the room so I can sneak around back." He flipped the queen, which Mirim snatched out of the air before turning to saunter toward The Riverstone.

It wasn't long after Mirim walked through the inn's doors that Robin heard a burst of cheers and laughter. He used the opportunity to race across the street on silent feet, slipping into the alley running along the side of The Riverstone. He rounded the corner and found the familiar footholds that would get him up to their room.

The climb was as strenuous as ever, and Robin felt a wave of relief as he gripped the open window sill and pulled himself in.

"Sorry that took so long," he said, as he brushed himself off. Robin turned to face an empty bed. He was completely alone in the small unadorned room.

Robin was so exhausted from the climb and the excursion, it took him a long moment to fully realize that the man he loved had abandoned him.

Brace Cobbit took a long draw of his pipe as he watched the chapel burn. The trees nearest the structure had been cut away to avoid catching fire, the wood to be used for the new cathedral's construction within the city walls.

Curling his lips to form smoke rings, Brace tried to make the terrible sight a little less harrowing by watching it through the smoky shapes his father used to make for them when they would fish out on the Green Lake on summer nights.

Unfortunately, it didn't help much. He still felt dread as the old place gave its legacy up to the flames. He had many memories of the Temple of Dawn. Growing up in a small cottage near the river, his family had made trips to worship at least once a week. They would pack up a meal and hitch a wagon to the tired old horse. Riding the long road around Sathford, they would make a day of visiting the chapel.

There were fond memories in the roots of this place, and Brace felt a vileness grow within him as he watched the desecration. He had helped his brethren put this holy place to the torch.

And why?

Brace blew out another smoke ring that would shame his father's legacy. That was perhaps what burdened him so much as he watched the flames reach higher into the night sky. He could not say for certain why the place needed to be burned.

He heard the footsteps approaching, but he didn't feel the need to bestir himself. No one else would be out here on the hill at this hour, not with the Collectors nervously watching the gates.

"Why do you watch this?" Darrance Moore asked, his armor creaking and clicking as he finally crested the hill. "This is not a sight to linger on, Brace. This is not our proudest hour."

"Is it our hour at all?" Brace asked.

Darrance didn't have an answer.

"Have you spoken with my cousin?" Brace asked, flinging out the contents of his pipe. "Since she gave the command?"

"I did."

Brace stood up to face his friend. "And did she give a reason for this madness? A true one?"

"She did," Darrance said, his blue eyes seeming to glow as they watched the angry flames below. Brace could tell the man was bothered, but he knew better than to ask. Paladins were by nature reserved when it came to their feelings—duty was their primary concern. "As to the truth, that is for the Light to decide."

Brace spat, adjusting the heavy green cloak that seemed to be choking him now. "Believe what you will about the vicar, Darrance, but I knew the man. Elf or no, he was devoted to the Luminaura. I refuse to believe this charge of apostasy."

Darrance turned his icy eyes on him. "I would guard your tongue, friend. The High Warpriest speaks for the Archbeacon in times of war. And we are at war, do not forget. Questioning Hope's judgment in this could in itself be seen as apostasy."

Brace chewed on his lip, wondering how he had gotten here. "You know why I joined the church, and I know why you did." He pointed to the fire that continued to blaze. From their place on the hill, they could see the shapes of acolytes moving to add more kindling to the inferno.

"This isn't it."

Darrance's stern expression softened slightly. "I understand how this is more upsetting for you—you have a history here. But the Lord Mayor has already approved the construction of the new cathedral, and the Archbeacon has already elected a beacon to replace Tomen as the Light's herald here in Sathford."

Brace's eyes narrowed on the paladin. "And you don't ask yourself why?"

Darrance looked genuinely perplexed and shrugged. "Why what?"

"Why were we rushed here, just in time for the assault?" Brace pointed again to the burning chapel. "Why did Hope have to spill Tomen's blood in the chapel? Burning this place—with so much history—so we can build a new place of worship." His shoulders sagged now in defeat. "What will the legacy of this new cathedral be, built on blood and ash?"

"What history would that be?" Darrance asked, his mouth tightening again. He nodded toward the blaze. "The elves built that chapel in worship of Oakus and it never truly abandoned its roots—the Order of Oakus even gathered beneath its roof once a moonturn. Hope charges that the vicar was stealing from the Luminaura's coffers to give to the druids, and you know as well as I the penalty for such blasphemy."

Darrance's fervor was rising, and Brace knew better than to feed its flames. He took a deep breath to calm his own anger. He was frustrated with Hope and the church as a whole, not Darrance, who was his only real friend within the ranks of the order.

He may have once called Hope a friend, despite their past quarrels. But after tonight he wasn't sure he would be able to confide in her again. It seemed her faith had consumed her, and whatever machinations were driving the Luminaura were kept secret from the church's lower ranks.

"It's late," Brace said, tucking his pipe back into the pouch under his cloak. His fingers brushed the keyshard that was there, and his eyes were drawn one final time to the fires down the hill. "Forgive me, Darrance. These burdens have affected my thoughts. I trust we can keep this between us?"

Darrance's face was stoic. "Of course."

Brace turned his back on the church and made his way back to Sathford alone, wondering if Darrance believed him. There was no room within the Luminaura for dissenting thoughts such as the ones he had expressed to his friend, and he suddenly feared that the two might be drawn into conflict.

As he passed through Sathford's gates, he watched the stonemasons—still busy, even at this hour—repairing the damage the harpies and goblins had caused. He considered walking straight to the stables to mount his horse and ride away from all this. The thought was comforting and exciting, but something—maybe the determined workers repairing their city—kept his path true.

For now.

Chapter Four

Awaiting Judgment

Blakehurst wasn't exactly what Brother Avrim had expected. He hadn't known Anika long, but something about her suggested nobility, not a woodland commoner. He thought of the sweeping paintings he had seen of Pyram, its great pyramid lit by a setting sun, shimmering across the gilded rooftops of the city built atop its steep inclines. That was what he pictured when he thought of Anika's origins.

Avrim's own imaginations were quite in contrast with the quaint backwater village that he strode through now. It had been two days since he had arrived in Blakehurst with Melaine and Deina, and their welcome had not been a pleasant one. After a dour ride from Oakworth—despite the lovely weather—they arrived as the sun had begun to set and were immediately accosted by Baron Caffery's men.

When they had explained their purpose, they were given escort to the Brightstar Sanctuary near the reeve's manor. There they delivered Matty's body to Mother Beatrim, a kind old elf to whom Avrim took a quick liking. The two of them had retreated to the glowery so they might talk of the recent events while the sisters prepared Matty for a proper burial.

"The Child of Light," Mother Beatrim said when they were confined in the candlelit chamber, as if she weren't surprised in the least. "I see."

Her acceptance of the fact had taken Avrim aback. "You don't seem surprised."

Mother Beatrim lit another candle, clearly not satisfied with the dozens that already lit the small room. "I am too old for shock, Brother. If you were wondering if I knew, I did not. But the girl was clearly important; though I suspected the Shadow had touched her—given what happened with her mother."

The thought of Renay had sent a pang of guilt through Avrim, and he knew he had to find Anika before she learned the truth of what had happened. She had fled thinking her brother had killed her mother, but really it was Avrim who had put that doom into motion. "Do you think she'll return here?" He had no idea where to begin looking for her. "There were those that claimed she flew from Oakworth, while others insisted that she murdered Renay." *I did,* he thought, focusing on the flame of a single candle as if it could burn away his shame.

Mother Beatrim silently considering the rumors. "I must pray on this, Brother," was all she said. "Come back to me on the morrow."

But the morrow had come and gone. And then the following morrow. Mother Beatrim assured Avrim that the Light would guide them, and Blakehurst was as good a place as any to await a sign.

Avrim was not sure he believed that as he strode down the town's cobbled road toward the reeve's manor. The townsfolk mostly stayed in their homes and shops, watching Avrim and his companions with nervous eyes. But he did not fault them for that as he watched Kasia Strallow exit the reeve's manor and stride toward him. Two of Baron Caffery's guards had been waiting outside the door, now joining her as Avrim stopped and awaited them.

"Brother Kaust," she said, regarding him coldly.

"Dame Strallow," Avrim replied. "I trust you have all the answers you need from us? Are we free to go?"

Her face stiffened slightly, as if she were fighting back a mocking laugh. "I'm afraid not, Brother. After consulting with the reeve, it seems there are still some questions regarding the Lawson girl and the events in Rathen. We believe you and your companions may be able to provide us with additional…insight."

Her last word felt pointed, and Avrim tried to retain his composure. He was beginning to feel like a prisoner. And he wasn't sure how much longer Melaine would endure these interrogations. "You were in Rathen as well," Avrim replied. "Before myself or Deina. What information would we be able to provide for your investigation here?"

Kasia gave him a knowing smile. "That is what we intend to find out, Brother." She stepped to the side of him with her escort, and added, "Please meet me at the reeve's this afternoon."

She left him there bristling.

It was hard for Avrim to accept that he and his companions were being treated this way. The Child of Light was out there, somewhere, and there may be more of these incarnates that could interfere with Anika's destiny. He had to help her—he had to convince Mother Beatrim that they couldn't just sit and wait.

He was beginning to feel like he was drowning in this small town, surrounded by people who looked at him with suspicion and doubt. When he had confronted the baron of Oakworth, he had felt like a hero, and now—what was he now? Some sort of conspirator, held captive by a witch hunter?

Avrim took a deep breath and surveyed the town once more. The only real movement he saw besides the armored Oakworth guards stalking the perimeter with the reeve's soldiers was at the smithy. He saw Deina inside speaking with the dwarven blacksmith. Seeing the two of them laugh and talk did much to relieve the dread he felt, and he decided to join them.

As he made his way, a tall figure stepped into view.

"Melaine," Avrim said, startled. "Where'd you come from?"

The half-orc motioned to the ruins of The Early Mule. "The reeve is planning on rebuilding the inn there—it was burned in the attack." She regarded the smoldering heap in sad recollection. "I used to help the lumberers in Wickham when they hauled in wood for repairs. Was seeing if I could be of some use while we're stuck here, but the carpenter would have none of it."

Not having a good reply, Avrim just looked at Melaine and wished he could fault the people of Blakehurst for their apprehension. His companion had the appearance of a monster straight out of an old book of stories where brave heroes vanquished legions of Shadow.

Melaine was taller than any woman Avrim had seen, and she was more orc than human. She had green-gray flesh and the smallest hint of tusks pushing her lower lip slightly forward. Since she was the first half-orc he had seen, Avrim had been taken aback during their first encounter, but he had come to see her as a person like any other, ashamed that he had ever considered her even remotely monstrous. Yet he would be lying if he claimed to be surprised by anyone else looking upon his friend in fear.

As if reading his mind, Melaine crossed her arms and said, "I shouldn't be surprised no one here had seen my kind before. There are few of us roaming about, and here in the heart of Vale...these people are so hidden from the world."

Avrim nodded, looking around the village. He noticed a hunter watching them from the dark edges of the forest, a bow slung across his back and several dead rabbits hanging from his belt. An apothecary worked in an open shed near her shop, watching them through the smoke of her brazier.

"They see a monster," Melaine said, without a shred of anger or bitterness. "It makes you wonder if they knew the truth of my kind, would it change what they saw?" She shook her head, doubting.

"I have heard tales," Avrim said, not wanting to pry.

Melaine regarded him now. "There are many tales, most false. Some say I am a result of orc warriors forcing themselves upon humans, but there is no proof of such couplings. Orcs are savage creatures of Shadow, and they hate those who are not orcs. Anyone who has seen how orcs live knows that they see their seed as a gift, and would not give that gift to those they hate."

Avrim nodded, glad to hear such horrific stories were likely untrue.

"The Sutheki tribes fought the orcs for ages, driving them to near extinction," Melaine said, turning toward the horizon. "When the Nether War unleashed the Shadow, it saw the orcs as its greatest champions—I'm sure you've read in your luminary that the orcs were the Shadow's children."

Avrim confirmed in silence.

Melaine shook her head. "They aren't the Shadow's children. We are. The ones like me—half-orcs, or half-breeds, whatever they call us—we are the result of the Shadow's perversions. The Sutheki were swallowed by the great cataclysm that split their lands, perhaps falling into the very Abyss itself. Orcs emerged. The wisewomen of Suthek say the Abyss twisted their ancestors into orcs, and only those who were strong enough to resist the Shadow's corruption maintained their humanity."

She motioned to her face. "But they still bear the scars of the Shadow's touch. My people may have resisted the Shadow," she nodded to the onlookers of Blakehurst, "but the world scorns us for our courage."

Avrim felt the pain in her words. The tragedies of Suthek were written in hundreds of ways, and Melaine's story confirmed his own interpretations of those many tales. "The luminary doesn't speak much of the Sutheki," Avrim said, as if in apology. "Your people's story should be added to its pages. There is a Bright Council each year in Andelor, where the Archbeacon considers revisions to the luminary…"

Melaine gave him a sad smile. "You are too good a man for the Light, Avrim. There's goodness in you, but the Light outshines it." She turned to leave, but stopped to give him one last look. "The Light exists only to counteract the Shadow—it does not exist to be good, nor does the Shadow exist to be evil. They exist to pit the world against each other. I hope your faith doesn't blind you to that."

As he watched her walk away, Avrim felt a fury rising within him similar to the one that overtook him in the baron's keep. Her words angered him, though he could not quite say why—he had listened to skeptics his entire life, and they never shook his faith. Something about Melaine's words cut him deeply, though.

Closing his eyes and taking a long breath, he reminded himself that she was entitled to her apathetic views of the Light. The rage slowly subsided, and he continued toward the smithy. The sound of hammer and anvil echoed from within the stuffy structure as Deina emerged to greet him. She looked strange not wearing her armor.

"Everything alright?" the dwarf asked, giving him a curious look.

Avrim nodded toward Melaine as the half-orc made her way toward the forest, likely seeking a bit of solitude. "She grows restless here."

Deina nodded. "Aye. She's not the only one. Any word from our gracious hosts?"

"It seems we're to be questioned yet again," Avrim said, not caring to hide his disdain.

"Bloody Oathers," Deina growled, scraping a boot across the cobblestone to show what she thought of the Arcania's enforcers. "You'd think surviving Rathen somehow made us fugitives. As if we caused the siege."

"From what I know of Oathers," Avrim said, lowering his voice, "they would rather put the wrong person in irons than return to the Arcania empty handed." Even speaking the words sent a chill down Avrim's spine. "What does the smith say of Anika?"

"Bruck knew the girl well," Deina replied, still scowling against the late morning sunlight. "Says her father, Bennik, was a good Eastlund man—once a king's man. Came to Blakehurst about fifteen years ago from the Westerran war with a Karranese babe in one arm and a blushing bride in the other."

"Must have been a strange sight," Avrim said. "You see a lot of Karranese sailors at the ports, maybe some merchants passing through. These folks must have found it a bit suspicious, no?"

Deina shook her head. "Bruck says things were different then—lots of refugees passing through. The northern holds in Karrane were just as affected by the war as Westerra. But any suspicions they had of an Eastlunder bringing a Karranese babe was quickly put to rest—seems Bennik was quite the tanner, and the village had need of 'im."

Avrim nodded, glad to hear that Anika had at least been more welcomed by these people than he and his companions had been. He suddenly got the impression that it was because she had been so accepted that the town was wary of their presence.

They think we brought trouble here, he realized.

Deina coughed and shifted her feet, clearly uncomfortable. "Bruck also told me about Anika's mother."

Avrim tensed, picturing Renay's bloody corpse on the floor of that wretched inn. He opened his mouth to divert the discussion, but was interrupted.

"Brother Kaust," a woman said breathlessly.

The dwarf and the priest both turned toward the sister. She was a middle-aged human with the pale complexion of a Guyenean. A woven shawl covered her braided, graying hair and her eyes were wide with concern as she hurried toward them.

"The Lightmother requests your presence at the Brightstar," she said breathlessly.

"It's about time," Deina grunted, stepping in that direction.

The sister held up her hand nervously. "Just Brother Avrim, my lady, if it please you."

"It certainly don't," scoffed Deina.

Avrim rested a hand on her shoulder. "Wait for me at the Brook & Stable." He followed the sister, leaving Deina to grumble behind them.

The Brightstar Sanctuary was empty when the sister led him inside, with the exception of two other sisters—a halfling and a younger human—near the altar replacing the candles that had burned too low. Avrim followed the sister to the side hall leading to the glowery. He turned to thank her, but she had already gone, leaving him alone.

"Come, Brother," Mother Beatrim instructed as Avrim opened the glowery's door, candlelight spilling into the darkened hall. There was an urgent edge to her voice. "Sit with me here."

Avrim crossed his legs and sat on the pillow next to Beatrim, his heart beating faster now in hope for any sort of news. He knew senior members of the Luminaura were granted visions through their practiced faith and their connection with the church's beacons scattered across all of Noveth.

"Have you seen the Child?" Avrim asked excitedly.

Beatrim's eyes widened and she shook her head slowly. "No, thank the Light; the Child was not in my visions."

Avrim's face twisted in confusion. He didn't understand.

"My father was a seer in Xe'dann," she said, swallowing as if the words pained her. "He was granted visions through the feysleep—the Light forbids me to partake, but some of my people experience prophetic dreams while they slumber this way. But none could call upon those visions like my father."

Avrim opened his mouth to speak, but no words came.

Mother Beatrim pressed on. "It is said that the elven bloodlines are connected through the Fey Domain, and that should my father die, his visions would pass to his heirs." She looked down at her hands, as if seeing them for the first time. "I fear this is true, and what I've seen may yet come to pass."

"What did you see?"

She looked up and Avrim saw terror in her wizened eyes. "The incarnates. The raw fury of the gods, wrecking our world." She pointed a gnarled finger up to the glowery's low ceiling. "I saw the storm from Rathen—Eyen, in the form of a grotesque bird with razor wings descending from poisoned clouds."

Corvanna, Avrim thought as he revisited that night in Oakworth in his mind, trying to blink away those awful memories.

"I saw black tendrils bursting from the ground," she continued, "wrapping themselves around a city's walls and pulling them down into the earth, swallowing all in search of a stone."

"A stone?" Avrim asked, leaning forward. "A keyshard?"

Beatrim nodded slowly. "A green keyshard. The halfling's stone."

Ruke, Avrim thought, remembering the incarnate they had encountered in the Old Ways. He cursed himself—*what if I could have stopped it?* His thoughts raced between guilt and anger as he imagined that great mass of mud and roots taking on the form of those black tendrils that Mother Beatrim described.

Before Avrim could find out more, the door to the glowery was violently thrown open. Nearly half the room's candles were gutted out, and Avrim turned to face one of Baron Caffery's armored guards in the doorway.

"You've been summoned by the reeve," the man said.

Avrim got to his feet, glaring. "Dame Strallow said we were to meet there this afternoon."

The guard stared blankly. "I cannot speak to that, Brother. I am ordered to escort you," his gauntlet was resting on the sword sheathed at his side, "one way or another."

Avrim took the meaning. Despite his annoyance, he would not quarrel in the Light's own home. He turned to Mother Beatrim. "We shall speak further of this later."

The old elf nodded, her eyes still fearful.

Avrim followed the guard outside to find Melaine and Deina, both women unarmed, waiting for him while flanked by two more guards on either side.

"This is quite the escort," Deina said, glancing sideways at the soldiers. "You'd think we were as terrible as goblins or harpies."

Avrim raised a hand to calm her. "Let us go see what this is about."

They were led briskly through town to the reeve's manor, where two more of Baron Caffery's guards waited on either side of the gate. They passed through and made their way up the stairs to the open door, where they saw Kasia Strallow waiting in the entryway with her arms behind her back. She wore her Oather's armor, ready for battle. She motioned for them to enter the den where a fire was burning in the hearth.

Reeve Rupert Warner was pacing the room as they entered, but stopped to welcome them. "Ah, thank you for coming," the man said with a flourish of his hand, as if he were inviting them to a dinner as guests.

"Don't see we had much of a choice," Deina offered, taking a seat on one of the cushioned chairs without waiting for permission. Melaine stood near the window, her muscular arms locked across her broad chest. Avrim did not miss the look that Rupert Warner gave the half-orc, and he was grateful that Melaine decided to remain quiet.

This would not go well for them if they did not tread carefully.

"Please make yourselves comfortable," the reeve offered, taking a seat himself in the most ornate chair by the fire. Avrim wondered why the man would have the brazier burning on such a fair day, but he took that to mean that the reeve viewed himself as a man of luxury. He made note of that as he found a seat for himself. Melaine remained standing, as did Kasia Strallow, guarding the room's only exit.

"How can we be of service," Avrim asked with as much kindness as he could muster. His mind was still wrapping itself around Mother Beatrim's visions.

"Well, it seems we've had quite a series of events," the reeve said, his expression changing from gracious host to dutiful lord. "Between the horrific attack on our town, it seems not only was Oakhurst besieged, but Sathford as well. And I won't have to remind you all about the tragic events of Rathen, where my…" The reeve looked away then to compose himself. "Where my son gave his life in defense of the city."

Deina shifted in her seat awkwardly, not able to touch the ground with her feet. "I'm sorry fer ye loss, m'lord," she offered. "Many loved ones perished in that madness—damned harpy scum, and damn the orcs with 'em."

The reeve cast a sideways look at Melaine at the mention of orcs, but then gave the dwarf a pointed look, swallowing as he nodded his head tightly. "Yes," he agreed. "Well," he turned to Avrim, "from Dame Strallow's report, you were the last outsider to enter Rathen's gates before the attack."

There was a sudden pause, as if the reeve dared not continue. Avrim looked from Rupert to Kasia; both of them stared at him with accusing eyes. He felt a panic wash over him, but tried to compose himself before opening his mouth. Unfortunately, Deina didn't bother.

"Just what are ye gettin' at?"

The reeve kept his eyes on Avrim, clearly not wanting to bandy words with the impudent dwarf. "What we are getting at," the reeve said slowly, considering each word, "is that while Dame Strallow held the city, Rathen was kept in order. But when you arrived and she had to depart, something ran afoul."

Deina visibly seethed, but Avrim motioned for her to let him speak. "We have already told you the account," Avrim said as calmly as he could. He shifted his gaze from Rupert to the Oather, who seemed to smile ever so slightly. "The duke's boy was possessed. Corvanna must have been drawn to the Shadowlord through him, so we took him out of the city so I could perform the necessary exorcism at the nearby priory."

The reeve looked toward Kasia, as if waiting for a cue. The Oather stepped forward, putting her hands casually on her hips. "Why would the Luminaura send you to the city while all of Rathen's priests were sent on to Wickham and Harkand?"

The question nearly took the wind out of Avrim. It was the same question that he had been asking himself on the Rathaway, while he and Deina discussed the dire request from Duke Ambrose. Avrim looked to his dwarf companion, feeling a sudden tension hanging on his next words. Deina looked as if she were about to offer her own opinion again, so Avrim spoke.

"To that, I cannot say for certain," he began. "Vicar Tomen bade me to make for Rathen—he seemed to know the duke would have need."

"Aye," Deina interjected. "That he did. I don't see why yer makin' us rehash this all again. There are more pressing matters—did you not see yer own burned buildings out there?" She pointed a stubby finger toward the reeve's window.

The reeve stood up then, his face reddening. "I don't need to be reminded of our perils here, lass."

Avrim stood up as well, but slowly, as to not stoke this fire more. "We have dealt with dire events," he said with as much softness as he could muster. "Deina, let us treat them with the patience they have shown us."

Deina snorted.

Avrim turned back toward Kasia. "I can see why you might be suspicious, given my presence in Rathen while my brethren there had been called away. But truly, I do not know what commands they were given by the church. I was there by my own temple's decree." Anger was slowly replacing calmness in his voice as he added, "I was there to help."

"Yes," Kasia said, still as a statue. "But to help who?" She gave no time for them to answer. "Your chapel. It was a shrine to Oakus, yes?"

Avrim scowled, seeing where the Oather might be going with this. "Before the Unthroning, yes. All churches that survived the Nether War were once devoted to the old gods."

Kasia turned to Melaine. "And you were pledged to a temple of Wick, yes?"

The half-orc was looking at the fire and remained still as she shifted her eyes to Kasia. "No. My order rebuilt the ruins of an old chapel to serve as our keep. I'm a ranger, not a priestess."

The Oather regarded Deina. "And are you a daughter of Myretha?"

"Me faith ain't none of your concern."

"Perhaps you could tell us what this is all about," Avrim said, sounding more of a demand than a suggestion.

Kasia did not like that. Her eyes bore into the priest now. "This is about the single greatest arcane threat to this land in the last hundred years. This is about someone either breaking the Oath of Sorcery or hoarding a pile of keyshards that could blacken the entire sky. This is about you three being the only known survivors of Rathen and admittedly being present for the attack at Oakworth."

As if Kasia's fervor had awakened a rage within Rupert, he stepped forward. "You all have to know something about all this! Tell her now—do you want to get taken to the High Sanctum?"

Avrim's rising anger was now mixed with fear as he realized they were not here to report on their experiences. They were here to be judged. And it seemed that Kasia had already decided that they were guilty. Wrestling with so many thoughts, Avrim couldn't think of anything to say in response—the black tendrils from Mother Beatrim's visions were wrapping themselves around his resolve, crushing it in crippling dread.

"Unless you have some sort of defense," Kasia said, still solid as stone, "we may as well escort you to the Arcania. If we leave now, we could make Sathford before nightfall."

The mention of home gave Avrim one last hope. He saw himself being dragged in irons before strange wizards to decide his fate, and the black tendrils squeezed tighter. "Yes, let us ride for the Temple of Dawn. You can speak to the vicar about all of this."

"Hadn't you heard?"

Avrim turned to the reeve. "Heard what?"

"The temple was burned last night," Kasia said slowly, as if to savor the words. "Your vicar was executed for apostasy."

The black tendrils were choking Avrim entirely now. He couldn't breathe. It was a long moment before he found his breath—a small ball of light that gathered in his chest and pulsed angrily, giving him life. He felt his hands tighten into fists, the world around him darkening.

His mind found a moment of clarity as he reminded himself that Anika would need him. The world would need him. He was the Light's chosen warrior, and he wouldn't let this miserable witch hunter stand in his way.

"Guards," Kasia called. She turned from the convening soldiers back to Avrim and his companions. "Do any of you think you'll need irons, or can we do this peacefully?"

Avrim's breathing quickened, feeling the Light calling him to action. "You can't do this, Dame. Mother Beatrim—her visions…I need to find Anika. What happened in Rathen is going to happen everywhere. Together—the Arcania, the Luminaura—we can stop it."

Kasia just gave him a condescending smirk. "I am stopping it. Right here, right now."

Feeling hope abandoning him, Avrim closed his eyes and gave himself over to the Light. The power swelling within him gathered into his clenched fists, and his fingers were thrown open to unleash blinding sunlight in the stuffy den. The reeve shouted as he was thrown back, knocking over his ornate chair. Deina cursed and Avrim heard the sound of Kasia drawing her sword. He leaped forward blindly.

He painfully crashed into Kasia's armored form, knocking them both to the ground. Opening his eyes, he could see the Oather still blinded, and raised his fist to smash in her face. Again. And again. His fist glowed brightly and left searing marks on the woman's face.

Blood pounded in Avrim's ears, but he could hear Deina swearing and furniture breaking. He stood up in time to see two guards charging him, their shields held up to crash into him. Raising his hands, he tried and failed to summon the Light again, and was painfully pinned against the wall by the charging barricade.

As he began to lose consciousness, Arim saw the Oather stand up, smiling at the priest despite her burned and ruined face.

In the Brightstar Sanctuary, Kasia waited while the Lightmother's acolytes tended to her face. She could feel the skin around her cheeks tighten as the Light mended the burns left by Avrim's blasphemous fists.

The priest's power had impressed her, and she felt a flutter in her stomach as she imagined how the scene in the reeve's manor would have played out if she had been alone with Brother Kaust. A smile touched her lips, wet and eager.

It didn't go unnoticed.

"It seems the pain has receded, Lady Commander." Mother Beatrim's voice was curt, and Kasia knew the woman did not care for an Oather's presence in her precious church. "Perhaps it is time for your company to depart, if you wish to reach Oakworth before nightfall. Goblins have been seen still prowling the backroads."

"May we speak for a moment?" Kasia pushed one of the young acolytes' bright hands away, not waiting for the Lightmother's answer. "Alone."

Beatrim nodded, motioning for the others to leave the glowery.

When the door closed, Kasia stepped up to the Lightmother, hands behind her back. "Do you know about the last prophet that spread their lies across Vale?"

Surprisingly, the old woman didn't flinch. "My father was hunted mercilessly, banished from the Joined Realms."

Only one of Sauthorn's wretched spawns would be so bold to reveal themselves, Kasia thought, impressed by the old woman's nerve. It was a shame she had to kill her. She drew her sword.

"I may have had to put you before the High Sanctum for harboring enemies of the Arcania," Kasia said without emotion, "but it seems you have been using forbidden magic—powers that warrant more severe restitution."

Mother Beatrim still seemed unbothered, her eyes boring into Kasia's. "You can take my life, Oather, but you'll never have the visions. They belong to Aetha, and you—"

Kasia's sword flashed in an effortless arc, cutting off the woman's final, cryptic warnings. Her old body crumpled softly as her head rolled across the floor, knocking over a tall candle. Kasia casually stepped on the flames out before they could burn the room's only rug, wondering if the vicar in Sathford had died similarly.

Before leaving, Kasia knelt to pick up the Brightstar amulet that had fallen off the elf's severed neck. She looked at the bloody medallion, wondering if Sauthorn had more aspiring prophets roaming the lands. She wrapped her fingers around the Brightstar, silently swearing to eradicate any of his surviving line.

They knew too much about her secrets.

Chapter Five

Ruined Legacies

Two figures burst out of the trees, both wearing gray-green cloaks that flapped wildly in their wake as they put distance between themselves and the tall sentinel pines of the forest. An echoing shriek followed them from those trees, a sound of primal agony that faded as the wind carried its suffering elsewhere.

Soon, the figures slowed their pace to better survey their new surroundings, but neither stopped running.

Bennik Lawson never thought he'd see the iron lands again. The sight of their rolling hills gave him a deep sense of nostalgia, as if he had never left. It was a surprisingly welcome sensation, especially given the horrors he had just escaped.

Feeling like he couldn't go on, Bennik finally stopped running and put his hands on his knees to brace himself. Gasping for breath, he turned to Lexeth. The elf was hardly winded, making Bennik feel even older than he had when the dryads had caught him off guard in the woods.

"It seems the Old Ways want us to be here," Lexeth said, surveying the land around them. The late afternoon sun cast only a few shadows across the rugged terrain. He gave Bennik a sharp look, his gray eyes looking for some sort of deception. "Did you not want to return home?"

Bennik spat, looking around. *Which home?* He never intended to return to his ancestral home; Blakehurst was his home. "Why would I not want to return home? And why would that matter? You were supposed to be my guide in there." He motioned back to the forest. "Don't you know where we're going?"

Lexeth calmly unslung his bow, checking its string. "No one truly knows where they are going in the Old Ways, especially now."

Bennik was sick to death of elven riddles and half answers. "You said we needed to find answers. Blakehurst is where your sister was killed. Why are we in Eastlund?"

Lexeth didn't blink. "You tell me. You brought us here."

"What do you mean?"

Shouldering his bow, Lexeth walked past him toward the awaiting hills. "The Old Ways draw on the traveler's needs and desires—it doesn't guide you where you want to go. It guides you where you need to go." Lexeth motioned north. "Whatever we need is here, not in Blakehurst."

More elven riddles, Bennik thought, standing up to follow. It was true he had his doubts that Blakehurst held any answers for them. He couldn't say why, but he knew that neither Anika nor Gage were there. When Lexeth had mentioned the Keyguard back in Lefayra, Bennik's first thoughts were of his boyhood home.

The Keyguard was a central piece of Eastlund culture. While each of the Joined Realms had their own stories and legends about the Keyguard, the people of Eastlund took a sense of pride that the original pact of the Keyguard was made in Menevere, before the Founding Throne.

When the Keys of Transience were first brought before King Matherik II, it was decided that Eastlund, Xe'dann, Laustreal, and Caim would set aside their differences and forge a fellowship devoted to protecting those godly relics. That was the first Keyguard, sworn to protect the Keys over a thousand years ago, if the legends were to be believed.

Bennik knew those stories well, given it was his legacy to follow in his father's footsteps as an honorary member of the Keyguard, despite the order being broken apart by the Purveyors.

"You were the one who mentioned the Keyguard in Lefayra," Bennik said, more accusingly than he intended. "How do you know you didn't bring us here? Either by putting that thought in my head, or perhaps it was your needs that guided us through the Old Ways?"

"No."

The dismissive tone only annoyed Bennik more. "Look, I've followed you since I woke up. I owe you and your kin for rescuing me from Rathen. But if we're going to find what we're looking for, you're going to have to speak plainly for me." He ran his hand through his thick hair, trying to keep himself calm. "I'm not an elf. I'm just a simple tanner."

Lexeth stopped and turned back to him. "Are you?"

"I am now."

"You were," Lexeth corrected him. "Just like you were to be a member of the Keyguard. Farrah told me of your past, and your connection to the man we seek." Lexeth's hard expression softened. "You are correct, though. I did put the thought into your mind. The Keyguard is not a name often spoken these days, and I hoped it would drive your thoughts."

Bennik considered that, frustrated over how brilliantly the scheme worked. If someone had asked him probing questions about the Keyguard, Bennik knew he would have been unlikely to divulge secrets, even in times of need. It was ingrained in him as a youth. *The Keys are gone, but the Guard is not*, his father had said often, *we wait in silence until the world needs us again*.

"We do not have the time to waste on second guesses and half-truths," Lexeth said. "I don't need to know your opinions or assumptions regarding the Keyguard, only the facts. Humans are not good at conveying those in a timely fashion."

Bennik couldn't argue that. "Well, here we are. What now?" He looked back at the woods, glad to find them still and silent. "Are those hags confined to the forest?"

Lexeth looked from the forest back to the northern hills. "I am unsure. I have never seen the dryads so...hostile."

There were tall tales of dryads lurking in the Westweald, but they were rarely believed. Bennik had never seen a dryad until they were ambushed by them in the Old Ways. The creatures drove them out of those strange, wooded halls and into Bennik's past. Or if Lexeth was to be believed, it was apparently Bennik who had driven them here.

"So," Lexeth said, "where do we go?"

Looking around, Bennik heard a distinct jingling in his mind—a sound from his childhood. That sound always reminded him of one place.

Fainly Lopke had no idea where he was. The Old Ways had led him completely astray, and he feared if he didn't find an escape soon, the gathering dark would consume him. Not for the first time since leaving the Arcania, he both regretted his impulsivity and cursed his hesitancy—he had delayed this task for far too many years, but he didn't know enough about what was happening to risk such a perilous trek.

His mind wandered to Ruke again. He foolishly expected to feel her presence down here, but if anything she had never felt so distant; down here in these depths she so loved, Ruke felt dead to Fainly.

"We always said we'd meet again down here," he said miserably, stepping over a blackened root that tried to catch his foot. He nearly stumbled as the earth itself heaved under him again. "I don't think you would hold it against me if I said I hoped to never come here again."

There was a putrid haze hanging in the earthen hall, as if the soil and roots were absorbing whatever life they could and exhaling corruption. Fainly found it hard to breathe. Knowing how this place worked, he focused on the things he needed, but they were compounding.

He needed to find the Child of Light before the queen. He needed to find Ruke's stone. He needed to recover *The Book of Stane*. But mostly—the earth shook again—he needed to get out of here.

"Guide me, Ruke." He had never felt so meek, so willing to drop to his knees and beg if it meant he could escape this deepening hell. The poisoned air thickened as if in response, but a subtle green light took shape in the murky distance. He narrowed his eyes, wondering if he was hallucinating. "Is that you?"

The light pulsed, quickening Fainly's heart that was already thundering in his chest. The earth shook again, but he was transfixed, stepping toward the mysterious glow. The unnatural mists parted for him, welcoming him forward. Even while in a trance, Fainly knew he was foolish for chasing a strange shimmering in the Old Ways.

But Ruke had always made him do foolish things.

He stepped forward. "Ruke?"

"You're here," Ruke answered. "I've been waiting so long..."

Her voice was weak, but it invigorated Fainly. He started to run and immediately tumbled forward as his feet became tangled in more writhing roots. The serpentine growths began to coil around his limbs, attempting to pull him into the loosening earth. Regardless, he clawed his way forward. "Ruke!"

"Not here," Ruke responded, but her voice wavered. Even after all these years, Fainly knew her voice well. But it sounded different here, taking on a strange rasping croak. "Was falling...falling. I saw her."

The green light intensified, and Fainly looked on desperately as Ruke took shape in the roiling gloom that separated them. "Ruke!" Fainly heedlessly reached for arcane power to free himself. The roots responded immediately as fire sparked to life above the palm of his outstretched hand, tightening and pulling him into the mossy sea below.

Before his head was pulled under, Fainly spoke a word and the fire took on the shape of a curved saber that he grasped by the hilt and slashed at the roots.

"Don't," the voice warned weakly. Fainly looked toward Ruke and saw her more clearly now, a shadow framed in a pale green light. But something was wrong...the halfling's body morphed into a stooped form stumbling forward. No—it was something crawling toward him, a frail and crooked form, not the vision of Ruke that Fainly had visited in the Fey Domain.

Heedless, Fainly carved at the grasping vegetation, the dry corrupted limbs yielding to the arcane fire with a piercing hiss. It sounded like a creature crying out as the gnome hacked off its limbs, but the sounds came from the earth itself.

"It's Oakus," the crawling form said, reaching out a hand. The shadow took form and Fainly now saw it was an old human woman, rotting clothes falling off her wrinkled flesh. She opened her mouth to call out to him; only two teeth remained to her. In response, the roots retreated back into the solidifying mossy ground.

Fainly released the magic, his fiery blade disappearing in a waft of smoke. He scrambled to his feet as the old woman began coughing violently, sapped of the strength she had used to pull herself toward the gnome.

Something about the woman reminded Fainly of an encounter he had nearly four hundred years ago, before his first long slumber. He was a young, ambitious mage back then, eager to join the Keyguard but too proud to follow their antiquated traditions. There was a woman then who showed him the deeper lores, allowing Fainly to push the limits of the feysleep.

"Kartha!?"

The old woman ignored him, still crawling. "I need him," she said between coughs. "Help me, please."

Dumbfounded, Fainly couldn't do anything but rush to her aid. He reached down to help her up—*gods, she weighs nothing!*—but her legs wouldn't allow it. She shook her head, motioning to the ground where the roots had retreated. "I need Oakus!"

Fainly didn't know what she meant, but he pulled her toward the mossy ground that had tried to swallow him. What clothes remained to her crumbled away under his touch, falling apart as if they were woven from dust. The living corpse that looked like Kartha was naked and withered, but she clawed desperately for the dark pool of growth.

When they reached the spot, Kartha shrugged out of Fainly's grasp and thrust her hands into the earth. The mossy ground gave way to her plunge and the dirt shifted in subtle ripples as if it were thick water. Kartha's mouth smacked open and closed as she spoke words that even Fainly couldn't discern. Some of it sounded like Ghultan, but he couldn't be sure, especially through her wracking coughs.

Whatever she said, the Old Ways reacted, the entire passage growing taught like a stretched bowstring. Fainly heard the sound of creaking branches as Karth began drawing her bare arms out of the ground. Her ancient body was caked in mossy earth as she drew herself back. When her hands emerged, they clutched a chunk of roots that writhed like snakes.

Kartha's mouth still worked wordlessly as her strength gave out and she fell to her side. "Help," she pleaded, motioning to Fainly with the roots in her skeletal fists. "Hold them."

Hesitantly, Fainly knelt over her and took hold of the roots. He looked to her for some sort of instruction, but Kartha's eyes were closed as her mouth worked a silent incantation. Fainly felt a tingle of power through his hands, followed by a quick surge. He closed his eyes against the foreign sensation and he saw Ruke in his mind, reaching out to him. Her face was twisted in an expression of rage and terror, but her screams were drowned out by the power deafening his mind.

Fainly opened his eyes and gasped. Kartha's hands had changed from bony hands bound in dry, leathered flesh to youthful, feminine fingers. Her arms were still old and feeble, but where she grasped the roots her flesh was smooth, strong, and the color of bark from a white oak tree.

"Focus," Kartha said with a dying breath. Her eyes had rolled back into her skull, her frayed, white hair falling out in clumps. "Channel…Oakus."

Fainly could feel her going limp, but he did as he was bade, imagining the branches were a keyshard of Oakus and he was channeling the power of growth. Immediately he felt the ancient magic, it gathered within him like a moment of climax and his body shuddered. A scream escaped him before he could grit his teeth. He could barely open his eyes, but he could feel Kartha thrashing from the surge of energy passing between them.

It was intimate and horrifying, something he had never experienced. In his mind, Ruke was with them, sharing in the moment, but screaming in protest. Whatever was happening, Fainly knew that Ruke did not want him to see it through. But there was no stopping it now.

As the overwhelming sensation passed through his body, Fainly could only watch now as it overtook Kartha. They both gripped the decaying roots so tightly that he was surprised they weren't crushed, especially in Kartha's powerful new hands that were now twice the size of his. Fainly watched as her wrists began to change shape, turning from weathered parchment to smooth, immaculate flesh. The energy that passed through him into Kartha was purging the years from her.

He was witnessing a rebirth, and from somewhere else he heard Ruke screaming a dire warning that he could not—or didn't care to—comprehend. He watched, eyes wide and mouth agape as Kartha's rotting corpse was rejuvenated, becoming something else entirely. The earthen, gray-brown flesh soon covered her whole body, luscious curves replacing bony joints, gnarled gray hair replaced by bushy, moss-like growths now sprouting from her head, under her arms, and just below her smooth belly.

The transformation was nearly complete. Fainly eventually felt able to let go of the roots, his body no longer locked in place by the powers that Kartha had summoned. He took a small step back, feeling smaller now as the witch had grown to the size of a hale, human woman.

He felt a strange flush creep up his face as he observed her form. Sitting there, gripping those roots with her head thrown back—*in pain? Pleasure?* Fainly assumed both, given his own experience—he couldn't help but marvel at the beautiful creature she had become. The rough, cracked texture of her skin began to smoothen, while her bony limbs had become thick, powerful, and lovely. Everything about Kartha's leathery body had been transformed into smooth, muscled curves and she bore the face of a twenty-year-old.

A long moment passed during which Fainly's mind finally cleared. He wasn't thinking of Ruke, or the corrupted state of the Old Ways, or even the perils facing Andelor. He was consumed by wonder.

But it was short-lived as Kartha began to spasm. She contorted, curling her limbs in as she hunched forward and pulling the roots to her mouth so she could begin devouring them. Her eyes were still white, the pupils rolled back into her head, but she savagely fed on the twisted branches that lashed around wildly in response to being consumed.

Fainly watched in disgust as Kartha shoved the last of the squirming plants into her mouth, chewing and swallowing, desperate to ingest every last fiber; and she did. When the feast was over—mud caking her lips and cheeks—Kartha's rigid body relaxed and she reclined against the earthen wall. Fainly couldn't turn away from the sight, despite the growing sense of propriety he felt as he gawked at a beautiful naked woman.

Darkness fell abruptly as the last echoes of the power left Fainly. It felt as if the world had taken a deep breath, and as it exhaled, a soft green light showed him the Old Ways had completely changed. The thick corrupted air was clearer now, returning to the gentle mists that Fainly had always associated with this place. He saw no more black, grasping roots coming from the shifting mossy seas; the ground was solid again, and plant life only swayed in slow rhythm like before.

His eyes shifted from the welcoming landscape back to his new companion. "Kartha, is that you?"

The woman's eyes opened, revealing vibrant emerald pupils that whipped from one sight to another. Finally they settled on Fainly, and she turned to face him. Sensing his unease, she looked down at her body and offered a laugh. "In a way." Making no move to cover herself, she sat up awkwardly, clearly unused to her new body. She inspected her arms, ran her hands over her breasts and then the soft flesh of her stomach, and finally along her legs, not finding whatever it was she sought. "I always wondered what they looked like..."

Fainly raised an eyebrow, still unable to take his eyes off her despite the flush that crept up his face as he watched her explore such a wondrous body. "What *who* looked like?"

She didn't take her eyes off the curves of her own flesh. "The Daughters of Oakus, as they called themselves."

Still confused, Fainly pried further. "The druids?"

"I suppose there are many who have taken the name over the years. But no—not mere druids. Ruke used to tell me of them. Before the elves came to Noveth, there were Eastlund maids who claimed Lohkrest Woods for themselves, living only to serve Oakus. Some say they were the ones who discovered these passages," she motioned down the infinite emerald hall. "They were something more than druids—they forged a bond with Oakus before he was Unthroned."

Kartha's gaze became distant then, her expression sagging with sudden sadness. "When the Keys were shattered, these ladies who had become so closely bonded with Oakus were transformed." She looked back to her own body, shifting to sit up taller. "It was said they had given up their own lives to take a piece of Oakus—the same power I imagine created the keyshards created the Daughters of Oakus."

Fainly considered that. It wasn't the first time he imagined the specifics of what had happened during the Unthroning. He liked to imagine colorful strands of energy—the essence of magic—coursing through the world as the gods were pulled down from the heavenly realms and bound to their Keys. When that power became too great, the Keys were violently shattered, and with them any relics, altars, or other objects used to channel or worship the gods.

He was surprised to realize that he never imagined any people—holy priests or shamans—being shattered or changed by that fateful ritual. It was commonly known that the Light and Shadow took hold within people and monsters, respectively, but Fainly realized he had never considered the implication of a person being shattered by an old god's power.

Kartha got to her feet, more gracefully than expected. Fainly's eyes were of a height with the patch of moss that had grown between Kartha's legs, and he finally gave into modesty, turning away in a show of investigating their surroundings. "What have you done? How did you come to be here, Kartha?"

There were too many questions swirling in his head.

"No need to be shy," Kartha said, taking her first step in a new body; she moved naturally albeit slowly. "This body isn't truly mine. I belong to Oakus now, for however long we find each other useful, I suppose."

Fainly looked back up to her, doing his best to ignore her nudity—*but she is gorgeous,* he thought miserably, hating this attraction he felt toward the old, cruel witch—while sorting through the jumbled questions in his mind. "How is this possible? Tell me where you have been all these years."

Kartha motioned for Fainly to follow as she walked slowly down the peaceful hall. She told the tale about the graystone and the demon Ithakan, then of poor Percy's possession and eventual death. "I followed Ruke's lead in binding myself to a shard—leaving my body down here in hopes I may someday return." She stopped walking and turned to Fainly. "I should not have been able to."

The Archmage considered her tale, thinking of how it aligned with the current events that had driven him from Andelor. "There are a lot of things happening right now that should not be possible. Though if you were expelled from that boy's body so near a passage to the Old Ways, it would not seem too extraordinary for you to return to your body." He gave her a sideways look. "Although this..."

Kartha nodded, looking at nothing in particular. Her mossy hair falling across her face. "It was desperation. My body was finished—it was rather miraculous I could move it at all. Though time passes differently down here, as you know. But since I awoke, I've had visions of a creature down here. A monstrous tree built like an armored giant."

"An incarnate," Fainly said, thinking back to his meeting with the Archbeacon. "If Eyen's power has been restored somehow, I can only imagine the others are finding their chosen. I suspected as much, but hadn't confirmed it." He looked up to Kartha again. "Until now, I suppose."

As if in response, the hall shook violently, knocking them both to the ground. The gentle mists grew heavy again, and a creaking sound in the distance intensified, growing louder as the ground shifted in undulating waves that closed in on them. Kartha grabbed Fainly, cradling him like a child as she started to run, sprinting gracefully down the hall.

Before Fainly could protest, they were turning down a different hall away from crooked roots bursting out the ground behind them, reaching.

"Someone is disturbing Oakus," Kartha said with a strange amount of calmness. Her words were punctuated by her quick strides. "We are no longer welcome here—think of where we need to be."

"We need to be everywhere," Fainly said as his face bounced against her bare chest. But only one place came to mind, and as much as he needed to go there, it was the last place he was ready to go.

Chapter Six

A Proper Greeting

Anika had lost track of time long ago. Since the events in Oakworth, the passage of a day meant very little to her. When once her thoughts were framed in days, weeks, and years, it seemed now they were instead shrouded in consuming, aimless oblivion.

She did fight against that darkness, not willing to give herself over to it completely. But there was a certain amount of comfort she found in letting her mind become lost in an impossibly deep sea of existential dread. Searching for meaning in her life while hugging her knees on the floor of a Karranese prison cell had a way of reminding her how little she (and her failed search for answers) mattered to the world.

The feeling of failure that consumed her in the wake of Corvanna's defeat felt less suffocating now as she sat and considered what her life had become. Having an abundance of solitude allowed her to ruminate on own thoughts and feelings, more than she ever had before, finding new ways to cope with all the compounded tragedies.

The only mother she ever knew was dead. The father who raised her was likely dead too. The Light would have her believe her brother was her sworn enemy. Her first love was dead, due to her belief that she could somehow fight against prophecies laid down centuries before her birth.

Anika was slowly beginning to accept these realities in a way that might let her forge ahead. The darkness gave her hope, and she found herself thankful that she had allowed it to envelope her.

But a newfound determination was waking within her, and she was ready to leave this dingy prison. She was the Child of Light, and she would never find her path down here in the cold shadows. However, she came here for a reason, and before she could think about the future, she had to find out where she came from.

She stood up suddenly, ignoring the pins in her legs and her numb backside. The jailor was nowhere to be seen, and one of the other prisoners had already been taken above. Anika wasn't sure what that meant. She was surprisingly unlearned in Karranese culture. While the baron of Oakworth routinely hanged thieves, it had seemed severe and uncommon, judging from how it had been discussed in Blakehurst.

Considering she was charged with thievery as well, she secretly hoped the other thief had survived his judgment. Regardless, she was tired of putting this off. "Hello?"

The other prisoner mumbled something at her in Karranese that Anika couldn't understand, but whatever it was, it sounded angry. Regardless, she heard footsteps from the dimly lit corridor. From around the corner, a pool of light drew closer. Soon, the jailor's broad form turned the corner and stalked toward her.

"Does milady need a new gown?" His mocking Eastlund accent was very accurate.

Anika swallowed and paused before answering. "I'm ready to speak with the nomarch."

Even in the darkness, Anika could see the man's shadowed expression shift from jovial to stern. "The nomarch doesn't serve at your convenience," he said in his normal thick Karranese accent. "Wait until she returns."

A sudden wrath came over Anika—like a crack of thunder in a calm sky—and she stepped toward the prison bars, wrapping her hands around them. "She's going to want to hear what I have to say." The jailor's lantern light intensified as her eyes narrowed.

He didn't seem to notice. "We'll see when she returns. Two days. Maybe three."

Anika saw something behind the jailor then, a shadow taking the shape of a woman. The Karranese woman from her visions; her birth mother. Or at least the way she imagined how her birth mother looked. No—she was certain the visage was her mother. The certainty was primal. It was the same certainty that came when she accepted that she was the Child of Light.

The vision of the woman strengthened her resolve and she reached out for the power that she had abandoned when she had been taken prisoner. A cool breeze came from down the hall, blowing her tangled hair back.

"I'm done waiting."

The jailor reached for the club that hung from his belt, taking an angry step toward her. But before his second step, a powerful gust came around the corner and knocked him forward off his feet. His lantern smashed to the ground and Anika had to tighten her grip as the wind hit her like a tidal wave.

Some time later, the nomarch strode into the prison, once again armored with a crimson cloak billowing in her wake. Wordlessly she instructed the jailor to unlock Anika's cell then motioned for Anika to follow her out of the dungeon. The jailor kept his distance from Anika, watching her nervously as he followed the two women.

"I'm ready to answer your questions."

The nomarch ignored Anika and kept her pace, turning the corner. Anika followed, uncertain what lay in store for her, but as she told the jailor: she was done waiting.

The two women left the dungeon via a spiraling stone staircase which started with dark, broken stone and after a few floors turned into aged marble steps with smooth, polished ebony banisters. After two more floors of silent ascent, the nomarch led Anika through an elegant archway that opened to a high-vaulted chamber.

The sunlight that came through the windows above nearly blinded Anika, but she followed the nomarch's footsteps that now echoed on the polished marble floor. Her own bare feet made slapping noises as she struggled to keep up, which—after her eyes adjusted and she saw the elegance of the hall—made her feel oddly embarrassed.

They walked the length of the hall, across decorative rugs and passing by giant sculptures of manticores, basilisk, and other desert creatures that were known to hunt the eastern sands. Anika felt a strange comfort from the deadly looking monsters, and was transfixed by each one as she passed.

The walls in the chamber were dark marble, with ivory pillars supporting a balcony above. Anika wasn't sure the purpose of such a hall, as there were no chairs or sofas, but it had a mystical quality that she assumed might make it a suitable ballroom or similar gathering hall.

"This is where your trial will be held," the nomarch said, as if sensing Anika's thoughts. She motioned to the statues. "Thieves found guilty are given a choice. Exile or servitude. Brave the eastern sands, never to return to Karrane, or serve five years in our mines on Suthek."

"I'm not a thief," Anika said, but the words sounded hollow even to her.

The nomarch responded with another wave of her hand, motioning to their right where two armored guards pushed open a set of heavy doors. The guards wore the same crimson and orange colors as the nomarch, and their cloaks bore the yellow pyramid and broken chain sigil of Karrane.

As Anika came to the open doorway, she saw a lavish study with more books than she had seen in her entire life. They lined the shelves on each wall, stuffed like bricks of every color—old leather tomes of various shades of brown, fat books with golden spines of flowing foreign scripts shimmering in the room's candlelight, and every other type of book she could imagine.

The sight shocked her; not just due to the extravagance of the room, but she never imagined books—even in this quantity and variety—would inspire such wonder in her. Unlike many of the other villagers in Blakehurst, Anika had learned to read at a young age. Her father had made it a point that Anika and Gage could both read the histories of Eastlund, Vale, and Westerra that he kept on the shelf above his bed. However, Anika had never lusted after books.

Until now.

"Welcome."

Anika turned to a young man dressed in the finest clothes she had ever seen. His deep ochre skin marked him as Karranese, and the elegant open vest that flowed past his knees marked him as a noble. His bare chest was adorned with several golden chains hanging from his neck, each one socketed with a ruby or a topaz that glimmered in the candlelight.

Suddenly very aware of the rags she wore, Anika crossed her arms and shifted uncomfortably. The doors behind her closed and the nomarch strode over to the table, where Anika now saw two other figures reclining in high-backed, ornate chairs. One was an elderly elf in a luxurious yellow robe clasped at chest, stomach, and waist with shimmering rubies. His shoulders were mantled in ornamental armor plates, tassels of silvery thread hanging from each.

The pale-skinned elf watched Anika with studied caution. His expression was not unkind, but the way he looked at her made Anika think she could be crowned queen of Vale or beheaded in front of him and he wouldn't be bothered either way. His old hands were steepled, fingers tapping in a slow and steady rhythm.

Two chairs away from the elf sat a more gracious figure, a holy woman if Anika would have guessed. She was Karranese, but her complexion was closer to the young man who stood before her as opposed to Anika's own. She wore priestly vestments similar to Mother Beatrim in Blakehurst. Anika's racing heart seemed to slow itself under the woman's kind and knowing gaze.

"I apologize you had to wait so long, my Lady of Lawson," the young man said, taking a step forward and clasping his hands as if in prayer. "Please tell me: may we call you Anika?"

Anika looked from him to the nomarch, who stood silently watching Anika with arms crossed over the swirling glyphs of her armor.

The man took another step forward, motioning to the nomarch. "Our honorable Jamira Kraiev has shared with us your name, but not your tale. We understand you would like to share that with us now..."

Anika shifted her feet again, not sure how to begin. She again felt overly conscious of her prison clothes. Something felt wrong. Shouldn't she be clapped in irons and questioned by a torturer? Instead, the man before her—who could only be the majest of all of Karrane—was motioning for her to take a seat at the finest table she had ever seen.

She made to move, but stopped herself. "Yes, I'm An—I mean, yes, you may call me Anika…" She didn't know how to address him. "Your maja—your majesty."

"Your eminence," the old elf said without breaking his fingers' steady tapping.

The man smiled at Anika. "Words can be quite funny, yes?" He motioned again to the table, pulling out a chair worthy of a queen. "Please have a seat. We only have a few questions, and then we will get you some proper attire." The majest clapped his hands and a Karranese halfling shuffled in through a triangular archway at the back of the room.

"Stevra," the majest said without looking at the short woman, "please prepare the lady's quarters. Have a meal brought up, and a selection of gowns befitting a royal guest. Also a bath."

"Certainly, your eminence," the halfling said with a jingling bow. She was dressed lavishly for a servant, in scarlet silks draped in orange scarves, tied with metal bands that were adorned with dangling jewelry. Stevra gave Anika a curious look, but her eyes darted away and she quickly spun around to disappear back through the archway.

Anika timidly took a seat. As she did, something pulled at her insides, upsetting her stomach. It was a familiar feeling, but not one she could assign a specific memory to—like déjà vu. She tried to ignore it as best she could as the majest gently pushed her chair closer to the table.

The familiar feeling of unease persisted as the majest and the nomarch found seats on either side of the table. Dreadfully, Anika only then realized that she sat at the head of the table. She felt absurd, despoiling such an extravagant chair with her filthy prison clothes while the ruler of Karrane folded his hand atop a royal table that she sat at the head of. Not for the first time, she silently wondered how she had gotten here. It was as if she no longer had even the faintest hint of control over her life.

"Now," the majest said, "where shall we begin?" He gave her a bright smile, which quickly soured when he saw her confused face. "Oh! Pardon my manners. You must think me a savage Sutheki or a fumbling half-orc." He laughed.

Anika couldn't help but smile in response. While she found the majest's bigoted remarks unattractive, his jovial nature was inviting and his beautiful face weakened her judgment.

"Allow me to introduce myself and my council," he said with a delicate hand placed on his bare chest. "I am Lekan Nafir, the Forty-Sixth Elected Majest of

Karrane, High Delegate of the Trivestiture, and Ambassador to the Chamberlords."

Lekan motioned toward the elf next to him. "My Grand Vizier Elrin Dothry. You've already met our most esteemed nomarch Jamira. And across from me is our Lightmother Taliah Renera, the High Beacon of the Sunstone Temple, the greatest monument built to the Light in all of Noveth."

Taliah swelled with pride as she offered Anika a kind smile and a nod of her head. The others kept placid faces as they watched in silent anticipation.

Anika felt like the silence that followed required her to say something. "It's...an honor." *Yes, it's been a real honor shitting in a bucket while you all kept me locked in a cage.* But she knew enough about royalty to know there was a game to be played here. The strange feeling in the pit of her stomach intensified, and she struggled to maintain her composure.

As if noticing, Lekan continued. "Perhaps, Anika, you could tell us how you came to our great city."

Not knowing how else to say it, and eager not to draw this out longer than it needed to be, she simply said, "I flew."

The claim didn't seem to surprise any of them, their expressions only slightly inquisitive, which unsettled her stomach even more. She began to wonder how much they already knew about her, and how many lies she could get away with.

"I am no stranger to levitation," the old elf said, finally folding his fingers together to stop their hypnotic swaying. "But to fly across an entire realm is not a feat even the Archmage of the Arcania could accomplish."

"It's said that some priests on Xe'dann are known to sprout black wings drawn from ancient Shadow magic," the Lightmother said. Her words had a poisonous tone, but she kept that gentle expression on her face which disturbed Anika more than the elf's accusatory stare. "Perhaps darker powers brought you here?"

"Come now, Taliah," Lekan said with a boyish charm that cut through the tension, "let us not make assumptions. I think we can all agree that we have plenty of time to sort through the details of our guest's journey here. What's most pressing is we discover why she's here and how we might resolve this misunderstanding, yes?"

The vizier and priestess nodded in unison while the nomarch shifted in her seat to face Anika. "You told the jailor that I would want to hear what you have to say. I'm listening."

Anika swallowed, trying to ignore the discomfort in her gut like an itch that she could not reach to scratch. Not giving herself any time to properly plan how she ought to respond, she began talking. "My home in Vale was raided by harpies, drawn to a keyshard that came into my village. The harpies were led by a monster named Corvanna who claimed to be an incarnate of Eyen."

Anika noticed Taliah's expression melt away with the mention of Corvanna, but she continued her story.

"The storm from Rathen was spreading south, and I saw her in the stone. She made it—the storm, I mean—and she needed the stone that was brought to my village." The yearning in her stomach intensified as she remembered that terrible vision. "I don't know how, but I knew she needed it. That's why the harpies came. That's why my father was…"

She paused, looking at the table and considering how much of her story these people needed to know. Would they believe her if she said she were the Child of Light? What would they do with her if they did? How else could she explain that she knew what Corvanna was and what she was after? She was afraid to lie, because she had no idea how she could answer all these questions while keeping all the half-truths straight.

"My brother, Gage, and I ran away, hoping to get the keyshard somewhere safe. But Corvanna came with her storm and attacked us at Oakworth, and…" she looked away, Matty dying once more in her mind, his body going slack as the sickening sound of his neck snapping echoed like thunder. The tears were like sharp needles thrusting themselves from the corners of her eyes despite her best efforts to keep them hidden.

"Perhaps," Jamira began, her voice gentler now, "you could begin earlier. With how you came to be living in Vale. You're clearly Karranese, that is plain to see. Who were your parents?"

The nomarch had cut to the quick of it, Anika realized then, relieved to not have to speak more of the prophecy she had been swept up in. The question was: what had brought her to Karrane?

"I don't know who my birth parents were," Anika answered. "I was adopted by an Eastlunder who found me in Westerra. I was taken to Vale to be raised." Despite the continued discomfort in her stomach, she gave the nomarch a steady gaze. "That's what I was doing in the chamberlord's manse. Like the visions of Corvanna, I've had visions of my true mother. The artists of Pyram are legendary. I thought maybe—"

The vizier interrupted her. "You thought your mother was a high lady in a chamberlord's portrait?"

The accusation shamed Anika when she heard it spoken aloud. "I thought, perhaps I might find a relation. Someone with a likeness." Her eyes fell down to the table again, defeated. "It was only a hope—foolish, I suppose."

Lekan leaned toward her, drawing Anika's eyes to his own. He offered her a small smile—his dark eyes threatening to melt her with the sympathy they conveyed. "It was not foolish. Clever, I might say. We do have the finest artists in all of Aetha, and—ah!" He sat up and snapped his fingers, his grin turning into the most captivating smile Anika had ever seen. "That gives me an idea—but one that we must prepare for."

The majest reached over and took Anika's hand in both of his, startling her at first, but his warm touch relaxed her body in a way she had not expected. "Thank you for answering our questions. I fear we may have many more for you, but first you need some proper food, a proper bath, and plenty of proper rest." He raised his hands to guide her out of her chair.

"Stevra," Lekan said while still smiling at Anika. "Please see the Lady Anika to her chambers and see that she is properly taken care of. If you will forgive me, my lady, I fear I must further consult with my councilors. But we shall speak on the morrow when you have had time to further recover."

Anika felt lightheaded, entirely charmed by the man. He was not what she had expected at all. She walked into this room ready to be tortured, tried, and possibly hanged by an angry tyrant. Instead, she felt as if she were a princess being courted by one of the most beautiful men she had ever seen. The discomfort in her stomach made her wary that this was all some sort of trap. And something about Lekan made her feel even more guilty about Matty's death.

"Oh," the majest said as he let go of Anika's hand and guided her to the halfling servant that awaited her. Lekan turned toward his vizier who slowly rose from his chair. Anika gasped as she saw the elf draw something out from his robes.

"I believe this belongs to you," the majest said, taking the item from Elrin in both of his hands as if it were a newborn babe and handing it to Anika hilt first.

The discomfort in Anika's stomach became a stinging pain, but then entirely dissipated as she took hold of Stormender. She felt complete again.

A heavy, blissful silence swelled within the room as Anika held the weapon. When she looked up at Lekan's kind face, she felt a sense of belonging beyond what she had ever felt in Blakehurst.

She was home.

Chapter Seven
Unrest

Sitting on a filthy crate, Gage watched the street as he pulled his hood forward to further shield his face from the rain and wandering eyes. He was transfixed by a certain stone in the middle of the busy road. Dozens of feet obscured that smooth jade stone from view, but he managed to keep his vision locked on it for almost the entire gloomy morning and on into the afternoon.

The stone looked nothing like the keyshard he had given his sister, but in his mind it was the exact one. And in that stone's depths, he could watch his mother die a thousand times. She died each time a wanderer's foot tread on that piece of road, then her bloody face would become Robin's and a chill would run down his spine as he watched blood drip from his lover's face.

His stomach groaned. He hadn't eaten since leaving the inn—*was that yesterday? Or two days ago?*—and his body was weaker than he ever remembered. The thought of food sickened him though, just like every other thought that passed through his mind sickened him. He was consumed with self-loathing, and when he occasionally saw his reflection in a puddle, he was compelled to stand up to stomp on it.

Fortunately, he didn't need to. The streets of Sathford were exceptionally busy, and there were plenty of travelers perfectly willing to tread on his visage. Gage watched more people pass by in an hour than he had seen in an entire year while living in Blakehurst. That should have excited him; he had always dreamed of living in a big city. Instead he felt pity for those people hurrying about, toiling away at their crafts. For what? What were they striving for? What could they hope to earn?

He saw a dwarven merchant struggling to guide her donkey through the bustling street, cursing as taller travelers mindlessly kicked muddy water in her direction. There was a Copera woman hawking beaded talismans from her traveling shop which was a cabinet strapped to the back of a hulking half-orc who clumsily shoved potential customers out of the way.

Gage wished he would be struck by the same wonder that he once expected to feel while tucked away in Blakehurst, dreaming of living in a bustling city. However, all he felt was pity and disdain, and a crushing sense of loss.

The afternoon dragged on, and soon Gage was struggling to ignore the hunger that was sending sharp pains throughout his body. He was about to get up from the turned-over crate in the alley when a figure approached, finding a seat next to him on another crate. Like him, the figure was covered in a dark, hooded cloak.

"Are you hiding as well?"

Gage tensed, unsure how to respond, afraid if he got up to run that the newcomer might suspect him of being a vagrant—which he was—and shout for the guards. Instead he just waited, keeping his face as hidden as he could.

"I don't blame you," the man said, reaching up to pull back his own hood. The dreary rain that had started that morning and continued throughout the day suddenly stopped. A roll of thunder in the distance marked the storm's next destination as a single ray of sunlight gradually lit the alley. "This city has lots of eyes."

Gage couldn't help but peer at the man from the shadows of his own hood. The stranger had scars running across his face and hands, as if he had been lashed a thousand times. His eyes were sunken in a grimy darkness, which ran down his face in black streaks. Silver streaks ran through his thin black hair, soaked by the rain.

The man reached his thin, pale hands into his robe and produced a package of waxy parchment tied with a string. He set it on his lap and slowly began to open it.

"Are you hungry?"

The very word sent another spasm of pain through Gage's stomach. Food sounded terrible to him, but his body vehemently disagreed. He watched hungrily as the man unwrapped a feast of three steaming chunks of bread, what looked like a white wheel of cheese, and a small roasted bird that was dripping with grease.

All apprehensions fell away, and Gage turned toward the man, reaching up to push his hood back just enough to reveal his ravenous eyes.

"I spent years in these alleys," he said. The man's voice didn't make him sound much older than Gage, but his face and eyes told a different story. He looked weary and defeated, but when he tore a piece of the bread that had soaked up some of the bird's grease and presented it as an offering, Gage thought he looked gracious and wise.

Gage reached out to take it, slowly at first. But when his fingers touched it, he snatched it quickly to his mouth and devoured it. As he chewed, he watched the stranger nervously, waiting for some sign of treachery. But his new companion just tore another chunk of bread apart, offering it to Gage as he took a bite for himself.

"Thank you," Gage finally said, taking the next piece while eyeing the steaming meat.

The man's mouth twitched as if he wanted to smile but had forgotten how. "Here," he said, picking up the entire meal and handing it to Gage. "I realize I'm not so hungry."

Feeling even more famished as he chewed the next mouthful of bread, he took the offering, placed it on his own lap, and began wolfing it down.

"I know they're looking for you."

Gage froze mid-bite, letting the juice from the bird slowly trickle down his chin as he watched the man warily. But something about the look he gave Gage made him relax, as if there were an unspoken agreement that passed between their eyes, promising that neither of them would expose the other.

"They're looking for me too," he said, looking at something in the distance above Gage's head. "That's why I came back here. I got lost here before, when I was younger; maybe I can get lost again."

A loud crash made Gage jolt, and he stood up. There were shouts out on the road, and two men in wild hair and bristly beards shoved each other as an armored knight on a horse kicked at them to clear the way.

"That's a good meal," the man said, as if he hadn't noticed the commotion.

Gage looked down and saw the food now scattered across the muddy ground, ruined. "I'm sorry," Gage said miserably. "I thought—"

He shook his head. "You thought they were coming for you. But they won't. They can post your face all over the city, but no one will see past the Luminaura here. Between the chapel burning down, the new cathedral's construction, and the incarnate attack, I hate to tell you, Gage..." he leaned back against the building, his eyes looking back to the distance above Gage's head, "...but you're the least of anyone's concern here in Sathford."

"How do you know me?" The question felt foolish—if he had seen Gage's face on the wanted posters, he would know his and Robin's name well—but he was curious how the man would respond.

His eyes remained distant. "I know your sister. I believe I hurt her; but she failed to heed my warnings."

My sister?

Gage swallowed, considering his chances of slipping away from this man without drawing undue attention from the guards that stalked the streets. But before he could act, the man's eyes met his.

"Tell me," he leaned forward, his thin limp hair falling over his pale, scarred face giving him the look of a ghoul rising from a damp grave. "Will you heed them?"

Gage's eyes fell then, looking into the man's hand where a jagged emerald keyshard beckoned him into its depths.

Robin's heart pounded. There was a commotion out the street, and he was certain someone had seen him. He tried to steady his breathing as he ducked between barrels in the alley behind a tinker's shop. There was shouting and shuffling around the corner, but he hadn't heard anyone call out to the guards.

He steadied his breathing, preparing himself for the moment when he'd be discovered and he would have to run through the half-flooded thoroughfare toward the bridge.

But the commotion died down. There were still a few nasty words thrown between a pair of arguing women, but no one came around the corner to confront him. Maybe he hadn't been seen after all.

He waited a long moment before he dared to creep out of his hiding space, but with the rain letting up, he had to get moving. Blindly hunting for Gage throughout the bustling streets of Sathford in the rain when everyone had their hoods up had gotten him nowhere. However, now that less suspicious folks were letting their hair down, he might be able to more easily notice a skulking fugitive.

After ensuring no one was watching for him, Robin emerged from the shadows with his hood drawn.

What were you thinking, Gage? He felt his anger returning now that he knew he wasn't spotted, and the same questions flooded his mind. How could Gage leave him like this? After everything they'd been through. *Can you blame him? You killed his mother, you monster!*

He turned the corner and slammed into a woman twice his size.

"Watch it!"

Robin was knocked back into the alley, ignored by the hulking woman who carried two bulging sacks over her shoulder. She pushed through several other people, shouting warnings after knocking them to the ground as well. Fortunately, no one paid Robin any mind as he scrambled back to his feet and arranged his hood over his blonde hair, making sure his elven ears were hidden.

Doing his best to weave through the bustling traffic, Robin made his way toward the only place he hadn't checked for Gage yet, hoping he wouldn't find him there.

"Raventhal Spire?" Brace asked, shaking the rain out of his long hair. He had missed the worst of the downpour, having spent the day sleeping off the ale from early morning.

Darrance Moore nodded and scoffed, directing his gelding through the bustling streets while keeping pace with Brace's more agile mare. "It seems the High Mage has been less than agreeable to Hope's commands. With the Archmage's recent departure, Andelor has less sway here. Move aside!" He checked his mount as a fish cart tried to cut through the congestion. "Hope has concerns regarding the Archmage—Luriah has assured us we have the Arcania's support, but with Fainly's disappearance...well, it's certainly strange."

Brace looked up at the tower as the clouds above began to part, letting a ray of sunlight through to brighten the strange avian statues adorning the school. All Brace could see were those damned harpies twisting in and out of those high windows. "So she means to have us demand entry?"

The paladin produced a scroll, sealed with Hope's yellow wax stars. "A holy writ, signed off by the Lord Mayor himself." He returned the decree to the leather pouch next to his sheathed sword. "We are to ensure the academy is willing to assist in the cathedral's construction, despite its own repairs. Fortunately, the Lord Mayor sees wisdom in striking while the iron is hot."

"Hail the Light!"

Brace and Darrance turned to see a stooped man in a leather cap standing atop a stalled wagon.

"Defenders of Sathford! Praise the Archbeacon and her warriors of Light!"

Brace saw Darrance smile as he waved to the man. "Tolle understands that the Light holds more sway here than the mages hiding in their tower." He looked back at Brace. "If it wasn't for that twisted harpy bitch, I dare say we wouldn't have been able to even ride through these streets without getting spat on. Sathford was always a haven for heathens, thanks to the Eldercrowns and that wretched Order of Oakus." Mere mention of the druids turned Darrance's smile into an ugly sneer.

The paladin's icy eyes looked up at Raventhal. "It's almost as if the Light sent that monstrosity just so we could show these faithless sheep how much they need us."

Watching as several more onlookers took up the cheers and glorification of their passing, Brace nodded grimly. "It certainly seemed to be a timely display."

The two men wove their way through the sea of bodies, across Sathler Bridge, and through Raventhal's ornamental gates, watched over by huge black ravens wrought out of iron with foreboding wings spread wide.

Hope waited for them by the tower's entrance, flanked by two paladins whose armor mirrored Darrance's, except for his sapphire shoulder plates that marked him as their commander. The High Warpriest had her auburn hair tied tightly back with a blue ribbon, wearing a long blue tunic instead of her armor, the Brightstar emblazoned across her chest. "Did you get the orders?"

Darrance nodded as he dismounted, handing his reins to the stable girl who rushed over. Brace followed the paladin, reaching into his pouch to touch his father's keyshard, suddenly feeling uneasy having it on him while entering the academy. He had heard rumors that there were glyphs in the Acrania that could detect keyshards and other items with magical properties. But looking to the paladins who moved to lead them to the doors put his mind at ease.

As they ascended the stairs, a large man waited for them by the huge doors. The High Mage of Raventhal Spire was built like a warrior, with broad shoulders, long brown hair streaked with white, and massive hands.

"Welcome to Raventhal," High Mage Konrath offered, though the expression on his face told the Luminaurians that they were far from welcome. He pushed open one of the huge doors as if it weighed no more than a curtain and it creaked inward to reveal a sprawling vestibule. "Thank you for accepting to meet. Please follow me to the Scrying Hall. Your guards can make themselves comfortable in the courtyard."

Hope led the party into the tower, followed by Darrance and Brace with her paladins waiting to secure the door. Konrath led them through the grand vestibule adorned with shelves of books, long sofas, and exotic rugs that Brace guessed came all the way from Caim, or perhaps Xe'dann.

"Where are your students?" Hope asked.

Konrath turned to her, regarding Darrance and Brace in turn as he said, "They have been confined to their quarters. We have had...complications."

Darrance looked to Brace, giving him the same quizzical expression that Brace was certain he gave in return. "What kind of complications?" Darrance asked, looking back at Konrath.

The High Mage didn't answer. His broad shoulders seemed to slump slightly, but then he motioned to an archway that spilled candlelight into the hallway. "Please. Join me here and I can explain."

Brace turned the corner and saw an elven woman in black robes standing near a long table. The room itself was decorated in high shelves stacked with books, statues, shimmering keyshards encased in glass, and other wondrous items.

"Dame Kandalot," the High Mage said, motioning to the elf, "this is Master Audreese Groaves. The High Warpriest's companions are Sir Darrance Moore and Chaplain Brace Cobbit."

Brace gave the elf a tight nod, but when she looked at him and betrayed a small smile, he felt his heart skip a beat.

"We bring an official command from the Lord Mayor," Hope began.

Konrath waved her away, motioning to the table. "I'm sure you do, but please. First, take a seat. Things have changed since our last meeting, and I apologize for my shortness before." He pulled out the chair at the head of the table and sat down, motioning again for them to join him.

After they had sat, the High Mage made a motion with his hand on the table, as if he were drawing invisible glyphs. As he finished his work, he explained, "Since the attack on Sathford, there have been several strange occurrences in the tower."

Brace gasped as he watched shadowy shapes appear in the air above the table. The conjuration looked like a series of tree roots, black and spreading out like corruption. The chaplain turned from the display to the High Mage, whose hand still busily drew unseen glyphs. The act looked like it pained Konrath, but the man kept his focus and continued speaking.

"It's no secret that the Old Ways connect our world in ways we don't fully understand. We brave their depths only under careful guidance, and we protect the gates with powerful spells forged long before our time. However, after that thing attacked us and brought that storm, something has changed."

"Here," Audreese said, motioning with a long pale finger to a certain point on the display—the lower "trunk" of the shadowy tree. "This is where the Onyx Gate below the spire provides access to the Old Ways. To enter through any other place would be extremely dangerous. The Onyx Gate is where we train our students in navigating those passages."

Konrath grunted suddenly, placing both hands on the table as he strained against some unseen pain. He looked up with grit teeth. "Sorry. Go on."

"Since the attack, something has been…growing from the Onyx Gate…" Audreese looked at Brace, as if expecting an answer from him. "We don't know what it is, but it's dangerous and it has affected some of our students."

Hope stood up, and Brace could see her eyes narrow on the conjured image of the black roots. "Is this Shadow? Can we see it?"

"No," Audreese answered immediately. "We can't see it, but we can reveal it through magic. Something spreads from the Onyx Gate, taking root in the Old Ways. I used to be able to roam those paths, deeper than anyone else in Noveth. But last I dared to enter, I felt a distinct corruption where I once felt a connection with Oakus."

The High Mage massaged his temples with thick fingers, looking ten years older. "Even visualizing this comes at a great peril." He looked up at Hope, motioning to the conjured display hovering above the table. "I can feel something is not right. I don't know if whatever this is can be involuntarily channeled through a mage, but as a precaution I've ordered Master Audreese to discontinue any studies in the undercroft and barred any students from practicing their crafts until such time as we can adequately resolve this threat."

"But is this Shadow?" Hope repeated with more fervor.

"That is why I summoned you." The High Mage waved his hand and the blackened veins above the table faded away. "We noticed this after the assault. It was subtle at first, like the dull aches an unmarked mage might feel while channeling near an Oather. But each day it became worse; myself and the other masters would become ill when we practiced our craft. The students do not draw from as deep of wells, so they were not a concern. But there are others of us..." He looked toward the elf as he trailed off.

Hope turned in her direction as Audreese stood up to speak. "I was returning from Andelor the day after the assault when I saw them: crooked figures with branches for limbs and glowing green eyes. It's as if they were guarding the way back to the Onyx Gate."

"Oakus." All eyes turned to Brace, who hadn't realized he'd spoken aloud. "The incarnate that attacked the city—a corrupted minion of Eyen. Perhaps these monsters were twisted by the Blooming One's influence in the Old Ways?"

"That beast Corvanna was an incarnate of Eyen," Darrance said stiffly. "Are you saying Oakus has several incarnates?"

"No," Audreese replied. "Incarnates are a concentration of magical energy; a singular form. I managed to fight my way through the creatures, but they were powerful and clearly born of the Old Ways. I felt the power they pulled from those halls, and the magic I was able to channel was certainly tainted. I can only suspect it was Shadow."

"What else?" Hope spun on her heels. "Lead us below."

"Wait!" Konrath's voice was deep and commanding, but Brace watched a weary man get to his feet, raising a warning hand. "You must hear this." He motioned back to Audreese.

The elf stepped toward Hope. "The Old Ways were fine when I left for Andelor, and I felt nothing on my way back. But when I felt the High Mage's warning about the assault," she reached up to the Arcanian mark that hung from her neck, "that is when I felt things change in the Old Ways."

"When you summoned the Light," Konrath added, drawing an acidic look from Hope. "When you stabbed that beast through the heart, I felt the first touch of this corruption."

Hope looked from the wizards to her First Paladin and Scoutmaster, then back to Konrath. "What are you saying?"

"I'm saying, whatever is down there cannot be fought with the Light. I fear it will only strengthen it."

Brace felt the keyshard in his pouch. It felt hot, as if it were about to burst into flames.

"If that is true," Hope said, staring at the high walls in the Scrying Hall, "then the Onyx Gate must be sealed until we can decide what to do. You can send your best students to assist with the cathedral's construction, and we can hold council with the Lord Mayor to decide on a course of action."

"That is another problem," Audreese said, looking at each Luminaurian in turn. "The Onyx Gate can only be sealed from where it was originally created: within the Old Ways..."

The two paladins in the courtyard turned to each other. Both held their helmets under their arms and rested their armored hands on the swords sheathed at their hips.

"You hear that?"

The other one shook his head.

"I could have sworn I heard a—I don't know—a scraping sound..."

"It's this place. All kinds of spells are probably running through the walls."

Neither of them saw the two figures that crept along the side of the courtyard toward Blackwing Hall.

"Desmond? How'd they hear us?" Gage felt a strange lightheadedness threaten his focus, but the Shadow seemed easier to command in this place, unlike in the baron's manor in Oakworth. He felt almost too empowered.

"It wasn't us. Something's happening," Desmond said, stepping closer so Gage could see him through the conjured mists. "I can feel whatever they heard...I think the glyphs are failing. Which means we don't have much time."

They crept faster, and Gage felt a purpose driving him now. But he slowed down as he neared the archway leading into the tower. "What about Robin?"

Desmond knelt next to him. "You said he needed to find Master Audreese, to take you through the Old Ways, right? As I said, I can show you how to navigate the Old Ways. Once we pass through the Onyx Gate, I can show you where the other gates are, and we can come back for Robin." There was a commotion outside the courtyard that drew the paladins away, rushing to investigate.

Gage made to follow, but Desmond caught his wrist in an iron grip. Looking at his scarred face, Gage saw restrained anger.

"But we have to go now, before it's too late."

Having felt like he had already come too far, and not wanting to go back to the streets of Sathford, Gage nodded and pressed on toward the darkened stairs that led toward the power the stranger had promised him.

Chapter Eight

The Voice of Stane

Layla's sleep hadn't been restful since Jath, where she watched Desmond's skin burst apart, splattering his blood across her face on the foothills of Dragonpeak. It wasn't the vision of the horrific act itself that necessarily haunted her. What truly unsettled her was the feeling of righteous satisfaction that overcame her during the grisly display.

She opened her eyes to the same dusty gloom of their small quarters in the berth below deck of *Severynth*—a ship morbidly named for the legendary sunken city—and felt a sudden and familiar relief to be far from Jath. She breathed in the stale air tinged with salt and old wood, leaving the dream behind.

It was the same dream: Layla watching Desmond die again and again while Valix reached her arms around, running her soft hands over Layla's body, covering her in smeared blood and ecstasy.

She still could not come to terms with feeling so pleased over the events. *Was it the Shadow that made me feel so...good about it? Or was it the feeling of justice? Was Valix right about Stane speaking to me through all that bloodshed?*

Every time she awoke, the questions were there. While she didn't think she should feel guilty about killing a man who would use another person in such a way, she also didn't think she should have felt so *good* about it either.

She rolled out of the damp sheets, her clothes sticky with sweat. The ship rocked steadily unlike yesterday, when the captain had to shift course to avoid a storm along the coast of Suthek. At one point, their quarters had rocked so violently that it had thrown them both from bed and Valix had cut her arm.

Layla saw that she was alone in the quarters now. Suddenly panicked, she got to her feet and moved the chest at the foot of their sleeping pallet to reveal the broken floorboard. The *Book of Stane* was still there. She breathed a sigh of relief and sat on the floor, feeling weak from such a small exertion.

She sat there staring at the book in silence, wondering if she should put on her robes to find Valix. Her companion had taken to lounging on the deck above with the crew. While Layla was rather reserved among the Xe'danni and Coperan sailors that crewed *Severynth*, Valix was as boisterous and vulgar as the worst of them. Something about it made Layla uncomfortable—jealousy, perhaps—so she remained in their quarters below deck most of the time.

Just as Layla was contemplating getting to her feet to find some food, the door to the room was pushed open and Valix slipped through its small crack. Layla was startled to see the tattooed woman's torso bared, with what looked like bruises on her arms and breasts. Layla got to her feet.

"Are you alright?"

Valix gave her a smirk. "Mostly." She tossed a torn rag aside and knelt down to the chest, which she opened and sorted through the clothing within. "That shirt was threadbare anyway." She produced a simple vest that she slipped her bruised arms into, grimacing in pain.

Layla laid a gentle hand on Valix's arms. "Are you sure? What happened?"

"Paying for our passage." She laid her rough hand delicately on Layla's. "The captain threatened to drop us at Suthek so he could use this room for tiger pelts from the barbarians unless we paid for the remaining voyage up front."

With a gasp, Layla drew her hand back, looking again at the wounds across Valix's muscled body. "Did he make you...?"

Valix gave her a curious look, which quickly turned to a smile as she shook her head. "He didn't *make* me, I volunteered. Of course, I didn't expect him to put two of his crew on me at once."

Layla was speechless.

Valix rubbed her neck as she continued. "That burly halfling with the missing ear," she gave Layla a wide-eyed look and breathed through pursed lips, "he was a rough one. I finished the human quick enough, but she wore herself out early. One of those Coperans jumped in then, and—" She cut herself off when she looked up at Layla.

Realizing she was gawking, Layla looked away. She was suddenly embarrassed that she was so shocked; it made her feel naive to the hard ways of the world. But there was a strange feeling that accompanied the shock. Was she truly jealous?

"I'm fine," Valix said, sensing the unease. "They didn't hurt me. In fact, you should have seen them—I think the halfling might lose the other ear." She reached into her baggy pants and produced a pouch from her smallclothes. It jingled as she shook it for Layla. "After paying the captain, I still have a queen and seven coppers for Velcarthe. I made more money from one night of fighting here than I made in a month in the pits of Unis."

Layla furrowed her brows. "Fighting?"

Valix tucked the pouch back in her pants. "Fighting. What, did you think I was up there pleasuring the entire crew?"

Too embarrassed to admit that's exactly what she'd thought, she smiled and shook her head. "I was just worried they might have hurt you. But I guess I forgot who I was traveling with."

Valix smiled. "Don't sell yourself short, Lady Abrigale. I may be able to hold my own in a fighting circle, but I've yet to flay a man."

Layla's smile died and she turned away. Almost immediately, she felt Valix's hand on her shoulder and she shrugged it off, taking a step toward the door.

"What is it?"

Layla stopped, but didn't turn to face her. "I can't stop seeing it. Desmond. I see him die every night, and he speaks to me while I tear him apart over and over and over again."

Valix waited for more.

Finally Layla turned back around, feeling tears well up in her eyes. "I can't stop hearing his voice. But it's not his. I'll never forget Desmond's true voice." She felt a warm tear creep down her cheek as she looked into the shadows of the room. "Desmond was cruel and sullen. When he speaks to me in my dreams, he is different—kind and encouraging. He says strange things…"

"Like what?"

Looking back at Valix, Layla tried to recall exactly what he'd said in her dream. "I don't always remember…but I think he said something about the pages…"

Valix stepped closer. "The pages?"

"He said my path was clear and the pages…bleed away?" Layla shook her head, struggling to remember. "That doesn't make sense. Bleed away?"

Valix's gaze fell to the shadows as well, as if looking for the answer. "The pages bleed away."

"Does that mean something to you?"

Chewing her lip in thought, Valix looked back at Layla. "I don't know what those words mean, but it sounds like maybe you heard the voice of Stane."

"In my dream?"

Valix went to the hole in the floor and reached down to retrieve the book. "There is power in dreams."

"Obviously, I know about the feysleep, but I wasn't—"

"Not the feysleep," Valix said, sitting down on their shared pallet and setting the book on her lap. "Sleep and death are so closely tied; our unconsciousness leaves us open to powers denied to the waking world. Dreams give us a glimpse into the Nethering, but most dare not look." She began flipping through the pages, as if looking for a particular passage that she would not be able to read. "More importantly, dreams serve as a connection to the Abyss, where Stane is trapped."

Watching Valix flip through the pages, Layla repeated the strange message in her mind. *The pages bleed away. The pages bleed away.* The more she mouthed the words, her lips found a new phrase. "The pages lead the way."

Valix looked up from the book. "Is that what it said? The pages lead the way?"

Layla blinked, trying to remember exactly, but it was no use; the dream was so distant now. But the words felt right. "The pages lead the way. I think so. I don't know why 'bleed' kept coming back to me."

"Dreams are strange," Valix said with distant eyes. "However, it must mean something. I do not doubt that you heard the voice of Stane, after that bloody business on Jath, and our joining ritual." She looked up at Layla as a proud mother might behold their child. "He's trying to tell you something."

"Something about blood and pages," Layla mumbled.

In the brief silence that followed, Layla remembered their bleeding hands during the joining ritual. A vision from her dream came to her in which a single blood drop from Layla and Valix's embraced hands fell onto the *Book of Stane*, which was opened to the pages that contained Desmond's blood.

Valix must have come to the same realization as her eyes met Layla's. She looked back to the book and began flipping through the pages quicker, coming to the spread of bloody pages. Valix gasped. Layla sat down on the pallet next to her and saw what had caught her breath.

The writing on the page was still illegible—sharp glyphs that flowed into elegant illuminations of various shapes—but the bloodstains had changed. Besides fading slightly, they had turned a lighter color in some places and a darker color along certain inscriptions on the page.

It was as if the blood was highlighting certain letters within the writing. *Are they letters, though?* Layla wondered if the Ghultan language was truly a language or merely a code that required some spell to unlock its messages.

"The pages lead the way," they both said in unison. Layla felt a familiar sensation spread through her limbs, similar to the elation she felt during the joining ritual. *Was this Stane?* She let all of her doubts about the Disciples and their faith fall away in that single thought of Stane being the source of such a wonderful feeling.

Valix slammed a fist down on the book, jolting Layla. "Dammit! We need to find Kartha!" She gave Layla an apologetic look. "If she's even alive."

The name Kartha brought back visions of Layla's meeting with Maze, warning her and Desmond that their actions might be fulfilling the witch's legacy. *But what legacy is that?* Layla wondered.

Confusion must have shown on Layla's face. Valix relaxed her fist and pointed to the indecipherable words. "She's the only one who can read this. No one knows how or why, but she meddled in enough different sorts of magic that it must have given her some form of understanding that even the most studied warlocks on Xe'dann could never achieve."

Layla knew enough about Kartha to know that half of the legends around her could not be true. Over the years—especially within academic circles—any inexplicable event, hex, or curse was credited to Kartha, the Last Daughter of Arkath. While Layla believed the woman was a powerful figure, it was in people's nature to attribute the unknown to something widely known.

"Do you think she still lives?" Layla asked. It felt absurd to her—how could such an ancient, renown woman still be alive and remain hidden. "There are tales about her consorting with Shadowlords and being dragged to the Abyss."

Valix shook her head. "She is so tied to Stane that I do not believe her role in this is done. I don't know if she's alive, but her influence will remain in this world in some form. We just have to find it."

That seemed like an impossible task to Layla. "What about the dragon?"

"Synderok?"

Layla stood up, thinking back on everything she had heard on Jath. "The dragon was said to have claimed this book during the Unthroning. Something must have drawn it to the ritual, don't you think?" She turned to Valix. "What if she heard the words that Kartha read from this book—that's what drew her."

That familiar look of pride and wonder began washing over Valix's face as she watched Layla.

"Whatever words are hidden in this book," Layla continued, "they clearly have power. And power clings. So whatever power this book holds likely clung to both the dragon and the witch. You said the dragon would be drawn to this book, so wouldn't Kartha be drawn as well?"

"If she lives," Valix nodded, "it would seem likely." Her face darkened suddenly, and she looked down at the page in the book that had changed. Certain symbols still gave off a faint glow in the dimness of their room. "But if the dragon is awake now and can sense power from this book..."

When she looked up, Layla could tell that Valix felt it too. Layla was no stranger to raw, unchanneled magical energy. It came off the book in waves now.

Suddenly, there were muffled cries outside their room followed by the sound of a powerful gust of wind slamming against the hull of the ship. The room rocked. Layla was thrown against the far wall and Valix braced herself, reaching for her companion while pulling the book to her chest. Both women were slammed to the floor as the ship shifted the other way.

Valix helped Layla to her feet and both women screamed as thin fingers of flame licked through the cracks in the wall. They raced for the door and into the chaos of the ship's berth. The crew were scrambling to get above deck. Voices screamed from the world above.

"Dragon!"

The cry was a knife in Layla's stomach, a confirmation of her fears. It was as if Synderok had heard them speak of her—as if Layla and Valix had cluelessly summoned a dragon to the heart of the Racivic Sea.

"Move!" A huge man shoved between Layla and Valix as they navigated the tight hall. The sailor carried a bucket over his shoulder, water splashing from it. The two women stepped aside as three other sailors hustled behind the larger one, each one carrying a bucket of water, heading for the deck.

Layla felt Valix's hand tighten around her wrist, the disciple's eyes were wide with uncharacteristic fear. "I can't...I'm not recovered from Jath." She hugged the book. "What can we do against a dragon?"

She didn't have an answer, but Layla was overcome with the conviction that had slowly been growing inside of her since Valix had freed her from Desmond's wicked grip. Knowing that if she thought too much about going above deck, she would end up dying, curled up helplessly on a burning ship.

"I don't know," Layla said, motioning to the book Valix cradled, "but if that bitch wants that book back, she must fear Stane." She put her hands on the tome, giving Valix a nod. The ship rocked violently again, and Valix let go of the book to brace them. Layla hefted the *Book of Stane* and turned to walk toward the stairs.

Above deck was chaos. Sailors were scrambling around with buckets of water or sand, putting out flames on the burning rigging. Layla was grateful to see that the ship itself hadn't caught fire, but that relief was short-lived as she saw the giant shape wheeling in the sky.

Synderok was more massive than Layla could have imagined, with great crimson wings that blocked out the sun, casting the world in shadow. Layla could see the dragon's flesh of fiery red scales was cracked and fissured, her entire body smoking in the sunlight. Synderok uncoiled her body and faced the ship, letting out a vicious roar as she beat her wings, sending gusts of wind that buffeted the already rocking ship.

Layla was knocked to the deck as several sailors went sprawling. The captain's voice bellowed across the crashing waves.

"Batten down the hatches and get those crossbows!"

Valix's desperate warnings were mingled with the captain's commands, but Layla only heard the voice of Stane—not his words, but his assurance that she could stop this monstrosity from capsizing *Severynth*. Emboldened by his presence within her, she stood up and faced the great wyrm in the sky, opening his book to the bloodied pages to which her dream had guided her.

The dragon's wings pounded the ship with more wind, but strangely the vessel steadied its course against it. Layla focused on the presence within her, letting the world fall away. She thought of her first years at Raventhal, struggling to channel magic through keyshards. There was a familiarity with the power she felt connecting her to the book, and as she focused on that bond, the voice of Stane came again. She didn't hear individual words; instead, it was the knowledge of what she needed to do.

As Synderok pushed her serpentine head forward, those fiery yellow eyes like the tips of molten spears, Layla closed her own eyes. In her mind, Desmond reached a repulsive hand to hers and lifted, guiding her open palm toward the sky. In the distance, she heard the captain shouting for his crew to brace for impact.

"To the gunwale!"

Layla felt other hands on her besides Desmond's, but she ignored the touch, maintaining her focus and connection. Power flowed through her and she felt the book's desperation to be kept away from the dragon's clutch. She latched onto that beckoning power, and felt her hand explode in pain and intense release.

The distant, echoing world came rushing back as she opened her eyes to see Synderok flailing away from the ship, her wings flapping wildly to find purchase as heavy black tendrils of smoke trailed from Layla's hand.

"Fire the ballista! Now!"

Layla felt her body give up, collapsing into strong arms as she watched the captain in his emerald and gold coat race across the deck to where several sailors were adjusting the giant crossbow at the stern of the ship. A muscular halfling was winding the device's arming mechanism while a burly human woman loaded a heavy javelin into its bolt track.

"Layla," Valix was breathless. "How did you do that?!"

Layla could hardly breathe, let alone answer. She struggled to maintain consciousness despite the searing pain in her hand.

"Fire! Now!"

Her vision faded as she saw the ballista unleash a bolt at the dragon that still struggled to stay airborne just above the crashing waves of the Racivic Sea. Layla blinked and heard a piercing shriek, opening her eyes in time to see the dragon crash into the water, its body hissing and boiling the ocean water. She gave into the darkness as the deck exploded into cheers.

"Layla!" Valix sounded as if she were drowning below the deafening waves that crashed against the ship's hull. Layla tried to respond, but it was no use. The Shadow consumed her.

You did it, a voice said from the darkness. Whether it was Valix, Desmond, or Stane, Layla would never know. But it was soothing, letting her drift further toward oblivion.

She dreamed of Raventhal and Desmond, her more pleasant memories now seen in a cruel new light. Desmond Everton sat in the darkness of his quarters, holding the charred corpse of his cat. Layla stood alone in the single ray of daylight that shone through the room's high window. He looked up to her, black streaking from those hollow eyes.

"You heard me."

The voice wasn't Desmond's. "I think so."

"You know, Layla Abrigale. You've known since Jath. You are the first to hear my true voice." Stane set aside Desmond's dead friend and got to his feet, his dark robes spreading across the entire floor, swallowing it all. "You have been chosen. And I am your final trial."

"What does that mean?"

Desmond smiled wickedly, bloody cracks forming across his face, pieces of his flesh falling away to reveal a stranger's face underneath. "The scions are the final test of your conviction. Only you can usher in my coming."

"How?"

The stranger with the bloody face gave her a sad smile, pieces of Desmond's visage still falling away like melting wax. He held his hands up in offering, catching the pieces of flesh that slipped off Stane's true face—a beautiful, long-haired Caimish man, pale like Desmond but full of life. "You will know. What you love in the world becomes what you hate, and what you hate..."

The room began to spin, and Layla felt ill as she watched Stane's hands collect the ruin of the man she had killed. Something began to take shape, and Layla knew she wanted to look away, but couldn't.

"...what you hate, Layla Abrigale," Stane's voice was a gentle whisper that slithered through her like poison, "is what you need." The pile of flesh took the form of a bald head with cascading tattoos and Layla felt tears well in her eyes.

"No..."

Valix stared lifelessly up at Layla, blood dripping from Stane's hands. He held the woman's head out to Layla and the elf recoiled. She tried to cry out, but she felt like she was suffocating now and no sound came. Valix's eyes blinked and the disembodied head's gaze fell on Layla. Its mouth spoke with Stane's voice.

"There is no love without hatred, but Light can exist without Shadow." Valix gave Layla a hideous smile. "The malice of Light needs a Shadow to banish, else it will only burn itself."

Layla turned away from the nightmare, trying to wake herself up. But she spun around into darkness, unable to escape. Stane continued speaking to her through the void.

"The pages lead the way, Layla. But you will bleed..."

Layla. A pale face appeared in the darkness. *Layla.* "No," she said, turning away from the voice.

"Layla..."

She saw Desmond atop her before she felt his thrust. His eyes were infinite holes of darkness, his lips mouthing her name as he thrust again. Smoking black tears streamed down his pathetic face.

"No!" She tried to push him away, but he held tight, thrusting each time he said her name. "Please..."

"Layla!"

Finally, she opened her eyes to see Valix, her head back on those strong shoulders. Layla tried to sit up, but her body resisted.

"Don't," Valix warned, tightening her grip on Layla. "You need to rest."

Blinking away exhaustion, Layla saw she was back in their room beneath *Severynth*'s deck. A lantern hung from a hook against the wall, bathing the room in a gentle orange glow. She looked up into Valix's eyes, reaching up to hold her face in her hands.

Valix smiled, putting a hand against Layla's as it found her cheek. "Dragon slaying is exhausting work, I hear." She was laying next to Layla on their pallet, propped up on an elbow. "You've been asleep all day, though I wouldn't dare call it restful. Bad dreams?"

Layla bit her lip, fighting back tears. As she stared up into Valix's face, she kept seeing the severed head in her dreams. *What did it mean?* She couldn't help but wonder if it was some dark portent. She stroked Valix's cheek, her other hand ran gently over the disciple's scalp. "I dreamt you..." Layla didn't want to say it aloud. "I dreamt of you."

Valix's smile faded slightly, her expression uncertain. Leaning forward, she put her lips delicately on Layla's sweaty brow. "I've been here waiting for you."

Overcome with warring emotions, Layla began to cry, her hands clinging desperately to Valix. She was terrified of losing the woman. These were unfamiliar feelings for Layla, and she didn't know what to do or say beyond tightening her hold on Valix. "I've been waiting for you."

Valix pulled Layla's chin up so they could look into each other's eyes. Wiping a tear away with her thumb, Valix ran another finger around the shape of Layla's eye. "We've waited long enough."

Layla shivered, but whether it was from fear, lust, exhaustion, or her new-found conviction, she could not say. Stane's words echoed in her mind, but she refused to be afraid of them—*I'm done being afraid.*

Grasping the back of Valix's head with all her remaining strength, Layla pulled the woman's mouth to her own, wanting nothing more than to consume every drop of her.

Finally, the voice of Stane quieted.

Chapter Nine

Behind the Mask

Knife crept along the rafters of the Lighthold, watching the figures below go about their duties. Silence came naturally to her, but the illegal blackshard she carried secured between her breasts gave her comfort. There was no way the Light would expose her while she carried such a blasphemous artifact.

Her target had yet to reveal herself, which didn't surprise the Guildmaster. She knew she would be waiting for most of the night before the Archbeacon made her move. The woman was nothing if not methodical.

Following Luriah Vaughn had revealed what Knife had already suspected: the woman kept to her schedule as if it were a practiced dance, never missing a step, no matter how complicated the rhythm. She attended royal functions with the queen's most leal lords and ladies, conferred with visiting dignitaries from Copera and Jath who worked to avoid civil war in the north, and spent the hours between dinner and sleep locked away in the Lighthold's fortress of ponderous religious texts.

Stifling a yawn, Knife silently cursed her sister's wretched curiosity. While it was perfectly within reason to keep an eye on potential rivals—something the Guild built a profitable enterprise on—Sopheena's concern over not knowing the Archbeacon's agenda bordered on obsession.

The Luminaura had always been the one institution in Vale that was above the throne. Since its conception, its power remained unchecked and unquestioned, and the Archbeacon commanded a seat on the queen's council with no need for deliberation.

Knife knew upsetting that balance of power was something they could not risk, especially with Copera on the brink of war and Karrane's majesty likely to be deposed. Vale needed stability, else those Eastlund brutes might see the fall of Rathen as an opportune time to reassess their borders.

Regardless, here she sat in the high shadows of the towering Lighthold searching for deception and finding nothing but tedium. While she watched a young chaplain stiffly walk toward the cathedral's massive doors, she considered following him out of sheer boredom, but instead she dangled a leg from the rafters and reclined against a stone buttress.

An unexpected weariness came over her, making her yearn for the feysleep. But she hadn't risked that since the day she died. She was a ghost now, as far as the world was concerned, and ghosts do not rest. Absently, she drew out the folded parchment from the place she had kept it for the last sixteen years, tucked into her leathers against her left breast. The place where she once had a heart.

As gentle as a beirmaiden preparing a king's corpse for a burial, Knife unfolded the old parchment. There was plenty of light from the glowing window panes, which projected the outside sunlight into the cathedral, but the Guildmaster didn't need it; she had memorized the words in the letter long ago.

She pushed her mask up to reveal a face split in three places by gruesome scars. One scar ran from her temple, across her brow, and all the way to her jawline on the opposite side of her face. The ruin of her nose had another slash running the opposite direction. The final gash was a diamond-shaped puncture wound in her cheek, just below the eye.

If she had still been able to cry, a single tear might have run from that eye and into the gory crevice as she read the words.

It was a mistake, but we weren't. I'll always love you, and we'll always have those nights in Merithian.

She stared at the faded letters, remembering the first time she had read them. It seemed so long ago, when the lands of Vale were so new and exciting—when *he* was so new and exciting. Now when she pictured him, she hardly remembered why she had fallen in love with him. Regardless, that love persisted, painfully so.

"Archbeacon!"

Knife folded up the parchment and tucked it away as she spun around to watch the commotion below. She lowered her mask, her thin hair falling forward like heavy, black spiderwebs.

She saw Luriah Vaughn striding down the blue and white carpeted aisle, a priestess in gold and white robes trailing quickly behind her.

Finally, Knife thought, hoping for a scandalous episode.

"How long has he been gone?" the Archbeacon shouted, sending several Lightsisters who had been praying scrambling toward a door to the side of the pews. Luriah and the priestess were the only ones remaining in the nave, aside from Knife who watched from the heavens.

The Archbeacon stopped halfway down the aisle and spun on the woman chasing her. "You just bring this news to me now? How long!"

"Vera—I mean, High Mage Mourgael did not say, your Luminous," the woman said meekly, both hands on her stomach. "The Archmage has been absent from his appointments for the past three days, so perhaps since then?"

"Three days?! And still you say nothing?!" The Archbeacon spun around to stalk to the doors, still shouting over her shoulder. "You knew Lopke is integral in finding the Child. I brought you to the Bright Council because I assumed that as the beacon of the Lighthold you might be able to handle the affairs in Andelor. Shall I send you back to Merithian, Constance?"

Almost running to keep up, the beacon shook her head. "No, your Luminous. I did not know the cancellations meant he departed—in your own words, the gnome is prickly and prone to missing engagements."

"You dare blame this on me?" Luriah's voice faded from the echoing nave as she pushed her way through the giant doors.

Knife crept along the rafters like a spider. While she was eager to hear the details of the argument, she had already gotten what she came for. The Guild already knew that the church was seeking the Child of Light with the Arcania, but now it seemed that Fainly had indeed fled Andelor without informing his new ally.

Which meant that either Fainly wanted to find the Child first on his own, or something much more pressing had pulled the Arcania's attention. Regardless, Knife would need to find out what the church would do in response, and hopefully discover what they wanted with the Child of Light.

As she lithely swung between the wood and stone abutments, Knife reflected on what she knew about the Children of Light and Shadow. There were Caimish tales about the inevitable war between Light and Shadow, which prominently featured the Children. In Fehir'whin, it was believed that whichever Child slew the other, the Light or Shadow respectively would become more powerful than the other.

However, when one Child fell, another would be chosen to take their place. Which is how scholars believed the world remained in balance between Light and Shadow, as each needed the other to exist.

Yet many believed—Knife included—that the Children were just an old wives' tale, and those who claimed the titles were usually just after fame or fortune from those who would believe their lies.

Regardless, belief was a currency that could buy power. So while Knife had no true convictions regarding the Children or the prophecies around them, she certainly appreciated the leverage that could be gained over those who did—such as the Archbeacon of the Luminaura.

As she crawled through the window pane that she had loosened along the Lighthold's bell tower, Knife could see Luriah Vaughn striding angrily across the courtyard below. She was heading toward the rookery, where the church kept their messenger doves. To Knife's knowledge, no one truly knew how the church had bred their doves to navigate as well as traditional pigeons, but the birds had become a symbol of the Light's decree, especially throughout Vale.

The sun was beginning to set, so Knife had adequate shadows to hide in as she followed the women below. Armored paladins strode across the courtyard, but they seemed more interested in avoiding the Archbeacon's curses than they were in performing an adequate patrol, so the Guildmaster had an easy time maintaining stealth.

The rookery was an elegant turret on the Lighthold's northern wall. Knife avoided a pacing sentry on the overlooking catwalk, slinking down the vines that had grown over the cathedral's tiered balcony and dropping silently to the ground. After waiting for the Archbeacon and her subordinate to slip through the doors, Knife hugged the outer wall to access a side window obscured by bushes.

Voices carried through the open window, so Knife knelt behind the garden's shrubs and listened.

"Seamus!" the Archbeacon shouted, her voice summoning a flutter of wings and aggressive coos. "Get down here!" There was a muffled crash from higher up in the tower, followed by the shuffling of feet scurrying down stone stairs. "I need to get an urgent message to Hope. Take this down."

Knife leaned closer to hear over the fluttering of more wings.

"Write that the Prophetess has spoken—she has seen the incarnate's demise in Oakworth, which can only mean the Child has revealed themself. The High Warpriest is to send First Paladin Darrance Moore to Oakworth at once to investigate and establish the Luminaura's presence. Write that Rathen can wait."

The Child in Oakworth, Knife thought. This could be no coincidence. Grip and Brood had been sent there only weeks ago to obtain Ruke's stone. To have not only the incarnate be drawn there, but the Child of Light as well...

As the discussion in the rookery turned to more mundane matters, Knife took the opportunity to slip away so she might take up her next position while the Archbeacon was still indisposed.

At least now she had some leverage.

Hours later, Knife waited again, watching with patient eyes behind a cold mask. The Archbeacon's suite was propped up above the eastern wing of the Lighthold and the sprawling Luminated Library. Among the other dozens of luxurious apartments for the church's highest officials, the Archbeacon's bedchamber was, for lack of a better word, divine.

Knife once again sat perched in the high shadows, the burning candles below created pools of light in which the servants carried out their nightly ritual of preparing the room for the Archbeacon's eventual arrival. A bath of boiling water was drawn by two muscular dwarf women, each one dressed in priestly garb. Trays of food were lined up on a long table next to Luriah's smaller dining table, and an elderly halfling cook barked orders at younger scullions.

The aroma coming off the feast reminded Knife that she hadn't eaten all day, and she was tempted to risk sneaking down to grab a few portions for herself. But before she could, the Archbeacon arrived. What followed was a whirlwind of activity with several vestals tending to Luriah Vaughn's evening needs. Knife watched with a grumbling stomach as the Archbeacon left her dinner untouched, instead allowing her vestals to undress and bathe her.

It was almost an hour until the chaste women finished scrubbing and rinsing Luriah's pale body, talking of nothing but weary piety. More hot water was brought in and then the Archbeacon waved them all away as she reclined in the steaming bath. Knife waited until long after the doors had been closed, when Luriah would be at her most relaxed, before she began her quiet descent.

While the blackshard she carried gave Knife the ability to channel the faint wisps of Shadow that allowed her to essentially disappear, there was rarely need for it. She traversed the darkness of the room like a prowling cat, and soon she was on the ground, creeping up behind the Light's highest chosen disciple.

Knife drew a knife.

The silence was split by a deep *thunk* that jolted Luriah's head up, searching for its source.

"Make a sound and the next one goes through your throat, your Luminous."

Luriah choked off a gasp as she straightened. She looked down at the small blade stuck into the side of her bath, wobbling slightly. The movement sent small ripples across the surface of the bathwater.

Knife already had a second blade out, deftly flipping it end-over-end between her fingers as she stepped into the candlelight ringing the bath. Luriah drew in a quick, stuttered breath as she tried to cover her breasts with one hand while the other went to the golden chain around her neck. There was a dull glow coming from the holy pendant.

Smiling behind her mask, Knife opened her vest, proudly displaying her own breasts and the blackshard that hung between them. The blackshard gave off its own kind of glow, but also weakened in the presence of Luriah's faith.

Luriah's face was a mix of rage and fear as she let go of the holy star, as well as her vain attempt of hiding any part of her that Knife had not already seen.

Satisfied, Knife spun the blade and sheathed it. "It looks like we're both a bit naked without our power, so let's call it a draw." She closed her vest and quietly pulled up a chair to sit next to Luriah's extravagant tub. "I was hoping we could confer, lady to lady."

Luriah tried to sit back in the water, but Knife could see she was still tense and afraid. "Ladies tend to make appointments," the Archbeacon said sternly, "and do not intrude upon other ladies in such a devious manner."

"Where has the Archmage gone?"

Feigning a look of ignorance, Luriah shrugged. "How should I know? I don't keep tabs on Arcania business."

"But you do keep tabs on incarnates and unsanctioned keyshard trading. Don't waste my time, Luriah. We know you are both looking for the Child. Has he gone to Karrane?"

A flush crept up Luriah's pasty neck. "I do not know. Truly. The last I spoke with him, he seemed intent on following up a lead there, so I can only assume that is where he has gone."

"Why does the church seek the Children? There have been dozens of false claimants of those titles in the last two years—why are you desperate now?"

"Who says I am?"

"I said don't waste my time. I know you'd never jeopardize your church's reputation." She pointed at nothing behind her. "Cleaning up your mess in Rathen, building a new cathedral in Sathford—those are the threats to your pristine image. Not rumors of the Children in Oakworth. Why do you need the Child of Light? Why now?"

A look washed over Luriah's face that surprised Knife. "Who said I needed the Child of Light?"

Grateful for her mask, Knife tried to keep her face passive as she puzzled over why the church might want the ultimate disciple of Shadow who they could not hope to capture or kill, if the legends could be believed.

"I won't pretend to know whose side you're on," Luriah said, her voice firm now, defiant. She stood up, proud, and bent to pull the knife out of the side of the tub. "But I can only hope you want what's best for the queendom. The Light is honest and just, while the Guild hides its purpose in the dark." She held the blade's handle out toward Knife.

Reaching over to take the blade, Knife looked up at Luriah with earnest eyes. "The Child of Shadow killed your father. Charlton Vaughn dedicated his life to finding the Child of Light and failed, killed for his efforts. Do you merely seek vengeance for your father?"

"Don't you?"

Knife held the woman's gaze, fighting back a sudden urge to slice her throat. "What would you know about my father?"

Luriah shrugged. "I can only imagine your father suffered some cruel fate. How else would a person wind up living behind a mask and selling secrets to the crown for a few coins?"

Overcome with frustration, Knife arose and lifted her mask to reveal her face.

While she did not plan to divulge her identity to the Archbeacon of the Luminaura this night, Knife secretly thought it may have been worth it merely to watch Luriah's pompous expression curdle before her eyes.

Which it did.

A long silence hung between the women.

"You're supposed to be dead," Luriah finally said.

"The Luminaura seems to be good at keeping secrets," Knife said, allowing herself a small smile. "Consider this one the most important. I am dead. My father killed me and my mother, Allista. Long before Charlton Vaughn began his crusade in Xe'dann, Count Delucar waged war with the vampire lords on Caim. The true heir to the High Elf crown, Delucar, descendant of Luishen himself, struck down Empress Vianka in Xoatia."

"I know the tale."

Knife stepped closer. "But not the cost. Delucar fought against the demons for years, never resting. And in that moment of triumph, when he finally returned to the Fey Domain for respite, the vampire thralls retaliated, turning my father into one of those Shadow-sworn bloodsuckers."

"Your father…"

"Like yours," Knife said, her voice holding less fury than her narrowed eyes, "fought the Shadow with everything he had. My mother bound herself to the Fey Domain to ensure the Shadow wouldn't allow the vampiric curse to pass on to all of Delucar's kin, like it almost did to me. So tell me the truth, Luriah Vaughn. Why do you seek out the Shadow?"

Lurian stepped out of the bath, water dripping to the polished floor in rhythm to both women's racing hearts.

"To destroy it, once and for all."

Chapter Ten

REUNIONS IN RUIN

The journey back toward Oakworth was made in doubt. Ransil didn't want to return there, but the strange foes emerging from Hollowood pursued him and his new companion northward, leaving them no other haven. Traveling without rest, they covered most of the distance before the sun went down. But with clouds consuming the moon, the night became too dark and they were forced to make camp near a vacant cave along a wooded stream.

Quinn Olivick slept peacefully, having drifted off immediately when his head settled on the pile of dead leaves. Knowing that the boy would wake up ravenous after some rest, Ransil began quietly preparing a meal while planning the next steps of their journey.

Ransil knew of several small mining settlements in the Horin Hills, but he felt an obligation not to lead the monsters that pursued them toward any small communities without a proper militia. Oakworth would be the nearest haven for them, as much as Ransil cared not to return there while Baron Caffery was still wary about the Guild—he didn't care to butt heads with that man again.

While he gathered a handful of dry branches and twigs, his thoughts wandered from his current plight to Grip. Even in the midst of pursuit and battle, he couldn't seem to shake the image of her face, offering him what he thought was a genuine smile.

It was just a mask though. There was nothing genuine about Griphelia Shu'wath. Ransil could hardly hold it against her; being the last heir to the Xoatian throne would not be a title that Ransil would be excited to lay claim to either. It wasn't as if the woman feared her lineage, but she was met with enough suspicion due to the legends surrounding dark elves being born of the Shadow, not to mention her own occupational choices.

As Ransil struck his flint to light the kindling, he supposed he couldn't blame Grip for her constant deceptions. He just foolishly hoped that he might be an exception, or that she might have some sort of limit to her untrustworthiness. But it turns out there was nothing the woman held sacred. Either that, or he truly didn't matter to her. The thought made him sadder than he had expected, but he shrugged the thoughts away and focused on the tasks at hand.

Letting the fire heat the flat stone he had laid above it, Ransil drew his knife and sorted through a patch of herbs—some nettle, sorrel, and, as luck would have it, some speckled mushrooms—and reflected on the last time he had gone to Sathford. The Guild had sent him to infiltrate Castle Tolle to recover some gems that the Lord Mayor had procured from their agents.

He deftly chopped the herbs and mushrooms on the edge of the hot stone, producing a shallow wooden bowl from his pack in which to mix the ingredients together. There was a rustling overhead and the halfling drew his other knife, bracing himself for an attack. A bird took flight from its nest.

Eggs, Ransil thought, sheathing his blades and looking for some branches to climb. The nest wasn't too far up, and Ransil was pleased to see seven eggs waiting for him. He kindly only took two, leaving the others to hatch and eventually provide another fortunate traveler some nourishment.

By the time Ransil had the eggs sizzling on the hot stone, Quinn was snoring loudly, dead to the world. Cautiously, Ransil crept over to the boy while their food cooked. With small and practiced hands, he picked through the boy's robes, easily finding what he was looking for. He pocketed his score, and shook his head in shame as he returned to cooking.

As naturally as pickpocketing had come to him, he had sworn that life off years ago. But things had gotten dire. He lost the information he had on the Shrouded and abandoned Anika when she needed him the most; he was running out of options. Using his knife, he carefully moved the eggs and mushrooms to the wooden bowl, sprinkling the herbs on.

Ransil hadn't realized how hungry he had gotten, and it took great restraint to not eat the entire bowl himself as he finally sat down to rest his aching legs. After eating his portion, he set the bowl aside and drew out his plunder. It was a small green keyshard. *Oakus*, Ransil thought, the realization sending a small chill down his spine. Remembering the Hollowood assailants, covered in vines as if controlled by the plants themselves, Ransil knew there was a connection—another incarnate stirring.

He could see something in the stone; not truly there, but the power emanating from the object put the visions in Ransil's mind. It was like the storm from Rathen, summoned by Eyen's fury. In the vision, something crept out from below the earth like corrosive weeds seeking to tear down the artificial world that had been built upon Oakus' natural splendor.

It was all tied back to Anika. Staring into the depths of that small stone, Ransil thought of everything that Anika had gone through since the attack on Blakehurst. She was swept away by those around her—including Ransil himself—and thrust before Eyen's incarnate without any true preparation.

I shouldn't have left her, Ransil thought, gnashing his teeth at the memory. *Damn you, Grip. You always lead me astray.*

"What are you doing?"

Rasil nearly dropped the stone as he was jolted from its hypnotic pull. He looked at Quinn in the faint firelight, his young face framed in disheveled brown hair was terrified. The boy had sat up as if awoken from a nightmare, and Ransil was truly surprised that he did not hear him stir amongst all those dead leaves.

But then he remembered whose stone he held.

"Did you bind yourself to it already?" Ransil asked, tucking the keyshard into his pocket. "Sorry. Had I known, I wouldn't have roused it. You need to rest." Ransil got up and picked up the bowl that had been warming on the edge of the hot stone, handing it to Quinn. The boy looked nervously at the halfling, but took the bowl eagerly.

"Why'd you take it? Are you robbing me?" His eyes never left Ransil as he shoved the egg into his mouth with his bare hand. The boy's eyes widened in shock as he chewed the food. "Mmm."

Ransil smiled at that. "If I wanted to rob you, I wouldn't have made you breakfast. I'm just holding onto it for you." He motioned to the sparse woods surrounding them. "A bandit out here would see a wizard traveling with a halfling cook and would mark you as the first target. Besides, if this keyshard is as important as you say, it's more dangerous in your pockets than mine."

Ransil sat down next to Quinn. "Your druid companion—Fallon Shaw. You're sure she has fallen in with the Shrouded?"

Quinn licked his fingers and handed the bowl back to Ransil. "That priestess Naya...she did something to her. I mean, Fallon had every right to be upset. She said the Luminaura killed her father for no reason." Quinn's eyes grew distant, staring into the fire. "But the things she was saying...about destroying all of Sathford." He looked at Ransil. "That couldn't be her. Naya did something to her."

Ransil wasn't convinced. "The Shrouded are deceitful and corruptive, but so is this." He patted his pocket that bulged with the keyshard. "Incarnates are vessels chosen by the old gods. And if you said she experienced her father's death through this keyshard...I can't imagine a more likely way for Oakus to find his vessel." He looked up at the faint hint of dawn on the horizon. "Regardless, we need to keep this away from both of them."

"We have to return to Raventhal," Quinn said, getting to his feet. "To warn the High Mage. Even if we keep this shard from Fallon, she knows there are plenty more at the spire."

Ransil got up as well, standing almost up to the boy's shoulders. "We'll have to go through Oakworth, find some mounts or hitch a merchant wagon. Got any coin?"

Quinn shook his head. "All I had was that keyshard. I didn't have time to pack anything before Fallon dragged me into the Old Ways." He looked north and then back at Ransil. "Wasn't Oakworth where you..."

Ransil nodded as he bent down to retrieve his pack, his low back screaming in protest. But there was no time to rest. The idea of returning to the place where Anika had defeated Corvanna—where he had foolishly abandoned her for Grip—filled him with dread, while also reminding him that this was his best chance to help Anika.

"Naya lost a hand in Oakworth," Ransil said, shouldering his pack. "I don't think she'll be eager to return. Whatever she is planning with Fallon, I think Oakworth is our best route if we hope to avoid them."

Quinn took a step and his body swayed as if his legs were giving out. Ransil braced him.

"You alright?"

Quinn nodded. "I don't think I'll be much help if we run into any more trouble. That wasn't enough rest, I guess." He looked back at the makeshift bed of leaves.

Ransil tightened his hold on the boy's shoulder as he straightened him, suddenly thinking of young Matty. Overcome with sadness and determination, Ransil patted the boy's shoulder.

"You're safe with me."

"I'm sorry, Deina."

The dwarf gave Avrim a sidelong look through a swollen eye. "Sorry fer what?"

Avrim nodded to the sizeable rump of the horse that Deina was tethered to. It released a timely clump of dung that the dwarf stepped over with a chuckle.

"I've seen worse," the dwarf said, adjusting her rope-bound wrists. "Besides, way I see it, if I'm lucky we might be facing a nasty sentence and I might just be out of your debt finally."

Avrim couldn't help but snort with a restrained laugh.

"Quiet!" One of the guards looked back from atop his horse, scowling at the prisoners through the open visor of his helm. The man had a blackeye as well, which looked worse than the dwarf's. "The dame says we can gag you if you don't walk in peace."

"Come try," Melaine said under her breath.

"What's that?!" The guard turned his spiteful gaze on the half-orc.

Avrim stepped ahead of his companions. "She said she'll try to be more quiet, sir."

The man slammed his visor down and turned back toward the quiet road to Oakworth. Avrim could see the column of soldiers that escorted them, four mounted guards in front and three behind. The prisoners were tied to the middle three, with Kasia Strallow leading the way further ahead, out of sight. The rest of the baron's men marched behind with the supplies.

When they left Blakehurst, Avrim had checked his own bindings and found them surprisingly loose. Now, as he discreetly adjusted them again, he was sure he could get at least one hand free. *But then what?* He wasn't sure he wanted to risk further violence visited upon his companions in any futile escape attempts, so he left the bindings alone.

They had left Blakehurst at dawn, with Dame Strallow hoping to reach Oakhurst by afternoon. The company had to ride a bit slower to accommodate the walking prisoners. When Avrim had asked why they couldn't ride the mounts they had taken from the baron's own stables, the Oather had told him they needed time to reflect on the severity of their charges—which told Avrim that their return to Andelor wasn't entirely urgent.

The prisoners kept their silence throughout the day, gladly accepting a small meal of dried bread and exceptionally sharp Westerran cheese. Avrim secretly gave Deina most of his portion as another small consolation for dragging her into this.

While they finished their meager meals, there was a commotion up the road that rattled the horses.

"Swords!" Kasia's bellow split the silence. The trees that flanked either side of the road were shaken to life as birds took wing in response to the command. "Mount the prisoners! Ride for the walls!"

Avrim couldn't see around the horses and the curving road, but he was yanked toward the mount he was tied to. The soldier grabbed him roughly by the wrists and he had no choice but to clamber awkwardly up the horse as it stomped its feet in frustration.

Deina and Melaine were similarly drawn up onto their guards' mounts and suddenly they were riding hard around the curve in the road. As the trees opened up, Avrim now saw what the commotion was about.

In the distance Avrim could see Oakworth, and it looked to be...growing.

There were figures outside the town's stone walls, but Avrim—struggling to stay on the galloping horse—couldn't make out what they were doing. *Fleeing? Fighting?* It was hard to tell from this distance.

As they neared, the sounds of battle became clear. Avrim awkwardly held onto the saddle with bound hands to keep from falling and watched as Kasia crested a hill and dismounted near the gates. Now Avrim could see there were writhing vines slithering across Oakworth's walls, snaking their way through crenellations and breaking through weakened sections.

There was a horrified cry as a guard in Oakworth livery was launched over the walls into the trees surrounding the town. *Was that a catapult?* Avrim's mind was struggling to grasp the reality of what he was seeing, but he didn't have time to dwell on it.

The guard in front of him leapt off the horse and then yanked Avrim down. "Stay here!" Drawing his sword, the armored knight raced toward the town gates where Avrim now saw Kasia slashing at one of the golems he had seen in the Old Ways.

"Oh no," Avrim said, turning to find Deina and Melaine. The two women had also been hauled off their mounts and left by the wayside as their captors ran off to join the defense of their town. Avrim scrambled over to them. "It's her!"

"The Shadow priestess?" Deina gnashed her teeth. "I thought this was over."

Melaine stepped forward as the sounds of crumbling stone were quickly followed by horrified screams. "I think it's just begun."

The three of them raced toward the shattered gates of Oakworth as its citizens began pouring out in a frenzied wave.

Anguished cries echoed through the halls of the baron's keep in Oakworth.

"Get to the children!" Baron Alburn Caffery cradled a broken arm as one of his personal guards hurried him through the door. "Go!"

Vivian gasped as another guard screamed. She watched in horror as a tree branch shaped like a serrated blade tore through the woman's armored chest. The guard spat up blood as her sword fell from limp fingers to clatter to the stone floor of the hall. Vivian wanted to scream, but her racing heart wouldn't give her the opening.

The heavy oak doors were slammed shut just as the lumbering tree-thing came into view and glared at the baroness with horrid green eyes. Vivian was pulled away from the door as it was being barricaded, her husband's strong hand spinning her to face him.

"I need you to go to the children, now. Get them out of here!" Alburn nodded at the door, which was now being pounded on from the other side. "These things are coming from below. That witch did this!" He put a hand gently on her cheek and pulled her face close to his, kissing her in a terrible way that made Vivian think it was the last time. Then the baron shoved her again. "Go, Vivian!"

Finally, Vivian complied, her mind shifting from the horrors of the assault to only Lenora and Viktor. She raced wildly down the hall toward the winding stairs. The children would be at their lessons in the upper study. She tried to shut out the terrible noises she heard from other parts of the keep, including her husband's panicked cries from behind her.

In her haste, Vivian tripped on her way up the stairs, smashing her knee into the corner of the stone. Screaming, she bit down hard against the pain and struggled up the next several stairs. She limped through the hall toward the study, its doors hanging slightly open.

"Children!" She nearly fell again, her legs tangling within her clothes. Lifting the hem of her skirt, she slammed against the wall and kept limping toward the doors. "Lenora! Viktor!"

Throwing herself through the doors, Vivian collapsed breathless to the floor. "Mother!"

Viktor's voice was choked and terrified. Vivian looked up and screamed again when she saw her children pushed up against the bookshelves, each of them tangled in a myriad of vines and roots, threatening to choke the life from them. In the center of the room was a figure from which the wicked plants grew.

"Renay!"

A horrid creaking sound, like snapping bones, filled the room as Renay turned to regard the baroness. The once-beautiful woman that Vivian and Alburn Caffery had loved deeply was now a ragged, decaying abomination, strangling her children with monstrous growths that had replaced her arms. While her body was repulsive to look upon, her eyes were almost worse—two vacant green orbs that were aglow with pure vehemence.

Vivian struggled to grasp what she saw, but when Lenora gave a choked sob, the baroness lost any desire to comprehend; Vivian lurched painfully to her feet and stumbled toward her children. There was another sound like creaking wood and a dark tendril whipped out toward the baroness, knocking her back to the ground.

"Mother," Viktor cried again, coughing as he struggled against the vines. "Why is she doing this?" Lenora cried weakly, her voice constricted by the groping, unnatural appendage.

"Please!" Vivian sobbed. Her arm felt broken, but she clawed herself forward on the rug. "What do you want?"

The creature that had taken over Renay's lifeless body kept its cursed green eyes on Vivian as it opened its mouth. "The Light did this...needs this..."

"No," Vivian said weakly, thinking of the Luminaurian priest who had saved them. She had watched as the blinding glow from his hands had brought her children back from death. She refused to believe it was only so she could watch them die like this. "Renay, please! You can't..."

Lenora screamed suddenly, a desperate shrill cry that caused Renay to jolt back. The girl was glowing like a small sun, lighting up the vast study that had previously grown dark as Renay's roots had crept along the floor, up the walls, and covering the windows.

The shrill cry from the girl turned into a weakened groan. Smoke began rising from where the roots touched her, charring and burning away from the power that was rising within her.

"No," Renay said weakly. She turned toward the Light-infused child, her neck straining.

"Mother!" Lenora's voice sounded distant. "I can't feel it anymore. What is she doing to me?"

"It's you, child."

Vivian turned toward the new voice and she saw a man in brilliant pearl armor, striding into the study with a sapphire cloak streaming from his shoulders. In one hand the paladin held a gleaming sword of Light that dripped dark blood and his other hand held the sun itself.

"The Light is within you, girl," the man said. "Stay strong!" He raised his glowing hand and Lenora grew even brighter. "This is an abomination of Shadow, and I need your help to banish it! You are so strong, my lady! Let the Light flow through you!"

Vivian stared slack jawed, unable to speak or act. All she could do is watch as this stranger saved her children from an otherworldly foe.

Renay opened her mouth to let out a horrific scream of pain. Her rotting jaw dislodged and fell to the ground as smoke came out of her exposed throat in puffs. The appendages growing out of her limbs began to contort and shrink, pulling slowly back into a hole in the floor. First Viktor was released, sliding to the ground in a heap and then crawling away from the monster. Then the blackened vines constraining Lenora began to crumble, allowing the girl to step away, still shining like a figure of pure energy.

Viktor was on his feet, helping Vivian to move away from the shrieking plant corpse. Renay's dead skin had begun to slough off the collection of mossy detritus within the twisted vines. Vivian had to cover her ears as the dying thing continued shrieking, slithering away from her daughter's heavenly aura.

She wanted to turn away from the gruesome sight, but it had transfixed her. Renay's lovely body had been ruined beyond belief, a mockery of what the woman had been in life. Vivian had cherished her, both as a sister and as a lover, and seeing her remains used by such foul powers made her insides twist.

Whether it was the physical pain from the monstrous thing's attack or pure agonizing sadness, Vivian could not move. Viktor pulled with all his young might to get his mother away from the dying, thrashing vines. Gradually he got her clear just as a flailing branch slammed down where she had been. The floor itself quaked in response, and Viktor fell to the floor.

"You're the one!"

Something about the desperate voice pulled Vivian's gaze away from the violently dying thing in the middle of the study. The armored man that had burst into the room to rescue them stepped carefully toward Lenora. He had taken his helmet off, revealing a mop of sweaty blonde hair and striking blue eyes.

Vivian looked to her daughter, whose form she could now see as her eyes adjusted to the brightness. Lenora's eyes were wide with terror as she looked from her former caretaker to the armored man staring at her in reverence.

"Please," Vivian finally managed to say. "Do not hurt her! She didn't do this!"

The blonde knight turned to her, letting his hand that no longer glowed fall, his sword relaxed at his side. His posture didn't imply danger, but his eyes were fervent and wild.

"She did," he said in wonder, turning back to Lenora. "She's the Child of Light."

Quinn didn't flinch away from the foes. Instead, Ransil was surprised to see the boy step forward to meet them. There were three dryads—or at least they once were, but these wielded cracked stone daggers and hissed like feral animals—moving to circle them.

Ransil and Quinn had been cutting through a small ravine toward Oakworth when they had suddenly gotten lost, which was strange considering how small the ravine was. But it felt like every way they walked they had ended up back where they had begun. It was around the third time they had returned to their starting point that the dryads had ambushed them.

Ransil had his knives out now, but waited to see what the women would do. He was not eager to see how he would fare against such a foe—or three such foes!

"Wait," Ransil warned, seeing the boy begin a motion with his hand. Something told him the boy was about to conjure fire again, but there was a competing, unfamiliar voice in his head warning him. He didn't understand the warning, but he felt it.

The dryads looked like gorgeous elven women, clothed only in delicate leaves that seemed to grow from the crevices of their bodies. He had seen one as a boy in the Acreage, when he was prone to exploring the Brandle Woods. He had lost his way and stumbled upon a mystical glade where a dryad sang to him. When he tried to follow her, she evasively led him back out of the woods and then disappeared.

Everything he knew about dryads came from whimsical stories, and if all those stories were to be believed, then dryads were both ravenous she-wolves who lured men into their dark glades to feast on them and frivolous exiles of the Fey Domain who existed only to pleasure adventurers.

As Ransil watched the emerald-skinned women leer at them, gnashing thorn-like teeth, he wished the latter stories were true.

There were sounds of battle beyond the trees, and Ransil could even see figures racing by between the leaves not far away. But he dared not move.

"What are we waiting for?" Quinn sounded like a nine-year-old boy staring death in the eyes. "They're going to kill us."

One of the dryads barked in response, a noise that sounded like a thick tree cracking in several different places at once. Her glowing green eyes bore into Ransil and her head tilted to the side, as if waiting for a response. The other two dryads still crept slowly in either direction, their crude knives held ready.

Whatever had warned Ransil to wait suddenly compelled him to reach into his pocket. Unsure what his other options were at the moment, he sheathed one of his knives and drew out the keyshard, knowing now it had been the source of the compulsion. With its weight in his palm, he experienced a wave of lightheadedness; something coursed through his body.

"Give us the stone," the dryad barked again, but now Ransil could discern the message being communicated. He didn't hear the words, but he felt them.

"I can't," Ransil replied.

"Can't what?" Quinn asked, now turning to look at the halfling.

"Quiet."

The barking dryad gnashed her teeth again and pointed at the stone with her knife. "We will not let her have it. Oakus denies her!"

The druid, Ransil thought. *They know of Fallon. Perhaps they know of Naya then as well.* "We took it from her, and we're taking it somewhere safe." Ransil saw Quinn looking at the keyshard and the dryad, understanding now what was happening.

"Tell her we're taking it somewhere she can't find it."

Ransil did, but the dryad barked angrily again. "It will not be safe. Give it to us!"

A vision suddenly came to Ransil of two women in a dimly lit earthen tunnel. One of them wore Vysarcian robes—Naya, the Shadow priestess—and the other was an elf wearing druidic leathers who Ransil could only suspect was Fallon.

He still heard the dryad's guttural raging, but it came to him in images now instead of words. Naya led Fallon through the twisting passages of the Old Ways, which darkened in their wake, rotting and withering. The dryad was showing Ransil how the women were corrupting the Old Ways.

The vision continued, showing Naya and Fallon now in a chamber that looked like an enormous hollowed out tree. They both stared in reverence at a massive figure—*the incarnate*, Ransil thought, somehow knowing for certain—that looked like a treeman out of the legends. It was over twice the size of both women, plated in armor forged from unnatural tree bark with huge lantern green eyes that duly glowed behind a mask of decorative oak.

Ransil was overcome by terror, unable to escape the image that spoke of world-ending peril. He understood the direness that came through the dryad's primal screams.

"Enough," he managed to say. But the vision persisted. Naya waved her one good hand while Fallon stood before the incarnate holding a keyshard. The treeman's chest came alive, gripping vines emerging from its mossy bulk to push the armor plates aside, revealing a hollow that looked like the size of a human or elf.

The dryad's voice became more desperate and angry, intensifying the scene that Ransil was forced to watch.

Fallon stepped toward the incarnate and pushed the keyshard into the dark crevice of the creature, above the hollow where a person might be held suspended within.

The incarnate's eyes brightened, blinding Ransil as the room was enveloped in angry green light.

"Stop!" Reality came back to Ransil as he fell to a knee, putting his closed fist that held the keyshard to his head. It seemed to help drive away the pain.

"You cannot stop her," the dryad warned again. "We can. Give us Oakus' gift. It was ours to begin with."

Ransil opened his hand to look at the stone. It was such a simple thing. He suddenly felt foolish for not just giving these women what they wanted. Who was he to interfere?

As he slowly got to his feet, Ransil saw the dryad who had spoken to him through the keyshard straighten. She lowered her knife, and the fury slowly melted from her face.

Just as Ransil was turning to Quinn to explain that this might be their best choice, the dryad screamed again, this time in anguish. Ransil recoiled and turned back to her in time to see a glowing arrowhead bursting from the woman's chest.

"Brace! Here!"

The other dryads turned to react, but similar missiles buried themselves into their chests as well. Black smoke coiled from their wounds as they fell to their knees, shrieking in Ransil's head.

"The Light!" Their voices echoed painfully in the halfling's head, and he fell to the ground, barely managing to hold onto the keyshard.

It took a long moment for Ransil to recover, but when he did he blinked his eyes to see Quinn kneeling over him, along with two strangers armed with longbows. The two human archers—a longhaired man and a young woman, both in green hooded ranger cloaks—both had arrows knocked, and each of those arrows had a glowing tip. Ransil knew them as Luminaurian acolytes.

Suddenly panicking, Ransil held up his hand to find it empty.

"I have it," Quinn said, giving the halfling a knowing look, flicking his eyes to the newcomers.

The cloaked man knelt down and held out a hand. "Brace Cobbit. The Luminaura is taking back Oakworth. You're safe now."

No, Ransil thought as he took his hand and was easily lifted to his feet. The vision of the incarnate still stained his thoughts. He looked at the dead dryads, their bodies burned by the Light; he wondered if they may have been their best hope against Naya and Fallon.

None of us are.

Chapter Eleven

A Grim Proposal

The sun woke Anika from a dreamless sleep. It sliced through the room thanks to a small gap in the curtains swaying gently in the morning breeze. Anika shielded her eyes against the piercing, radiant blade of light and rolled away from its reach. The bed nearly swallowed her.

She was buried in soft blankets that felt like little clouds and she sank into a cushion of air. It was comfort that she had never experienced or even dreamt of, and she honestly did not care for it. As she crawled from the soft abyss, her thoughts went back to her mornings in Blakehurst, when she would wake up and hear her father already working outside. There would almost always without fail be a steaming cup of tea waiting at her bedside.

Memories of Blakehurst were painful, even more now that she was pampered in the high palace of Pyram. It made her feel guilty, enjoying such luxuries while her former life lay in absolute ruins. She sat up in the bed and observed her chambers.

The floor was gleaming marble, polished to such a shine that it looked like still water. Atop the hard floor were rugs of such exotic patterns that Anika felt she could stare at them for hours and not be any closer to puzzling out how they were designed.

Near her curtained, four-post bed was a cabinet, atop of which sat a basin filled with tepid water. Anika's eyes became fixed on that still water. She saw the ocean in her mind, vast and silent. Above it was the sky, clear and patient, waiting for her. She closed her eyes and suddenly it all came back to her.

Anika was flying.

Leaving the horrors of Oakworth, Anika was weightless and free. But directionless, she flailed in the air, her limbs reaching for any purchase as she began to spin further upward. She screamed, but no one could hear her as the world shrank away below, flashing between distant green and infinite blue.

A knock at the door jolted Anika from the vision and she nearly fell out of bed. She tried to catch her breath as she got to her feet. The feel of solid ground slowed her racing heart.

The knock came again. "Lady Lawson?"

"Yes?" Anika looked down, suddenly remembering she was naked. The door creaked open and she turned to find her clothes, but they were gone. "Wait!"

"Lady?"

Anika grabbed two handfuls of the fluffy blanket from the bed and covered herself with it awkwardly, spinning around to see a shocked Stevra standing in the doorway. The halfling was holding a stack of folded clothing. She gave Anika's makeshift garments a curious look.

"Where are my clothes?" Anika demanded, instantly regretting how much she sounded like a royal snob. She was more than a little flustered.

"Where they belong," Stevra said with a placid face, "in the burn pits." She lifted the clothes. "These were not worn by a prisoner in our dungeons, so I had thought they might appeal to you more."

Anika felt abashed. She nodded, averting her eyes from the woman. "Thank you."

"Are you cold, my lady?"

Anika looked at her and saw genuine confusion on Stevra's face. "No, I...I just." *Do I really have to explain this?* "I am not accustomed to being unclothed in front of strangers." But now that she thought about it, she hadn't even remembered undressing for bed; the last thing she remembered from the night before was drinking the wine sent to her room.

Stevra considered that with a flat stare for a moment and then shrugged. "Well, I don't consider us strangers, Lady Lawson. Even so, Vale must be a strange place if you have to hide yourself from the servants."

"I don't have servants," Anika said with a small amount of pride. "If I did, I wouldn't expect them to have to dress me."

Stevra smiled finally. "Well, you certainly haven't seen some of the more elaborate Karranese gowns, my lady." She entered the room and presented the clothes, holding them up for Anika.

Anika stared at them, feeling a bit foolish but not wanting to feel even more foolish by dropping the blankets. "You can set them on the bed, thank you."

Her tight expression fighting back a smile, Stevra set the clothes on the bed. "I trust you'll be able to figure these out. I don't suppose you would let me bathe you then?"

Anika smiled at that. "I'm still clean enough from the bath last night, thank you." She was suddenly very glad to have been left alone last night to scrub the dungeon's filth from her body. She had never been so filthy in all her life, which, as a tanner, was saying a lot.

As she thought back to the grime she had scrubbed off her naked flesh, she felt a new sort of shame. The night she had spent with Matty in Oakworth, she had been overcome with confidence, which she had attributed to some hidden power lurking within her, desperate to find its way out. She had been proud and certain of herself in that moment, and right now—cowering in the presence of a kind halfling woman who had seen it all before—Anika felt meek.

She let the blankets fall, swallowing the discomfort she would normally feel from being laid so bare. Stevra gathered the blankets without a word, as if she had expected it, and began making the bed.

Relaxed, Anika dressed herself as Stevra fluffed the heavy covers while whistling a foreign tune.

The clothes were colorful and silky. While most of the decorations around the palace were shades of fiery oranges and reds, Anika's wardrobe was emerald greens and sapphire blues, with silver filigree along the hems. She was provided with no small clothes, which shouldn't have surprised her given the sweltering temperatures that Karrane was known for.

As she slipped her arms into the loose, sleeveless top, she turned to face Stevra. "Does the majest...require my presence this morning?" *Was that how ladies spoke in court?* And just like that, she felt insecure again.

"He has requested that you join him for lunch," Stevra said, with a curious glance. "Until then, the guards outside your doors have been instructed to escort you wherever you wish to go." The halfling gave her a raised eyebrow. "Provided you stay within the palace walls."

Having seen the perimeter of the palace from her balcony, Anika couldn't imagine wandering further than the royal terrace which ran around the pyramid directly below her chambers in the apex terrace. Each terrace of Pyram was built atop the sides of the great pyramid that the city was named for. Anika knew of the stories told about the wonders that dwelt below that pyramid, but she knew better than to ask about them.

She slipped her legs into the pants that only came down past her knees. There were slits along the sides, making it feel like she wasn't even wearing anything. But she liked the touch of the light fabric against her skin.

"Does he think I'll run away?" Anika asked, feeling suddenly brazen.

Stevra gave a chuckle. "Do you think we could stop you from running away? You came here for a reason, my lady. You need something here, yes? Why should he fear you fleeing? If he did, you'd still be locked up in that cage."

Anika cinched her top with the belt the majest had provided. Its buckle had a scorpion fashioned into it with tiny yellow gems. "Why am I not locked up in that cage?"

Stevra stopped bothering with the bed's covers and looked at Anika with a playful gaze. "I guess you'll find out at lunch, my lady."

Once she was finished dressing, Anika left Stevra to her duties and walked toward the doors. When she opened them, she saw two armored guards standing sentinel to either side of the doorframe, facing each other. One was a gruff dwarf man with a fiery red beard that marked him as a northerner and the other was a darker-skinned Karranese woman with broad shoulders and tightly braided hair that fell over them.

Both guards nodded when they saw her. They were armored in crimson plate mail edged in gold with orange cloaks falling from their swooping shoulder plates. Anika gave them an awkward nod in return, but stopped short just as she was about to step out of her room.

There was an uneasy feeling in her stomach, and it reminded her of the day before when she had met with the majest and his councilors. She spun around and returned to the bedside cabinet, opening the drawer to where Stormender rested in its new sheath—a gift from the majest. She affixed it to her belt and then returned to the doors.

With no immediate destination in mind, Anika walked down the hall from her chambers to the outer terrace. A pristine morning view welcomed her. She faced southward, toward the Auleric Ocean. She could see activity down at the city's sprawling docks, with huge galleys being loaded by stevedores that looked no larger than tiny insects at this distance.

Anika put her hands on the terrace railing, closing her eyes and letting the wind blow through her hair. She thought of flying again, losing control in the atmosphere. At the slightest hint of dizziness, she opened her eyes.

She heard a guard shift behind her. "Is milady unwell?"

Anika looked over her shoulder at the woman. "No, I'm just not altogether used to this...height."

"That is not uncommon here," she said kindly. "May I suggest we walk on the other side of the terrace. You will still have the view, but it will feel less overwhelming."

Anika obliged, once again not sure where she was going. She followed the guard's advice and walked along the slanted face of the city's pyramid, watching the sea and slowly hearing people begin their day on the terrace below. The distant sounds of the markets far below on the lower terraces were barely audible over the suffocating peacefulness of ocean and wind.

With no particular destination in mind, she walked and thought, resting a hand on Stormender and feeling a sense of completion that was foreign to her.

Even when she felt like she belonged in Blakehurst, there was something always incomprehensibly missing. As she touched the enchanted blade at her hip, she couldn't help but wonder if it was what she had been missing.

During her meeting with the majest, the discomfort in her stomach—the pull—was relieved when the knife was returned to her. When her father had first given it to her on her cursed birthday, she had also felt a void filled.

Thinking of her father filled her with fresh, unexpected grief. She still had no idea what had become of him, but she couldn't imagine him surviving captivity among the harpies. Still, her father was once a king's ranger, as much as he declined to speak of it. Anika always suspected he had been a great warrior, but kept that part of his life secret, especially after their mother left.

She missed her father, more now than when he was first taken. Having kept him out of her thoughts made her ashamed; but between her mother, Matty, Gage...it was too much.

A flock of strange birds squawked as they flew overhead, bringing Anika out of her thoughts. She tried to focus on the serene skyline to keep the grief at bay. Aside from her escorts, she was still alone on the terrace. They continued their walk toward an elaborate staircase, not unlike the one she had ascended the night before. Only this one led down to the lower terrace, where she could see signs of life.

Two pairs of guards paced along the terrace in opposite directions, dressed identical to her own escorts. She saw a young girl and boy in vibrant colored silks racing down the stairs to the next terrace, their sandaled feet slapping loudly against the sandy stone.

"What's down there," Anika asked her guards.

"The royal terrace," the dwarf grunted. "Some apartments for the dignitaries, the majest's theater, the dining hall, the grand ballroom, and the archives."

Something stirred in Anika. "The archives?"

The woman answered. "Yes, milady. The most expansive in all of Noveth, if the Archivist is to be believed."

The dwarf grunted again at that.

Without knowing exactly why, Anika stepped down the first stair. "Take me there."

The archives took Anika's breath away. She thought the room where she had met the majest had more books than she would ever see in one place again. There was so much she had to learn about the world.

Passing through the towering doors of the chamber, Anika felt like she was stepping into the past, where ancient lore promised all sorts of wondrous things and held infinite mysteries. She felt completely insignificant in the presence of such architecture and high-reaching shelves completely packed with timeless volumes of the world's history.

There were two other figures in the archives, an older elf woman who sat at a desk and paid Anika no mind when she entered with her entourage, and a human nobleman with ruddy skin who gave her an evaluating stare before he turned back to continue searching for a particular book on a lower shelf.

Still not knowing exactly what drew her here, she strode past the rows of shelves toward a large round desk in the center of the hall. Craning her neck to truly appreciate how many books lined the walls, Anika accidentally walked straight into the desk, causing a loud thump.

A head suddenly popped up behind the desk—a middle-aged gnome woman with pale skin and a set of elegant spectacles on her bulbous nose. "Mind the noise, dear," she whispered in an Eastlund accent. "If you need something, just take a chip and I'll come find you." She nodded to a bowl on the desktop that contained a bunch of obsidian disks.

Confused, Anika reached for the bowl and picked up a chip with two fingers. She felt a strange aura coming from it and knew it to be enchanted.

The gnome scoffed as the small purple stone that hung from her necklace pulsed with a weak glow and produced a subtle jingling sound. "Well not while I'm right here, certainly." She motioned for Anika to return the chip.

Dropping it back into the bowl, Anika gave the woman an apologetic look. "I'm sorry, I…"

"You're a prisoner?"

"No, I'm just—"

"Here to arrest me?"

The dwarf guard gave a light snort. "We're just her escort, Saleen. She is a royal guest and wanted to see the archives. Lady Anika, this is Archivist Saleen."

The gnome gave a curt nod and motioned to the sprawling chamber. "By all means," she whispered, "have a look." She raised an eyebrow at Anika. "Unless you were looking for something in particular?"

Instinctively, Anika's hand went to her father's knife. But instead of Bennik Lawson, she thought of the halfling Ruke and her brother Gage. She hadn't thought of Ruke's words much since facing Corvanna. But now she realized the echoes of the halfling priestess' words were what drew her here.

"The Children of Light and Shadow," Anika heard herself say.

Saleen's eyebrow fell. "Some light reading for the morning?" She waved a hand. "Pardon the pun." With a small hop, she disappeared behind the desk, but Anika heard the gnome's footsteps as she came around the other side. "I suppose you'll want *Ehury's Accounts on the Unthroning* and *The War of the Children*?"

Anika heard the guards behind her move away toward the chamber's only exit as she followed Saleen. "I don't know," she answered honestly. "Whatever you suggest. I've never read either."

"Don't tell me you're one of those Stane fanatics." She waved a hand above her head, dismissing such folks. "I don't have time to disprove that nonsense regarding the Children. I specialize in history here, not religious foolery."

Anika didn't know how to respond, so she followed quietly. The archivist led her toward the opposite end of the chamber, where the room broke off into several alcoves. Saleen guided Anika along the leftmost wall where the morning sunlight spilled in to illuminate a tiered shelf.

"Here," Saleen pointed to the lowest shelf, "are the volumes recovered from Velcarthe detailing some of the earliest mentions of Light and Shadow. Back then it was mostly good versus evil mythology, nothing much substantial. But here," she moved her small arm up to point to the second tier of shelves that began at Anika's shoulders. "This is where you'll find more recent writings from some of the best scholars in history."

She turned to face Anika. "You'll find Ehury's books here, as well as *The War of the Children*. There, the one with the golden spine."

Anika saw the red book the gnome motioned to with a golden device on it, half blazing sun and half-moon.

"I'll leave you to it. There are reading desks over there. Come see me if you have any questions, and stay where your friends can see you—I'll have no trouble here, mark my words."

Anika smiled, appreciating the woman's bluntness. "Thank you."

Easily finding the books that Saleen referenced, Anika also gathered a few other hefty tomes—including *The Light in Ghulta* and *The Children's Balance*—and carried them to the desk. She hadn't read many different books in Blakehurst; her father had kept an old copy of *Legends of Noveth* that contained various tales from before the Unthroning, which he used to her learn to read. But beyond that, most of her reading was limited to brief tanning instructions and lists of supplies.

She took a deep breath and opened Ehury's thick tome, flipping through the first few pages of ponderous writing, wondering if she was in any mood to do any focused reading this morning. But she felt she had to learn something. Too many coincidences had happened since her brother had given her that keyshard; she had to at least try to understand her purpose.

As much as she wanted to deny the fact, she knew she was the Child of Light. But she didn't fully understand what that meant.

She spent the rest of the morning poring over the books. Breakfast was brought to her, a meal of spicy sausages, fried eggs, and a fresh crumbly bread, along with a steaming cup of coffee—a drink she had heard about from Neff the trader, but she had never tried.

After she finished her first cup of the dark, bitter liquid, she kindly asked the guard for another as she continued reading about her destiny.

Stevra came when it was time for lunch. The halfling servant found Anika standing over a desk in the archives with a mug of coffee in one hand while her other hand flipped through a huge book that was stacked on top of another book, which was stacked on several other books.

Anika was led back out to the royal terrace and up to the apex terrace. It was a long walk around to the northern side of the pyramid, but she welcomed the shade as they made their way into the solarium. Set within a concave opening near the top of the pyramid, the open courtyard was divided by several sets of decorative pillars.

Anika was guided to the end of the solarium that was shaded from the sun, and there sat the majest.

Lekan Nafir was even more handsome in the open daylight. He had a youthful mop of wavy black hair, upon which sat his elegant crown. The sheer, silken vest he wore did little to conceal his tight body. He was not muscular like Matty had been, but Anika's eyes did not shy away from what Lekan's clothing left revealed.

"My lady of Lawson," Lekan said with a bright smile. "Even in the grime, you took my breath away. Now, though, you stop my very heart."

Feeling a blush creep up her neck, Anika returned the smile awkwardly. Unsure how to respond, she simply said, "Thank you for the clothes...and the room...and, well, thank you for releasing me."

"To be clear," came a voice from behind her, "you are not released."

Anika turned to see the Grand Vizier Elrin. The old elf wore a strange robe of bright yellow, mantled in orange feathers. He walked around Anika to stand beside the majest's table, vials of colorful fluids tinkling from his belt. *An alchemist,* Anika thought, having never met one before.

"You are here by the grace of the majest," Elrin told her, motioning to the guards. "You are under watch."

"Yes," Lekan said sternly, "she is aware." The majest motioned to a chair at his table. "Please, my lady, join me. You must excuse my council—we are facing trying times and nerves are not exactly steady, as they say."

Anika made her way to her seat, casting a nervous glance at the vizier who openly glared at her. As she sat down, she saw another figure near the balcony railing. An ashen-skinned dark elf; Anika could not decide the person's age or gender, but they reminded her of Grip. The dark elf held what looked like a canvas and a box tucked under their arm. Anika supposed they had to be an artist. Karrane was well known for its wealth of artists.

"I heard you visited our archives," the majest said as he claimed the seat across from her. "Tell me it was to your liking?"

Lekan had a nervous energy about him. He didn't seem as confident and calm as he had during their first meeting.

"It was incredible," Anika said honestly. "I never thought I'd see so many books at once. It must be the biggest collection of books in the world."

The majest smiled proudly. "I dare say it is! And I challenge you to find a more studied archivist than Saleen. She has been to every library from here to Xoatia and Ghulta to Eastlund. Scholars come from all over Aetha to behold her collection." He cast a nervous glance at Elrin, then looked back at Anika. "Tell me: are you a book lover?"

Anika shook her head shyly. "No, I—well, my home only had a few books. But I'm fascinated by history." Something about Lekan relaxed her, and she wanted to confide in someone, even if she could only talk tangentially about the subject matter she had been engrossed in—she still didn't think she should go about telling everyone she was the Child of Light. "Ever since that storm up north, there has been a lot of talk regarding the keyshards and the old gods. I find it all very compelling."

A strange expression passed over Lekan's face, but it was quickly replaced by his charming smile. "I'm sure Saleen could fill your ear on that topic."

Anika smiled uncomfortably, feeling her eyes drawn to the dark elf who seemed to be waiting for something.

Following her gaze, Lekan caught sight of the artist and stood up. "Please excuse my lack of decorum," he said to Anika, motioning for the artist to step forward. "This is Wyndie, my finest court artist. He comes to us from Xoatia."

The artist stepped forward and promptly set down his box, opened it, and began assembling an easel.

"This idea came to me from your story last night," Lekan continued, sitting back down and holding his hands out to Anika.

Unsure of the customs in Karrane, she stiffly put her hands into his. Once again she noticed how incredibly soft his hands were. She shifted in her seat, flustered.

Lekan didn't seem to notice. "It is a tragedy to not know one's own lineage, and my heart was breaking all night thinking about how you were only here looking for your family."

The word seemed to drive a dagger into her heart. She knew her family, but when she thought of her father, she imagined his broken body in the wilderness somewhere, and when she thought of Gage she saw the memory of her mother's corpse. But she didn't interrupt him, and she kept her hands still.

"When you were found in the chamberlord's manse, you were looking for your mother's likeness—I understand you have had visions of her." He squeezed her hands. "Do you think you could describe her to Wyndie?"

The question sent her right back to The Early Mule, when she had imagined the Karranese woman sitting with Elza. Then, she saw the woman again in Oakworth. Something in her core told her the woman was her birth mother.

"Yes," Anika said distantly. Though she was unsure if she could put the vision into words, she knew this would be her best chance for an answer.

Lekan released her hands and motioned to Stevra. "Please bring out the food. Wyndie, heed our lady Lawson's words and let us see if we can lead her home."

Anika's stomach rumbled at the mention of food. All that reading must have worked up more of an appetite than she realized. Or perhaps her stomach was just roiling from anxiety, as she had no idea how to begin describing the woman in her mind.

As her eyes shifted between Lekan, Elrin, and Wyndie, Anika let an awkward silence hang over the table. Finally, she looked out across Pyram and took a deep breath as she let the majesty of the place embolden her.

"Her skin is like mine," Anika began, holding up one of her hands and inspecting it as if seeing it for the first time. "And her hair was the same. She looked like an older version of me, but her nose was wider here," she pointed to the side of her nose where her nostrils flared out less than the woman in her mind.

She continued describing the vision as best she could while the food was laid before her. Lekan sat silently, his gaze encouraging and comforting. He sipped juice from a chilled glass beaded with condensation, glistening in the morning heat.

Anika was served a light salad of purplish greens tossed in a citrus dressing, dusted with crushed nuts and seeds and topped with exceptionally sweet yellow fruits.

The meal continued with a cold soup, with Anika's descriptions of her mother occasionally interrupted by Lekan sharing a brief jest or random fact about Pyram or Karrane. Wyndie continued dutifully painting, not speaking or looking away from his canvas. His hands were deft, mixing paints, switching between charcoal and brush. Anika had never met a true artist, but she imagined she was watching one of the best in the world.

Finally, as Anika and Lekan finished the last bites of the exotic fish soaked in butter and lemon, Wyndie set down his brush. Anika felt like they had been at the meal for hours, but the sun still looked to be at its zenith. Her stomach twisted in nervous anticipation again as Wyndie began removing the canvas from the easel.

But when he turned it around to show them, Anika was more confused than anything else. The face staring back at her—while expertly depicted, a wondrous work of art—did not look familiar.

Anika heard Lekan gasp. She turned to see him rise from his seat slowly, entranced by the artwork, stepping slowly toward it.

Elrin stepped up to the table. "Is that—?"

"The last domina," Lekan said in disbelief. "Mavala Drastil..."

"This can't be," Elrin said, turning toward Anika accusatorially. "This is who you saw in your vision? This is your mother?"

Anika turned from the old elf back to the portrait, about to admit that it was not. But the majest turned to face them.

"Don't you see?" Lekan's eyes were wild, boring into his vizier. "It's been over fifteen years since the uprising." He looked toward Anika, gaping at her like he had never seen her before. "I can see it now. You're her."

"Who?" Anika asked, looking again at the portrait of the woman whose face looked less foreign now. Something about the painting made her question her own memories. *Was that who I saw? The skin and the hair look right...*

"The dominess." Lekan stepped toward Anika and dropped gracefully to one knee. "My betrothed. Kalany Drastil. Heir to the Trivestiture of Karrane." He once again held out his hands to her. "You were lost to us, but you have returned."

Anika stared at him in shocked silence, wanting to look back to the painting but afraid if she did it would shatter this surreal moment. Secretly, deep in the shadows of her heart, she had dreamed of being a lost princess—that her true parents were great people from a faraway paradise. It was a dream she would never admit to anyone, not even herself. But now it seemed to be coming true.

Here she sat, atop the greatest pyramid in the world, looking out over a paradise. A beautiful man knelt before her, promising her a life of luxury. It was all too much for her.

"My dear Kalany," Lekan said gently, still holding out his hands for her. "We were once to be wed; our families dreamt of uniting our rivaling houses and joining the three great cities of Karrane once more as a single empire." His smile nearly melted her. "Shall we fulfill our destinies together? Will you be my royene?"

Anika swallowed. Her eyes drifted from Lekan to the painting, and she saw her mother staring back at her.

Chapter Twelve

The Last Guard

They traveled through the night, staying clear of the Eastlund Road at Lexeth's urging. It would make their journey quicker overall, yet Bennik's knees were not happy with all the hills they had to climb. But the elf insisted.

"There have been skirmishes along our borders," he had told Bennik with a certain amount of bitterness. "The Briarhold fell two years ago to some sort of treachery, but the young heir to House Thornton blamed my kin in Gladwater."

"I remember," Bennik had said sadly. Conceding to Lexeth's insistence, he followed the elf into the hills.

Bennik had heard of that massacre. Sir Patrick Thornton had such a prickly reputation that word of his recent antics had spread all the way to Blakehurst. Bennik had met the boy at Lord's Faire in Menevere nearly thirty years ago. At the time, Patrick was a pudgy boy who whined when he failed to make the lists in any of the trials. Even back then, Bennik could tell the boy would go on to do no good for the world as a man.

From what Bennik had heard of the Gladwater Massacre, a small band of elves that refused to adhere to the Eldercrown's decrees made a camp along the Evansly River, and Lord Marten Thornton reluctantly gave them leave to dwell within his borders. However, not all the Thorntons were as accepting of the elves, as they were a mysterious people that the Eastlunders never fully embraced, even when they stayed in their trees.

When Sir Patrick Thornton had returned from campaigning in Guyen and found Brairhold in ruin and his father murdered, it only took a few elven arrows found amongst the dead for the new lord to condemn the Gladwater elves.

Patrick had led an army consisting of his own house's knights and footmen and slaughtered the peaceful elves to whom his father had provided refuge.

Bennik had remembered being enraged upon hearing the news, not only due to the tragic nature of the event, but also how it would further divide the elves and Eastlunders. As a result, he now had to scramble up and down hills instead of easily walking along the Eastlund Road just to avoid being caught openly traveling with an elf in Eastlund.

"I don't suspect I'll be any more welcome here," Bennik had told Lexeth. "Bannerlords that defect from the king's army aren't normally welcomed back to the iron lands with open arms. I'm more or less a traitor now."

"At least you'd be able to blend in easily," the elf responded when they had begun their trek into the Fowler Uplands. "We should be able to avoid any homesteads or hovels if we follow the hills to the sunken tower."

Bennik heard that jingling in his mind again.

Even the name of the place had been enough to rekindle the guilt that had kept Bennik from ever dreaming of returning home. The sunken tower was once an exciting landmark for him. As a boy, he would explore the old place with his cousins, defying Jarrod Lawson's decree that no one should enter the dangerous edifice. Kobolds had once come up from Guyen and claimed the place as their own before Bennik's father had driven them out.

The sunken tower had earned a foul reputation since it fell from grace during the Nether War. But for a group of adventure-seeking boys, the half-buried turret had been a promise of adventure. Years later, Jarrod Lawson's friend and advisor, Reston Mauer, would be given rights to the tower for his faithful service to the bannerlords. Bennik had known it was a poisoned gift, one to set the old man aside when his eccentricities could no longer be tolerated.

Thinking of Reston reminded Bennik of when he had received word of his father's death. The letter had come from Reston himself, the man who was meant to train the next Lord of Gavelston in the ways of the Keyguard. But the letter had instructed him to forget about the Keyguard—or the *obligation* as Reston had called it—and to forge a life far from the petty courts of Eastlund.

Sweat stung Bennik's eyes—which could just as easily have been tears from the bitter memories—and he wiped it away as he crested another hill, exhausted and aching. He breathed a sigh of relief at the sight.

With dawn breaking ever so slightly over the eastern trees, Bennik could now see the silhouette of their destination. It was as if he had stepped back into the past. The dread he had felt revisiting the place was suddenly replaced by a surge of excitement, as if he were a child again, beholding a dark keep of ancient wonders.

"You see it too?" Lexeth's voice betrayed a hint of concern as he slowed his pace.

"I may not have elf eyes, but I'm not blind." Bennik followed his companion down the hill, touching the hilt of the curved elven knife out of instinct. Something about Lexeth's tone set his nerves on end. "The tower is where it has always been."

"Not the tower," Lexeth said, looking over his shoulder at Bennik. "The vines around it are...moving."

The elf picked up his pace then, his bow held at his side while he shifted his cloak behind his quiver. Bennik saw him draw an arrow, and he in turn drew his knife, holding it blade down while he pushed himself into a quick trot to keep pace with the elf.

They closed the distance quickly, and as they neared, Bennik saw what Lexeth had spied earlier. There were thick veins of overgrowth climbing up the tower from years of neglect. And now those roots were writhing over the stone like ponderous snakes, slowly climbing the sunken tower.

Daylight broke as they crossed the shallow creek that marked the Lawson's ancestral borders, but Bennik didn't have time to savor the nostalgia of finally returning home. Instead he raced up the embankment, jamming his knife into the muddy ground to serve as a handhold as it got too steep. Lexeth walked weightlessly up the incline, nocking an arrow as he neared the broken piles of stones that once served as the tower's outer boundary walls.

"Stay alert," the elf said softly, motioning where Bennik couldn't see. "Dryads."

"Again?" Bennik grunted, finally cresting the hill and preparing for battle. But then he saw the charred corpse. "Someone's here."

Lexeth nodded, motioning further along the wall where more dryads lay slain. They looked like young elven women, but their skin bore the coarse texture of tree bark, and their hair, in hues of autumn and spring, lay like tangled moss. The dryads they had encountered in the Old Ways were feral and savage; but in death, these looked like slaughtered children.

Bennik swallowed his sadness and pushed on, Lexeth falling behind with his bow held ready. The pair walked along the broken stone walls to where several dryad corpses were strewn in a heap.

"There was a chase," Lexeth said softly.

Bennik saw it too. Tracks led up the other side of the hill, lots of them, a clear sign of a pursuit. Whatever the dryads had chased into the tower had used the fallen walls as a choke point to unleash some sort of terrible fire magic on their pursuers.

"Is this the work of the man we seek?" Lexeth asked, nodding to the bodies.

Bennik shook his head, unsure. "Reston was no wizard. Perhaps he had some sort of weapon? A keyshard?"

Lexeth looked across all the bodies, observing the singed stones along the broken walls and the tower itself. The living roots crept around several burned spots on the tower's stones as if they feared whatever had caused the marks would return.

"This was not caused by a mere keyshard," Lexeth said, his voice certain.

Bennik held his knife in front of him as he crept forward, suddenly feeling less than equipped for whatever was in the tower. He paused as the elf gently laid his hand on Bennik's shoulder.

"Something's coming."

Knowing his ears could not compete with an elf's, Bennik waited to follow Lexeth's lead. But the elf had just drawn his bow and stood still as a statue. A long moment passed during which Bennik held his breath, but just as he was about to release it, Lexeth released an arrow that disappeared into the tower's arched doorway with a silent hiss.

There was a gentle thud, a pathetic whimper, and the sound of something falling down stairs. Three sets of glowing green eyes appeared in the shadows of the tower, coming closer.

"Behind me," Lexeth said, just as one of the approaching sets of eyes let out a feline snarl and bounded forward. Nocking and loosing another arrow as fluidly as Bennik might skin a rabbit, Lexeth dropped the shadowy cat and it fell in a black heap.

Panthers?! Bennik couldn't believe what he saw. One time he had seen such a creature caged on the docks of Menevere, but to his knowledge the beasts were mostly found in the distant jungles of Laustreal. Whether or not he believed his eyes, the two panthers speeding out of the shadows toward him and Lexeth were certainly real.

Lexeth managed to loose another arrow, striking down the first cat, while the second leaped over its fallen companion, extending its knife-like claws. The elf leapt aside, just barely avoiding the attack. Bennik sidestepped and slashed clumsily at the leaping panther with his knife. Unaccustomed as he was to dueling a jungle cat with such a short blade, he managed to slice the beast's side.

Unfazed, the panther landed and spun, letting out another vicious snarl. Bennik froze as the emerald glowing eyes settled on him. He had fallen to a knee after the awkward attack and was unprepared for the pounce he knew was coming. Fortunately, Lexeth put the frenzied beast down with an arrow through its skull.

"Syrina's horn," Bennik cursed under his breath. "Panthers here in the wild?"

Lexeth slipped a hand under Bennik's arm and helped him to his feet. "These were no ordinary panthers. You saw their eyes? Oakus has taken them. Just like these," he motioned to the vines creeping up the tower, still slithering slowly like conjoined snakes.

"What does that mean?" Bennik wiped the blood from his knife onto the panther that had died slumped on the nearby stone wall. He looked at its wide eyes, now lifeless but still faintly green. It was a tragic sight. Even though the creature had just tried to maul him to death, Bennik couldn't help feeling sad—such a majestic beast, driven by some unnatural power.

"It means that Eyen sent a storm," Lexeth said, motioning to the distant sky, then to the panther, "and Oakus sent this, and those dryads—driven mad by the old god's fury." He nocked another arrow and stepped toward the tower. "It means an incarnate is stirring already."

The words confirmed Bennik's fears and brought back terrible visions of Corvanna. Suddenly, he was no longer back home in the iron lands; he was in that ruined manor in Rathen held captive by a cruel demigod and her ruthless legions. He felt his knees weaken as he took a step toward the sunken tower, his chest tightening.

He cursed himself for being a coward—for letting the memory of Corvanna and her horrid orc witch torturing him haunt him still—but it seemed to only make his breathing that much more difficult. Soon he was on all fours, struggling to shake away the suffocating dread to no avail.

What's wrong with me? Bennik had fought in two wars and seen more terrors in his life than most men. Yet the mere memory of Corvanna and her minions had brought him low like a child. There were distant voices competing with the trauma broiling in his mind, but the world was falling away with each breath Bennik failed to catch. He felt like he was falling until a large hand reached under him and drew him back to his feet.

Managing to open his eyes, what he saw snapped him out of the panic attack. A woman nearly the same height as him stared at him with emerald pupils—not burning green orbs like the dryads or panthers that had attacked them, but green eyes still meant foe to him.

He reached for his knife, but a hand caught his wrist. He turned to see Lexeth, his bow over his shoulder.

"She is with me."

Bennik looked down to the source of the voice. A small balding gnome with a pinched face stared up at him. The man looked familiar to Bennik, but he couldn't put a name to him.

"This is the Archmage of the Arcania," Lexeth said, as if reading Bennik's thoughts.

The gnome gave Lexeth a curious look. "Have we met before?"

Lexeth ignored him, looking toward the woman, who Bennik just realized wore no clothes. Her skin looked gray in the morning light, and she had mossy hair like the dryads. He averted his eyes when he realized he was staring at her curves.

They were in what had become the tower's new entrance: an archway that once served as a balcony until the tower had sunk so low that it was now at ground level. The gateway no longer had the rusted portcullis that Bennik remembered from his final visit to the place, and the balcony's floor had become a heap of rubble.

"You are no dryad," Lexeth said to the woman. "I've read tales of the Daughters of Oakus…"

"Come," a familiar voice echoed from inside the tower. "We'll talk in the solar, before these pesky roots bring the place down."

The jingling sound was real this time.

Reston. Bennik knew the voice better than he knew his own; he had spent so much of his youth listening to the old scholar's stories and lectures. Part of him wanted to race ahead of the others and greet him, but he was also nervous facing the man again after all these years. Instead, he waited, his eyes wandering down to the Archmage.

"Did you do this?" Bennik asked the gnome, motioning to the burnt dryads that littered the grounds outside the tower.

Fainly gave him a flat look before regarding the dead creatures. "They started it." He turned to follow his mysterious companion into the sunken tower, openly admiring his view. Lexeth motioned for Bennik to enter ahead of him; the elf had his curved knives drawn, ready for anything.

Inside, the tower seemed unchanged. The walls were slick with moisture, with occasional stones broken or missing, moss and weeds sprouting from the damp crevices. Between the sounds of footsteps, he could hear the distant echoes of water dripping from every direction.

As he made his way to Reston's solar—as the man liked to call the old room—Bennik pictured the lower floors of the tower. The water levels changed occasionally depending on rainfall, but on most visits there were two floors that were not flooded. Most of the rooms still had standing water, murky and infested with snakes, but they would be accessible by the old stairs. The sounds of dripping water were accompanied by the occasional clattering of rocks.

"This place will fall," Fainly's companion said, her voice echoing down the curved hall that wrapped around their destination.

"Aye," Reston said from beyond the wall, "but there's time for a bit of wine and words. There's much to discuss."

Bennik felt butterflies in his stomach as he rounded the corner to enter the solar. He felt transported to his youth. A round chamber that may have once been an impressive great hall for study was now crammed with shelves, chests, and crates of books and parchment. The hearth had a weak fire burning below a mantle packed with leather-bound tomes. A long table sat in the middle of the room atop a dirty rug that may have once had a discernable pattern.

Reston Mauer stood at the head of that table, pouring wine into five tin cups. Bennik was shocked; the man didn't look a day older than the last time he had seen him. But then again, Reston had a way of seeming older than he was. The sudden realization that Bennik himself was now probably older than Reston had been when they had last seen each other hit him like a mailed fist in the gut.

"Reston." The name came to Bennik's lips unbidden, and he realized he was staring with mouth agape while Fainly and the strange woman stepped toward the table.

The old man looked up, giving Bennik a familiar arrogant smile. "The young lord returns. You must forgive me—the place is certainly in no condition for a grand reception." His eyes shifted to the woman. "As I was saying before the interruption, you might find a cloak and tunic amongst the rubble there." He motioned toward the assorted boxes along the wall. Reston himself wore an old gray cloak over his broad shoulders, the brown tunic beneath was covered in stains. "I'm an old man, prone to leering…"

"I'm quite comfortable," the woman said.

"Ivy, please," Fainly interjected, motioning for her to go find some clothes. "You're a distraction. There are urgent matters to discuss and we need to focus."

With a shake of her head and a rueful smile, she turned and obeyed. Bennik noticed the woman moved a bit awkwardly, as if she was more uncomfortable in her strange skin than she would have them believe. He let the thought go as he made his way to the table.

Reston came around toward him with two cups in hand. He handed one to Lexeth and set the other on the table near Bennik's chosen seat. "It's been a long time, my boy." He threw his arms around Bennik and lowered his voice. "I'm sorry about your father, lad. Jarrod was my dearest friend." The leather pouch at Reston's waist jingled, reminding Bennik of simpler times.

Before Bennik could respond, Fainly urged them to begin their council. "There's much to discuss. Firstly, perhaps: what do you know of these roots tearing your tower apart?" As if in response, there was another knocking of stones in the distance as a piece of the tower fell away.

Reston released Bennik, but kept a firm hand on the man's shoulder. The older man had wild gray hair and a bristly beard. Bennik had always remembered him keeping his beard trimmed, much like his own, but he now looked like a crazy hermit—which Bennik supposed he might just be nowadays.

"It's Oakus," Lexeth answered for him, draining his wine in a single gulp and setting the cup down on the table. No one except Fainly sat in their chairs, but the gnome needed the boost to see over the table, his eyes fixed on Lexeth as the elf continued. "The storm that took Rathen was Eyen fighting against the incarnate claiming his power, now Oakus is doing the same."

"Against?" Ivy asked, adjusting a faded red tunic that covered her torso but barely covered anything below. She had cinched it with a belt. "I say the old gods are using the incarnates to escape their bonds."

"And who are you?" Lexeth snapped.

"A friend," Fainly responded, waving away the concern. "I don't care about the ambitions of the old gods. I care about what these incarnates are capable of. Corvanna was defeated at Oakworth by the Child of Light, I have heard."

"Releasing the scion," Reston added, removing his hand from Bennik and moving back to the head of the table. "The first, but not the last."

"The scion?" Lexeth's voice rarely betrayed emotion, but he sounded genuinely confused.

Out of the corner of his eye, Bennik noticed Fainly recoil at the word.

"What do you know about the scions?" the woman named Ivy asked.

Reston looked toward the fire, his eyes distant. Another rock tumbled in the distance. "Anthur Pembrook told me about the scions. His father, Sir Dennis, a descendant of Sir Branton the Betrayer, was given a vision when he burned his feet performing the Walk of Wick. For each of the Keys of Transience to be remade to Stane's design, he required a scion."

"The incarnates are not the scions?" Bennik felt completely out of his element here, but something told him this concerned his children, so he was determined to understand.

With a slow shake of his head, Reston looked toward Fainly, absentmindedly jingling that damn pouch. "No, the incarnates are primal reactions to other machinations at play. The scions were chosen long ago, weren't they, Archmage?"

All eyes turned to Fainly, who glared at the old man.

Ivy moved quickly, startling them all. She grabbed Fainly by his robes and jerked him up so they could look into each other's eyes. "It was Ruke, wasn't it?"

"You'd do well to put me down," Fainly warned. "Else I'll tell them who you really are…"

Ivy's green eyes subtly flicked toward Reston and then back to Fainly, furious. She slowly lowered the gnome back to his seat.

The Archmage fixed his robes and looked back to Reston. "I don't know when they were chosen. I suspect I slept through those years, and when I try to remember, it feels…hazy."

"Ruke," Ivy said under her breath, putting her hands on the table and hanging her head. "How could you?"

"I chose the final scion," Fainly admitted, "though I was led to believe at the time that I was helping Ruke to escape from Elysun where she had become trapped."

"Trapped?!" Ivy snapped. "Did she tell you she was a *prisoner* in the heavenly realms? Tortured by lack of any possible want?! Suffering through the misery of eternal splendor?!"

The woman seemed to immediately calm herself when Reston raised a hand. "We don't have time for whatever vendetta you have against Ruke." He stepped around the table toward her, his icy blue eyes stripping her bare again. "Although I would be curious to find out what connections you have to Ruke. And to Oakus for that matter…"

Ivy straightened at that and turned away, pacing as she said, "You likely have just as much animosity toward Ruke as I do, along with the rest of the Purveyors. But you're right, we don't have time right now. The incarnates are stirring." She turned to look toward Bennik. "You were in Rathen, imprisoned by Corvanna. Why?"

"I…" Bennik didn't want to tell the whole world who his children were, but he wasn't sure if Corvanna's legions still had the truth that they had extracted from him, even though their master was dead. He knew if he wanted to protect Anika or Gage, he would need help. "Because, I am the father of the Child of Light and the Child of Shadow."

The room fell silent. Drip, drip, drip. The echoes of the sunken tower accompanied the crackling flames in the hearth for a long moment. Then, Fainly laughed.

Lexeth stepped toward Bennik, his expression uncharacteristically emotional. "The Chi—both of them?"

Bennik nodded while Fainly composed himself.

"I should have known," the gnome said.

"Known what?" Bennik leaned over the table, eager to learn what the man found so funny about the situation.

"That's how she did it," Fainly said as if to himself. He looked at the table as if it were covered in arcane glyphs he was trying to decipher. "Luriah said the Shadow was gathering its power—I had taken it for just another one of her sermons. But her priests helped arrange for Corvanna to gather enough of Eyen's keyshards to allow the harpy to become an incarnate."

Bennik looked to Reston for some sort of understanding, but the old man looked as confused as he felt. "You think my children were the cause of that?"

"Maybe," Ivy said, but she gave Bennik an empathetic look. "Your children…were they both born naturally to you?"

Another stone fell, followed immediately by another. Time was running out.

Bennik quickly explained how he had found Anika in Westerra and raised her as his own with Renay. And then about the previous Child of Shadow that had tried to kill Anika while Renay was pregnant with Gage. As he told the tale, he felt a certain amount of dread settle over them, and something told him that Fainly may be right—Anika and Gage were brought together by some force.

Fate. Destiny. Prophecy. Whatever it was, his children were in its grasp, and the world was falling apart around them. He had to help them—he wouldn't allow them to fall victim to whatever Stane had planned.

Another stone fell.

"We have tasks laid before us," Reston said, straightening himself and producing that old leather pouch from his waist. "Fainly, you and your...companion must assist Bennik, help him protect these. The elf is to escort me to Lefayra; the Eldercrowns will need to know about this." Reston upended the contents of his pouch onto the table. Nearly a dozen small red keyshards spilled out, giving off a distinct magical aura.

Ivy stepped forward. "Are these..."

"Pieces of Kindler," Reston said. "Anthur Pembrook and his ancestors all spent their lives recovering Sir Branton's Key...the sword that ruined him and may have brought doom on us all."

The entire tower quaked then, a chunk of stone falling from the ceiling and smashing onto the table. Lexeth swiftly scooped up the keyshards and put them back into Reston's pouch.

"There's a passage to the woods below," Reston said, but turned toward Bennik, thrusting the pouch into his hands, "but you must go with Fainly and find the scion—remember all I've told you about the Keyguard, boy. You are all that's left. And protect those shards with your life."

"Why not bring them to the Eldercrowns?" the elf said, nodding toward the pouch. "Wick's incarnates will come after them."

"Exactly," Reston agreed. "Which is why we must keep them far from Lefayra—there is a betrayer in your midst."

Lexeth's eyes went wide, but there was no time to discuss it further. Bennik grabbed Reston's arm to guide him out of his solar as it began falling apart.

"That bastard Oakus," Reston grumbled, "we still have so much to discuss."

Ivy slipped ahead of them, giving Reston a glance over her shoulder. "He knows. Why do you think he's driving us off?"

Lexeth and Reston made their way down the decaying tower, with Bennik trailing behind, uncertain yet determined to join his peculiar new allies on a quest to rescue his children.

And maybe the world.

Chapter Thirteen
Left Behind

Robin wrapped himself in the threadbare blanket that they had allowed him, shivering—not against the cold, but out of pure miserableness. It had only been two nights in the cell, but it may as well have been a year. Gage could need him, or even be dead, and Robin would never know, locked away in the Lord Mayor's dungeons.

"Stop clattering your teeth, would ya?"

Robin peered over his shoulder at the fat halfling who occupied the cell across from him. Unlike the baron's dungeons in Oakworth, at least the Lord Mayor kept his pens well lit, with a sconce between every other cell.

"Sorry," Robin whispered meekly, not wanting any trouble.

The halfling stood hanging his arms through the bars of his cell. He wore a comically small vest that did little to cover his hairy belly. His face was framed by two bushy patches of light brown hair on his cheeks and a few strands of wiry hair sprouting from his shiny pate. His nose looked almost three times the size of a normal nose.

"Whachya get pinched for, pretty boy?" The short man stuck one of his fingers in his belly button and dug around. "Breakin' the Lord Mayor's curfew?"

Robin sat up. He didn't like the man's attitude, but he hadn't really spoken to anyone since Gage disappeared and he felt eager to talk to someone. "Sneaking into the spire."

The halfling burst out laughing, nearly doubling over. It took a moment for him to recover himself enough to look at Robin with a raised, bushy eyebrow. "You're either a liar, a fool, or a brave son of a bitch, boy, and I'm not sure which one I'd like better."

Robin grinned. The man did have an infectious laugh. Something about his demeanor reminded him of Brood who he had abandoned in Oakworth with the rest of his friends. *Were they truly my friends though?* He wasn't so sure.

They had protected him and Gage, but if they knew what he had done—how he had killed Gage's mother—he wasn't sure he could call any of them friends any more.

"What were ya looking for in the spire? Some of them magic gems?"

Robin shook his head. "My friend. I think he went in there, but never came back."

The halfling spat. "Well, good riddance, I say. You don't want to mix yourself up with any of them mages. Nothing but trouble in my experience." He leaned his face against the bars, his eyes shifting back and forth down either row of cells before settling back on Robin. "You in the Guild?"

That's a complicated question, Robin thought. But he just shook his head. Although his mother held the position of Guildmaster, he was not officially a member of the Guild. "No, I'm just an apprentice cook from Blakehurst."

"Blakehurst?" The halfling screwed up his face. "You know Ransil Osbury?"

Robin nodded. Thinking of the man made him feel suddenly ashamed. While he hadn't come to be exceptionally warm with Ransil—a practical and strict master—Robin knew that the halfling had saved him from the baron's gallows in Oakworth. And how did Robin repay that?

The halfling across from him let out a chuckle. "That little bastard owes me fifty queens! In fact, I was meaning to go collect before I got tied up here."

"For what?" Robin asked, genuinely curious now.

The man looked slightly abashed before saying. "Looting, they say. But me and the others were just helping the merchant return his wares to his cart after the harpies attacked. I only took a bit of coin to pay for my services, but the Collectors got the wrong idea and killed me gang and shackled me up." He spat again. "Shoulda left when I had the chance."

Robin nodded, feeling the exact sentiment. If he and Gage had left Sathford and made for Andelor across land, he wouldn't be locked up. He had foolishly tried to sneak his way into Raventhal when he *felt* Gage nearby. The feeling had come suddenly as he had crept along the outer walls around the spire. It was like something was calling out to him in his mind, and he was drawn further and further.

In retrospect, he credited the strange feeling to his own frustration. He had wanted Gage to be nearby so badly that his mind had forced his body to feel something. That had to be it; it was the only logical explanation.

Regardless, he had made his way over the spire's walls and immediately tripped the glyphs that he knew would be there. The Luminaura's own High Warpriest was in the courtyard with her sword already out, as if she had anticipated a foe. Her paladins were on him before he could even react, and he had been sulking in a cage ever since.

The halfling quieted when a large woman with a tray and a club came to deliver their evening meal. It was the same as last night, cold porridge and crusty bread. At least the bread tasted somewhat fresh. Robin pushed his gruel around with a bit of bread before setting it aside.

"You gonna finish that?" The halfling's own bowl was licked clean. "My name is Tomby, by the way. Tomby Cordle."

"I'm Robin." He slid the bowl across the damp stone floor between their cells. "Just Robin."

Tomby scooped up the bowl and shoved a handful of porridge into his mouth. "That a common elf name?"

Before Robin could answer, both prisoners turned toward the sound of armored footsteps echoing from down the hall. Tomby set the food aside and wiped his hand on his dirty pants as he got to his feet.

The High Warpriest strode toward their cells, her armor gleaming even in the dungeon's faint torchlight. She wore a blue cloak from her shoulders and her blonde hair was tucked behind her ears. Her face was slightly marred by a patch of discolored skin around her eye and scalp, but her expression made her seem proud of it.

The woman stopped as she reached their cells. She looked down at Tomby. "Can you wield a hammer?"

The halfling licked his lips and looked to Robin for an answer. Not finding one, he shrugged. "Aye, a reasonably sized one I suppose."

More footsteps followed the woman, who now motioned toward Tomby's cell. Robin saw two jailors approaching, one carrying a huge iron ring of keys and the other a copper lantern.

"Get this one out of here and put him in irons. He is joining the builders at the cathedral."

"I won't need no irons," Tomby promised, "I ain't gon' run nowhere. I'll happily work off my sentence."

"You'll work regardless," the warpriest snapped. "Leave us." She rounded on Robin and crossed her arms as the jailors hauled Tomby off.

She stared at Robin, as if waiting for him to speak. But he didn't even know what he would possibly say. After a long moment, she broke the uncomfortable silence.

"Did you know about the troubles in the spire?"

"What troubles?"

Her eye twitched slightly as she bit her lower lip. "Why did you come to Raventhal? What were you looking for?"

Robin momentarily considered his options, but chose to stay close to the truth for now. "I was looking for my friend. I thought he went into the spire. I didn't know about any troubles. Unless you mean the harpy attack?"

The woman stared at him, unflinching. "Do you know who I am?"

Robin nodded.

She stepped forward. "I think you know *what* I am, but I don't think you know *who* I am." When Robin didn't respond, she took another step forward and laid one gauntleted hand on the crystal hilt of her sword and reached the other hand up to the Brightstar that hung around her neck. "My name is Hope Kandalot, High Warpriest of the Luminaura."

Robin saw the necklace she wore begin to glow, a simmering coming from between her clenched fingers. He felt an uneasiness growing within him, like a compulsion that he couldn't satisfy. His eyes remained fixed on Hope's glowing fist, shifting uncomfortably under the woman's gaze.

"Tell me your name."

Robin swallowed, trying and failing to look away from the intensity that came from her necklace. He had planned on giving her a false name, but suddenly he was compelled to say, "Robin. Just Robin."

"And who was your friend?"

Again, several lies came to Robin's mind, but as he stared at the light coming from Hope's silent prayer he said, "Gage Lawson, a trapper's apprentice from Blakehurst."

From the edges of his vision, Robin could see Hope's face react to that, but he couldn't read her expression. Whatever she was doing with her hand was muddling his mind.

Hope stepped closer again, now within Robin's reach. She knelt down to cast the light glowing from her chest on his face. Then she gasped and released her grip on the Brightstar.

Robin was finally able to look away from Hope's summoned light, looking up into the woman's shocked face. He took a bit of comfort in seeing the woman's stoic exterior fall away, but found her astonished reaction to his face to be almost more disturbing. Robin remained silent as she stared at him.

Hope didn't blink, staring intently into Robin's eyes. "Tell me about Gage."

"He...he's..."

"He's your partner."

Robin swallowed, suddenly feeling naked. "Yes." He was relieved she answered for him. He felt unable to lie, and he didn't want to expose Gage as the Child of Shadow, especially not to this woman.

"And you," Hope said, still boring into him with her cold eyes. "Tell me about you."

Robin felt a cold bead of sweat trickle down his brow and sucked in a breath between clenched teeth as he saw her hand go back to the star dangling around her neck. "There's not much to tell," he managed to say before she wrapped her hand around the holy symbol again.

The Light came back and chased away his ability to deceive.

"Where do you come from?"

Robin wanted to blink, but couldn't. "Andelor."

"And who is your mother?"

He whimpered pathetically. "Nipheena, the queen's sister." He could see Hope begin to smile.

"And your father?"

The Light seared his mind, burning away any chance he had to lie. Desperate, defeated, with no other recourse, he wept.

"The king of Vale."

As they navigated the Old Ways, Gage felt a sudden stab of guilt that nearly doubled him over in the shadowed tunnel. He felt Desmond's bony fingers wrap around his arm, keeping him on his feet.

"What is it?"

Gage shrugged out of the man's grasp. "Nothing. Felt something, that's all." He could sense Desmond's eyes narrow on him.

"Down here, your feelings are anything but nothing." He motioned to the surrounding darkness, which produced eerie creaks and the sound of stretching leather, as well as the occasional bestial howl. "You are connected to these paths, and whatever you feel is an extension of what the old gods feel."

"Is that why you brought me here?" Gage asked with a hint of annoyance in his voice. "To instruct me how to serve the old gods?"

Desmond gave him a vile grin, which looked more sinister due to the gruesome scars across his face. "I brought you here to instruct you on how to subjugate the old gods. You're the Child of Shadow, Gage. Do you know what that means?"

Annoyed, Gage shrugged. "No, why don't you tell me."

Desmond took the bait, rounding on Gage. "It means you can change the world. The incarnates are echoes of the old god, but you are what bound them to the world. You have the power to do what your sister failed to do."

Gage narrowed his eyes. "Which is?"

"Resist Stane."

The name sent a cold chill down Gage's spine. It wasn't the name itself; if anything, the name Stane had lost any sense of importance it may have once had—at least to Gage's perception—as it had become repurposed by bards and scribes as a sort of title for any mysterious figure. Stane was an anchor for wayward tales needing a familiar harbor.

Whatever dwelt within Gage—Shadow, Light, or some other accursed thing—responded to the name Stane differently now that it had been awoken.

Desmond must have noticed Gage's discomfort written across his face. He leaned closer and said, "His disciples say he is inevitable—the one true god destined to unite the world under one benevolent rule."

Gage turned away, looking out into the deepening mists that surrounded them. His eyes saw only swirling oblivion, but his mind forged pathways extending out from him, some clearer than others. He began walking down the brightest path.

"What if it's true?" Gage kicked aside a groping plant that seemed to reach for his ankle. "What if he truly aspires to be a benevolent god? Should I resist that?"

"You know there's no such thing," Desmond said, following closely.

"No such thing as what? A benevolent god?"

Desmond laid his thin fingers on Gage's shoulder and gently turned him around so that their eyes met. "Benevolent aspiration. To aspire is to yearn for conquest and subjugation—to crush others beneath you. It is a wicked desire, born within all of us." His intense eyes shifted to the nothingness beyond them. "Stane is anything but benevolent. He is the epitome of insatiable ambition."

Another sharp sensation cut through Gage and he pulled away, spinning around. Despite the paths laying clearly before him, he was beginning to feel more lost than ever. *What am I doing down here? Why did I abandon Robin?*

A flood of questions suddenly surged through his mind, but he focused on one as he looked over his shoulder at his new companion. "And you?"

Desmond gave him a curious look.

Gage rounded on him now, the mix of emotions within him becoming undiluted anger. "Certainly you didn't lead me down here out of sheer benevolence. You told me you knew where Anika would be—you said you could show me how to control these powers." He raised his hands, feeling it gather in his fingertips.

"My ambition aligns with yours."

Gage felt the sudden urge to unleash wherever collected in his fingers, but he took a steady breath, genuinely curious. He let his hand fall.

Desmond's eyes softened. "Like you, I am an instrument of Shadow. It used me, twisting me into a monster." He looked back toward the Onyx Gate that Gage had unknowingly sealed. "I had dark thoughts, but I wasn't a monster. Just like how I can only assume that goblins or orcs or harpies or kobolds weren't monsters, but the world around them was hard, and the only hand that extended to them was cloaked in darkness...promising them a way to avoid the crushing boot that loomed over them."

The pale man's words moved Gage, reminding him of the dark thoughts he would occasionally have as a boy. He remembered being spiteful of his sister in times of jealousy—saying hurtful things to her about how she didn't belong or how they weren't really family. That fateful morning when he stole the piece of Skythe from Elza's shop and cursed them all, everyone he knew—even then, something deep down told him the stone was poison, but he foisted it on Anika regardless.

He knew now that was the Shadow then, manipulating him with a tongue so convincing that he believed it to be his own. Gage even felt its touch now, trying to twist Desmond's words around to mean something more beneficial to its cause. But Gage felt stronger now, able to push against its corruption.

"You feel it, don't you?" Desmond asked, still watching the path behind them back toward Sathford. "It's bending to your will. You can master it—you won't be like me."

Staring into the deep mists, Gage wondered if it was this place that gave him strength; he wondered if Desmond had known what would happen down here. A sense of clarity was settling within him, and he looked back at Desmond.

"What are you?"

Desmond met his eyes. "I am the first of Stane's scions, meant to usher in his ascendancy." He stepped toward Gage, his face tightening. "And I will show you how to stop me."

Fallon struggled against the dead weight of the Mawsurath's limbs. She felt life within the thing, but it was weak and resistant. She focused all of her power—all of Oakus' power from the keyshards Naya had managed to accumulate from the Shrouded—and forced the incarnate to take a single step before her vision faded and her mind exploded. She screamed against the sudden agony.

"Enough," Naya said. "Just feel the connection. It will take time."

Fallon pushed open the armored plate on the Mawsurath's chest so she could properly scowl at the priestess. "How much time? You said I had been chosen—it feels like this thing wants to kill me." She began climbing out of its hold, feeling lightheaded. "It's like it can't hear me."

"You're still learning its language," Naya assured her, motioning to the golems that stood sentry around them in the chamber. "There is no common tongue shared amongst Oakus' legions. Each has their own understanding. The incarnate must not only speak and understand all these myriad tongues, but also the languages of Light and Shadow. It is the same for you."

Tired of the woman's constant riddles and vague instructions, Fallon strode away in frustration. She felt the surrounding mists reacting to her mood, becoming thicker, roiling.

Naya followed. "You remember what's at stake here, yes?"

Rubbing her temples, Fallon nodded. She closed her eyes against the headache she felt brewing, silently reminding herself why she was here; unbidden, an image came to mind of her father's head rolling down the aisle of the chapel he so loved. It was not a true memory, but an obscene imagination she had created from her father's keyshard.

"The Light cannot be allowed to continue its malicious ways," Naya warned. "Your father will not be the last to be sacrificed to the Luminaura's lust for power. The Shadow does not overreach—just imagine what the church would do if they took control of the incarnate! You have to focus."

"I know!" Fallon snapped, rounding on the woman. "I know what has to be done! I'm the one that Mawsurath responded to—not you!"

Naya recoiled from the outburst, but was immediately distracted by a sound behind them—snapping branches and the serpentine hiss of one of Oakus' countless appendages bracing itself against a powerful intruder.

"Mawsurath is a Shadowlord's name."

Naya spun around, reaching for the Shadow as she faced two men approaching from the blackness.

"Desmond Everton?!" Although the scars made him look half a stranger to her, Fallon knew him by how he held himself—fragile but determined. He was her only lasting memory from the spire, before she left to follow Archdruid Wrenda's teachings in the Order of Oakus. "Is that you?"

The man squinted at her for a moment, likely searching his memories for a vision of the girl that she used to be. It didn't take long for recognition to wash over his face—she never remembered him smiling like that.

"Fallon Shaw...are you—?"

"She is the chosen," Naya interjected, but any other words she was about to say were caught in her throat. "The Child!"

The priestess' one hand shot out toward the boy that stood just behind Desmond. He had the look of an Eastlunder, with shaggy hair and dark eyes. Something about his presence twisted Fallon's insides.

Desmond stepped aside, motioning to his young companion. "This is my friend Gage Lawson. He guided me here, sealing the Onyx Gate behind us so that the dryads could not get to the spire's keyshards before us."

The boy stepped toward Naya with fury in his eyes. "You would have had me kill my mother."

The priestess seemed to physically shrink before the boy. "She would have killed you, Gage...the Light would have had her smother you as a babe."

"You lie," Desmond said.

The way he said the words drew all their attention. There was a certainty to his tone, a promise of revelation.

"It was not the Light that blinded his mother, poisoning her thoughts." He looked toward the boy named Gage with sadness in his eyes. "It was the Shadow that consumed her. A stain left on her by an unwanted child..."

"No." Gage shook his head, his eyes becoming distant as Desmond continued.

"The Light may have guided the woman, but she would never have heeded its call if she had not been infected by the Shadow. The two forces forever play off each other, and the cycle cannot be stopped until either side embraces itself instead of ceaselessly trying to consume the other." He looked toward Naya. "And the Light will never yield."

The vision of her father's head rolling down the aisle came to Fallon again as she listened to Desmond's words. Somehow, she knew he was right.

"What does that mean?" Naya asked.

"It means the Shrouded are wrong," Desmond said. "They will never compel the Light. I was wrong. I thought I could use the Shadow to force Anika's hand in claiming Stane's aspect that dwells within me; to grant me the freedom of death—to unchain me from constantly being pieced back together no matter how many times I try to kill myself.

"But the Light exists to consume Shadow. Its very nature is to banish any force that may oppose its reign; I see that now. Anika is not the one who can stop this. She doesn't have the strength."

Fallon felt a chill creep up her spine as she watched Desmond turn toward the Child of Shadow.

"The power to extinguish the Light is here. We have sealed the Onyx Gate, which means we can unseal it." He looked toward Fallon. "You'll need keyshards to truly awaken the incarnate, and you know as well as I that the spire holds plenty." Then to Naya. "You have Shrouded agents in Sathford—once we breach the Onyx Gate, you go rally them and infiltrate Castle Tolle."

Fallon swallowed, feeling the reality sinking in that vengeance may be within reach. But when she looked at Mawsurath, she remembered the searing pain that had stabbed through her head.

"I don't know if I can," Fallon said weakly. "I don't know if I can control it..."

Desmond stepped over to her. "You can with this." He held out a fist of thin fingers. When Fallon put her own hand out, he dropped a green keyshard into her palm. There were bits of dried blood on it.

"Is that...?" The Child of Shadow stepped around to see, his eyes wide.

"Ruke's stone," Desmond said, rounding on Gage. "Two thieves stole it from your sister after the attack on Oakworth. I felt a strange connection to it, so I tracked them, killed the shardbearer, and took it." He looked back at Fallon. "Ruke bound herself to this stone, I could feel her. It should be more than enough to carry out our plans."

"*Our* plans now?" Naya stepped forward. "So you are with us?"

All eyes fell on Desmond, but he looked toward Fallon. "We are with you."

Fallon looked at the bloody stone in her hand, feeling a purpose beyond her comprehension. But the vision of her father's head came again and she clenched her fist, ready to tear the world down to its foundations if it meant she could have her revenge.

Chapter Fourteen
Seeds of Vengeance

The dragon began to fear *Severynth*. Occasionally she would pass over the ship's course, shrieking threats from afar, even spitting flames where they would have no chance of touching the sails, but there had been no further attacks.

Layla had become something that dragons feared.

The crew had also treated their passengers with more reverence. Their meals had improved, and when Layla and Valix would grace the deck to enjoy the fresh air, they would earn nods of respect from the crew, especially the captain. And when Valix would wind her fingers through Layla's or the women would hook their arms together, they would earn looks of endearment.

Layla couldn't remember ever being happier, and she didn't want the voyage to end. Unfortunately, dark clouds on the horizon had forced the ship to divert toward the Wane Coast, and now land watched their passage. It was like an approaching doom, threatening to wake Layla from a dream that she desperately wanted to savor a bit longer.

"We can find another ship," Valix said, leaning over the rail, her eyes on Noveth's shores. Her left arm twined itself through Layla's right and eased the tension of the journey's end. "The docks of Waneport are teeming with Xe'danni trade galleys."

Layla had only been to the city once, while ridding the Wane Coast of the troglodytes that had been amassing to form an unprecedented army. She had been under Desmond's thrall then, but she remembered it vividly—how she had channeled more fire than she thought possible and how she would willingly give herself to Desmond every night.

Her body became tense and Valix loosened her grip on the elf's arm.

"You still want to go, right?"

Layla turned to her and forced a smile, her mind still back in a time when Desmond ruled her emotions. "Yes." She nodded toward Noveth. "There's nothing really left for me there." Layla grasped Valix's hand in both of hers and kissed it. "You saved me and I'm yours."

Valix returned the smile. "I was not the one who chased away a dragon. But we are both Stane's now—you've heard his voice, so you know why we must continue down our path."

As if in response, the dragon let out a bellowing cry up in the clouds, drawing their eyes to the sky. Layla could see its obscured form like a hazy shadow. She knew it would not stop pursuing them. And the book.

Layla held Valix's hand and thought of that dark tome down in their cabin. She had spent the last two days flipping through its pages, desperate to make sense of any of the markings, to no avail. In fact, Layla could have sworn that the pages changed each time she flipped through them, noticing new markings that she swore were not there before.

When she had asked Valix about the shifting writing, the woman nodded. "I have noticed as well. It can only mean that the pages are protected, and the language truly is locked away by spells or ancient knowledge."

Thinking back on that, Layla turned toward Noveth again, considering both Maze's and Valix's words about Kartha, the legendary witch. If it was true that she was the only one who had ever read Stane's words, then finding her should be their purpose. And from what Valix had said of the woman, Layla did not believe they would find her in some Xe'danni city.

The witch's legacy was in Noveth. But so was Desmond's, and Layla was not eager to return.

The dragon's wail came closer now, causing a stir of activity on the ship's deck. The women turned to see the captain emerge with his green coat, barking orders for everyone to prepare for another attack. But for some reason, Layla was not concerned. She knew the dragon would not come.

She held Valix's hand and drew her down below.

The rough streets of Waneport were a welcome sight for Grip, who had felt hounded since emerging from the Old Ways outside of the Steddlewood. Under normal circumstances, she would never have risked going into that place, given what she knew lurked down there, hunting for her. But the situation had grown dire.

The satchel she carried under her arm held her salvation, but it also held the heavy guilt she had carried since abandoning Ransil.

Thinking of the halfling made Grip angry; not just angry at herself for treating someone she loved so badly, but also angry at Ransil for being so damn benevolent. As much as she loved the man—and she knew that she truly did, more than anything in this wretched world—she could do without his annoying conscience, constantly interfering with any chance they had to be together.

Grip tried to shake away those thoughts and focus on the task at hand, keeping her good eye peeled for any sign of Prath amongst the bustling dockworkers. But if she was honest with herself, she wasn't even sure if she'd know her by seeing her. The dwarf hadn't been the most cooperative member of the Guild—never visiting the conclave in Andelor—but the wayward agent would be Grip's only chance of securing access to the new Lord Mayor, Jaffron Casryk.

Ever since she had passed through the Waneport gates, she felt the eyes on her. As a dark elf in Vale, she was accustomed to being leered at, but it still made her feel as reviled as ever. A human woman passed by dragging her chubby little whelp with one hand and lugging a haul of fruit with the other. The little boy pointed at Grip when they passed by.

"What is that, momma?"

The woman tugged his arm, keeping her eyes averted from Grip. "Come along, Toby, mind your step."

Grip gave the boy her most menacing stare, gnashing her teeth as they passed. She smiled as she turned away from the sound of the boy whimpering behind her. Continuing on through the press of people, she came to the city's beating heart: Wharfside.

It was a wonder to behold. Grip had originally come to Noveth through Waneport, and Wharfside was where she first met Ransil—*Ruse*, she thought, fondly remembering their young and reckless days. Back then, the port was filled with suspicious eyes. But now she received significantly fewer glares and gawks as she descended the wide stairs that led to the markets.

Wharfside was built into the lower cliffs of the Wane Coast, providing a breathtaking view of the Racivic Sea below. There were a series of very wide stairs and even wider, winding inclined roads leading down to the docks. But the splendor of Wharfside was the market, where traders from Copera, Karrane, Xe'dann, Jath, Suthek, and even distant Caim brought their wares.

While the queen's consortium would sort through the imports and send a significant portion to Merithian and Andelor, Waneport was known to be the place where shrewd traders would go to ensure they had the choicest pieces of what wider Aetha had to offer.

"You look lost, my lady."

Despite being taken by surprise, Grip turned calmly to see a cloaked man whose hood hid most of his face, except a bird-like nose that stuck out noticeably. Even though she could not see his eyes, she could feel their intense gaze.

Grip knew the code, but did not know the man. "Not lost, but always looking. Can you help me out of a pinch?"

The man was still as a statue for a long moment, the bustle of Wharfside carrying on as Grip and her fellow agent each seemed to be waiting for the other to make a move. Finally, the man gave a curt nod for her to follow him down the stairs toward the market.

As Grip followed, she noticed the graceful way the man moved. If he wasn't an elf, she would be quite shocked. He swept down the stairs as if he meant to lose her, and Grip got the sense that she was being tested somehow. That rankled her. She was Knife's first choice for the Guild's most important task, not some fresh recruit to be hazed.

Swallowing her pride, Grip stuck to the man like a shadow and reached the bottom of the stairs, weaving between shouting merchants and burdened dockworkers carrying goods to one of the countless ships docked at the harbor. The agent led her between a smithy and a quaint little halfling bakery that reminded Grip of Ransil's place in Blakehurst. The man finally lost her when he disappeared around the back corner of the building.

Feeling some sort of trap, Grip slowed her pace and tucked her satchel tighter under her arm. But when she turned the corner she saw the man with his hood down, revealing a full head of graying hair and a gaunt bird-like face to match his beak nose.

Definitely not an elf, this one.

"If you're looking for Prath, you're two weeks late."

"What happened?" Even before asking, Grip could only assume it had something to do with the dwarf's drink. If she recalled, Prath was sent to Waneport for drunkenly compromising a Guild operation in Andelor.

The man shrugged. "Can't say for sure, body never turned up. She was gambling with some of the Lord Mayor's house guards, but never returned. Was hoping maybe you were here with some news about it."

Grip didn't like that one bit. While she wasn't going to mourn Prath, she was here to confront Jaffron, and this complicated matters.

"Did the Lord Mayor have any reason to want her dead?"

The man shrugged again.

"We haven't met. Are you Knife's replacement here?"

"I suppose so," the man put his hands on his hips, revealing a brace of several small knives at his waist. "Name's Price. You're the dark one, huh? Grip?"

Dark one. For a fraction of a moment, she considered producing her own throwing knife hidden between her breasts and then burying it in the man's shoulder as a lesson in politeness. But the weight of the documents under her arm reminded her there were more important matters to tend to.

"I need to get to the Lord Mayor," she said, looking over her shoulder just to be sure there was no one within earshot. "No witnesses."

"Out for some revenge?"

She shook her head. "Jaffron was just appointed by the queen to oversee all of Noveth's trade. We have no need for him to die."

Price crossed his arms. "Well, he's going to be hard to get alone today. His galley is being prepared for departure; the big one—*Revery*. He's probably already boarded."

Can't catch a break. "Can you get me aboard? I have information he needs."

Raising his eyebrow, Price gave a twitch of his head as if to say "that's a shame." But instead he said, "Might help both of us if I knew what this was about?"

"It's enough to know it's Guild business and I outrank you."

Price nodded with a condescending smile. "Ranks don't mean much outside the conclave, but I'm not looking to piss in Knife's porridge. Maybe you just tell me if this has anything to do with Ruke's stone."

Grip tried to keep her expression steady, but she cringed inwardly. *How could he know? Who are you, Price?* "In a sense, yes. Let's leave it at that."

Something that might have been fear crossed over Price's face, but he just nodded and pulled his hood back up. "Well, it must be important then. Wouldn't want to upset the queen, would we?"

Grip did not like how much this man seemed to know about her business. She was led to believe that only herself and Brood knew about their purpose in Oakworth. Knife specifically said she didn't want anyone else in the Guild even whispering about the job. Paranoia took root within her as she followed him out that shadowed alley.

"Follow my lead," Price said, and she did. They wormed their way through the loud and crowded market, both of them moving with a mixture of casualness and stealth. Any Guild agent knew how to blend into a crowd—moving without notice often required being seen, which normally proved difficult for Grip. But the swath of people in Wharfside gave her a much wider palette in which to lose herself.

As they reached the docks, Grip saw *Revery*. I was a true war galley, with several ballistae along its bow and stern. The sails weren't yet raised, but Grip noticed the sea green colors of Waneport and knew that the city's wreathed anchor and scales were hidden in those folds.

"Looks like we still have some time," Price said over his shoulder, slightly slowing his pace. "Anchors are still down, but there's our man." He nodded toward the ship.

It took a moment, but Grip finally saw him. Jaffron wore an elaborate admiral's coat of sea green with a matching hat fringed in gleaming silver tassels. He wore a curved saber at his hip and high boots, his thumbs casually hooked on his belt. Standing at the edge of the gangplank leading up to his ship, he looked like he was posing for a triumphant naval painting.

Grip sighed, not looking forward to their encounter. In addition to the dockworkers scurrying about to load the ship up with supplies, Grip noted the guards at either end of the dock as well as on the ship's deck.

"How do I get on board without causing a scene?"

Price gave her a vile smirk. "You a good swimmer?"

Layla awoke to distant shrieks of Synderok and started to rise. But as she felt Valix's fingers brush the hair from her brow, she relaxed, knowing there was still no danger. She reached out and placed her hand on Valix's bare thigh where it was wrapped over her waist.

"Never a dull moment." Valix began to sit up, but Layla rolled over and pinned the woman back down, refusing to give up this moment.

Layla ran a hand over Valix's bald head, feeling the stubble of a new head of hair growing in. "With you? No." She smiled and kissed the woman.

The dragon roared again, this time closer. The ship itself quaked in response.

Valix gently pushed the elf away, still smiling. "We should make sure there's no trouble. You're the only one aboard who has almost slain a dragon."

Layla stiffened. The word dragon brought sudden and unexpected memories of Jath under the shadow of Dragonpeak. Flashes of Desmond's face mixed with Valix's in her mind, and they both meshed together until they took on the form of an elderly elf begging for his life. He was a stranger to Layla, but somehow she knew him to be Sauthorn, the Xe'danni seer that Maze had spoken of.

"Layla? Unless you want someone else on this ship doing this..."

Fingers gently ran up Layla's bare side. As the vision of the elf pleaded, blood dripping from his mouth, the voice of Stane returned in her mind with indecipherable messages. They were words of warning that she could not understand. She felt a hand cup her breast, but she was still too deep in her own thoughts, and Sauthorn's face turned back into Desmond's, who was opening his mouth to latch onto her once more.

"No!" Layla jerked back, the visions and voices falling away. Valix had her hands up defensively, a look of apologetic fear on her face.

"I'm sorry." She began to sit up, untangling herself from Layla. "I was only teasing."

"No," Layla began. "I mean, it's not that." She ran her own hand up Valix's side, tracing several of the swirling patterns tattooed on her lovely flesh. She wanted to dig her fingers into the woman, to hold her tighter than she'd ever held anything. But she settled for palming the small of her back and pulling Valix into her lap. "Stay. Can't we stay?"

Something terrible awaited her up on the deck, it was the only reason for the visions and mysterious words. There were more shouts above, and a dragon's roar that sounded like it came from the ocean itself.

Valix scrambled out of bed, grabbing a pair of pants from the table by the door. "Come on!"

Layla had no choice. She found her own robes and slipped into them, hurriedly pulling the heavy black book from its hiding spot and cradling it to her chest. As she ran down the corridor toward the stairs, she saw Valix up ahead struggling to put a pair of baggy pants on, forgoing a top—her tattoos seemed to shimmer with dark power.

Panicked voices mingled above as Layla neared the hatch, and she saw dark smoke obscuring the world outside. But she caught a few commands rising above the wordless screams.

"She doesn't want us to reach land!"

"More sand!"

"Bring the buckets, now!"

They emerged onto deck to see flames consuming the sails. Huge clouds of black smoke swallowed the sky when Layla first came on deck, holding onto Valix for support. But the dragon's wings cut through the hazy atmosphere, sending acrid gusts that rocked the ship violently.

Layla, Valix, and the rest of the crew were sent tumbling to one side of the ship, drenched in ocean water that came splashing over the railing. But the crashing waves that were summoned by the rocking vessel served as a blessing. As the deck steadied itself, Layla got to her knees and heard the hiss of dying flames—the sea itself had extinguished the worst of the dragon's flames.

But Synderok was coming back around.

"To the ballista!" The captain was shrugging out of his green coat, scrambling toward the stern of the ship.

Layla felt Valix's hand on her arm, but didn't hear whatever she was trying to say. The elf was already standing, opening the *Book of Stane* to the page that called out to her. Once again, she lost herself to the mysterious text, the world around quieting and slowing. A vision came to her of a deep, dark cavern where the ground suddenly split to reveal a fiery maw. From that burning crevice came Synderok, her enormous claw crashing down on the tome Layla now held.

In response to the vision, Layla felt the book in her hands resist, as if it tried to slam shut on her. But she held it, feeling a dagger thrust into her mind.

Something ran from her nose, tracing a wet line around her lips. Whether it was blood or seawater, she wouldn't know—her lips were mouthing an incantation that Layla did not even understand.

She felt the familiar power surging through her as she flipped through the pages, finally stopping when the presence within commanded her to. That same presence turned the confusing symbols on the page into another vision of the old elf, Sauthorn. He looked at Layla with fearful eyes, blood running down his wrinkled face.

"Vengeance comes." Sauthorn mouthed the words again, the phrase echoing in Layla's mind. But soon the blood drowned the vision, and Layla was staring at the pages stained with Desmond's blood.

Suddenly Layla lost the power. It left her like snuffed candle, leaving only the feeling of hollow smoke in her still aching mind. She turned to Valix, whose grip had tightened on her arm. Layla now saw why Valix was still holding her—there was a piece of splintered wood the size of a human arm jammed in Valix's side, blood streaming out of the wound to mix with the flood of saltwater sloshing around on deck.

Layla dropped the book and knelt down to Valix just as the blasts of wind told her that Synderok was descending again for another attack.

A voice thundered through the chaos. "Fire!"

It wasn't the captain's voice, or Stane's.

Grip had been violently shaken from her hiding place when it felt like *Revery* had capsized. She was thrown from the high shelf in the cargo hold and her side slammed against the low overhang above. Her reflexes were quick as ever, allowing her to brace her head from cracking open or causing some other severe injury. She escaped her little nook with a bloody lip and plenty of bruises.

It took her a long moment to get her bearings—weariness had taken her by surprise after sneaking aboard the ship and she had almost let herself fall asleep in her quiet nook. Unfortunately, it seemed like the ship was sinking now, so she grabbed her satchel and crawled over the huge crates of supplies in the hold. Above, she could hear muffled commands, an eerie shrieking, and boots stomping in frantic rhythms.

Please don't tell me that's a wyvern, Grip thought, not wanting to ever encounter one of those again. But that wouldn't make any sense—wyverns were relatively common on Caim, but weren't seen around Noveth, certainly not lurking above the ocean with nowhere to perch.

Grip was somewhat grateful for the commotion, as it seemed to have emptied the lower holds of *Revery*. She crept silently and carefully along the corridor to the stairs until she realized that she was alone. Relief was short lived though, as she was thrown violently against the wall when the ship rocked again to the side.

"Fire!"

The voice split the commotion above her, commanding and slightly shrill. She knew it was Jaffron just by how the words *felt* to her. Oddly she thought of Ransil then, and secretly wondered if that vain elf sealord would have claimed her heart if the halfling hadn't beaten him to it. She pushed the thought aside and slipped up the stairs to the main deck, no longer concerned about the Lord Mayor's guards.

Grip was welcomed to black smoke and a gout of fire spraying from the sky. She saw the blood red wings behind those flames and nearly laughed due to shock.

But before she could do anything, the snapping sound of a ballista unleashing a javelin pulled her attention. She watched as the missile struck true, knocking the dragon back and extinguishing the jet of flames.

With the flames gone, Grip could see another ship nearby, slightly smaller than *Revery* but not by much. Its sails were mostly scorched away and the mast still burned like a candle. Some of the crew had been set ablaze as well from the dragon's last breath, and several flaming figures threw themselves desperately into the ocean.

It was madness.

The dragon struggled to gain purchase as its massive wings pumped up and down, its muscular body twisting against the pain of the long wooden stake through its chest.

"Again!" Jaffron's voice cut through the cacophony, pulling Grip's attention from the burning ship getting dangerously close to *Revery*. She saw Jaffron with his cutlass drawn, pointing it at the wounded dragon. He had lost his hat and his long dark hair flew wildly against a spray of the ocean.

The next heavy bolt was hastily fired and missed the dragon. As Grip watched the wayward missile disappear into the distant waves, she saw a robed figure on the other ship begin levitating, an open tome floating before her. The book emanated dark energy, and Grip knew what it was immediately, though she had trouble believing it would be possible.

In the air, the dragon's wings had finally caught the wind and steadied the creature's ascent. Grip stared at the thing in wonder and horror. She had seen a young dragon once in Fehir'whin, but it didn't compare to this magnificent beast. Grip could only imagine this particular dragon was unique amongst its kin. It had a god-like quality, not only in the fear it inspired, but also because the scales covering its immense body were like thousands of crystalized flames.

Black tendrils suddenly exploded out of the rough waters below, reaching up and wrapping themselves around the dragon's limbs. The monster screamed in protest, unleashing wild sprays of fire uselessly into the sky. Grip heard many members of the crew on *Revery* gasp.

"Look! Black sorcery!"

Grip's heart froze, expecting to see the crew all turn to face her now that she'd been called out. But relief washed over her as she followed several pointing fingers to the rocking ship adjacent to *Revery*. She had become so accustomed to being associated with darkness and forbidden magic that she had assumed someone was accusing her of summoning those black appendages. But she now saw the source as well.

The robed woman floating above deck of the other ship was radiating Shadow magic; a dark aura hung around her and the open tome that floated before her. With the dark energies of that book, she was strangling the dragon, pulling it into the sea. As the magnificent and terrible flying serpent struggled with its huge wings to escape its fate, the sea itself rose up from below, taking the shape of a terrible maw that opened up to swallow the dragon entirely.

Grip stood breathless, in awestruck terror. She couldn't believe what she had just witnessed, and if it weren't for the cheers erupting from the nearby ship, she might have assumed she imagined it.

As the sea began to calm, Grip watched as the mage in the pale pink robes fell to the deck, looking altogether lifeless. The crew of the burning ship rushed to the mage's aid, and that was when Grip felt a hand on her shoulder.

She turned to see a familiar face from her past.

"Your majesty," Jaffron said with that rakish smile, "I didn't know we had royalty aboard."

The last thing Layla had known was the smell of smoke, the sight of a drowning dragon, and the sound of victorious cheers. But blackness had consumed her completely and she felt like she had fallen for days. When she felt rough hands on her, she began to weakly open her eyes.

Through her hazy vision, she could see a burning ship beyond the wooden rails of the deck. It took her a breath to realize that she was on a different ship, much more splendid than *Severynth*. She heard distant voices that became clearer as her vision focused.

"...but you knew my father." A dashing, regally dressed elf held a curved saber at Valix's throat. The naked disciple still had the piece of wood stabbed into her side, her tattoos now vividly glowing. Even in her current state, Layla could tell the wards were the only thing keeping her alive.

"No..." Layla said weakly, but when she tried to move, her limbs wouldn't work. She also saw that she was restrained by two burly sailors dressed in the same sea green that the elf wore.

"Tell me," the man said to Valix, "did you forget to cut out his eyes and bury them in grave soil?" He slashed his saber and cut off one of Valix's arms. Layla choked on her breath as she watched the limb that had once lovingly traced the curves of her body flop obscenely onto the ship's deck, splattering blood.

"No! Please!" This time Layla found her voice and drew the man's attention.

"Jaffron!" A dark elf woman stepped forward, a leather satchel clutched to her stomach.

But Layla's eyes couldn't stray from Valix long. The woman she loved looked at her without an ounce of pain in her eyes. Her expression was one of apology.

"Must you do this now?" The dark elf motioned to Layla. "Did you see what she did? To a dragon?!"

Jaffron smiled at Layla. "Oh, I have plans for this one, too. But her," he turned back to Valix who silently stood her ground as blood seeped from her body. "She kidnapped my father, murdered him, and then cursed me with his bloody visions. That, I just cannot allow."

"...please..." Layla still couldn't move, her body completely drained from defeating Synderok. She tried to summon any magic that would save her love, but she felt as useless as Valix looked at the moment. All she could do was weep.

"...I love her..." Her voice was a choked whimper, unheard.

"But, I am in a charitable mood," Jaffon said, with a playful wave of his saber. "Do you have any last words, Disciple? One last prayer to your limp cod of a god, Stane?"

Valix looked at the man with seething eyes for a moment, but then turned to Layla. Her eyes softened, and she opened her mouth to say something. But before the words came, the sword slashed and Valix's bald head went soaring from her shoulders, spinning into the now peaceful waters of the Racivic Sea.

All life left Layla's body as she collapsed and let the darkness take her again, hoping she would never awaken.

Chapter Fifteen

A False Idol

Ransil found Quinn in the baron's library—the one above ground—sorting through the piles of books that had been thrown from the shelves during the attack. The boy seemed to be looking for something specific, shoving aside tomes and piles of bound parchment that kicked up dust in their wake.

"Can I help you find something?"

Quinn didn't look his way, still rifling through the remains. "I'm just curious if there are any copies of *Grumrik's Runecrafts* here. The only copy we had at the spire was taken to Andelor by Master Audreese."

Scratching his head, Ransil couldn't help but smile. "Is that what you're truly worried about at the moment? I seem to remember dryads trying to kills us to get that stone in your pocket."

Quinn looked up at that, glancing over Ransil's head to make sure no one was listening.

"Relax," Ransil said, sticking his thumb over his shoulder, "they're all getting ready to meet in the baron's—or the baroness' I should say—court. They believe they have the Child of Light to thank for the city's defense."

Quinn stood up, abandoning his search. "Will you tell me now?"

He scratched his chin, still a little unsure about the boy. "What do you want to know? I told you what I saw—what the dryads showed me."

"Not about that," he said, "I mean about this place—what happened here before. And you clearly don't believe they have the Child of Light here." He sat down on a huge chunk of the library's ceiling. "We're in this together now, right? You're helping me get back to the spire—shouldn't I know?"

Ransil ran a hand through his hair, feeling defeated. He didn't want to betray any of his friends' secrets—especially Anika and Gage—but the boy was right. He was clever beyond his age, and clearly gifted with his magic. Ransil knew he would need Quinn's help.

He told him everything.

Vivian Caffery felt ashamed for not weeping, for not ripping out her hair in agony and throwing herself on Alburn's cold, stiff body. But she felt reborn since last night, for better or worse.

She had barely slept. All the tears she had held back to be strong for her children she unleashed when she was alone in her chambers. The bed she had shared with Alburn and Renay was now cold and passionless.

Seeing Renay's body desecrated like that in the library had made everything worse. Vivian could lay in bed and imagine Alburn there with her, his face stern and dutiful but his hands tender and loving. But if she dared imagine Renay, who was once soft and ravenous, she could only see the monster that tried to strangle her children.

Vivian managed to drift off to sleep between sobs several times only to awaken immediately, gasping and screaming for her guards to check on the children. After those vain attempts to rest, she decided to drink herself to sleep. But she only managed to get drunk enough to dull the pain.

And then the morning came, and her duties began.

Her first order of business was making herself presentable. Her normal maid, Brumhilde, was killed in the attack, so Vivian was attended by a young girl named Chloe. She was a nervous thing, with large soft limbs like Vivian's and a face that seemed slightly too small for her head.

Vivian allowed Chloe to bathe her and dress her in silence, which gave the baroness time to clear her head for the morning's events. She would not have time to properly mourn for her husband or the others killed by those foul intruders, not while she needed to take on the duties that her husband had once shouldered.

She closed her eyes while Chloe finished with her hair, feeling a pleasant emptiness inside. Although she knew it was just because she had become numb from sobbing all through the night before, she welcomed it.

After she was made presentable, Vivian left the mausoleum that her chambers had become, thinking how each attack the city had suffered had taken away one of her loved ones. She dare not think of another attack claiming either of her children; there was no time today for such dreadful thoughts.

Vivian focused on the two more certain dreads that awaited her: viewing her husband's body and sitting in his chair to attend the press that awaited. Surprisingly, it wasn't fear she felt welling up inside her as she made her way down the stairs toward her duties. She wasn't certain what the feeling was that had replaced last night's sorrow, but she welcomed it.

Perhaps it was the faintest hint of excitement.

She dared not question her own emotions—how could she be excited when her husband was dead, their lover returned as a vile corpse to kill their children?—but she held onto whatever that feeling was, drawing strength from it as she followed her guards to her husband's temporary resting place.

The Baron of Oakworth had been laid on the table in the apothecary on the main floor of the keep. Vivian's personal guards remained outside as the healer—an old, gruff dwarf named Gregor—bowed and left the baroness to her grief.

But in that dimly lit room, where bottles of various colors of liquid and vials of herbs adorned the numerous shelves, Vivan found something other than grief. Seeing Alburn laying there, his closed eyes sunken and his mouth slightly leering as if he had died how he wanted to die, Vivian did not weep.

The sight of Alburn Caffery's peaceful corpse was in stark contrast to the memory of Renay's horrible remains given a dark new life, and Vivian found herself grateful for her husband's rest. She saw great care was given by Gregor in patching up the poor man's final wounds. His grotesquely broken arm was mended, the exposed bone tucked back under flesh, which was stitched back up and hidden in the sleeve of his favorite coat, decorated in the brown and orange hues of autumn.

Vivian didn't feel the pain from last night as she admired Gregor's work. If anything, she felt emboldened. Her husband had his flaws, but she had loved him relentlessly, as he loved her. Together they had made two wonderful children and shared more joys than most people could even imagine in this world.

That subtle tinge of excitement blossomed into an overwhelming sense of pride. Vivian knew she was who all of Oakworth would look to for leadership, and she would not let Alburn's death be in vain. She stepped forward and grasped his cold fingers in her own. The feeling of that lifeless hand nearly broke her resolve, but she closed her eyes and remembered when her husband's fingers had been strong and full of life, grasping hers. The memory strengthened her, and she bent to kiss her husband on his forehead before turning to face what lay ahead for her.

Avrim was awakened by two sharp clangs on iron bars. The sour smell of his clothes mixed with the stench of the dungeon's refuse quickly reminded him where he was. He sat up from the crude straw bedding, shielding his eyes against the glare of a lantern.

"Thank you, Thomas, that'll be all."

As Avrim's eyes adjusted, he saw a tall woman wearing the robes of a Lightmother. After a moment, he recognized her as Mother Agathene from the Temple of the Lightborn here in Oakworth.

"Mother Agathene," he said awkwardly, not feeling they were acquainted well enough for her to remember him—Avrim had only been a boy the last time he had made the rounds to her temple. "You look well."

"How I wish I could say the same, Brother Avrim." Her voice was curt and her face stone. She held the lantern in a strong hand, but the way it lit her face made her seem ancient. "You stand accused of wicked crimes against our order. I would hear your plea myself."

Avrim didn't know where to begin. His devotion to the Light felt at odds with his devotion to the Luminaura. It seemed there were so many conflicting rumors and splitting alliances within their order that he couldn't be certain where this woman stood. But sitting in a cell awaiting judgment for heresy and worse, what did he have to lose?

After a long moment of silence, the woman shifted, as if ready to leave. "I fear you may have fallen victim to unfortunate mentoring. It seems Father Tomen may have led you astray, and you must now face the consequences of his follies." Her face softened as she began to turn away.

"Wait," Avrim said, choking on the dry word. "You said you would hear my plea. My plea is mercy, Mother," he shifted to a knee, his limbs still sore from the fighting yesterday. "I have found the Child of Light, and to protect her, I fear I have put the Luminaura in a precarious situation."

"Lenora?" Agathene asked incredulously. "That is quite a claim to make, given our First Paladin Darrance Moore has revealed her just yesterday, while you were still in irons trying to escape the Oather's justice."

Avrim was taken aback. *Lenora?* He had saved the baron's daughter when Gage had tried to murder her. *Why is Darrance proclaiming her the Child of Light?*

"That can't be..." Avrim struggled to find the words, wondering if there were any words that could help the situation. "That girl is not the Child of Light, Mother. She was nearly killed by the Child of Shadow, but I healed her..."

"Was that also while you were held captive by Dame Kasia?"

"No," came a gruff voice from the darkness beyond. "It was when we saved yer damn city the first time it was getting sacked, ye old withered cunt."

"Deina, please."

"Fine company you keep, Brother," Mother Agathene said, sounding unbothered. She gave Avrim a hard look. "What do you know of the Child of Shadow?"

Once more, Avrim considered his words, staring down at the filthy stone floor of his cell. "He was here, a boy from Blakehurst. He tried to murder the baron's children in their beds, but I was able to bring them back from Mural's Gate." He looked up at Mother Agathene's dimly lit face. "You know as well as I, the Light has limits to what it will heal. That girl should have died. But the Light chose her to live."

The old woman's expression changed, a look of fear etching heavier lines on her face to make her look even older. "Did you say Blakehurst? A boy?"

Avrim nodded, creasing his brow. It was then that it became clear to him. *She knows something about Gage.*

Mother Agathene's lips tightened and the concern on her face suddenly melted away, along with the additional years it had brought with it. "Well, you have pled for mercy—as the guilty are wont to do—but it is not mine to give. You three are not held by the Luminaura, but I felt it was my duty to hear your words before the baroness decides your fate this morning." She lifted her blue skirts trimmed in gold and began to turn away.

Avrim felt a sudden darkness within him. "Aren't you going to ask about her?"

Agathene froze.

No, Avrim thought, trying to resist the urge to think of her again. "The mother..."

"Avrim," Melaine said from the side of Avrim's cell opposite Deina. "Let us save it for the baroness. She will remember..."

When Agathene turned to look at him, Avrim stood up, the darkness turning into a low, smoldering fury. "You knew, didn't you?"

Agathene seemed to shrink in front of the priest, although she was free and he was locked in a small cage. Her withered lips trembled as if she were going to speak but forgot how.

"She came to you, didn't she?" Avrim slipped his fingers around the rusty iron bars, leaning his face through them. He couldn't tell if the woman's lantern grew brighter or if he had, but the lines in Agathene's face deepened. "She confided in you about the Light, desperately begging her to kill her child—the Child of Shadow." His hands tightened around the bars as he remembered seeing the woman's bloody body in the inn, murdered by the Shadow. "Did she sit in your glowery and beg for forgiveness? Asking why the Light would have her do such a thing?"

Mother Agathene's lips parted further, but she still couldn't find the words. She stepped closer toward Avrim's cell, as if hoping it held some sort of absolution.

"Avrim, enough."

He couldn't tell if it was Deina or Melaine or both of them, but the fervent rage building within him drowned their voices out. Avrim felt fire in his eyes, and he reached out a hand toward Agathene who seemed blinded by something she saw in Avrim's burning gaze.

"Avrim!"

Agathene took a step closer and Avrim lurched forward, wrapping his hand around her neck. The old woman finally snapped out of her trance. She dropped the lantern, reaching both her feeble hands up to Avrim's wrist.

"How long did you ignore the Light?!" Avrim's voice bellowed down the dungeon's hall. Despite the smashed lantern, the damp hold was illuminated by the priest's unleashed rage. "You knew! I knew when I saw her—I felt the Shadow hanging over her! The Light begged me to give her relief! You knew!"

"Avrim, release her! Guards!"

Agathene choked, mouthing words that Avrim knew were worthless excuses. He knew she was culpable for Renay's death, as much as he was.

"You could have stopped it!" Avrim screamed. "But you made me do the bloody work! And now she's dead! Dead!"

Mother Agathene's eyes began to roll back in her head by the time the guards arrived. Avrim didn't see them, the world was a blazing inferno to him, but he felt the club that fell on his wrist, breaking the bone.

The Light left Avrim in a rush, and all he knew was pain and shame as he fell to his knees, cradling his broken arm. He had let the divine power consume him again, just like when he had nearly beaten the baron to death, and when he all but shoved a burdened mother to slay her son in the name of his religion.

Avrim fell back, his body weak and his mind broken. It took a moment for his senses to return, but when they did he could hear the guards fumbling for the cell keys, probably to lead him to his now certain execution.

"Wait," a hoarse voice said, wheezing. "I'm alright. Let him rest. Fetch Gregor to see to his arm. They are to be judged shortly."

Avrim let exhaustion take him. The Light had completely faded and left him in harrowing darkness.

Ransil and Quinn were the first ones to arrive to lunch, the former was welcomed specifically by the baroness who recognized the halfling and declared him a guest of honor, with Quinn earning the designation by association. The Luminaura Chaplain, Brace Cobbit, had accompanied them since they left the library that morning, but Ransil couldn't tell if it was a courtesy or a precaution by the church.

It certainly seemed like the Luminaura was truly in command of Oakworth, even though Ransil and Quinn were present during Vivian Caffery's investment. Normally, the queen would carry out any formal investiture, but under such pressing circumstances—or in the case of an heir coming into their inheritance—a group of nobles can serve as a proxy council, as long as the proper documentation was approved and signed by the crown.

However, despite Vivian's legitimacy as the ruler of Oakworth, the church had staked an early and distinct place in the woman's court. The paladins who had come to Oakworth's aid from Sathford nearly outnumbered the household guard, and the chaplains and acolytes easily doubled the city's meager watch.

Something about it made Ransil uncomfortable, but the halfling did not let it show in his interactions with Brace Cobitt, who he quite liked.

"At least the kitchens survived the assault," Ransil said to Brace, patting his stomach as they left the great hall. Most of the attendants were just sitting down to their meal following Vivian's investiture, but Ransil, Quinn, and Brace were the first to eat and the first to leave. "I haven't eaten that good since the last harvest festival back home."

"Aye, the Acreage?" Brace asked, producing a pipe from the pouch at his waist.

Realizing he didn't want to invite certain questions, he nodded. "I do miss the place," Ransil said, without having to lie. "But Vale's treated me well."

"And you, boy," Brace asked, puffing his pipe. "You're a spireling, I see. But where'd you come from? You have the look of an Eastlunder."

Quinn looked to Ransil, as if unsure if he should lie or tell the truth. The halfling gave him a shrug and a slight shake of his head to tell him it wouldn't matter.

"I...I don't know," Quinn said. "I'm an orphan. I was left at Raventhal and have been a student since I could walk."

Ransil got the sense that Quinn was being truthful, and he found he wasn't altogether surprised. The boy struck him as a bit of a savant—he'd never heard of a child that age wielding such magic. Looking at him now, Ransil realized how truly young the boy was, and he felt sorry for such a burden to be laid on his shoulders.

"Well," Brace said between puffs, "there are certainly worse lives to fall into." He turned to Ransil. "Yesterday you said you two were needing to head to Sathford rather urgently?"

Ransil nodded, hoping he didn't have to explain the reason.

"Seems I may be able to get you an escort, if you're looking to hitch a ride."

Giving Quinn a quick sideways glance, Ransil looked back at Brace and nodded. "That we are. When can we leave?"

Brace motioned toward the baroness' audience chamber. "There's to be a short council, with some local knights and lords who've come to pledge fealty to the new baroness. The church has been charged with escorting the Child of Light to the Brighthold in Andelor, so I suppose there will be a bit of discussion on that point, and Sir Moore may need my support."

Ransil froze as Brace and Quinn continued walking toward the audience chamber, but he quickly recovered and hurried to keep pace with them. "The Child of Light?" He feigned a disinterested tone.

Brace nodded, motioning dismissively with his pipe. "The baroness' youngest, Lila? Lydia?"

"Lenora?"

Brace snapped his fingers. "Yes. It seems she fought off whatever Shadowfiend burst up from the baron's secret chambers below. Sir Moore, our First Paladin, witnessed the girl's power with his own eyes." He looked down at Ransil, his eyes shifting to either side to ensure no one else could hear. "If you ask me, all this talk of the Children is making people quite eager to be the one to find them.

"I remember as a boy, there was a lot of talk of the Kingfin—a massive fish that lurked in the Amber Grove Lake." Brace puffed his pipe again. "So many fishermen claimed to have seen Kingfin, and any time someone brought a sizable catch back to town, it was hailed as the elusive legend of the lake." He sighed, letting out a long puff of smoke. "I trust Darrance. I just hope he's not pawning off some carp as Kingfin."

Ransil's mind was racing. Mostly he thought of Anika, only half hearing Brace's story about some fish. Wherever she was, she was being hunted. He had no notion what the Luminaura would want with her, but it was no surprise that they would be looking for her, especially in the wake of recent events.

But now it seemed that the church had convinced itself that Lenora Caffery was the prophesized Child of Light. Ransil wasn't sure he should be the one to correct them. In fact, he wasn't even sure if they were wrong. He knew little about the realities around the Children, so who was he to say what they believed was wrong or misguided?

Regardless, he bit his tongue. He wished no harm on this young Lenora Caffery, but if he could maybe see the church's intent toward the Child of Light with the girl serving as Anika's proxy, he'd be in a much better place to help his friend.

If she ever returned, that was.

"If it's all the same, my lord" Quinn interjected.

Brace chuckled. "I'm not lord, boy. Just a chaplain."

"Well, if it's all the same, we should be on our way immediately. I need to get back to the spire."

Ransil coughed. "I think it's best if we attend this council, Quinn." He shot the boy a hard look, hoping to keep him quiet. "Besides, we would be much safer traveling in the church's company along the Valeway."

"Aye," Brace said with a nod. "With all these cursed fey-devils creeping out of the woods, I wouldn't advise traveling without a bit of company. Especially you." Brace looked at Quinn. "The spire will need you there in one piece. Seems there's some woodland fiends causing trouble there as well."

Quinn and Ransil shared a look, but before they could press the man for more details, a voice spoke behind them.

"You, chaplain."

The three of them turned, and Ransil felt his throat close up at what he saw.

Dame Kasia Strallow strode toward them, her eyes fortunately set on Brace. "Where is your paladin?"

"Sir Moore is attending to church matters." Brace's voice was steady as he blew out smoke almost directly into the Other's face. "You will find him in the audience chamber shortly."

Kasia held her gaze on him, her gauntleted hands clenched into fists. Ransil kept his face downturned so as not to draw her attention. The last time he had seen her was in Andelor when he and Dolly—Scratch at the time—had blackmailed the woman for a cache of blackshards. He doubted she would have forgiven him.

Finally, Kasia's hands relaxed. "Perhaps you could tell me why my prisoners are being kept from me. I am expected in Andelor, and I've already delayed my return due to helping your people clean up this mess."

Prisoners? Something felt wrong, and Ransil had learned to trust his instincts; they had saved him more times than he could count. If the Arcania was escorting prisoners through Oakworth, there could only be a handful of places where those prisoners could have come from. He hoped Brace's attitude would throw the woman off balance. She was as cunning as they came, but her pride would be her undoing.

"You have no authority to hold prisoners here," Brace said, his voice still calm and dripping with disdain. "The three you brought from Blakehurst are now in the baroness' custody. And as the Luminaura is serving as the temporary stewarding power for Baroness Caffery until such time as the queen properly invests her, Sir Moore has been appointed the town's justice."

The mention of Blakehurst made Ransil's lunch turn upside down in his stomach. Avrim, Deina, and Melaine had departed for Blakehurst to see to Matty's remains. Once again, his instincts were right, and now he had to figure out how to free them under the church's militant eye.

Suddenly Ransil felt meeker than he ever had, not just due to this constant scramble to figure out what he should be doing to help Anika—wherever she was—but now he was literally hanging his head to avoid Kasia's notice.

"We will see what Vivian has to say," Kasia said tightly, taking a step toward Brace. "And as for the church, you had best hope when I return to Fainly that I forget this folly. There was a time when not even the faith was above the Oath's authority."

In response to the threat, Brace took another long drag off his pipe.

Then, Ransil's stomach lurched again as he saw Kasia's legs bend, shifting in his direction.

"You never kept the best company, did you, Ruse?"

Finally, Ransil looked up, letting out a steady breath. The Oather's face was carved from angry stone, eyes furious slits. Ransil had hoped the years between them and the scruff that now covered his pudgier cheeks would have allowed him to avoid notice, but he should have known better—Kasia Strallow did not become Lady Commander of the Oathers without an excess of shrewdness.

"You must have confused me with someone else," Ransil said in a tone that also said, *I know secrets, too.* "Lots of halflings in Vale these days."

Kasia seemed to take the meaning, but held the halfling's gaze for another moment before adding. "Your cousins send their regards from Andelor."

Ransil immediately feared for Rosh and Dolly. The last he had seen of them was when they had all parted ways here in Oakworth—with everything that had happened since, he had assumed they would have been laying low at the Breeze. But he didn't give the Oather the satisfaction of a reaction.

Kasia stood up, gave Brace another hard look, and then turned to Quinn, evaluating the mage for a moment. "Are you from Raventhal or the Vestige?"

The boy shot Ransil a quick look; the halfling nodded for him to tell the truth.

"Raventhal," the boy said meekly, clearly understanding the woman's authority. He struggled with the collar of his robe to produce his Arcanian mark. The small crystal caused the black etchings on Kasia's armor to gleam slightly. "Here's my mark."

"What is an Accepted doing in Oakworth with his mark? Are you planning on casting magic outside the spire without authorization?"

"Konrath assigned him to me," Brace said, calmly exhaling another cloud of smoke. "There's trouble in the spire and they wanted the students to be kept busy. And as you can see," Brace motioned toward the keep's main doors, "we had need of his magic."

There was another awkward silence between Brace and Kasia as the former took another slow drag from his pipe.

Finally, Brace added, "Seems like Raventhal might have need of your expertise, given their distinct lack of Oathers these days. You can leave your prisoners here. The church can help the baroness see to their care."

Kasia gave him a poisonous smile. "I think I'll lend my voice to this afternoon's council. The baroness needs to hear my account."

As she strode away, Ransil felt even more burdened. Anika, Gage, the druid's keyshard, and now the Oather and his wayward cousins; he felt like he was losing focus, not knowing what role he played in all of this. And why did this stranger feel the need to lie for Quinn? More and more he felt like he was in the midst of a grand conspiracy.

"I think I'm in love with that woman," Brace said suddenly, with a much too thoughtful expression.

Despite the circumstances—or perhaps because of them—Ransil guffawed.

Later that afternoon, the council convened in the audience chamber, a place Vivian now saw in a much different light. Before, she had sat behind the baron's high seat during such gatherings, along with any visiting lords, ladies, and other dignitaries. But now that she sat at the high seat, the hall felt somehow larger and more ominous.

Unlike Alburn was accustomed to—making a show of entering the hall after everyone else had already settled in—Vivian arrived early, so attendants would see her sitting when they began to gather.

"They should see you first," Mother Agathene had advised the night prior. "Rather than a vacant chair, the people should see you sitting there, ready to rule."

Vivian had agreed, but she couldn't help feeling a strange sense of guilt when she first took that chair, as if the act was motivated by ambition and not duty. Regardless, she was glad to have the old woman's council. Her husband had preferred to rule on his own, trusting his own instinct, guided by his own ambitions. But Vivian hoped to rule differently.

Not only because she doubted her own instincts—she was no Alburn Caffery, lacking that inherent shrewdness—but she had always wished her husband would have conferred with her more. She meant to listen as well as lead.

"Your Ladyship."

Vivian blinked, realizing she had been staring at the guard, lost in her own thoughts. "Yes, Derik?"

The guard wet his lips, looking nervous. "Shall I open the doors?"

The question set loose the butterflies in her stomach. "Yes, of course." She felt Mother Agathene's hand on her shoulder, giving a light but reassuring squeeze. Vivian nodded in appreciation.

As Derik and his brother Cobb opened the doors, Vivian was shocked by the gathering of people waiting out in the antechamber. At the front of the press, Vivian saw the familiar face of Lord Byron Vickers and his three knighted sons, each of them in full armor with their helms tucked under their arms. Their house colors were represented in the deep forest green of their armor, each piece of platemail trimmed in polished copper.

As the Vickers men strode in, inclining their heads to honor the baroness, they were followed by several well-dressed lords that she was passingly familiar with. Reeve Rupert Warner from Blakehurst strode in, his puffy red face pinched in an expression of self-importance. Accompanying him was the Widow Ackerly, an elderly human woman who retained the fallen estates of her dead husband's family. Vivian always felt sad for the woman, ruling over nothing but ash and bone while still playing these courtly games.

An exceptionally pale elf—who could have passed as man or woman—dressed in exotic finery entered through the gates next, as other more familiar figures followed, each finding a place to stand on either side of the aisle.

Vivian noted many members of the Luminaura, most notably the dashing Sir Darrance Moore who had rescued her and her children, as well as Derik's gruff-looking cousin who sauntered in with a young mage and the old halfling who Vivian recognized from the last assault on Oakworth.

Remembering that there were multiple attacks on her home suddenly made Vivian feel lightheaded. But she closed her eyes and took a deep breath, reminding herself that this would probably be the single most important appearance she would make in front of these people. It would define her legacy.

Such heavy thoughts surprisingly comforted her. She felt how she imagined Alburn had felt at times like this.

Powerful.

She opened her eyes to see the flood of people had ceased, and the young page—another one of Derik Cobbit's many cousins Vivian believed—announced the proceedings. "Lords, ladies, and gentlefolk, allow me to present your ladyship, Baroness Vivian Caffery, vassal lord of Oakworth and its surrounding lands, to be invested by the sovereign queen of Vale."

There were several customary shouts of, "Long may she rule!" The Vickers all went to a knee, while many others merely inclined their heads or gave a brief applause.

Vivian took another deep breath and placed her hands firmly on the armrests of Alburn's great chair, gripping the burnished iron tree ornaments. "Your presence here shall be noted and properly documented. All in attendance have either defended our glorious town with their very lives, or risked great harm by traveling here in such perilous times."

As she gave her prepared introduction, she noticed the Oather stride in, and something about her presence unsettled Vivian greatly. But she maintained her composure and finished welcoming the great council.

"Our first and most pressing order of business is the safety of our town," Vivian announced. She motioned toward either side of the hall where the paladins, acolytes, and chaplains were convened, supplementing her household guard. "Due to their timely aid and our own compromised defenses, the Luminaura has been given full martial authority until such time as our own militia is fully garrisoned."

There were a few murmurings, but no outward objections. Vivian was afraid Sir Byron's bristling mustache was an indication that he might make an argument. The knight was a firm proponent of the old faiths; his house's arms bore six stars above a tower on a hill, praising the six old gods and the mortals who fought for their glory. To Vivian's relief, Byron finally inclined his head in a tight nod.

"With that in mind," Vivian continued, "let us proceed to the trials." She motioned to the side of the hall where one of her guards stood ready by a door. At the signal, the woman turned around and pounded on the heavy oak door before turning its key and opening it to reveal the torchlit stairs leading down. Footsteps echoed into the chamber.

Vivian looked toward the Oather, reluctantly raising a hand to beckon her forward. Dame Kasia Strallow approached the seat. The baroness did not like the insolent look the woman gave her, but she reminded herself that the Oathers were above even the Luminaura when it came to matters of unsanctioned sorcery.

"Our first accused are brought to us by the Arcania," Vivian began, as she turned to see the jailor lead three shabby figures up the stairs. The first was a man, his head hanging and shoulders slumped, as if the irons on his wrists were too heavy to bear; one of those wrists was wrapped in bandages. Then came a dwarf woman who glared at the gathered nobles as she stepped into the bright hall. A flash of recognition caused Vivian to trail off her decree, and when the half-orc woman emerged, the baroness shot to her feet.

"What is the meaning of this?!"

Several gasps swept the hall as all eyes turned to the prisoners. When the first shackled man looked up, Vivian knew immediately it was the priest who had pulled her daughter back from the jaws of death.

"Why are these heroes bound?" Vivian demanded of her jailers, before turning the question to the Oather.

Kasia looked at her prisoners, then back to Vivian. "These individuals stand accused of illicitly dealing in keyshards, conspiring against the throne, and heresy against the Luminaura."

Another wave of gasps. Vivian's own breath was caught in her throat as she looked back at the three people who had defended her home and family. She refused to believe such charges. Certainly there was some confusion.

"What proof have you of these charges?"

Kasia regarded her coolly. "When I was passing through Oakworth on my way to Blakehurst, I became suspicious that some thieves meant to rob your late husband of his keyshard. As I understand from speaking to your household guard, these three traveled with those thieves and they did in fact carry out their larceny."

During the presentation of evidence, Vivian watched the prisoners. While the man looked ashamed and defeated, the dwarf gnashed her teeth and the half-orc woman just watched Kasia with cold, dark eyes.

The Oather continued. "Their conspiracy against the throne was hatched earlier in Rathen, when they thwarted my associate's defense of the city by robbing him of the keyshards that were meant to be used against the harpy menace that would later threaten Sathford and Oakworth."

Someone from the gathered shouted. "Traitors! Hang them!" It took a moment for the murmurings that followed to quiet down enough for Kasia to continue her accusations.

"And finally," the Oather said, looking at the priest in irons, "this is Avrim Kaust from the Temple of Dawn in Sathford, which was recently burned down for its heretical vicar's blasphemy. It is only reasonable to assume that his only errant priest carried out the defiant vicar's treacherous machinations."

More voices took up the cries of "Heathens" and "Shadowfiends!"

Vivian looked to the prisoners for some defense against these charges. When the mob's cries for justice quieted, she finally spoke. "You, Brother Kaust. How do you respond to these charges?"

The priest looked up to her. "I have no response. I will accept the—"

"The hell you will!" The dwarf stepped forward, her face turning red and her eyes smoldering on the Oather. "This bloody bitch spins quite the tale for someone who abandoned Rathen to its fate!"

The jailor raised his club to strike the dwarf, but Vivian stayed him. "Hold there!" The man looked abashed, but lowered the weapon.

"Your ladyship, may I respond to the charges?"

All eyes turned on the tall half-orc woman who seemed to loom over the entire gathering. Of the three prisoners, she wore her irons almost proudly. Vivian nodded.

"The charge of illicitly dealing in keyshards is only partially true," the half-orc said, causing another murmur amongst the gathered. "We did not buy or sell any keyshards that belonged to the Arcania, but I was one of the rangers from Wickham that encountered Corvanna before the fall of Rathen. The harpies were gathering keyshards, much like the dryads are now. It seems fruitless to charge anyone with dealing in keyshards when such foes are using them against the realm."

Vivian heard Byron Vickers mumble something to his sons that sounded like agreement.

The half-orc continued. "We merely obtained the keyshard in Rathen to keep it from Corvanna. And in regards to your late husband's keyshard, we suspected it would likewise be a target and we interceded."

"How did you come to suspect such a thing?" Kasia's voice was steady, unyielding.

"We traveled with the Child of Light," the half-orc said plainly, eliciting a surge of disbelieving gasps. "The girl had visions, and we followed them to stop the incarnate."

"False."

Vivian's heart raced as she turned to see the stunning face of Sir Darrance Moore step forward. She had trouble catching her breath, and not because the paladin was probably the most handsome man she had ever seen, but because she knew what was coming. The paladin's cool blue eyes fell on her.

"Your ladyship, I have heard these prisoners' claims and have since conferred with your daughter, the Lady Lenora. She had not seen these individuals before Corvanna's attack."

"Lenora is not the Child of Light," the half-orc said, stealing the words out of Vivian's own mouth.

Darrance stiffened. "She is. I felt it when she defeated the monster that emerged from below. She possesses the Light itself—there is no other way I could have summoned such power without aid."

"What you felt was an echo of what I felt," the half-orc replied. She motioned toward Vivian with her shackled hands. "What her ladyship felt, when my companion brought the girl back from the brink of death. This man," she motioned to the priest next to her, "is the most devout priest of the Light I have ever witnessed—a soldier purely devoted to the Luminaura—and the Light chose him to save the girl. That is what you felt, sir; the life that this man saved still carries his undying conviction."

Vivian's mouth was dry. Something about the half-orc's words and how she delivered them, the baroness knew them to be true. In addition to how much she *wanted* to believe those words, to save her daughter from being thrust into a perilous prophecy, Vivian certainly *felt* them to be true, deep in her bones.

Darrance didn't reply. He looked from the half-orc, to Vivian, and then finally to the ground. A long moment passed where the only sounds were a few whisperings among the waiting nobles.

Finally, Kasia broke the silence. "Who is the Child of Light that you claim told you of the visions?"

"That is not for me to say," the half-orc said, stepping back. "I only respond to your charges, to which we plead innocent."

"Here, here." Byron Vickers twitched his beard and nudged his sons to join his decree.

Vivian turned to Kasia. "Do you have any additional charges, Dame Strallow?"

The Oather's eyes narrowed on the baroness, but she only said, "No."

"Then if no one objects," Vivian said to the others, "I hereby declare the accused innocent of their charges. Release them immediately."

"Your ladyship," Mother Agathene whispered, leaning toward her chair. "The priest..."

"Is free to go," Vivian cut in, giving the priestess a cold glare. She felt authority brewing within her now. "Along with the other two." She nodded toward the jailor, who turned to begin removing the prisoners' shackles.

"I shall report this to the Arcania, my ladyship," Kasia Strallow announced, inclining her head with a mocking smile on her face. "I am sure we shall speak again soon when I begin the investigation on your husband's missing keyshard."

Vivian's chest tightened as she watched the woman leave, wondering what kind of foe she had just made.

Chapter Sixteen

A Past Brightened

The east wing of the Drastil manor was musty, and Anika felt like she was walking back in time as she strode slowly down the halls toward the gallery. She felt Elrin's watchful eyes behind her, judging every step she took. But she tried to focus on Lekan next to her.

The majest made her feel like a princess—which is what she supposed she might be soon. Every few steps, he would cast a glance toward her and smile that shy smile of his, making her blush and smile in turn.

She thought she had been in love in Blakehurst, swooning over Matty Cullen and dreaming of one day maybe having a small family with him. After laying with him in Oakworth, she was certain she knew what love was. And when Matty died in her arms, she believed she would never love again.

What she had begun feeling for Lekan felt different. It felt less urgent and safer, which is not something she thought she had desired; but after so much loss and Gage's utter betrayal, she desperately craved some certainty in her life.

Anika was also honest with herself. The promise of a luxurious life as a Karranese queen—or royene, as they were called—certainly had a lot to do with the desire she felt for the man walking beside her.

As if reading her thoughts, Lekan reached out an expecting hand. Anika gladly took it, giving him another smile. She twined her fingers through his, feeling each of the five ornate rings he wore.

"Tell me," the majest said, pulling her closer so the vizier or their guards wouldn't hear. "Do these halls feel familiar at all? I know you were just an infant when they took you away, but sometimes we recall the places—the smells—of our infancy without realizing we do."

THE WITHERED ROOTS

Anika looked around. The high ceilings were supported by wide pillars, inlaid with patterns of thorny vines. Ancient rugs lined the floors, their feet leaving streaks in the collected dust. There were cobwebs in every corner and between every piece of furniture.

It felt to Anika like a coffin, and she was suddenly glad she had no memories of it. But feeling Lekan's thumb stroking the back of hers made her spine tingle, and she didn't want to make him sad.

"I don't know," she said instead, making a show of looking hard at each unlit candelabra and empty vase. "It's hard to tell with everything looking…"

"Old?" Lekan finished with a soft chuckle. "Fifteen years is almost a lifetime, especially for you and me. This place has been left untouched since the domina disappeared with her lover, taking her only child with her to avoid the uprising." Lekan looked at something unseen in the shadows. "We were just babies then."

The majest had told her the story, and Anika had made sure to inquire about the domina's fate. Curiously, the archives did not have any writings about the uprising or the Drastil family around that time, but Elrin, Stevra, and even the nomarch, Jamira Kraiev, had plenty to share about Mavala and the Drastils.

Mostly, what she could gather followed the majest's tale. When the uprising threatened the domina's rule over the Trivestiture—which Anika learned was the term used to describe the shared governance between the three cities of Pyram, Truine, and Ithyra, overseen by the chamberlords—Mavala and her bodyguard and lover, Saviz, fled their home with their infant daughter, who just happened to be promised to the next majest of Pyram.

When Anika had asked Saleen, the archivist, about Mavala's tale, the gnome had looked uncharacteristically flustered. "We don't keep the histories of the uprising. They are kept in the vaults where they will never inspire such violent insolence amongst the good people of Pyram."

While Anika had found that slightly curious, she could understand the royal archives not wanting to make such writings available for anyone to see.

"Has no one lived here since?" Anika asked.

"Oh, certainly," Lekan said, motioning with his free hand down the hall behind them. "The other halls have been used for various functions, and we allow the theater troupes to use the ballroom occasionally for their performances. But this wing has been sealed…as sort of a monument to the domina's memory."

"There has not been a domina since Mavala," Elrin added in a lecturing tone. "The uprising was a result of the chamberlords circumventing the Trivestiture's own accords, and the domina was held at fault for the economic collapse when trade between the three cities and the Xe'danni merchant guilds fell apart."

"A sad story, to be sure," Lekan said, squeezing Anika's hand and flashing her another charming smile. "But we are not here to mourn, are we, my…Kalany."

It wasn't the first time he had called her that name, but each time it felt like a cold touch on her neck. The image of Mavala's likeness from the painting floated before her. Anika tried to conjure up the image of her the woman from her visions, but now she only ever saw Mavala's face.

Anika loosened her fingers and gently pulled her hand away. "My name is Anika."

Lekan's eyes maintained their kindness, but his smile seemed more forced now. "Of course, my Anika. It is a powerful name. Is it Valen? Or Westerran?"

Anika wasn't certain, but she was certain it was hers. "I don't know. As I said, my father is an Eastlunder."

"Your father was Karranese," Elrin said sternly. "A mighty warrior and noble protector of the domina. His name was Saviz Gamal, and he probably saved your life from the rebels."

The words were probably meant to sting Anika, but she had trouble feeling a connection to these names they kept placing on her. As much as she believed she wanted this life they were promising her, it felt like they were slowly trying to erase the life she had known. Her past may be complicated and tragic, but it was her own, and she wouldn't have them erase it. She simply nodded for now and kept walking toward the doors.

The gallery was sealed behind two heavy, ornate doors decorated with silver and bronze floral designs. The two guards that led them through the hall pushed those doors open, shaking loose years of dust and cobwebs.

The doors creaked in protest, and Anika thought she heard the faintest of whispers behind that sound, but as the light from the guards' lanterns spilled into the room beyond, Anika gasped. She immediately forgot about the ominous voice accompanying the door's screeching hinges. A rush of what she could only assume was nostalgia threatened to knock her to the ground.

A looming face stared down at Anika; her mother's face. The uncertainty she had felt when the majest's artist first presented his interpretation of the woman from Anika's vision had faded completely. She felt tears welling up in her eyes as she stared up at the magnificent work of art.

She had found her mother.

"The domina was a benevolent ruler," Lekan said, stepping forward and turning to face Anika. He motioned a hand to the enormous portrait of Mavala Drastil behind him. "Pyram's most legendary painter—Esmira Vontane—gifted this to Mavala for providing artists a sanctuary to practice their crafts. Mavala loved the arts above all."

Lekan flashed Anika a smile and motioned to the other wall. "That is, until Kalany was born."

Once more, Anika thought she heard a distant whispering voice, but regardless she turned and choked on sudden tears. A smaller painting adorned the wall next to the gallery's doors, but it sat in a more ornate frame with two tall bronze braziers on either side of it.

The painting was of Anika—or Kalany—as a baby, bundled in soft purple velvet against her warm chestnut skin. Anika knew she would not be able to see her own defined features in a newborn baby, but the image was of her, she felt a strange sensation that she took for certainty. Those tiny eyes were barely open in the painting, but Anika felt an overpowering sense of nostalgia.

Next to the painting of the newborn was another framed painting of a similar size. This one was of Mavala again, draped in a single piece of sheer orange silk. In the painting, Mavala stood naked, the orange scarf wrapping itself around one shoulder, cascading down her leg. The domina's breasts were left revealed, one feeding a newborn Kalany—again bundled in soft purple, cradled in one of Mavala's arms—and the other seemed to be the centerpiece of the painting, drawing the eye. A stream of pale white milk ran from the domina's large, dark, perfect nipple. Mesmerizing.

Anika felt an unfamiliar sensation looking at that painting, and she looked down to the plaque below it which had a single word in a foreign script.

"Life," Lekan said from behind her. "That's the name of that painting. I understand it was the domina's most prized piece. Another of Esmira's, who sadly died shortly after completing this one."

"It's amazing," Anika said in a trance, her voice breaking. She felt a stirring within her belly, and oddly her thoughts went back to that night in Oakworth, in The Harvest Breeze with Matty. She only seldomly pictured herself as a mother, but something about the painting made her aspire to it. Perhaps she merely aspired to be a radiant giver of life like her mother.

The barrage of unfamiliar feelings left her weeping now. On the edge of her vision, she saw Lekan take a lantern from the guards as he ushered them and the vizier out of the gallery, leaving him alone with Anika. As the doors closed, Anika thought she saw a figure in gray robes, but when she blinked there was only Lekan in the room with her.

Together, the two of them walked around to admire the other pieces decorating the maze-like hall. Each time they turned a corner, their path split in two directions, then three, then four. After only a couple turns, Anika felt lost, but she let the majest guide her on as she walked through her mother's life; a life she could have had—may still have.

She slid her arm through Lekan's, wiping her tears away with her other hand. The gallery had begun to feel cold as they passed by more abstract pieces of art that Anika didn't care for, but the majest was warm, and the light from his lantern comforted her against the dimness hanging around the art.

"Are you alright, my Ka–my Anika?"

Anika would have stiffened at the slip, but even thinking of the name he almost called her felt more natural here, as if it were a shoe that was once too tight but had begun to loosen after wearing, and it might be a perfect fit after enough steps.

"Yes," she said, taking a deep breath. These tears felt good, but her mind was almost numb at the moment. The sudden flurry of emotions fought a gruesome battle within her, but it was over as swiftly as it came and now she felt exhausted. "I just feel...so lost."

"I as well," he said, moving the lantern to either side as they came to another split in the hall. "I think I may have led us astray." He gave her a sideways glance and a mischievous smirk.

She couldn't help but laugh, welcoming the levity.

"I like when you smile," the majest said, taking the left path that led to a small round chamber. "You look so much like the domina."

Anika saw statues in the room beyond, contorted figures hidden in shadows. "What else do you know about her? You make her seem too good to be true—doesn't everyone have their flaws?"

"To that, I cannot say," Lekan said, admiring another painting that Anika couldn't understand—formless shapes and ugly colors, not to her taste. "I was obviously too young to know her personally, but my predecessor, Royene Yasmin Be'hir, spoke only of her grace and beauty. And as you can see," Lekan motioned to the room ahead, holding up the lantern, "her beauty is quite evident."

Anika blushed when the light revealed the chamber for her. The statues she had seen were of Mavala and a man—she could only assume her true father—in erotic poses. There were several pairs of statues, each one lifelike, carved from polished marble. Each pair of statues were a different frozen moment of intimacy between man and woman, and with each pair she saw, whatever modesty she gained from her small life in Blakehurst melted away.

The pair of statues nearest her, Mavala wrapped her legs around the waist of a standing muscular man, her back arched in ecstasy. Another, the domina was crouched down low, this time the man arching his back. The two marble figures at the far end of the chamber were twisted together, their limbs resembling one of the giant pretzels Ransil had made in The Early Mule using a recipe he said came from Xoatia.

On the walls encircling the statues were colorful paintings of Mavala and Saviz pleasuring each other with their hands and mouths; in some paintings there were other figures present as well. Anika never considered herself a prude, having shared in ribald tales with her friends Jema and Wilma, who taught Anika the ways in which she could pleasure herself. However, the round chamber of lust was enough to make her uncomfortably pull her arm out of Lekan's, swallowing a lump in her throat.

Lekan didn't seem to notice, raising his lantern so she could see better. "Your parents were beautiful, and they loved each other well." When his eyes fell on Anika, his smile faded slightly. But after only a moment, it grew even wider than before. "Oh, I apologize. I had almost forgotten you come from Vale. They are a bit skittish about physical love there, as I understand."

"Well," Anika said, crossing her arms. She tried to look at the statues and paintings with the same wonder that Lekan did, but something inside her felt wrong. "I don't know if skittish is the word. But some things are kept private. Is this," she nodded toward the statue of Mavala kneeling down to pleasure her father with her mouth, "common? Seeing your parents like this?"

He chuckled slightly. "Certainly not in the act, no, but this is only art. It represents love and passion, and it captures their beauty in that moment, no? Many nobles celebrate their heritage, and this is part of it—the true essence of it, you could say. I have many paintings of my parents joining in efforts to bring me into this world. I cherish them."

While Lekan explained, Anika tried to look up at the pieces again, feeling less discomfort with each word the majest said. It definitely put her feelings in a different perspective. Maybe it wasn't shame or modesty that made her feel uncomfortable.

"Just as I would cherish you, Kalany."

She looked back at Lekan and she realized what it was she felt now, and she stepped toward him. Instinctively, her hand went to Stormender at her waist, brushing her fingers over it, feeling its inspiring presence and drawing strength from it as she took another step toward the man who could give her everything.

The majest looked at her with those dark, intoxicating eyes, his smile slackening slightly, his lips inviting.

Anika stopped in front of him, their faces only a hand's span apart. "Tell me," she said, her voice growing husky as her body responded to the atmosphere, "what is expected of a royene?"

He responded with his easy smile, revealing perfectly white teeth. "Power. Peace. Luxury." He reached a hand up to trace his finger over one of her eyebrows and down the curve of her cheek. "Only what you deserve."

Her legs felt weak, but that didn't matter as his hand went around the back of her neck, pulling her mouth to his. He tasted like herbs and fruit, and his tongue was a tender serpent. The kiss felt like it lasted too long and not long enough, but when Anika realized she was being lowered to the ground she put a hand on Lekan's chest.

She looked down and saw that the majest was already mostly disrobed and she couldn't help but think about Matty. The thoughts came unbidden, but she would not deny or bury them. Although her body was certainly ready for this, her mind was not.

"We do not have to," Lekan said, tucking himself back into pants that did little to conceal his excitement.

Anika's eyes drifted to a painting that had drawn her gaze before. In the piece, Mavala was on her back, her fingers twined through a head of dark hair down between her legs. When Anika looked back at Lekan, she saw that he had followed her gaze to the painting and was now giving her another one of his smiles before kissing her stomach gently and making his way down.

Laying her head back, Kalany looked upon her mother, seeing herself now in each of the statues and paintings, Lekan in place of her father. Despite the rising ecstasy, she couldn't help but wonder why this all felt so right.

Stormender begged for her to touch it, but instead her fingers curled around Lekan's hair and she let everything else go.

The figure in gray robes went unnoticed, retreating back to the gallery's shadows.

That evening, Anika confined herself to her quarters while Lekan tended to royal matters. If given the choice, she would have spent the entire day with the majest in her mother's gallery, but as it stood, she would wait for him alone, giving herself some time to sort her thoughts and emotions.

She failed miserably at that, spending too much time laying on her bed and remembering every tremble of pleasure that Lekan had given her that afternoon. Soon after dinner was delivered to her room, Stevra brought her evening attire.

"The majest has requested your presence in his solar," the halfling said with a suggestive raise of her eyebrows. "Would my lady take a bath after the meal?"

Anika sat down at the prepared table at the foot of her bed, only just then realizing how famished she was. "Yes, I think I will."

Stevra seemed taken aback by that, but smiled brightly. "I shall make the arrangements." She spun on her broad feet and walked swiftly to the doors, shutting them behind her.

Anika tore into her dinner, unsure where her sudden ravenous appetite came from. She supposed she might have Lekan to thank for that. There was a brothy soup that wasn't warm, but tasted marvelous, filled with chunks of little green soft fruits, with lime and zesty herbs. She drank every last drop of it.

The meat was the ribs of a small beast, slathered in a sweet honey sauce that tasted like pineapples—which she hadn't known existed until she had them in

Pyram, but now were officially her favorite food. As Anika sucked the last of the meat off one of the bones, there was a soft knock on her door.

"Come in," Anika said between bites, apparently unable to sate her appetite. But the knock came again. "Stevra, come on in."

The door creaked open but the face that peered in was not the halfling's, but one that Anika recalled seeing when she had first met Lekan. "My lady, may I come in?"

Anika suddenly realized she had sauce dripping from her chin and reached for the napkin to clean up. "Yes, come in..." She couldn't remember the woman's name.

"Taliah, my lady," the woman said, slipping inside the room and closing the door behind her. "I'm a Lightmother with the Luminaura, and I..." She looked nervous. She was a pale-skinned human, with close-cropped auburn hair that framed her square face. "I come to give you a warning, my lady..."

Suddenly Anika's appetite withered. Her day had been a whirlwind of warm emotions, but this woman's words sent a slight chill down her spine.

"Do not return to the domina's manse."

Anika waited for more, but the woman just stared at her, as if expecting a response. "My mother's manse? Why not?"

The woman's eyes darted to the walls, looking for some hidden foe. "I fear saying more, my lady. Can you come to the glowery? The temple on the third terrace, facing the sea. Midnight. I can explain more there."

Anika got up from the table, her legs feeling weak as she stepped around it toward the woman. "Tell me. What's wrong with the domina's manse? I was there today with the majest."

The woman looked terrified, her eyes wide. "I felt something. It's the Shadow—"

Another knock at the door interrupted her. "Lady Anika, are you ready for your bath now?"

The Lightmother straightened at the sound of Stevra's voice and moved toward the door. "Midnight," she whispered. "The glowery. Please come."

Anika took another step, but the woman was already opening the door, letting Stevra in with the two porters who carried huge casks of steaming water. Stevra stepped in after Taliah departed, giving Anika a raised eyebrow.

"Saying a few prayers before bed?"

Anika smiled awkwardly and sat back to finish her meal, but her appetite was sufficiently gone. She laid her napkin over her meal and watched Stevra prepare her bath, pondering the woman's mysterious warning.

That evening Anika drank plum wine and ate sweet pastries with Lekan in his solar. She had dressed in the fine gown he had sent to her, but neither of them remained in their clothes for long.

They kissed, held, and touched each other, but did not make love—Anika still did not feel ready for that. She had still felt guilty enough for the other physical contact so shortly after losing Matty, but something about the place inspired her to savor whatever pleasures she could find before they were ripped away again.

As they laid back on Lekan's sprawling couch that faced the breathtaking open view of the dark, peaceful ocean, its waves shimmering in the moonlight, thoughts of Taliah's warnings were distant but still present in Anika's mind. The majest was breathing heavily, adjusting his thin silky pants that still left him mostly exposed.

Anika still had the surprisingly sweet taste of him in her mouth as she laid down next to him, the cushions threatening to swallow her. The sight of the moon's fractured form reflected in the waters below made her think of candles in the darkness, and the Lightmother's words began echoing in her thoughts.

"You are quite good at that, Kalany," Lekan said, his voice still heavy with lust. "Did you have much practice with the boys in Blakehurst?"

The name still didn't feel right to Anika, and neither did the majest's tone. The implication that she would do *that* for just anyone, made her feel—well, she didn't know exactly how it made her feel, but it certainly did not make her feel like herself. But she tried not to dwell on it, wanting to continue enjoying this escape from reliving the events of Oakworth.

"No," she said, maybe too stiffly. "It doesn't seem to be that complicated."

Lekan laughed, rolling over to face her, looking even more lovely in the warm light from the braziers to either side of the couch. "No, I don't suppose so. Also, these things come more naturally to people who feel so powerfully connected to one another."

Anika smiled at that, feeling more like herself again. The way the light bathed Lekan's face made a question come unbidden to her lips. "Was the domina—I mean, my mother...was she religious at all?"

The sweet expression on Lekan's face slowly shifted to confusion. "I—I can't say I know with certainty, Kalany. The temple has been here since the Nether War, so I can only imagine she would have made appearances there, if only for political purposes. But I won't claim to know much about her beliefs. Honestly, most of my people follow the Gloaming Word, but the gray priests won't win us any favors with the other Joined Realms."

Anika nodded, looking again out to the ocean.

"Why do you ask? Are you sworn to the church? Do I have to compete with the Light for your affections?"

She returned his teasing smile with one of her own, but it felt forced; her mind had already begun to take her away from the moment. Anika had hoped that she could shut out any wandering thoughts and just enjoy the evening in this paradise, but something kept pulling her back. First it was the pull from Stormender and now it was the Lightmother's strange words.

"No," Anika finally answered. "To be honest, I rarely visited the chapel in Blakehurst. Mostly, I only ever went to the glowery for holidays, when we would light our own candles." She smiled at the sudden memory that came to her. "Once, Gage tried to take his candle from the room without Mother Beatrim seeing, but he burned his finger and dropped it, nearly setting the whole room ablaze." Anika chuckled. "He was always a problem."

But her laughter faded fast and she felt her face slacken.

Lekan took notice. "Do you miss him?"

She realized how little she had thought of Gage recently, especially since finding her mother. In a way, when Gage killed Renay Lawson, he severed their familial bond and made Matty's sacrifice meaningless. Anika only refused to kill the scion to possibly save her brother, but now—thinking of him from the comforts of Pyram, with the memory of Renay's lifeless body still haunting her dreams—Anika couldn't make herself care about Gage's fate.

"No," Anika said, still staring into the distance. It was only partially true. She did not miss seeing him as they had last parted, with the Shadow taking root within him. But she missed her brother. Regardless, she looked back to the beautiful, nearly naked man lying next to her and pushed the concerns away. "I don't miss anything right now."

He leaned over to kiss her and they once again gave themselves over to their passion.

Anika excused herself from the majest's chambers well before midnight. The same two guards who had watched over her since her release from the prison were waiting outside. Lekan followed her to the door, wearing an open robe for the world to see how he was made, which Anika did not mind. The majest kissed her one last time and then motioned for the dwarf guard.

"Strolm, a word."

The guard bowed slightly and stepped into the majest's room; Lekan gave Anika a smirk as he slightly shut the door for a private word.

Anika gave the other guard, Macy, a curious glance, but the woman just shrugged. A moment later, the dwarf returned, nodding to Macy, and Lekan reappeared to give Anika one last last kiss blown from his hand.

As foolish as it felt, Anika gave a small chuckle and waved goodnight.

"Problems?"

Anika heard Macy's low voice as she walked ahead of the guards, back toward the stairs. Strolm just grunted in response.

As they neared the stairs and Anika began to descend, Strolm grunted again. "Milady's quarters are this way."

"I would like to visit the glowery," she said, not stopping, her hand tapping Stormender on her waist. "I know the way; you can wait here if you'd like." She heard the guards' armor clank as they followed her down.

The lower terrace was more active than those above, with small gatherings of painters and musicians practicing their crafts long into the night, great oil lamps lighting the narrow plazas on either side of the stairs. Anika couldn't believe she hadn't ventured out at night before. *How did I not hear this wondrous music?*

There were stringed instruments accompanied by soft drums with bells that jingled. And even though disparate groups of musicians played across the plazas, it seemed as if they were all locked into the same tune, contributing to a dissonant orchestra. She saw painters and sculptors creating breathtaking works.

She wanted to linger and watch, but she could not deny the weariness she felt. Also, she was eager to speak with Taliah about her cryptic warning. She promised herself she would visit the plaza again tomorrow night, if Lekan did not invite her to his room again that is, because she was not sure if she had the strength to refuse him.

As she made her way to the temple, Anika held onto the recent memories of the majest's touch. It was like a dance in her mind, Kalany and the majest, perfectly in step with the enchanting music that filled the night, like the rhythms and melodies were written just for them. It was all more intoxicating than Lekan's wine. She arrived at the temple in soaring spirits.

However, as she stepped through the threshold, there was a dark aura in the bright room. Candles burned through the vaulted chamber, giving off a warm and welcoming energy. But despite it, a chill gripped Anika's heart, and she felt that familiar yearning to unsheathe Stormender.

She resisted, stepping cautiously through the doors that creaked closed behind her. Strolm and Macy waited outside the temple doors after Anika had told them she meant to atone in the glowery. She was surprised to see the temple deserted.

"Hello?" Her restrained voice echoed loudly through the vaulted ceiling, bouncing around between the carved reliefs of stars and flames. She heard muffled footsteps sliding on stone, and then the soft groan of a door.

"Lady Lawson?'

Anika walked through the pews and around a pillar to see Taliah peeking around a door nervously. She jolted when Anika came into view.

"Are you alone?"

Anika shook her head, motioning to the door. "The guards..."

Taliah's eyes darted from those closed doors back to Anika. "Come this way."

The shorter woman led Anika through a tight hallway, also lit with many candles. There were several alcoves that contained altars upon which sat ornamented copies of the luminary, a book she never became too familiar with.

Anika followed Taliah through a double door that was only slightly creaked open. After she slipped in, Taliah shut the door, leaving them in near darkness. A single candle burned in the room, casting strange shadows along the undecorated walls. The lifeless candles that lined the room had turned into black fingers reaching up to clutch the women in a shadowy grasp. The chill inside Anika deepened.

"I am sorry to keep you at this hour, my lady," Taliah said, turning to face her. In the faint light, the lines on the woman's face aged her by almost a decade. "I did not know how else we might avoid the majest's spies."

Spies? Suddenly Anika was suspicious of this woman. What did she want from her? Clearly she was trying to scare her, or pit her against her betrothed. But she waited for Taliah to continue.

"You went to the domina's manse?" It was spoken like a question, but she did not wait for Anika to answer. "You must not go there again."

"Why not?" Anika's hand inched its way to Stormender, wanting desperately to feel the knife but not knowing why.

"The Shadow—did you see anyone there? Other than the majest's entourage?"

Again the woman spoke of Shadow, and almost immediately Anika realized she had stepped right into a fervent sermon. The woman had made her suspect some sort of treachery lurked in Pyram's dark corners, but she was just a priestess giving warnings about the Shadow. Even the memory of the whispering and gray robes she had experienced in the gallery felt like paranoia. *I'm just tired,* she told herself, wanting to get to bed.

A small part of Anika wanted to tell the woman who she really was, *what* she really was, but she did not want to go back to what she was. Even if she was the Child of Light, here she could just be Kalany Drastil, the Royene of Karrane, not some dirty orphaned tanner from Blakehurst, running from some wicked prophecy.

"There was no Shadow," Anika said, her voice more condescending than she intended. "It was dark, yes, but the place had seemed abandoned since—"

"Since the domina was overthrown by the Shrouded."

The word felt like an icy blade in Anika's bowels. The Shrouded. She pictured the woman Naya from the baron's chambers, who tried to get her to kill her own mother. She knew the Shrouded was a secret society of Shadow worshippers who sought to darken the world to their wicked ways.

"What do you know of the Shrouded?" Anika's voice grew hard, and her hand was tightly clenched around her enchanted knife.

"I know they rule here in Pyram," Taliah said, her eyes still wide. "The majest and his vizier...I had my suspicions before—that they only allowed me on the council to gain favor with the Archbeacon in Andelor. That gray priest from Truine has returned."

Anika suddenly felt dizzy. "Are you saying Lekan is a member of the Shrouded?"

"Y-yes," Taliah said nervously, her voice lowering each time she spoke. "As I said, I had my suspicions, but it wasn't until I heard them plotting to take you to the domina's manse—to convince you to marry the majest."

"What does that prove?" Anika asked, her voice rising in anger. She was angry at this woman for trying to ruin her happiness, and angry at the thought of being deceived, even if it was out of love or passion. "What does the Shrouded or the Shadow have to do with the domina's manse? He showed me my mother's art."

"You don't understand," Taliah began, but a knock at the door made her gasp. The door opened to reveal Strolm's scowl.

"My lady, it is late. You must return to your chambers."

"In a moment," Anika said, about to turn back to Taliah.

"No," Strolm said bluntly, stepping into the dark glowery with a hand on the axe at his waist. "I insist."

"He's right," Taliah said, her voice sounding more assured now. Anika turned to see her smiling. "It's late, my lady. We can continue your atonement tomorrow. First thing though."

"Yes," Anika said, knowing that no sleep awaited her that night.

Chapter Seventeen

Hidden from Harm

Knife crumpled up the parchment, walking toward the hearth. The fire within had burned down to a single weak flame. She tossed the wadded-up message into the glowing ashes and watched it slowly curl and accept its smoldering fate.

The other message she tucked into her vest so the man behind her couldn't see.

"What do we do?" Bloom asked. The half-orc's voice threatened to make Knife laugh, despite the grim circumstances. Since the man's nose was broken, he spoke as if he had two fingers shoved up his nostrils, and Knife tended to have trouble taking the big man seriously when he sounded so ridiculous.

"We do nothing," Knife said, pulling up her mask to take a drink of wine. She could feel Bloom stiffen behind her. She knew all of her agents were desperate to see her face. *They'd be disappointed,* she thought to herself, sadly reflecting on how beautiful she once was.

Unfortunately, whenever she reflected on her youthful beauty, she only saw visions of her sister. And then she thought of the king, and that would not do. Lowering the mask again, she turned to face Bloom. "Price has proved his worth, but it seems Grip has failed us. We are strapped as it is, though. She can wait. What of Brood?"

"Still no word," Bloom said, though it sounded like he said "kill no bird."

Knife suspected he had died. If he had not sent a bird back, or reported to Crane's, he was likely caught or killed. She would not mourn the halfling. He was a sorry replacement for Ruse, but Knife would not allow her thoughts to dwell on Ransil Osbury at the moment.

"I will confer with the throne on the matter of Ruke's stone." Knife strode down the long table that sat in the center of the conclave's parlor. There were six chairs, one for each of the Guildleaders from the six Joined Realms. Currently they were all empty, because three of them were dead, two of them were busy counting their coins, and the remaining one had to take care of fucking everything.

"I thought we were supposed to sail for Suthek."

It took a moment for Knife to decipher what the hell Bloom was trying to say, but when she did she just flashed him a look with her expressionless mask. "Things change, Bloom. Get back up to the streets and find me something useful. We may not have Ruke's stone, but we can certainly find a few keyshards to offset the queen's loss."

She strode out, knowing it was fruitless to send Bloom looking for keyshards. That was not a job for a brute like him. Besides, it was not keyshards they needed; it was Ruke, and that little bitch was locked away in her little rock.

Knife slipped out the parlor doors and into the damp grotto of the conclave. Dozens of tunnels that served as Andelor's sewers connected here where the Guild guided all of Noveth's enterprises amongst the stenches of the rank refuse from the nobles above. Although, that wasn't entirely true; the stench, at least.

Knife was always grateful for the conclave's enchantments that allowed anyone carrying a Guildmark to smell the fragrances of ale, meat, and sex instead of the shit that piled up below them.

The conclave—as the Guild called it—was more like an underground market specializing in black market paraphernalia that the Guild agents brought in from all over the world. The parlor, where Knife conferred with her lieutenants, was really the only enclosed room in the conclave. The rest of the Guild's establishments were crude stands with ragged awnings and shrewd dealers sharpening their daggers.

Knife saw the regulars convening around the table, sharing short glasses of dark liquor from Guyen called bogwater. Wisp was pouring a drink while singing an awful sea shanty, the bulging dwarf's chins quivering as she tried to force her low voice into something a goblin might produce.

The human woman, Crawl, slammed her empty glass down. The gruesome scar that severed her lower lip in two glistened as the bogwater dribbled through the wound. She was a swarthy Coperan pirate that had once been lovely, but some Jathi saber had made her a bitter drunk.

The gnome twin cutpurses, Flip and Flop—whose names Knife both despised and could never get right—sang along with Wisp, Flip's higher register adding a bit of feminine grace to Wisp's braying. Flop seemed half a girl himself with all the paint he wore on his face and his singing voice nearly matching his sister's, but they both earned more than their share at the docks, so Knife tolerated the gnomes' whimsical nature.

"Give it a rest, Wisp," Knife said as she approached the table. She ran her fingers over her vest, feeling the message pressed against her breast. "Who do we still have in Sathford, Crawl?"

The woman ran her tongue over her ruined lips as she struggled to think through the bogwater. "I reckon no one after the attack. Bloom had a cousin there—Brick? Block?—can't remember, but I heard he got crushed under some roof when that harpy started dropping stones."

"How fast can you get there?"

Crawl didn't look happy about the prospect, but knew better than to ask questions. "Might be a few days by ferry, four or five if I ride. Twins said they'd been under the Arcania before, with the gates."

Knife shook her head. Not only was she hesitant to ever send her agents in the Old Ways, she knew that was no longer an option anyway—not with the reports she had been receiving.

"Ride," Knife said. "Meet me at the stables before dawn. Pack light and keep this quiet." She glared at the twins from behind her mask. "Quiet, which means you both heard nothing, understood?"

Flip and Flop nodded their matching heads of red hair, returning to their drinks.

She left them and made her way across the rickety bridge that connected the conclave's market with the various passages leading to the hundreds of hidden doors that allowed her agents to secretly slip into just about every corner of Andelor.

Knife took the path toward Valiant Keep.

Queen Sopheena Durrask stared at the plain woman, considering her response. It was a completely unprecedented request, which was both enticing and more than unsettling. As she understood, there had only ever been one Archmage of the Arcania, and there was no official method that she was aware of in regards to selecting a new one.

"You're quite sure this is necessary?"

The woman in the red robes nodded her head, unenthusiastically.

Sopheena found that bothersome. She was known to hide her own emotions from her subjects, so she wanted to appreciate the woman's restraint. However, this mage was asking to take control of the most prestigious and important magical institution in all of the Joined Realms. A little zeal would be welcome.

"To your knowledge," the queen asked her, "how is the Archmage sworn into their role? Is there a ceremony? Who beyond the throne should be involved? The Luminaura? The Consortium?"

The dark woman's placid face remained unchanged as she blinked. "Fainly assumed his role out of necessity. The role of Archmage was one that grew organically from within the Arcania, when the bickering of the High Mages became too tedious and the tower began taking the other academies around Noveth into the order."

That made sense to Sopheena. She couldn't imagine the academy operating without some figurehead to steer its operation, especially with the other institutions like Raventhal and the Vestige to coordinate. It was the same with a realm. She ruled Vale and each of its individual baronies, cities, and territories. Every institution needed someone to blame when things went wrong.

"And I apologize," Sopheena said, "what was your name again?"

"Vera Mourgael."

The name sent a shiver down Sopheena's spine, and she sat up straighter in her throne. She was suddenly worried that the woman was working some kind of magic on her, but she pushed the thought away. *It's merely a haunting name,* she assured herself.

"And tell me, High Mage Mourgael, why should I appoint you as interim Archmage?"

The woman's emotionless face twitched at that. "As I've said, your majesty, I am the most accredited High Mage in the Arcania, and I personally served alongside Archmage Lopke for the past seven years. I am trusted within the order, and I can ensure that operations of the academy continue uninterrupted in the Archmage's absence."

Sopheena was surprised to find that she was convinced by the woman. Honestly, she had little concern for the Arcania, especially with the prospect of Fainly gone. She was more concerned with what the rogue mage was up to. It was no small feat that he had discovered her secret, but she could only hope he didn't know the whole truth of why she had come to Noveth all those years ago.

"Very well," Sopheena said, standing up from her throne. She began to descend the dias, her boots clicked on each marble stair, echoing in the mostly vacant hall. Guards lined the aisle, but fortunately she was free of courtiers and other dignitaries. The queen stepped gracefully toward Vera, waiting for the woman to kneel; it wasn't until she was within reach that Vera stiffly took a knee and inclined her head. "Your request is granted."

Vera took Sopheena's hand and kissed it gently. The elf queen thought the woman's lips felt icy cold as she drew her hand back, but certainly it must have been her imagination.

"There is one other matter," the new interim Archmage of the Arcania began as she rose. She looked up in the queen's eyes, fearless. "The Oathers."

Don't you dare, Sopheena thought, thinking of how long it had taken her to wear the gnome down regarding the Oathers she had sent to Suthek. "What about them?"

"With what has happened in Rathen, Sathford, and now Oakworth, it would be prudent to assign an Oather to Sathford, at the very least, to investigate any connections beyond the harpies."

"I permitted the Archmage Lopke to send the Lady Commander Kasia Strallow to Blakehurst before he departed. It seems she had failed in Rathen, but we can send word for her in Sathford. Surely she should be passing through on her way back to the city."

That did not seem to please the woman, but at least she had the sense to nod in agreement. "Very well, your majesty. Thank you."

When she didn't leave, the queen gave her a look of impatience. "Was there something else, Archmage Mourgael? Do you require a signed writ? I'm sure my clerk can draw one up this evening."

The woman seemed unbothered by the queen's impatience. "I have a notion, your majesty. I was curious if I could share it with you?"

Mostly, Sopheena just wanted this audience done with. "I suppose."

"I have spent the last two nights in the Archmage's personal study," the woman began, "hoping to discern why he would abandon the Arcania after so many years, especially at such a time of need."

"And what have you found?"

The woman finally looked bothered. "Not as much as I would have liked; the Archmage had taken to keeping his journals in a ciphered language, one that even I could not discern despite my specializations in glyphs."

The queen blinked, waiting.

"However, there were many books on the Keys of Transience in his study, particularly a certain study on Oakus' Key, known as Elysun."

"You suspect he went in search of it?"

The woman shook her head. "No, I think he has it. He has spoken of Ruke before, only in passing but I could sense that the man had something more than a scholarly interest in the Purveyor."

Sopheena was lost, and even more eager for this audience to be at an end. "What of it?"

"Your majesty," the woman began, motioning to the ground, "there are gates below the Arcania, passages to the Old Ways. The Archmage has had them sealed, fearing students may abuse them. But I'm sure you're aware, the Arcania's other academies are accessible to each other through the Old Ways."

Truly, the queen hadn't thought much about how the mages traveled between the schools. She was no stranger to teleportation, but she personally refrained from using it unless she knew specifically who had prepared the passage. There were tales of ancient Ghultan warlocks creating passages to the Nethering, tossing sacrifices to whatever twisted gods lurked in the oblivion beyond. Sopheena had no desire to step through any dimensional door anytime soon. But she nodded regardless, knowing that the Old Ways connected the world; she was not shocked to hear that they were associated with teleporting between the schools.

"Well, it's said Oakus built the Old Ways," the woman continued. "I'm not religious, but it's clear his magic is tied to it. I suspected that Fainly had used the Old Ways to go wherever it is he went, but when I examined the gates, they were sealed."

She paused.

"And what does that mean?" Sopheena asked, suddenly dreading the answer.

"That remains to be seen," Vera said arrogantly, "but I suspect Fainly has the Key and is in the Old Ways, which means he may have almost limitless access to the entirety of Noveth."

It was quite the notion, and one that Sopheena liked not at all. "What do you suppose the new Archmage of the Arcania could do to ensure such a rogue mage did not operate with such unchecked power?"

The woman regarded the queen coolly, as if requesting a glass of wine. "I suppose the new Archmage should seal the Old Ways entirely as a means of protecting Andelor and all the Joined Realms from such unsanctioned sorcery."

Queen Sopheena smiled at her new Archmage, suddenly picturing the little old gnome buried in dirt, being torn apart by foul creatures of the earth.

When Knife entered the room, she heard the king before she saw him. He was murmuring, as he tended to do when he was reading. The Guildmaster slipped out of the passage, easing the pillar-that-wasn't-a-pillar back in place to hide the gap in the wall. But then she stood and waited, listening to the king's soft, wordless voice.

Something inside of her melted, and she savored the feeling of vulnerability that she could only feel around Markus Durrask.

The king was poring over what looked to be letters, though Knife found that a bit strange considering how much of the kingdom's rule was out of his hands. Usually she expected to find the king with one of his ponderous histories, drinking wine while he explored the ancient glories of men long dead.

To be honest, Knife found that charming, but she supposed it was only because it was Markus. Any other person being consumed by such frivolous pursuits would normally earn her disdain and pity. But with the king, she found his devotion to legacies of old to be endearing.

That thought made her wonder—not for the first time—how this otherwise simple man had come to build such a foothold in her heart. Despite the physical pleasures she had explored across the world, somehow they paled in comparison to the companionship she craved but could not have.

After a long moment of observing him, Knife sauntered over to the king, letting her soft boots drag just slightly so he could hear her coming.

"Good afternoon," the king said, not turning to see her coming. He knew her ways. "The queen has been summoned by one of the High Mages. Should I deliver your message?"

Knife had no clever retort.

This got the king's attention. He straightened in his chair, pushing himself away from the table covered in sheafs of parchment. When he turned to her, his face was a mix of concern and surprise.

Knife lifted up her mask.

Eyes wide, the king arose and looked toward the door which was securely closed. He looked back at her, taking a step forward. "What are you doing?"

Something about being in front of him without her mask—something she had not done in years—made tears suddenly well up in her eyes. Infuriated that she couldn't keep her emotions in check, she reached up in the blink of an eye and grabbed the King of Vale by the throat. She could kill him with a twitch of her wrist if she wanted.

Markus' eyes went wide, but he didn't resist. His face began turning red as air was restricted by Knife's tight grip.

"You made me send him away, and now they have him."

Markus reached up a hand, gently touching Knife's fingers that squeezed his throat. Despite being unable to breathe, his touch was tender and caring. His mouth formed words that he could not turn into sounds.

"Our son could be hanged on the morrow, Markus! And he would never know his parents...he would die without knowing..."

She struggled to form the words, her voice becoming thick with emotions as tears now flowed freely. Knife loosened her grip slightly under Markus' caring touch and the king drew in a long breath.

"What's happened?" Instead of pulling away from her, he put his other hand on the small of her back. "Where's Robin?"

"The Luminaura," Knife said, her eyes looking past the king, focusing on the dying flames in his hearth. She thought of her meeting with the Archbeacon, and a feeling she hadn't experienced in years bloomed inside of her like a parasitic flower—shame.

In a strange moment of weakness—whether it was the Archbeacon somehow using the Light to pierce her blackshard's protection, or just her own desperate need to confide in someone—Knife had told the church who she was. And if the report in her vest was true, then it was likely that they would soon know they had her son.

Her son could tear the kingdom apart.

Knife had never thought what the queen would do should she find out about Markus and her own sister, but she did know that Robin would not survive whatever it was. Sopheena was barren, and it was no secret amongst the nobles. Markus' offspring would be a clear sign of treason.

Aside from that, Knife knew what a descendant of Count Delucar would mean for their aspirations in Caim.

As it all came boiling up, she collapsed in the king's arms, weeping for the first time since she was a girl. Her mask clattered to the ground. The years of hollowing herself out and playing the part of the ruthless crime lord had finally taken their toll.

Markus held her, whispering calming nothings in her ear as she showed a side of herself that no one else in Andelor had witnessed.

"Sathford," Knife managed between sobs. "He's in the Lord Mayor's pens—if the church finds him..."

She felt Markus stiffen. "Why would the church care about him?"

"Because I gave them reason to."

There was a moment of silence as Knife let the emotion slowly drain out of her. Thinking of Luriah hardened her again, replacing the agony with a flicker of rage. She focused on it, allowing it to burn away her tears.

"I'll go," the king said finally in a firmer tone. His hands went to the back of her neck so he could turn her face up to his. "I'll go to Sathford myself and get our son, whatever it takes."

The absurdity of the statement made her step away from him, narrowing her eyes. "You don't think that would be suspicious? The king of Vale interceding in the Lord Mayor's justice? On account of some half-elf bastard?"

Markus' brow furrowed. "I only want to help..."

Knife bent over and snatched up her mask, slipping it back on. "You shortening my sister's reign will help no one except those who wish to supplant her. You don't think Karlton wouldn't look for the slightest offense to rally the pesky eastern houses against the foreign elf queen who sends her lord husband to meddle in their affairs?"

The king still stared, seemingly immune to her barbed words.

He knows I'm scared, she thought, becoming even more annoyed with the man. He knew her too well; it's like he knew her better than her own—

The door swung open and Knife did her best to look casual, slumping her shoulders slightly and cocking her hip.

"Sister."

Queen Sopheena gave her a curious glance. "Oh, I see I have intruded." She closed the door and removed the jeweled crespine from her hair. "News from below?"

"Some," Knife said, flicking her eyes to Markus to make sure the king knew to hold his tongue about their son. "There's been a bird from Price. He confirms that Grip's alive but travels alone, without the stone."

Sopheena sighed. "I suppose we shouldn't be surprised, what with all that trouble in Oakworth." She strode over to the table where the king had been reading, pouring herself a drink. "Wine, sister?"

"No, I have places to be."

"Sathford?" Sopheena took a delicate sip as her lilac eyes peered over the glass at Knife, watching her response carefully.

Knife felt her stomach heave and she bit the inside of her lower lip to keep her eyes from flicking back toward the king. *She heard.*

The queen lowered the glass, still waiting. She licked a drop of wine from the corner of her lip. "Trouble down the river?"

Knife took a steady breath, feeling all of her guile and wits drain from her, replaced by panic and desperation. *How much did she hear?*

Before Knife could think of a lie, her lover rescued her.

"Well," Markus said, turning toward the table to pick up his own glass, "it seems the Lord Mayor has not been entirely cooperative with the cathedral's construction." He took a sip and leaned over to kiss the queen on the cheek. "I wanted to go myself to explain in person the Luminaura's presence in the city."

Markus turned to Knife, slipping his hand around Sopheen's waist. The Guildmaster did not fail to see the king's hand slide down to caress her sister's ass while he raised his glass toward her.

"But your sister makes a fine point," the king continued. "It would not serve for the king to handle such nonsense. She has volunteered to personally ride to Sathford where she can kindly explain to Karlton that the throne has swift need of this cathedral."

Despite the king's smug look as he took another sip of wine—his hand still fondling Sopheena's backside—Knife loved him fiercely in that moment. The man was more cunning than many in Valiant Keep realized. With the simple lie, he gave Knife a very legitimate reason to leave the city to personally handle a situation that the queen would likely not entrust to someone else.

And yet the queen's eyes lingered on Knife, suspicious. *She must have heard something.*

Knife feigned nonchalance, shifting her posture. "Would you rather I not go? Should I send Crawl in my place? I'm not sure her face will win any favors with the Lord Mayor."

"You would tell me if you ever used the Arcania's waygates, wouldn't you?"

The question disarmed Knife, unsure what that had to do with anything. But at least she wasn't asking if she had fucked the king recently. "You know I've kept the crew away from Fainly's towers. We don't need that sort of trouble."

The queen's face seemed to relax and she gave her sister a wry grin before taking a sip of wine. "Well, see that it stays that way. Our newly appointed Archmage seems to believe she can dismantle the Old Ways to prevent Fainly from doing whatever it is Fainly might do when left to his own devices."

That sounded like madness to Knife. Despite her fey lineage, she disliked the prospect of teleportation—something about trusting her body to the whims of magic, not knowing where she might end up, never sat right with her. And yet, the Old Ways were ancient, primal. Even with the reports she had heard—corrupted roots reaching out to pull people into dark, misty oblivion—the thought of those iconic passages being destroyed unsettled her.

"I've never needed the Old Ways before," Knife decided to say. "The fewer wizards we have sneaking around down there the better, I suppose. Good riddance." Still, something twisted in her stomach at the notion of meddling with such vestiges to the old gods. But looking at Markus Durrask, she was reminded how small and insignificant she truly was. "I'll leave for Sathford at once, not by the waygates."

The queen set down her empty wine glass. "See that you don't, sweet sister. Do not linger there, I will need you in Suthek before the winter. Safe travels—but what am I saying?" Sopheena turned to give the king a delicate, lingering kiss before casting Knife a final coy glance over her shoulder. "You've always been a better rider than me."

Knife found Crawl at the stables, brushing a gorgeous mare that was saddled and ready to ride. The big woman turned, a dark green cloth mask covering her nose and ruined mouth.

"I'll take this one," Knife said, reaching up to gently run her gloved hand up the horse's long forehead. Her fingers were exposed, and the feel of the animal's coarse fur on her fingertips seemed to settle her stomach. "You take the gelding."

Crawl nodded, but held the Guildmaster's gaze. "Are you sure you want to leave? Whatever is going on in Sathford, I'm sure I can handle it."

It was a simple question, but for some reason the woman asking what *she* wanted made Knife crumble inside. She choked on a restrained sob and then fell into Crawl's arms to cry once more.

As the sun finished its descent behind the stable, Crawl held her master in powerful arms. Knife let her body rid itself of all these useless emotions before embarking on Guild business. There were thousands of Crawl's secrets inside of Knife that would protect this vulnerability, but Knife felt safe in the mutilated woman's arms beyond that.

They were both mothers. So together, they shared in misery.

But at least this time, Knife kept her mask on.

Chapter Eighteen
The Ruins of Arkath

Despite Ivy's reassurances, the three travelers avoided the woods as they traveled south. After the ravenous wild animals that attacked the sunken tower and the perilous trek through the Old Ways with Lexeth, Bennik was in no hurry to venture into the trees again.

"Trust me," Ivy said stubbornly, "I would know if the dryads were close. If anything, they are probably chasing after your elf friend and the old man. We could be back to Vale by the afternoon."

"I share the man's concerns," Fainly said. "A few days shouldn't make much of a difference, and the waygate in Arkath will take us directly to any of the academies."

"Arkath?" Bennik, who had been walking aimlessly away from the sunken tower, spun around in surprise. "You suggest we go to Arkath?"

Ivy laughed. "You're scared of the forests, but you want to go to Arkath?"

The ruins of Arkath were infested with undead, the restless citizens of the old empire now under the thrall of the serpentine lich known as Fendra. Bennik had heard tales told throughout his youth about brave Eastlunder knights venturing into the harrowing remains of the first empire, seeking glory and forgotten treasures. But few had ever returned, and those who had spoke only of death, decay, and misery.

"No one spoke of fear," Fainly said matter-of-factly. "It is simply logic. Even with your guidance, stumbling through the Old Ways is dependent on the whims of our unspoken desires. If we wish to have complete control over our destination, we will go to the nearest waygate, which is Arkath." He spun around to give Ivy a raised eyebrow. "Unless you prefer we present our motley selves to King Cedric in Menevere and ask if we can perchance use *his* waygate?"

Bennik ignored the jest, stepping between the two. "And just where is our destination? I would prefer we return to Blakehurst so I might see what has become of my home. Perhaps my children have returned…"

"The old man said to find the scion," Ivy said. "Your children's fates are entwined with the scions, so the sooner we find the first scion the sooner we will find your children."

"What scion?" Bennik asked, still not clear on how his children were associated with these mysterious figures. "How do we find them?"

"That is our destination," Fainly said, pointing west. "Raventhal Spire in Sathford, where we'll find the sixth scion—or where we'll at least pick up his trail."

They traveled the rest of the day in relative silence, following the bank of Westarrow River until it split into the Hook and the Graywaters. The sun was beginning to set as they approached the outskirts of a small village, each of them beginning to feel the weariness of the journey.

"We could use some mounts," Fainly said, motioning to the thatched roofs in the distant, smoke billowing out of several chimneys. "If we rest there, acquire a few horses, we could be at Arkath before nightfall tomorrow."

Bennik knew the village, though it had grown since he had last passed through on his way to Westerra all those years ago. The pastoral fields surrounding Mistbrook had grown in all directions, with several farmsteads bordering the river and even more toward the eastern hills.

"I would prefer to avoid a settlement," Ivy said with a sigh, "but even these legs are beginning to wear out."

"These legs?" Bennik gave her a questioning look.

Ivy seemed to stiffen and cough, but then flashed him a wry grin. "I had to carry the gnome most of the way to the tower."

Fainly's head whipped around, but when he looked at Ivy, his face changed and he swallowed whatever it was he wanted to say.

Curious, Bennik though, wondering if the two were hiding some sort of relationship. He was still unsure about Ivy—whatever she was, the Archmage seemed to trust her, but after having been nearly killed by dryads, her appearance made Bennik more than uncomfortable.

They pressed on toward Mistbrook as the sun hung heavy along the western tree line. Bennik was surprised they hadn't encountered any travelers since leaving the tower, but now that they were nearing the town, they could see riders and wagons heading down crude trails toward the Eastlund road.

From the corner of his eye, Bennik saw Ivy draw her hood, covering her mossy hair and tucking it out of sight. He was thankful that she found enough clothing to cover up her peculiar flesh (as much as he didn't mind its curves).

"Careful here," Fainly said, nodding toward a farmer who was riding toward them on a weary donkey.

Bennik ignored the gnome and waved in greeting. "Good afternoon!"

The Archmage flashed him a venomous look over his shoulder, but Bennik pretended not to see. He knew these people much better than his companions, and being unsociable this far south in Eastlund would draw more attention than if they all dressed up in motley and danced into Mistbrook.

"Hello there," came an eager but nervous voice. As the figure neared, Bennik could tell it was a young human man, probably not much older than Anika. He had darker skin, too, which was more uncommon in Eastlund than in Vale, and he found a melancholy taking root, reminding him just how much he missed his daughter. "Has the king sent you?"

The king? Bennik looked to Ivy who had lowered her head to conceal her face. Fainly peered over his shoulder again and frowned at Bennik.

"No," Bennik said, "I'm afraid we are just travelers, looking to rest our feet."

That seemed to deflate the man, whose shoulders sank as he nodded in understanding.

"May I ask why you might be waiting for someone from the king?"

The man dismounted his donkey; the creature immediately began mouthing around the grass for something to chew on. "The reeve sent a raven to Menevere three days ago, asking for aid. We've sent riders to Roskaway, too, but they've just arrived with the gold they left with. Mistbrook is growing desperate."

"Bandits?" Bennik asked, knowing that the further south you go in Eastlund, the more havens there are for cutpurses and raiders.

The man shook his head. "The dead walk here. I've seen them myself."

"Arkath," Ivy said, still keeping her head low.

"The ruins are quite far from here," Fainly said. "Where are they coming from?"

The man gave Fainly a surprised look as if he hadn't seen him there—or had mistaken him for a human child—and then said, "They come from the ground. You can see the empty graves in the cemetery. My grandfather who's been dead for over five years attacked Ulrich the smith just two nights ago!"

There was a moment of silence, the only sound was the donkey chewing on a choice weed.

"Perhaps we can be of assistance," Bennik said, drawing glares from both his companions. "Can you take us to the reeve?"

The man shook his head. "I can't at the moment. I have a long ride to Hookport." He swallowed, looking back over his shoulder. "And to be honest,

I don't care to be in Mistbrook at night anymore. But you'll probably find the reeve in The Rainy Shore." He pointed toward the only two story building in Mistbrook. "You can tell Wanda that I sent you—that Morty sent you. She runs the Shore and can introduce you to the reeve."

The man mounted his donkey and wished them luck if they planned on spending the night in town.

"I'm not sure what your angle is, Bennik," Fainly said as they continued toward Mistbrook, "but I don't mean to delay ourselves on account of some piddly, backwater necromancer. Let the reeve sort it out."

Bennik quickened his pace out of spite, forcing the gnome to nearly run to keep up. "You don't find it suspicious that we're heading toward an undead-infested city and there are corpses coming to life this far from it?"

"Not at all," said Fainly. "I'd say it's almost expected this close to such an accursed place. That kind of power flows outward like tainted water, soaking into the land around it."

"He's right," Ivy added, sounding more indifferent about the matter. "And don't forget. Oakus is restless. An incarnate is awakening him, causing violent reactions. Those beasts that attacked you at the tower were driven mad by the corruptive powers of Shadow at play in the Old Ways."

"More reason for us to investigate," Bennik said. "Besides, we need mounts, supplies. Unless you have some queens stuffed up your crevices, we'll need to do a little work." He looked back at Fainly. "Or perhaps you can magic us to the ruins? Or conjure up a horse or two?"

That seemed to anger the gnome, who lowered his head as he struggled to keep pace.

"Leave him be," Ivy said. "He saved my life, and it will take him quite a while to recover fully. For now, let us do things the old fashioned way."

They arrived in Mistbrook to find it seemingly abandoned. There was a wide thoroughfare through the village that would probably serve as a small market during harvest or if a merchant wagon happened through. But aside from an old gnome woman sweeping her porch and a dwarf laborer dragging two huge bales of hay toward the inn, there were no signs of life.

"There," Fainly said, catching his breath after having to nearly run to keep up with Bennik's long strides. His stubby finger pointed toward the town cemetery. The iron gates looked damaged, one door hanging from its hinges. Beyond, they could see several piles of loose dirt with shovels stuck in the ground; it looked like there were graves either being freshly dug or repaired. "See the roots?"

It was then that Bennik noticed the blackened roots reaching up from the graves, like tendrils of black smoke frozen in time.

"Oakus," Ivy said. "I suspect what we are dealing with here is not really the undead, but parasitic vines using these corpses as puppets. I saw many shambling skeletons in the Old Ways—the rage of the Blooming One."

"Let us find out," Bennik said, nodding toward the inn.

The Rainy Shore looked like the newest building in town, built with a timber frame and wattle-and-daub walls. The widows had finely ornamented shutters adorned with patterns resembling rippling water during a rainfall. The sign that hung above the door depicted a lily pad near a shore with a frog atop it and a moon above slightly obscured by a raining cloud.

Bennik pushed the door in and was greeted by the sound of a lively melody plucked on a harp, accompanied by a boyish voice singing a heroic anthem. The room was lit with several lanterns, with windows on three of the walls allowing the remaining sunlight in. A portly dwarf woman behind the bar laughed at a young human woman's story. At the sound of the door, the dwarf waved the newcomers in.

"Greetings, strangers," the dwarf said in a deep voice drenched in a southern accent. "Name's Wanda, so we ain't strangers no more, eh? Grab a seat and tell me what you'll be having."

Bennik felt a warm sense of nostalgia, which was curious because he had never been to this particular establishment. He strode toward the bar, nodding to the short table with the two halfling farmers who both raised their tankards in greeting.

"We'll each have an ale," Bennik said, fumbling in his pocket to make sure he had enough copper kings to cover a meal. "And any bread and meat that you may have in the kitchen."

"Got some fresh potatoes and buttered beans," Wanda said as she turned from the young woman who had been regaling her and disappeared through the curtains into the kitchen.

Bennik's gaze was drawn to the woman as he heard Fainly and Ivy find seats at a nearby table. The woman was a pale-skinned laborer with strong arms, fiery red hair, and freckles spotting her face. She smiled warmly at Bennik and said, "Well you three make quite the party."

Glancing over his shoulder at the red-faced Archmage who looked like he might die from exhaustion and the hooded woman who was mostly still a stranger to him, Bennik felt he could only nod. "Troubling times can forge uncommon companionships, it seems." He took a step toward the woman. "My name is Bennik..." He suddenly remembered where he was. "Tanner. Bennik Tanner."

The woman stood up—almost as tall as Bennik himself—and extended a calloused hand in greeting. "Pleasure Mr. Tanner. I'm Madison Wright."

Bennik shook her hand, her strong grip reminding him of Bruck, Blakehurst's dwarven smith.

"What brings you to Mistbrook?" Madison crossed her arms over her chest, assuming a challenging posture that Bennik found odd.

"Just simple travelers seeking our fortune. We've had enough of the bickering houses in Eastlund, so we thought we might work our way toward Vale." The lie had enough truth to it that Bennik easily made it sound earnest. "We were informed of some trouble in town by Morty, who sent us here—hopefully we can help. Perhaps you could tell me where we might find the reeve?"

Before Madison could answer, Wanda appeared through the kitchen's curtains with three tankards of ale. At her heels was a young halfling boy in an apron carrying a tray of steaming food. Bennik had not realized how hungry he was until he smelled the feast.

"That'll be me," Madison said.

Bennik turned back to her, half in a daze from the smell of dinner. "Sorry. What will be you?"

Madison grinned. "I'm the reeve. Morty probably failed to mention that both former reeves had died in the past three weeks. Reeve Stroth was murdered by some bandits that burned down his estate with him locked inside, and the former Reeve Wright, my bastard uncle Myron, died during the first attack trying to play the hero while drunk."

There was an awkward silence and Madison laughed, taking another drink of her ale. "You look quite surprised to see a maid steering this little ship."

Bennik felt rather embarrassed for being so shocked that this woman was the reeve. Perhaps it was because he had already pictured a tired old man or puffed up noble like Reeve Warner in Blakehurst, or perhaps it was because Madison was so lovely. Most likely it was because something about the woman's demeanor reminded him of his wife Renay, and any thoughts of her usually resulted in him feeling shame or remorse.

"I'm sorry, forgive me," Bennik said abashed, hoping to win the woman's favor so they could get what they need for the rest of the journey. "I supposed I pictured some tired old man like myself." He gave her his most dashing grin.

"Oh, you're not so old," she said, smiling back. "But you certainly look tired, so tell me: how can the reeve serve you this evening? You've probably seen coming in that you won't be getting the royal welcome—folks are pretty on edge with everything that's happened. But Wanda's place here is as cozy as it gets, so you should be able to rest off your travels at the very least."

"Actually, we were hoping we might be able to serve you."

Madison raised an eyebrow, giving Bennik another grin. "Pray tell."

"We have heard of the troubles, and we are no stranger to such woes. Perhaps if you were to tell us more about these undead that have threatened Mistbrook, we could help put an end to it."

"Three brave warriors, have we?" Madison stepped closer, looking from Bennik to his two companions. "An Eastlunder veteran, a gnome wizard, and..." As Madison's gaze settled on Ivy for the first time, the kindness drained from her face.

Bennik turned to see Ivy lowering her head and reaching for her hood to better conceal her face, but it was too late.

"Wanda, fetch your axe," Madison said, stepping cautiously away from Bennik, reaching back to the bartop to grab the nearest weapon: a rusty knife covered in gravy from her dinner plate. "This one wears clothes."

"It's not what you think," Bennik began, holding his hands up in a well-meaning gesture. But he heard Ivy's chair skid against the floor as she stood up.

"I'm no dryad," she said, lowering her hood to reveal her thick mossy hair. "I'm an old woman that's just borrowing this body. Although if you're this fearful of dryads, I suspect I may be able to explain what troubles you."

Madison stood frozen, holding her pitiful weapon up in defense. Her eyes went to Wanda who waited by the bar, the halfling cook hiding behind her formidable form. Slowly, the reeve lowered the knife and looked back at Ivy. "What are you?"

"That's not important right now," she said, returning to her seat and taking a drink of ale. "Have a seat." Bennik and Madison joined her and Fainly at the table as she continued. "I have a suspicion that you were recently visited by a dryad—maybe several—that came from the west and infested your dead with unlife."

Bennik and Madison both looked from Ivy to each other, as if either one of them had the answers to the other's questions.

"As you can see now," Ivy continued, motioning to her oaken skin, "I have a connection to the creatures of the forest, and there have been...unsettling events that have turned many devotees of Oakus to the Shadow.

"I can feel them now beneath the earth, roots writhing for anything to destroy. The dryads blame all of us for what is happening, and they are driven by a primal rage to tear the world apart to avenge their loss."

"Their loss?" Madison's eyes were wide.

"The natural order," Ivy said, once again motioning to herself. "What once was is now being undone, changed forever. The old gods are being despoiled by the incarnates, and their provinces shall suffer."

Madison looked at Bennik, confused. "What does this mean? Why are our dead rising from the cemetery?"

"Because of Kartha," Ivy said, her eyes distant. "Kartha, the last child of Arkath. The cursed one. It all started with her. She drew the Shadow upon the First City before it was even born, cursing all who dwelt there with the affliction of unending life—but not true life, only a perverted and rotting vestige of life."

Bennik cast a glance at Fainly, who simply frowned at Ivy, as if trying to solve a puzzle locked within the green woman's face.

"But the undead do not leave the ruins," the reeve said, hooking a thumb to the dwarven innkeeper. "Wanda has been there. There are skeletons and more fresh corpses wandering around those halls, but it is said they are bound there and cannot leave."

Ivy nodded, her gaze returning and settling on Madison. "That's true. The dead do not leave there, but the curse can. And there are pathways deep in Arkath that lead to the most primal parts of the world, where the dryads dwell. Such ancient creatures can carry that curse and inflict it elsewhere." Ivy's eyes drifted to the window. "When I saw those withered roots in the empty graves, I had a vision. A lone dryad, green eyes glowing with ancient, primal hatred. She carried the curse of Arkath here—the curse of Kartha the Wretched."

"How can ye know all this?" Wanda asked, eyes wide with horror.

Ivy's gaze went from the reeve, to Wanda, and finally to Bennik. "Because I am Kartha. And only I can break the curse."

Chapter Nineteen

Shrouded Promises

Gage had lost track of the days, but Naya assured them time passed much slower in the Old Ways than it did in the world above. He hoped that was true. The longer he had been apart from Robin, the more he worried what trouble the half-elf would get into if he began looking for Gage.

His mind had become more hazy down here, as if he had no true memory of why he left Robin in the first place. He still remembered what had happened in Oakworth, with his mother—the tension he felt between himself and Robin still tightened his stomach—but he struggled to recall what drove him from Sathford that night.

"I need to get back," he told Fallon as they sat next to Mawsurath's lifeless form. The thing stood like a terrible and majestic suit of organic armor. Gage imagined the creature pulling Raventhal's towers down with its corrupted roots, giving him a chance to return to Robin so they could escape in the madness that followed. "Do you think you're ready?"

Fallon turned to look at him. "Are you?"

He felt uncomfortable under her gaze, but he couldn't quite decide why.

She was a lovely young elf, and she had determination in her eyes, a trait he found admirable. His own determination had been waning since the events of Oakwoth. The further he retreated into his own thoughts, the more futile everything seemed. Which—now that he thought about it—was probably why he had fled from Robin. Their path once felt certain, but it slowly became clouded to the point where he couldn't see it anymore.

Maybe it was Fallon's determination that he found so uncomfortable. She seemed so assured of her own path, her purpose. When she spoke of the Light, it was with vehement conviction; she knew the Light was the true reason people did evil things. She believed Shadow may result in evil, but it didn't inspire evil in the same way the Light did.

"Your mother and my father were both deceived by the Light," she said, as if sensing his unease. "They're both dead because they put faith in a false belief. If it wasn't for the Light, do you think your mother would have tried to kill you as a child? Or abandon your family for a new one?"

Gage closed his eyes and watched Robin kill his mother again, Renay's eyes wide with both relief and sudden, overpowering compassion. He felt more love in that moment than he ever remembered feeling in his whole life, and when he opened his eyes to look at Fallon again, it was as if he suddenly realized why he had been driven away from Robin.

Fallon stood up and turned to Mawsurath. "I spent a lot of time down here, thinking about what has to be done. I never thought the Child of Shadow himself would show me my path." She stood before the incarnate—*the weapon of the incarnate,* Gage told himself, for he knew that the young elf before him was the true incarnate—running her hand lovingly over limbs as thick as trees.

She turned back to face Gage. "Why'd you come here? What did Desmond say to you that made you follow him?"

Gage had no answer. He frowned, having just now realized he wasn't truly aware of why he was here—what had driven him to follow a total stranger. Or maybe he did know, but he loosened his hold on the Shadow just enough for it to cloud his memories again.

He thought back to that day in the alley in Sathford. It was as if his mind had buried the memory, but now deep in the Old Ways, he began to loosen the dirt and dig up the truth, feeling a sense of foreboding as the dark underworld began to fade away, replaced by the repressed memory.

"What warnings?" Gage had asked back in Sathford, taking a step away from the ghoulish man. He was a passenger within his past self.

Desmond stood up, his eyes growing intense now. "I warned her that I would kill all her friends and family. I...don't remember why."

Gage froze, not in fear but in confusion. "So you're here to kill me? Why feed me, then?"

Desmond smiled, but with difficulty. The scars across his face seemed to pain him. "No, I don't mean to kill you. Besides, you don't fear death. The boy you love is out there looking for you—it's him you fear." Desmond stepped closer. "It seems you would prefer death over being found."

The truth of the words cut him. He had been sitting alone in The Riverstone, waiting for Robin to return with a plan of departure. It was during that time alone that he began to feel the suffocating dread. At first Gage thought it was the dread that had hounded them since fleeing Oakworth. But now that he was alone in the dark, he convinced himself the impending doom he felt was Robin.

Robin had taught him how to steal and pick pockets. If it hadn't been for Robin, Gage would never have stolen that damned stone from Elza's wagon, he wouldn't have had to kill the gnome, his father would not have gotten savaged by harpies, and he may not have had to watch his mother be killed before his eyes.

"There's no shame in running away," Desmond said, his eyes drifting back to the city behind Gage. "I ran away, too. When your sister failed to heed my warnings, I fled." He looked back at Gage. "I was lost, like you."

"So why are you here?"

The man drew a green keyshard from his tattered robes. "I learned the truth."

Looking at the stone took Gage right back to Blakehurst, when he saw Eyen's stone dangling from its rack in Elza's shop. It called to him, reminding him of the desire his sister had for it. He felt the same pull now, gazing into the emerald depths of the keyshard.

"That's Ruke's stone," Gage said, suddenly remembering it from the baron's chambers in Oakworth. "How did you come by it?"

"It came by me," Desmond said, holding the stone out for Gage. "Just like that shard of Eyen came by you in Blakehurst."

Gage looked from the enchanting stone to Desmond's uncomfortable gaze. While he didn't consider himself an excellent judge of character, there was something in Desmond's eyes that seemed earnest, sincere. Gage reached out a hand to take the offered keyshard.

When he touched Ruke's stone, time froze and the world around Gage darkened. He was alone in oblivion.

"Hello?" Gage's voice echoed, its sound growing fainter and fainter but never truly ending. Looking around, he saw nothing. He took a step, and his foot pressed against something that he couldn't see; perhaps it was ground, but when he looked down he saw vast empty space.

After what felt like far too long, a ghostly green light pierced the darkness and a small figure took shape. The blackness began to take shape as the emerald glow radiated slowly from the little woman's form.

"Ruke," Gage said, though he had no true idea what the halfling looked like.

"I should have expected you." Her voice sounded harsh and angry. "The Shadow has consumed almost everything here, it was only a matter of time before you found your way to break this paradise altogether."

"I don't want to break anything," Gage said, truthfully.

Ruke scoffed. "Maybe not yet, but the time will come. The Light seems dormant in your sister, so the Shadow may not have fully taken root in you, but in time you will spread your filth all across the Nethering."

There was a ghoulish shriek in the distance followed by a gruesome ripping sound. Ruke ignored it, stepping closer to Gage, the ground below finally taking the form of a dry, cracked desert. A few strands of dried grass sprouted up through the various fissures in the earth.

This is supposed to be paradise, Gage thought, knowing that he now stood in Elysun, or at least a vision of it. *That's what this must be,* he thought, *a vision.* He had once heard that keyshards had the power to make the wielder hallucinate. There were some nefarious mages who only sought keyshards so they might get drunk off their visions, losing themselves completely to the real world so that they may live in a wonderland of their own imagining. He supposed that must be kind of what the fey sleep was like, and he suddenly wondered if Desmond had cast a spell on him.

"The man," Gage said, looking around for anyone else in the materializing wastes. "Is he..."

"The scion?" Ruke stepped closer, her eyes solid emerald orbs behind narrowed lids. "He brought me to you, because only you can draw Anika to him."

"Why does he need Anika?"

Ruke's expression went from angry to puzzled. "So she can kill him. He will find no other rest. If he is killed, Stane will only keep sending him back, painfully. True rebirth is the most traumatic feeling a mortal can experience, and Stane's scions will be trapped in their cycle until all six are finally gathered for his coming."

Gage didn't understand. "If he'll just come back, why does he want my sister to kill him?"

Ruke's face softened. "The Shadow hasn't quite taken you, has it?" She took another step closer, now leaning her head back to look at him with those glowing green eyes. One of her eyelids twitched, creating a pulsating rhythm in the soft light around them. "Your sister knew, I could see it in her eyes. The Light gave her knowledge, but it seems the Shadow is still hiding it from you."

Gage had too many questions, but he only asked, "Hiding what?"

"They may call you the Child of Shadow, but truly you are the son of Stane."

The name hit Gage like a hammer to the chest. His breath left him in a sense of painful clarity. Sudden visions played in his head of a masked assassin in the woods at night, crouched low and following three figures, a cloaked Eastlund woodsman and a Westerran woman holding a young Karranese girl's hand. Gage got the sense that he was watching himself, but when he saw the woman's swollen belly he knew what he saw.

He was watching his family in Blakehurst before he was born. The assassin crept along like a spider, a jagged knife in either hand.

"You are his legacy," Ruke's voice was distant now, on the edge of Gage's hearing. He could barely hear her over the thundering of his own heart as he watched a killer stalk his family. "A curse on the world, meant to inspire fear and desperation."

Gage closed his eyes, but he couldn't block out the scene. He had to watch as the assassin leapt toward his mother with its blades raised to kill the young Anika, who clutched her mother's leg desperately. Bennik barreled into the killer and they both thrashed to the ground. Gage felt dull aches like sore muscles as he watched his father beat the Child of Shadow to death. As the screaming stranger died, Gage saw darkness pool below their body; it wasn't blood.

The Shadow oozed its way across the ground like a living puddle until it settled below Renay, who clutched her daughter desperately to her pregnant belly. The pool of darkness shrunk below them as it took root within Renay, choosing her son to be the next Child of Shadow.

Gage felt something dark awaken within him then, and he finally opened his eyes. But now he didn't see Ruke, or even Desmond.

Fallon's eyes were narrowed in concern. "Can you hear me, Gage?"

"I remember," he said, snapping back to the present. "Desmond showed me Ruke's stone, and..." Gage's eyes went to Mawsurath, feeling oppressive dread emanating from the monstrous form. It was similar to how he felt in Oakworth in the baron's chambers. Now that he remembered why he followed Desmond out of Sathford, he was beginning to wonder if Fallon remembered why she had followed Naya. "I know why we have to do this."

Fallon nodded, giving him a slight grin. "Good. So you're ready?"

"I am," he said, knowing that there was only one way to draw his sister out from wherever she was hiding. He wasn't sure he wanted to use Fallon in whatever way Demond had planned, but he was sure now that this is why he had come here. He found comfort in remembering, and in having a purpose. "I know what has to be done."

Fallon turned and laid a hand on Mawsurath's chest. The creature's bulk opened up to reveal the hollow that looked like the exact size of the elf's body. As Gage watched, another vision of that alley in Sathford flashed in his mind—he watched a dark cloud pool below him and Desmond as Gage touched Ruke's stone. The darkness gathered under him, just like it had under his mother.

He blinked the memories away and could only stare in dread as Fallon entered Mawsurath, a dark pool gathering below the creature. Ruke's stone shimmered at Fallon's throat, dangling from a leather throng, and the Shadow drew into the incarnate.

Do not fail us, Anika.

Chapter Twenty

An Unquiet Night

Melaine woke up to pleasant aches, the echoes of last night's embraces. She felt rested, but from the gloom surrounding the bed she could tell that she couldn't have slept for more than a few hours. There was a chill under the soft sheets, her bare skin covered in goosebumps. She rolled over to see the other side of the bed was vacant.

It was then she felt the gentle breeze through her loose hair. Looking toward the windows, she saw the balcony door thrown open and Deina stood naked, looking out over the sleeping town.

The half-orc admired the dwarf for a moment. The shorter woman's body was bathed in moonlight, each curve, scar, and imperfection accentuated in the faint glow. Deina's limbs were stout and broad, her belly thick and tight. Everything about her was powerful.

Melaine hadn't been with anyone—not truly—until Deina; and it was still a strange concept for her, wanting to touch, feel, and hold. But the awkwardness of that physical attraction didn't keep her from rising out of the bed, despite the chill, to join her friend.

Deina turned to watch the ranger approach, her hard expression softening. The dwarf's hair—which was usually tied back—hung in voluminous curls, and Melaine couldn't resist twining her broad fingers through it as she bent over to kiss the top of Deina's head before sitting cross-legged on the balcony.

"Sorry if I woke ye," Deina said softly, turning back to look out over the peaceful town. Several pools of torchlight marked the guards patrolling the empty roads below. "Couldn't sleep."

"Is something wrong?" Asking the question made Melaine suddenly dread the answer.

This was the first time she and Deina had made love, and Melaine had wanted to savor the experience. But now she drew her hand back from the dwarf's hair, suddenly nervous that she had failed somehow. She had been with a human man once, but she did not have to do anything—it just sort of happened *to* her. It was different with a woman, especially one she cared so much for, and now she feared she hadn't performed well.

But all Melaine's concerns were put to rest when Deina lowered herself into the half-orc's lap. The dwarf leaned back, her bushy hair covering Melaine like a blanket. Deina hugged one of the half-orc's muscular arms, carefully positioning Melaine's hand to cup the dwarf's large breast.

Melaine shuddered slightly in relief.

"There's a lot wrong," Deina said, stroking her friend's arm, tracing her muscles with a caring finger. "That damn Oather isn't done with us, and we still have no idea where Anika is. And I'm starting to think Avrim's noggin ain't as clear as it used to be."

"What do you mean?"

Deina sighed. "I've only known the man a little longer than ye, but he's changed. I still owe him me life, so don't think me disloyal. But I still can't shake that image of him murderin' that one-armed dwarf." She laid her cheek against Melaine's arm. "Maybe it's just being back in this place, but every time I close me eyes, I see Avrim crushing that poor bastard's head."

"I won't condone what he did," Melaine said. "But after meeting that man's master, I think the world is better off being rid of such Shadowfiends."

"Aye," Deina said, resigned. "Don't mean I ain't worried about that priest and where he's leading us."

Melaine stared at the smoke billowing out of The Harvest Breeze's chimney, trying not to imagine the memory Deina described. She distractedly ran her thumb over Deina's nipple, stiffening it, hoping to lighten the mood. But Deina just softly grunted in her throat, hugged her arm tighter, and motioned to the town.

"This be a cursed place, Melaine. And while I'll never kick the likes of you outta me bed, you could be free of this dreadful town—free of whatever dark path this priest be leadin' me down. Have you considered returning to Wickham while ye still can?"

"That's a long road," Melaine said, now pinching Deina. "I would probably need a bodyguard."

Deina squirmed slightly with a restrained laugh, grabbing Melaine's hand. "I swore a vow to Avrim, and I mean to keep it. But I don't feel right about dragging you further into this. Especially now."

"Now?"

Deina spun around, wrapping her legs around Melaine's torso so they were face-to-face. The dwarf's hands slid up to the half-orc's face. "Well, that fool of a priest may already own me life, but me heart…"

Melaine kissed Deina deeply as she stood up, carrying the other woman to the bed.

Ransil grumbled over the state of the pantry. He could hardly believe he was standing in a baron's kitchen and there wasn't a speck of dried parsley to be seen—not to mention no marjoram or thyme.

"Humans," he scoffed, settling for the single crock of sage tucked between the oats and barley.

No halfling cook would tolerate such a sorry excuse for a pantry—*not even a proper spice rack,* Ransil thought to himself—but the Cafferys entrusted their kitchens to a brutish Valen butcher named Gregan, who seemed to be skimming the keep's supplies from the look of things.

Ransil returned to the pot on the stove, climbing the stool that allowed him to reach the burner and adding the sage to his midnight concoction. He hadn't been able to sleep after meeting with Avrim in the church.

"You were there, weren't you?" Ransil had asked the priest after Mother Agathene had retired to the glowery, leaving them alone in the chapel.

Avrim didn't seem able to meet the halfling's gaze, his eyes downcast as he knelt before the hundreds of candles in prayer. Silence lingered between the two men until Ransil took a step forward, his fists clenched.

"The Oather didn't know about Renay," Ransil said coldly. "I'm sure the Cafferys hid that little crime…it would have led to too many questions regarding the Oakhold below. But you were there—you went with her when we split up. Grip told me she saw you speaking with Renay while escaping the Oakhold."

Another long, quiet moment passed.

Avrim finally turned to face Ransil, and the halfling could see tears welling up in his eyes. "It was the Light," he whispered, as if afraid the candles might hear. "Being back here, I can feel it again…it's all I can do to not be completely overwhelmed by it." He wiped a tear away, hardening his expression. "I told her to kill her child, but it was the Light's decree…not mine."

In the kitchen, Ransil stirred the bubbling contents of the pot, remembering the pity he felt in that moment. He had sought out the priest to confront him over the death of Anika's mother, but he left the church realizing that Avrim was just a man like him, being led around by forces beyond their understanding.

After the encounter, Ransil knew he would find no rest, so his feet brought him to the kitchens instead of his bed, where he might find a little bit of solace against the oppressive dread that continued to hound him.

Despite the lack of seasoning, the smell coming from the pot took him back to Blakehurst. As he absently stirred its contents, he reflected on some of the best years of his life, tucked away in the small village, away from the Guild and its plots and Grip and her games. But as he thought of The Early Mule, his mind inevitably drifted back to Robin.

He was the closest thing to a son Ransil would probably know, and not knowing where the boy was deepened the sense of failure that hung over his heart. The victory over Corvanna was the beginning of a series of shortcomings that Ransil felt ill-prepared to overcome. Troubles were growing like maggots on a corpse and Ransil had no shovel to bury the thing.

While he continued stirring, he felt his mind going in circles just like the stew, around and around, coming to no conclusion, but hoping that if he kept moving he might encounter some solutions. But his thoughts froze when he heard a sound. He instinctively drew one of his daggers and shifted his feet on the stool, only to nearly fall off as he gasped in surprise.

In the kitchen's shadowed entry, he saw an unexpected familiar face.

Deep below the kitchens, Brace and Darrance descended the scorched stairs, following the two guards who each seemed to tremble with every step they took.

"How long has it been?" Brace kept his voice low. He was the only one without a sword drawn, but his hunting knife was within easy reach on his belt. Both guards ahead carried torches to light the way.

"We haven't heard from them since this morning," the smaller guard said. Her voice was choked with fear, but she hid her expression behind a full helm.

Her companion looked over his shoulder; even in the low light, Brace could see the man's terror writ across his face. "They were to follow the trail and return...six of them went down but just Veyman returned..."

Veyman had been stammering about dryads down below, but Brace didn't have the luxury to sit and hear the man's story as Darrance armored up and volunteered them to look into the matter. The passage itself had been found last night by the baroness, having heard scratching from the walls in her bedchambers. The household guards had investigated and found a hidden staircase leading down below.

The baroness sent a small group of her own soldiers to discern if that was where the invaders had breached the keep. She kept the rest of the Luminaura forces above ground to watch the halls.

But when Veyman's return had caused a panic, the Luminaura had taken over command of the situation.

Brace looked to Darrance as they followed the guards. His friend's jaw was set firmly, eyes narrowed, ready for whatever horrors awaited below. "Should we go rally the others?"

The paladin shook his head. "Not yet. First we see what's down there." There was an unmistakable glow to his eyes and Brace knew not to argue, so he followed the three others into the darkness below.

As they descended further underground, the world was even more burned. The black ash deepened the shadows along the walls, swallowing the torchlight. Brace felt a palpable dread and instinctively reached a hand to his belt, drawing out his father's keyshard rather than his knife. He rubbed his thumb over the rough edges, tempted to conjure a spark, but he resisted, relying instead on the guards' torches.

A bestial hiss suddenly split the silence, both guards nearly falling on their backsides as they held their torches forward hoping to burn away the sound.

"We should go back," the man ahead of Darrance said.

"No," the paladin replied, putting an armored hand on the guard's shoulder and steading him forward. "Go, we can't let them escape."

Brace knew *them* to be the dryads. He closed his fist around his keyshard as he gave Darrance a sideways glance, seeing those fiery orbs for eyes. He feared the Light was consuming his friend, as it already had his cousin. For years Brace had viewed Hope as completely lost to him, swallowed whole by the Luminaura's zealotry, but it had thus far spared Darrance.

Until tonight, it seemed.

Darrance shouldered his way through the guards as the tight stairway opened up to a wide chamber. Their torchlight—and Darrance's glowing eyes—revealed blackened shelves of charred books. A long table sat in the middle of the hall, only partially burned, and black stains marked where several fires had been lit in an effort to burn the contents of the hall.

Three archways led deeper underground, each one partially obscured by huge twisted roots that seemed to have burst up from the ground, pushing away the floorstone and cracking through the wooden door frames.

"I...had no idea this was down here," the guard said, her voice still barely a whisper. A crash echoed from one of the corridors, but Brace couldn't tell which one. It was followed by another monstrous hiss and then clacking footsteps, which grew louder as they drew closer.

"Someone's coming," one of the guards whispered, raising her sword.

Brace felt his keyshard grow hotter as his heartbeat quickened. "It sounds like a knight—the paladins..."

Darrance shook his head, the footsteps almost on them. "Not mine. They're watching the gates." He stepped forward, hefting his shield and readying his sword for an attack.

Brace didn't know if he should laugh or curse when he saw who stepped into the torchlight.

———◆◇◆———

Melaine arched her back, grabbing handfuls of the sheets as her body convulsed. She felt blood in her mouth as she bit her upper lip, but she couldn't remember tasting anything half so sweet. Deina's powerful arms gripped her legs, restraining her to the bed as she continued working her magic.

In their passions, Melaine barely heard the rapping at their door, but when Deina pulled her mouth away, the knocking intensified.

"Myretha's swollen tits," the dwarf growled as she slid off the bed, begrudgingly stomping toward the doors. "The damn keep better be on fire—it was almost my turn!"

Melaine was so flushed she couldn't contain the laugh—she couldn't remember the last time she had ever even heard herself do such a thing. Deina looked over her shoulder as she reached the door. "Don't you move." Melaine covered herself with a sheet just as Deina whipped the door open to reveal Avrim and two halflings.

"This better be damned important," Deina said with a fist on her hip.

"Deina, I..." Avrim averted his eyes, but when they fell on Melaine his face reddened and he pretended to inspect the ceiling. "There's trouble...perhaps you could dress yourself so we can talk."

Deina motioned for them to come in. "Me clothes are somewhere 'round here. Come in. Is this about them guards finding that passage? If they were useful guards, they might've known where their master hid his secrets." Deina casually plodded toward the bed to sift through their garments, looking for something to wear.

Melaine typically wasn't modest, but she felt a strange sense of shame on account of this intrusion and wanted nothing more than her leathers. But something about Avrim's demeanor made her anxious, and she stood up, letting the bedsheets fall away. The halflings didn't seem as bothered by their nakedness as Avrim had, but she supposed the priest might be more surprised to find them naked together.

As the women dressed, Avrim began. "You remember Ransil Osbury, Anika's companion from Blakehurst. This is his cousin Dolly." Avrim motioned to the woman who limped into the room.

Melaine tried not to gasp. The woman named Dolly steadied herself with a walking stick. Her leg looked mangled, as if it were broken and not set right. She also had a gash along the side of her face from her hairline to her chin, which was crudely stitched shut and gruesomely scabbed over.

"Ransil, please," Avrim motioned to the bed, "bring Dolly here...careful." Ransil helped his cousin to the bed, the woman grimacing in pain. Avrim looked toward Melaine. "I haven't had time to heal her yet. Ransil found her hiding in the kitchens just now and he came to find me."

"Why not take the poor lass to the temple?" Deina was hiking up her pants as she came over to help the halflings get situated on the bed.

Ransil shook his head. "We can't let anyone know she's here, not with the Oather around."

"Why not?" Melaine asked, adjusting her leather breastplate, trying to grasp this unfortunate turn of events. She found her eyes straying toward Deina's exposed torso and grit her teeth, trying to focus on the situation at hand despite yearning to be back in bed with the woman she was falling in love with.

"The bitch kidnapped my girls," Dolly said between broken gasps. "I don't know what she'll do to them if she finds me here, not doing her dirty work in Andelor."

"Quiet," Ransil said. "Avrim, please. Tend to her wounds." He patted his cousin's hand and gave it a kiss before turning toward Deina and Melaine. He lowered his voice as Avrim began praying. "You were with us when Anika faced Corvanna on the walls. Afterward, it seems Dolly and my cousin..." Ransil looked down, visibly overcome with emotions. "Her brother, Rosh, they took a keyshard from Anika."

Deina bristled, looking at the wounded halfling as she struggled to get her top on.

"They were blackmailed," Ransil said, stepping in front of Dolly as she arched her back and hissed through clenched teeth. Avrim's steady prayers came in murmurs behind him. "The Oather...Lady Commander Strallow; she had her squire kidnap Dolly's girls, holding them captive in Andelor waiting for Dolly and Rosh to deliver the keyshard."

"Then why is she back here?" Melaine asked, adjusting her belt that held two shortswords at either of her hips. "Where is the keyshard?"

Ransil's head fell again. "They were attacked. Rosh died and the keyshard was taken."

"By who?" Deina said, hefting her axe.

"The scion of Stane."

"What are you doing down here?"

Kasia Strallow gave Darrance a contemptuous look. Her face was smeared with blood and dirt, and the dark lines of her armor seemed to writhe in the torchlight like shadowy worms. "I don't answer to paladins."

As Brace watched the intricate designs of the Oather's armor, he felt his keyshard begin to cool, a dull ache blooming in his head. He carefully returned the stone to his pouch as Darrance stepped toward Kasia.

"Where are her ladyship's guards?"

Kasia removed one of her gauntlets to wipe the sweat from her brow. "Among the dead or lost. It looks like the baron had himself an unsanctioned gate. Gave the dryads direct access to the keep from below." She slid her hand back into the gauntlet and rested it on the pommel of her sword. "I believe I killed the last one back there though."

A sudden earth shattering growl shook the corridor. Both guards went sprawling, Kasia fell into Darrance's arms, and Brace crouched low to retain his balance. Debris fell from above.

Brace saw Kasia look curiously up into Darrance's eyes—now glowing again—before pulling away from the paladin and turning to face the darkness.

"That was no dryad..." The Oather drew her sword, the patterns on her armor alive again with its anti-magic enchantments. The guards scrambled to their feet, their torches now burning weakly on the ground.

Another low growl echoed from within the darkened corridor, and heavy footsteps began to shake the ground in a steady, dreadful rhythm. Something very large was coming toward them, shaking the world with each step it took.

"We should fall back," Brace said, finally deciding to draw his knife, knowing full well it would do him no good against whatever was coming toward them. "Back into that chamber!"

The guards were the first ones to obey, scrambling behind the huge table in the center of the room. They each held their swords out defensively in nervous hands, and Brace knew they would be no good if it came down to a battle.

Darrance only took small steps backward, his glowing eyes fixed on the gloom beyond as if he saw their foe perfectly. The Oather took steady steps back as well, graceful and reluctant.

As the steps grew louder, shaking Brace's very bones, he felt a coldness near him, as if a ghost slipped by while the world quivered under whatever doom came from that corridor. The eerie sensation passed as a soft green glow appeared from the shadows, revealing a treeman that filled the entirety of the massive corridor.

"The incarnate."

Brace wasn't sure if it was Darrance or Kasia who said it, as the word filled his head like a divine message.

"Oakus save us!"

Brace knew that was one of the guards, as he heard both their swords clatter to the stone floor right before he heard their boots scampering up the stairs.

As the creature stepped further into the torchlight, Brace saw now that it wasn't just a treeman. The massive figure that stomped through the burnt vines and twisted roots lining the hallway was a godlike creation—a huge golem forged from tree bark, gnarled roots, and knotted vines.

But most curious was the woman's face he saw where the being's heart should be. *An elf,* Brace thought, in a surreal moment of calm. A beautiful young elf stared at him with emerald eyes, her body held within the strange being as it stomped toward them like some inexorable giant. It appeared the girl controlled the monster, like some great suit of armor.

"What is this?" Brace heard himself ask nobody in particular. His mind was racing and he seemed completely entranced by the woman's green eyes.

"As I said," Dame Strallow said as she took several steps back to let the massive thing push them further into the chamber, "it's the incarnate." Kasia spun her sword and pointed it toward the thing in challenge. "Your power wanes here, fool! Go back through your gate before we chop you down!"

The creature stopped, its limbs creaking loudly as it stood up to its full height so that the elf woman stared down at the Oather. But her eyes went from Kasia to Darrance, and those emerald orbs became wicked green slits.

"You." The elf's voice thundered in the chamber, causing Brace to grit his teeth against sound. The creature's tree trunk-like arm raised, its thick fingers curling into a fist with one long appendage pointing toward the paladin. "The Light must be put out."

The words sent a chill down Brace's spine and he had to tighten his grip on his knife to avoid dropping it. Fear was creeping through him, as if the very ground infected him with it. Perhaps it was the constant rumbling, even after the monster had stopped its thunderous walk, or maybe just the sight of something so terrible and godlike simply unmanned him. Whatever it was, he was completely terrified.

"You are welcome to try," Darrance said, his own voice a booming roll of thunder in the hall. "I can see the Shadow hanging over you, fiend. The old god's power may flow through you, but darkness guides you, and I shall not let it pass." He stepped toward Kasia, standing with the Oather, ready to meet their mutual foe together.

Brace took a step back without even realizing it, feeling an overwhelming desire to join the guards that fled up the stairs. But he stood firm, refusing to leave Darrance.

"You killed my father," the elf girl said from the monster's chest. "For what?! He was ever faithful! Fool as he was, he served the Light, and for that you took his head!" She raised the monster's arm, and Brace saw that each of the thing's fingers were razor sharp like swords. "Now I'll take all your heads and the world will be better for it."

"You're an abomination," Kasia said calmly, "and you wield unsanctioned magic that I shall not abide. You must face me before claiming any other heads."

"Who are you to sanction magic!?" The towering creature stomped, shaking the ground again and bringing more stones down from above. "I served in your precious Arcania and saw how you selfishly locked power away from the world. No more! I'll tear your academies down as well once Mawsurath and I stand on the ruins of the Brighthold!" The girl's voice was a roll of thunder.

"Brace," Darrance said, casting a look over his shoulder. "Go! We'll hold this thing off. Report to the baroness and call the paladins. Now!"

But just as Brace was turning toward the stairs, he heard the pounding of many feet. He imagined the Caffery guards coming down in full force, but instead he saw the halfling he had rescued from the forest. Along with him came a haggard-looking halfling woman and the Oather's captives who were freed the day before.

Each of their faces went slack in surprise when they saw the incarnate, except for the dwarf who stepped forward as if not at all bothered by the scene. She hefted her axe and spat.

"Was wondering what was causing all this racket down here."

Chapter Twenty-One

BEFORE THE ALTAR

It was the same dream she had last night, vivid and foreboding.

In it, Gage crept through the darkness with his wretched companions, Matty's killer on his right and the priestess on his left. They skulked down a hall toward her bedchambers in the great pyramid with a heavy shroud around them.

Anika watched with ethereal eyes, unable to call out to them or question their motives. All she could do was watch, knowing they went with ill intent.

Her brother looked as if he hadn't eaten or slept in days, his hair hanging in limp tangles over a sweaty brow that was furrowed in determination. The other figures had faces that were blurry to Anika, even though she would never forget what either of them looked like. Her brother's appearance unsettled her, since she had never in her life seen him look that way, and yet her mind was able to form a likeness so unmistakably Gage.

It gave the dream a prophetic quality that left her puzzled, worried, and anxious. It had to mean something, but she didn't know what that was.

As with the previous dream, she knew she was sleeping and yet the dread she felt was all too real. Her pace quickened with each step the figures took, and as they neared her door she knew she would wake up at any moment.

But each of those moments dragged on entirely too long, and she tried and failed to force herself awake as she watched Gage's hand clasp the ornate, golden doorknob that would lead to her slumbering body.

Just as her brother began to turn the knob, his head jerked toward her, his eyes two black slits boring into her formless presence.

This wasn't like the last dream—last time she had managed to wake up before Gage's hand had reached her door. His eyes chilled her heart, and she felt as if she were sinking, a thick oblivion pulling her deeper into the dream just as she was about to escape.

"It's your fault, Anika."

Gage's voice was a whisper, but it cut through her like an icy blade.

The pale, scarred man who killed Matty turned toward her as well. "You made me kill him. All you had to do was put me down—a flick of your wrist and Stormender would have sealed mine and your brother's fate. You and Matty could have been happy together."

No! Anika struggled with everything she had to wake up and banish this nightmare. But she felt something pulling her down into the roiling sea of her own fears and doubts.

"How does it feel?" The priestess' face was still blurry, but she raised the stump where Ransil had cut off her hand. The shadows took shape and formed a misty, black hand that pointed a smoking finger at Anika. "Knowing that Gage has embraced the Shadow, despite your pathetic sacrifice. You could have saved Matty and your mother, but instead you chose to play hero."

You lie! Anika felt rage replacing the dread and doubt. She was no ancient sage who had studied every prophecy. But she was the Child of Light and she knew—she could literally feel—what the Shadow dream told her was a lie, meant to torment her. And yet it rang with just enough truth to cut her.

Her anger burned away the suffocating weight that was pulling her deeper into the dream, and she embraced it, feeling her fingers slowly clench into fists as she pushed the dream away. The three figures became more distorted so that even her brother's face was unrecognizable.

And yet it wasn't enough. She focused on the wrath she felt deep inside—drawing on powers that she had nearly forgotten during her stay in Pyram—and she began to feel lighter, almost floating. The dread and guilt fell away and she felt like her eyes were slowly—

"Kalany!"

The voice jolted her back to reality, and as her eyes jerked open she saw the majest below her, standing naked and shocked as he looked up at her with wide eyes. "Wh-what are you doing?" Winds were whipping the bedsheets, knocking paintings off walls, and almost knocking Lekan off his feet. He held up an arm to defend against the buffets of air.

Anika's head was both spinning and throbbing as she immediately realized she had unknowingly levitated herself above the majest's bed in her sleep. The power she had summoned to awaken felt dreadfully familiar, and suddenly memories of flying over Vale, Westarra, and Karrane all flashed through her mind making her feel ill. She grit her teeth and tried to clear her mind.

"Kalany, stop!"

She felt overcome with rage again, trying with everything she had to cut herself off from Eyen's power. "My...name...is...Anika!"

She clenched her fists and realized then that she held Stormender in her right hand. She immediately let it fall from her grip as if it were a burning coal, and instantly she dropped back to the bed, limp, exhausted, and naked.

While her head was pounding with rushing blood and uncontrolled powers, she couldn't hear Lekan as he tried to sooth her with distant words, his hands gently cradling her. The bed felt wonderful, and she let herself melt into it while ignoring the rest of the world around her. Soon she was so exhausted that she may have fallen asleep again if the door wasn't thrown open.

Anika's senses rushed back as she sat up in bed, covering her nakedness with the bedsheet. Lekan stood up to meet his guards, neither of whom acknowledged their lord's state of undress. Each armored soldier had their halberds lowered to meet whatever foe caused the commotion.

"At ease," the majest said quietly to them. "The lady just had a nightmare. We thank you for your vigilance, but that will be all. Good night."

Anika found herself strangely embarrassed. Not only had she caused such a needless disturbance, but she did not like how the guards had eyed her as they turned to leave, as if they didn't trust her—a mysterious outsider—with their liege.

She knew the power she wielded would cause division, and she had taken great care not to call on it while she explored the possibility of a life stolen away from her. Knowing now that she could call the same winds that carried her from Vale to Karrane in her sleep, Anika feared she was losing any control she might have over it all.

"My love," Lekan said, pacing over to the table near the bed. "I am sorry if I angered you."

"Angered me?" Anika shifted to face him, confused.

He poured dark red wine into a small glass, strangely taking care to put himself between Anika and the table so she could only see his back and—well, Anika was hardly bothered by the view. "It seems you are not ready for your true name, and I apologize if I have been forcing it upon you."

My name?! Anika was flabbergasted that he wanted to speak about her name after he had just watched her fly and summon a storm in his bedchamber, all while sleeping.

And yet, she didn't want to press the matter on him, afraid of the questions he may begin asking about her true nature.

"It's alright." She feigned apprehension, hoping to disarm Lekan from pressing too much about her little flight. But she was almost more bothered by his lack of interest. "It's still a lot to get used to."

He turned around with a drink in hand, his expression tight. "I understand. And I admit, my...," his eyes strayed toward her body now that she had let the sheet fall away, "...desires have gotten the better of me. My enthusiasm for our possible betrothal may have become tedious for you, I fear."

She shook her head. "No, I am excited, too." She motioned around his luxurious bedchamber. "This life you've shown me—I never would have dreamed this is where I came from. The life I could have had."

Lekan sat down next to her, offering the wine. "The life you *can* have, Ka – Anika."

She took the cup, looking into its dark red depths and suddenly remembering the nightmare. The liquid was so murky that she could almost picture Gage's shadowed face in it, staring at her with those hollow, cruel eyes. It was not her brother staring back at her, not truly—it was a hard truth her dreams were trying to force her to accept.

"Call me Kalany," Anika said, looking up into Lekan's eyes. What she saw in the majest's gaze was deep love—compassion, excitement, lust, and everything else she could possibly want. Her life as Anika had ended in misery, and she suddenly wanted to let it all go. "I am Kalany Drastil."

Lekan flashed that smile that weakened Anika. "Yes, you are." He nodded toward her wine. "Now drink that; it will calm your nerves and quiet your nightmares."

Anika lifted the glass to her lips, but paused suddenly, feeling compelled to tell Lekan everything about her—who she really was. Whether her name was Anika Lawson or Kalany Drastil, she could not escape her fate. She was the Child of Light, and if she were to marry him, he had to know the truth.

"Lekan, I need to tell you something...about what happened."

Lekan touched her leg gently, running his soft fingertips up her thigh, making her tremble. "I understand. I won't ask where you found that blade."

It was then Anika realized she was still clutching Stormender in a white-knuckle grip. The blue stone in its guard pulsed a subtle glow in the wrinkles of the sheets and she felt the familiar fullness of Eyen's power as she looked into its depths.

"We all have our secrets," he said in a whisper, his fingers working their way further up her leg. "Drink, and let us forget it even happened."

Anika did, gulping down the sweet, burning liquid as Lekan's fingers brought her the relief she needed. Kalany dropped Stormender and the wine glass so she could grab the majest by the head and pull his mouth to hers.

Elrin was in the archives, alone amidst a pile of books and an oil lamp, when the nakys found him. He was a human boy of thirteen who the vizier had often seen in the upper terraces, and he was the only nakys that Elrin had ever seen carry a blade. He had dark Karranese skin and lengthy hair that was bound in thick braids.

"What is it?"

As was custom, the nakys knelt quickly—a quick dip of his knee and nod of his head—and clasped his hands behind his back before speaking. "Your excellency, I have come from the mines. There's been a...discovery." He licked his lips, choosing his words carefully. "The High Hewer has requested the majest personally, but...I, uh...I thought it wise to consult you first."

Good, Elrin thought. He preferred to be the one to bring discoveries to the majest. And at this hour...he was glad the boy knew better.

The vizier cast a final glance at the tomes. He had asked Saleen to show him which books the majest's little toy had been reading—ponderous tomes about Stane and his old prophecies. With that weapon the girl carried and the books she had chosen, there was some connection Elrin had not entirely worked out yet. But he pushed himself away from the table as he made a silent promise to himself to return to the task as soon as he could.

Slowly, the old elf followed the boy down the great stairs to the lower terrace where they could access the lift. Once they were safely aboard the platform, Elrin waited until the doors were secured by the operator and they were descending the shaft before he questioned the nakys.

"I can't say, your excellency. I didn't see whatever it was. But there was quite a commotion among the hewers. Lurgan—that's the High Hewer—asked me to fetch the whole council, knock on the majest's door."

Elrin knew Lurgan Fossbane well enough to be surprised that the nakys was able to keep the dwarf from impulsively marching his way up to the high terrace to deliver the report himself. The vizier was suddenly impressed with whatever cunning the boy possessed that allowed him to keep the hewer in the fathoms.

"What's your name, boy?"

The nakys kept his eyes lowered. "Phaeston, your excellency."

"Tell me, Phaeston, were you born in the fathoms?"

The boy risked a glance toward Elrin, but shifted his eyes back to the floor before he answered. "Yes. My father is a corvee. He was banished during the uprising, sentenced to a life of hewing." He swallowed before adding, "I serve to restore my family's name."

Elrin ground his teeth. He had little sympathy for the rebels who had tried to turn Pyram into some lawless ruin, but he couldn't deny the respect he had for a boy trying to right the wrongs of his father. Regardless, he maintained a hard expression to keep the boy nervous and eager to please the majest's most trusted advisor.

"Seems to me like a nakys stationed in the fathoms would be hard pressed to avoid hearing the murmurings about the world above."

Phaeston looked up, giving the elven vizier a tight nod. "They speak of the girl."

"What about her?"

The boy shifted on his feet, visibly unsure how to respond. "Many say that she...that the last domina has returned..."

Elrin couldn't help but smile. The lift shuddered and began to slow. When the doors opened, Elrin had almost forgotten what he was doing down here, being so relieved to hear that their trip to Drastil manor served its purpose. He turned to Phaeston. "Lead the way."

The fathoms was the name commonly used to refer to Pyram's vast underworld. While the city itself thrived above ground, the depths below was where the city's true wealth came from. The hewing tunnels were bursting with precious metals and gems, and there was no shortage of proud dwarven hewers or disgraced nobles serving life sentences of hard labor as corvees to provide Pyram with a steady stream of trade.

Ithyra and Truine could combine all their wealth together and it still wouldn't come close to matching what Pyram could produce from its mines. Even Copera had trouble keeping pace, but the chamberlords had little to fear from the merchant princes of the north.

Elrin stepped off the lift into the dusty landing, passing two guards who saluted him as he followed Phaeston into the nearly vacant Hewer Hall. The miners worked in shifts, with half the members of the hewer's guild working throughout the day while their fellows slept and the other half working through the night. The hall's antechamber was lined with tables and benches, where the hewers would gather for meals and revelry.

They passed through the silent hall, their footsteps echoing into the vast nothingness above. Phaeston guided the vizier down several spiraling stairs before they began to hear voices; a dwarf's bellowing laughter overpowered them all.

Elrin had to hold Phaeston's hand as they crossed a crude wooden bridge spanning a wide chasm. The old elf tried not to look down into the void; deep down, he knew he could whisper a word and avoid falling, but his habit of not relying on magic was a hard one to break.

The voices grew louder as they passed through another high archway, each one less decorated and more crude than the last. This one was formed out of lumber and rope instead of carved, polished stone, meaning the mines that lay beyond were fresh and not yet fully prospected.

"I said don't ye touch it!"

Elrin recognized Lurgan's unmistakable voice, barking orders at what sounded like a large gathering of defiants. The hewers were a curious bunch who didn't abide by normal hierarchy. The High Hewer wore the title more as a necessity rather than as a badge of authority; the guild of hewers operated more as a loose rabble, with only the corvees—those forced into labor for criminal offense or family debts—truly subjugated by the High Hewer's decrees.

"It's doing it again! Look!"

As Elrin rounded a corner in the narrow tunnel, stepping around jagged stones that lined the mule path, the walls began to glow with a soft blue light. Almost instantly, the vizier felt the presence of magic. A lot of it. He quickened his pace, pushing past the nakys who had been leading the way.

Bright blue light blinded him as he turned another corner, bumping into something in his haste. He heard a snort and felt something hard push back against him. Opening his eyes, he saw a mule hitched to a stone cart shaking its head as it turned away from the elf. Elrin shoved past the beast into a circular chamber where the hewers were gathered.

Lurgan caught sight of Elrin at once. "Your excellency! Where is the majest? He must see this." The dwarf was filthy, covered in dirt and dust that came off of him in clouds as he motioned to the center of the gathered hewers. "Step back, dammit! Make way!"

As the hewers parted, Elrin saw what had drawn the crowd and he gasped.

"We must get the majest..."

Jamira Kraiev was no assassin. However, the nomarchs of Karrane served under the rulers of the cities, in accordance with the Trivestiture. So when Elrin—the majest's premier advisor—had commanded Jamira to rid Pyram of its Lightmother, she knew it could mean her life if she defied the order.

The nomarch had to tread carefully. Ever since that damn girl had shown up, things in the city had felt less and less certain. The chamberlords had called a summit, which most nobles had taken to mean there would be a shifting of powers. Jamira herself welcomed a new majest, as something about Lekan's impetuous nature had always grated on her.

She would not lie and pretend that she did not want the honor (or sentence, depending on perspective), but volunteering for such a position was simply not done. Still, her desire to see Lekan removed from the station had little to do with her own ambition and more to do with her simply not liking him.

"Can you remove this?" Taliah asked in almost a whisper. "I have no desire to harm you, or force the truth from you. I accept that you mean to kill me." She motioned to the black stone hanging around her neck with her bound hands. "I would just prefer my last moments not be encumbered by such filth."

The nomarch ignored the woman's protests. The Shadowmark that hung around the Lightmother's neck would keep her from channeling, but in truth, Jamira did not fear the Light. She had no secrets she feared exposed, and there was no Shadow within her heart, waiting to be burned away.

The wagon hit a bump in the road and both women were rocked nearly off their seats. In the back of the wagon, the women were alone except for the crates of vegetables, oats, salted meats, and a few hidden keyshards bound for Jamira's nome of Cassith.

"Leave it for now." Jamira began to remove her armor, feeling too hot in the stuffy confines of the wagon. "And if I wanted you dead, I would have seen to the matter by now." She felt Taliah's eyes on her, but refused to meet the gaze. Despite the woman being cut off from the Light, she had a quality that inspired confessions and Jamira was in no mood to get in touch with her feelings.

Besides, it wasn't her own confession Jamira sought.

"What do you want with me then? It's abundantly clear I have been relieved of my station." Taliah leaned back against a sack of grain, looking exhausted. "I can't imagine what Elrin plans on telling the Lighthold—this will not go well for anyone."

"I don't imagine our young majest cares much about Pyram's standing in Vale," Jamira said, unbuckling her breastplate and letting it clatter to the floor. The sudden air on her sweaty tunic was exquisite. "His aspirations don't seem to take into account the happenings beyond his own city. But to answer your question, I require your loyalty in exchange for your life. I risk much by not slitting your throat."

"How much do you value loyalty pledged at swordpoint, dear nomarch?"

Jamira finally glanced at the Lightmother, narrowing her eyes. "Do you see a sword in my hand, woman? I'm not threatening you. I'm asking for your help in exchange for my own defiance of the majest. Saving your life could cost me my own; if that does not earn a shred of your precious loyalty, what will?"

Taliah laughed. "I suppose you have the right of it. Take off this cursed relic and I am your woman, then."

"You can't even touch it, can you?" Jamira looked at the smooth black stone etched in gray runes that were barely visible through the darkness that hung around the thing.

After a long pause, Taliah sighed. "I can, but if I choose to touch it, the Shadow will haunt me long after I rid myself of this thing. I will not be able to channel the Light until I can rid my thoughts of it. Some priests are unbothered by these old trinkets, but those of us with doubt in our hearts have trouble shaking off the Shadow's stain."

Suddenly overcome with sympathy for the woman, Jamira reached over and took the thing off, tossing it into a corner of the wagon. "Give me no trouble and you'll not see it again."

"I am your woman," Taliah repeated. "Where are we going?"

"To visit an old woman in Cassith," Jamira said, removing another leg guard. It would not serve to look too threatening this time; she had relied too much on intimidating to get to the truth. It was time to see what faith might reveal. "To learn if this girl is worth prying from the grip of Lekan Nafir."

Lekan was pouring himself another glass of wine from a fresh pitcher when the knock came. It was a soft rap, but given the hour he suspected it may be a pressing matter. Regardless, he sauntered calmly to the door, not bothering to dress.

He opened the door to Elrin, who was nearly doubled over panting and sweating. The old elf's eyebrows raised as his gaze caught something over Lekan's shoulder. The majest turned to see Anika sprawled obscenely on the bed, naked with legs spread.

Lekan turned back to Elrin, sipping his wine. He gave the elf his most insidious smile. "My blushing bride."

The old man took two more heaving breaths before asking. "She's still alive, right?"

Lekan walked back to the bed, motioning for his advisor to come in. "Your concoctions seem to be losing their strength, old man. She was flying in her sleep tonight. It was fortunate I was awake—she summoned that damn knife of hers and it came whipping across the room." He sat down on the bed, pushing Anika's leg out of the way. "If I hadn't rolled out of the way, it would have buried itself in my head. I thought these potions were supposed to suppress her abilities."

The elf looked at Anika warily, a mix of embarrassment and fear on his face. "They should. I mixed Blackshard powder with several other tonics, used to cut mages off from their powers. She shouldn't have been able to even use the blade's power."

Lekan drank again, annoyed. He regretted not keeping a true alchemist at court, but the Apothecary Guild was in Ithyra and out of his reach. "Well, at least it still seems to sedate her. But she may be developing a tolerance to the stuff. We need to expedite our plans. The chamberlords have called the summit, so the wedding needs to happen well before the gathering."

The vizier didn't respond, and Lekan turned to see the old man leering at Anika's naked form. "Shall I summon a painter, Elrin? Have her likeness framed for you so I might have your attention?"

Blinking, Elrin turned to him. "I believe it may be something else, your eminence—not a tolerance, but..." He looked over his shoulder at the doors.

"Out with it," Lekan said, feeling the hour weigh on him. He needed his rest if he was to perform like a trained monkey again for his guest all day. "What is it?"

Elrin blinked again, his mouth hanging open as if he had forgotten how to speak. Finally, he said, "You must come with me to the fathoms. I believe I know what may have caused her episode and her sudden resilience against the potions."

Lekan was both bothered and intrigued. He had no desire to descend into the filthy depths below the city, but there was a sense of wonder, fear, and discovery in Elrin's voice.

"Very well."

After Lekan dressed, they made their way to the fathoms in silence. The majest brought the pitcher of wine with him to make riding the lift down into the depths of the city bearable. By the time they reached their destination, Lekan felt quite lightheaded and completely out of wine.

Elrin guided the majest through the dirty halls and crude tunnels of dirt framed by simple lumber. This was not the night Lekan had hoped for, already missing his betrothed's eager body. She was a clumsy lover, but something about that made it more exciting for Lekan, and he looked forward to returning to her when the potion had fully worn off. But for now, he was stepping over stones and mule turds in the pyramid's most rank depths.

"This way," Elrin said, guiding them around a turn. Lekan started to hear hushed voices and the soft light from the lanterns began to give way to a soft blue glow.

"What is that?"

Elrin didn't answer, but quickened his step. When they rounded the final corner, Lekan's eyes widened.

The hallway ended in a circular chamber, similarly walled off with crude lumber, several arches built for what he assumed would be future tunnels. But what truly drew his attention was the huge blue stone that jutted up from the ground, as if it had been thrust up violently from the depths of the earth.

Lekan had no words. He simply stepped drunkenly toward the massive—*is it a keyshard?*—blue rock, afraid to get too close to it.

"Your eminence," a gruff voice said from amongst the gathered figures, but Lekan was too fixated on the rock to see who it was. "We found this earlier today, but it be dull and wane." Several mumbling voices agreed on that point. "But tonight it came to life, damn me kin if it didn't."

"What is it?" Lekan asked, to nobody in particular. He stepped even closer to the thing, peering into its swirling depths. He was no wizard, but he certainly felt power coming from the thing. "Some sort of keyshard?"

"We don't know," Elrin said from close behind. "It was discovered this afternoon. Lurgan said it was dull and gray, but not quite like any normal rock. But it just...appeared. And then it changed. There were reports of a small earthquake tonight, so the mines were evacuated. When they returned, it was...well..."

Lekan paced around the thing, searching his spinning mind for any memories of such anomalies in the many histories he had been taught. Nothing came to mind. "It's blue, like her knife..."

The mumblings grew quiet then, and Lekan felt a nervousness fall over the gathered. He looked up to Elrin whose gaze was locked on the giant stone, something like recognition in his eyes.

"What?"

Elrin looked at Lekan. "You said Anika floated tonight? In her sleep?"

Lekan nodded, unsure what had taken root in his advisor's mind. "Yes, the knife, it..."

A silent understanding passed between them. *She summoned it,* he realized. Whatever had happened in her dream had caused her to awaken whatever this thing was. Which could only mean one thing.

"This is tied to her blade," Elrin said, speaking Lekan's thoughts. "Which means she carries a Key of Transience."

Anika awoke with a start from a groggy, dreamless sleep. She was naked and shivering, alone in the majest's bed. She glanced around the room for Lekan, but he was nowhere to be seen.

There was a feeling of emptiness in her stomach as if she were hungry, but she knew it wasn't food she craved. She reached out for Stormender and felt nothing. Looking down at her hand, her fingers were outstretched waiting for the blade to come to her.

She still felt nothing.

A panic rose within her, and she got to her knees, looking around the bed, pulling the sheets away. She heard a clatter on the other side of the bed and climbed over to see the blade spinning slowly on the ground, the blue stone winking at her dully.

Something felt incredibly wrong. She called the blade again, and it only spun slightly faster, nothing more. Frustrated and confused, she scooped it off the ground. Instantly, she felt restored, as if she had momentarily forgotten how to walk but found her footing after a couple stumbles.

The faint morning light was beginning to creep into the room, and she slowly got dressed, wondering where Lekan had gone. But it wasn't long before she heard footsteps outside. Anika hurriedly finished getting dressed and sheathed Stormender at her hip before taking a seat at the table near the bed.

Lekan burst into the room covered in dirt and smiling wildly. "My love! What a glorious morning! I hope you slept well, because today we are to be wed! And wait until you see the altar I found for us…"

Chapter Twenty-Two

THE PATH OF DOUBT

Bennik barely slept, despite the comfortable accommodations Madison Wright had provided them. Mistbrook was a quaint town, reminding him of Blakehurst, but it had luxuries beyond its means. Despite the soft bed and cozy room, Bennik spent most of the night staring blankly at the old leather pouch Reston had given him.

Now that he actually had a moment to rest, his mind refused to quiet. Foremost were his feelings of guilt for not being present for Anika and Gage. At the same time, he struggled to remember all that Reston had instilled in him about the Keyguard, not to mention the numerous tales involving Kartha the Cursed.

Mostly, though, he truly began to fear that he might not survive their trek through Arkath, a place that inspired dread within any Eastlunder. Even the terrors of Rathen and the cruelty of Corvanna paled in comparison to the thought of venturing into the undead city. It wasn't his death he feared; he had led a more fulfilling life than he thought he deserved. What he truly feared was that he wouldn't be there to help his children when they needed him.

He was so consumed with his thoughts that he barely heard the soft tapping at his door.

At first, Bennik's mind associated the light raps with the thundering of horse hooves as he imagined racing to Arkath with his strange companions. But when the knocking grew louder, he quickly got up to answer the door.

For some reason, he expected to see Ivy—or Kartha, as she claimed to be—but Madison Wright stood before him in a light shift, stepping back and crossing her arms over her stomach.

"Did I wake you?"

Bennik shook his head. "No, I, uh…I haven't been sleeping well."

She laughed softly. "Oh, have your dead townsfolk been climbing out of their graves as well?"

Feeling abashed, Bennik scratched the back of his head, thinking of a reply.

Madison laughed again, louder this time, but she quickly covered her mouth and stepped forward, resting a gentle hand on his chest. She leaned in to whisper. "I apologize. I'm told my humor is darker than morning moods. I've never slept well, and waking is a perilous task for me."

The reeve stepped into his room, leaving Bennik gaping at the empty hallway outside wondering what was happening. He turned to see her taking a seat on his bed.

"Do you mind if I keep you company while neither of us are sleeping?"

Bennik slowly closed the door, feeling a bit uncomfortable. He wasn't quite sure what the woman's intentions were, but he hadn't been intimate with anyone since Renay, so he felt wholly out of his element at the moment. "I certainly don't mind. Thank you again for putting us up here."

"It'll be morning soon," Madison said. Bennik moved to take a seat in the chair at the foot of the bed, not failing to notice how the woman's shift rode up as she crossed her legs toward him. "Do you truly mean to ride into Arkath? On account of that…she cannot truly be Kartha, can she?"

Bennik shook his head in response to both questions. "I have no desire to go to Arkath, but the gnome I travel with is Fainly Lopke, the Archmage of the Arcania. He assures me that she is indeed Kartha, and she can get us through the city to hopefully put an end to its curse." He looked up into her eyes. "I don't quite know why…but I do trust him."

He couldn't quite read her expression as she nodded. "Well, Bennik Lawson, I don't know you well enough to know if I can trust your judgment, but there's something about you…and I have a bad habit of putting my faith in handsome Eastlunders."

Bennik smiled. "Well, if it's any consolation, I won't be lingering about, so I won't have much chance to tarnish that faith. When the sun comes up, we'll be on our way."

"To Arkath," she said, her gaze drifting to stare at something that wasn't there. "I can't imagine. You three are very brave. At least promise me you'll return so we can properly reward your heroism—or at least tend to your wounds if things run afoul?"

Bennik's eyes fell, knowing that one way or another, they would not be returning.

After a short silence, Madison rose. "I see. Well, we had best make the most of it then." She lifted the hem of her shift and pulled it deftly over her head, revealing nothing but a soft, strong body beneath.

Bennik stammered and rose awkwardly, trying and failing to avert his eyes from her welcoming flesh. "My lady, I..."

"Save your pleasantries," she said playfully, "and take me properly, like a warrior who plans to face death on the morrow. The dead walk, ancient witches lurk about, and strangers are risking their lives to protect my village." Madison stepped toward Bennik and grabbed the front of his pants. "Let us have tonight, at least."

As she undressed him, Madison held his gaze, the playfulness melting away into something more serious that pushed all other worries out of Bennik's mind.

"How else are we to sleep soundly on such a night?"

Afterward, Bennik slept like the dead—the ones that remained in the ground.

———◆○◆———

The ride to Arkath was much less miserable than Bennik feared. After his night with Madison, and a warm, delicious breakfast of eggs, sausage, and dark ale at The Rainy Shore, he met with Fainly and Ivy in higher spirits. Even if they were mounting up to meet their death, at least he felt satisfied and content for the first time since he could remember.

They rode hard for the first few leagues south of Mistbrook, finding no need to speak to each other. They had broken their fast in silence as well, but Bennik couldn't help but cast the occasional glance at Ivy, who was more appropriately dressed after Madison lent her some riding clothes. The plain brown fabric made her skin look even more green and mystical.

Whether or not she was truly the same Kartha who had broken the world and brought the curse down on Arkath, she was clearly not a normal woman. Bennik wanted to ask her or Fainly how they came to meet, but he supposed it didn't matter much at this point. He was tasked by Reston to find the scion, and that would most likely bring him closer to Anika and Gage. So for now, he reined in his curiosity.

He patted the pouch of keyshards secured to his belt.

"I know you don't mean to return," Madison had said to him at the edge of town, mounted on her own gray mare, "but call on me if you ever pass through." She smiled coyly before nudging her mount to turn back toward town. "I could always use another restful night's sleep."

Bennik smiled at the memory as he urged his mount faster, keeping pace with Ivy who rode a larger, much faster horse. Even while sharing the saddle with the gnome, she still outrode Bennik. They rode along the banks of the Little Hook, which was more a creek than a river. When they came upon a roving band of troglodyte raiders, Ivy waved a glowing green hand and thorny vines burst from the ground scattering the creatures.

They began to slow their pace when they neared the first of the statues.

"It still stands," Ivy said as Bennik finally matched pace with her. "I haven't been back this way in over a hundred years—I would not have expected the lady to still keep watch."

The lady was an armored woman wearing an eagle helm, standing nearly twenty feet tall. Bennik knew her to be one of the First Mothers who had established Noveth. The land was called the "nova earth" by the first settlers from the sunken lands, seafarers who fled their flooded empire to seek a new world, and the words had meshed together to form the land's current name.

Arkath was one of the oldest cities on, built on the shores of Noblelake thousands of years ago. The giant First Mothers were set along the empire's original borders. The statues were said to be enchanted by sigils that would alert the Arkathians to any fiends crossing into their lands.

As Bennik stared at the eagle-helmed First Mother—who was named Dame Heather Falkry—he suspected that whatever wards had once blessed her weathered, near featureless face had since waned. He stared at her proud, dead stone form with both sadness and reverence. He had grown up with tales of Arkath's former glory and the First Mothers' heroism, and staring at this relic from the past served as a reminder about the dread he was riding into.

"We aren't far now," Fainly said, his own lined face dark with worry. The little man looked as if he had not gotten any sleep in Mistbrook, and Bennik began to worry that all they had to defend themselves against a city of undead was the old sword Madison had lent him, a dryad claiming to be an ancient witch, and an old mage who looked like he had one foot in the grave.

The Keyguard, Bennik thought morosely. *My children's lives are at stake—perhaps the entire world—and we motley three may be the only hope...*

"We can let the horses rest," Ivy said to the gnome as she turned theirs around. "Even at a trot, we'll be there well before dark." She patted the horse's neck. "But these poor creatures should save themselves for their flight from Arkath."

Bennik held his gaze on Heather Falkry's likeness, his curiosity starting to boil again, threatening to anger him on account of Ivy's—or Kartha's—deceptions. As he turned his horse to follow his companions, he gave voice to the nagging thoughts. "Any relation to the First Mothers, Lady Kartha?"

The woman didn't turn to face him. "Yes. Dame Falkry was my paternal grandmother, as it happens. My father, Karrik, was her third son, the only one to survive the Founding War."

From the stories Bennik had heard of Kartha, he had no way of discerning her claims. For all he knew, Kartha was indeed the granddaughter of First Mother Falkry, but the woman's lineage wasn't the matter. "That would make you, how old then?"

This time she did turn, smiling over her shoulder and peering into him with those ghostly green eyes. "I am newborn in this form, so you could say I'm only a few days old." She gave Fainly's balding head a playful rub before the gnome shooed her hand away, "And here sits my venerable father."

I'll only get riddles from this one, Bennik thought with growing disdain. "Fine. Keep your secrets, as if we're not risking our lives for the same cause. My own children hang in the balance, and you expect me to believe you're a long-dead witch taken up in a dryad's body. And I'm to follow you blindly into the most accursed city in all of Noveth..."

"They aren't just your children, Bennik." Ivy's face hardened. "I was there when they were first born. I delivered them. I carried them out of Myrethold as it crumbled around us and Synderok awoke from her fiery depths. I found them homes so they might one day grow and put a stop to the foul presence that I helped unleash on the world."

Bennik stared at the woman, their eyes locked on one another's. Gazing into those green depths, he truly believed and accepted that she was Kartha. In her eyes, he didn't see the mystical shadows from before. He saw a mother, scared and concerned and desperate.

"You may have raised Anika," Kartha added, "but I brought her into this world, for better or worse." She turned back to their path then. "So believe what you choose, because truly it doesn't matter who I am right now. The only thing that matters is we find the scions before they begin to hear the voice of Stane."

They continued in silence, and Bennik's thoughts moved from Kartha to their destination and the tasks before them. Kartha had claimed that she could both navigate Arkath and lift its curse, so he chose to trust her in that while he focused on remembering everything Reston had taught him about the Keyguard.

He couldn't say yet how his knowledge about the legendary order devoted to protecting the Keys of Transience would have such relevance to their current plight, but he trusted Reston, and spent the remainder of their ride focusing on separating the old man's teachings from the various heroic ballads that had spawned over the centuries.

Contrary to what all the Eastlund bards liked to sing about, Bennik knew the Keyguard wasn't just a band of parading heroes who rode around the realm slaying monsters and wielding their magic relics. The reality was, they were a relatively secretive group without a name until King Elton gave them one when his nephew, Sir Branton Pembrook, joined the order. The order was formed to protect the Keys from falling into the wrong hands, but by the end the order had become a disparate collection of factions devoted to each Key.

The Keys of Transience were said to be gifts from the old gods, given to the mortals as a reward for their devotion and proof of their divine existence. But each of the Keys eventually spawned their own splintered internal factions within the Keyguard. Over the years, each faction of the Keyguard developed a reverence for their own specific old god and its Key, oftentimes putting each other at odds until the order's greater purpose was all but abandoned.

That was when the Purveyors of Light were formed in secret, and the Keyguard's undoing began.

Once more, Bennik heard the jingling sound. But this time, it was him who was shaking Reston's old pouch. He released it, letting it dangle again from his belt as he gripped the reins with both hands, urging his mount to keep pace.

Bennik eyed Kartha now, considering her claims of being there when the Purveyors brought low the old gods. He urged his horse forward, a flood of questions racing to his mind, but only one escaped his lips.

"Are you a Disciple of Stane?"

Kartha's shoulders fluttered in amusement as she laughed softly through her nose. "The Disciples are an aimless lot of deceivers. They know nothing of Stane's true purpose. That old sack of bones Gravern claims to be his champion, but he is Stane's one true foe."

Bennik could tell he had touched a nerve. He considered his next words carefully, because this may be the way to get her to truly divulge her secrets to him. His eyes went to the horizon where dark clouds were gathering over the distant trees. He could see the stone edifices of Arkath now barely peeking over the leaves, watching him like snakes rearing up in the grass.

"You know Stane's true purpose, don't you?"

Kartha cast a glance over her shoulder. But before she could answer, Fainly peered around her arm at Bennik. "It's no secret, Lawson. Stane aspires to be the one true god of Aetha. It's why he fooled our friend here into carrying out his desperate gambit."

"Believe what you will, Archmage," Kartha said, still holding Bennik's gaze, "but if all he wanted was godhood, he would have destroyed the gods long ago and claimed their dominion. Stane's true purpose runs deeper than that."

"Deeper than godhood?" Bennik raised an eyebrow, waiting for some joke. "And what would that be?"

Kartha smiled, turning back toward the darkening sky. "When I first learned of Stane, I was so fascinated by him. I'm sure most are stricken with wonder when they learn of such a man whose reputation spans thousands of years. A legend. But I knew in my heart that he was real—not just a name that was borrowed by ambitious men." She hung her head slightly. "I can't say why, but I believed in him. Which is why he came to Arkath."

Bennik didn't see him, but he could sense Fainly stiffen at that, and what followed was a short, uncomfortable silence.

"Stane came to Arkath?" The gnome's voice was more than skeptical.

"You saw him?" Bennik felt an overpowering sense of wonder, so forceful that he believed her claim almost immediately. Because he wanted to believe it. Tales of Stane were as old as time, and his name had been used by many men—beasts as well—though no one truly believed whoever claimed to be Stane was truly the first mortal to walk the physical world. "In the flesh?"

"He wasn't like the paintings," Kartha said, her voice losing a bit of its cutting whimsy. "He had pale skin, which would later mark him as Caimish to me, but at the time I had never seen a man so deathly white. He had long black hair; it always hung limply over the sides of his face." She ran her green fingers through her own coarse hair. "His eyes are what I remember most, though. They were not human—nor of any other lineage I have ever known. They were both divine and profane, full of life while clouded with death."

Bennik watched the distant clouds continue to gather. *A storm*, he thought, suddenly feeling the same oppressive dread he had felt in the ruins of Rathen. The memory of last night with Madison felt like someone else's now, and all Bennik could feel was pure fear. So he focused on Kartha's story.

"Is that how Arkath fell?" Bennik pictured a pale, black-haired man striding through the dwarven-built city, pulling its great statues down one by one, dark magic swirling around him like some evil sorcerer from a song. "Did he bring the curse?"

"No," Kartha said swiftly, "I did."

Fainly laughed. "So it's true?"

Bennik urged his horse forward with touch of his heels, eager to better hear what the Archmage found so humorous.

Kartha didn't respond, her eyes held on the fallen city ahead and the storm that gathered over it.

"Ruke had told me she suspected as much," he said through laughs, "but by the Old Six, I refused to believe it."

Bennik was lost. "Believe what?"

Though Kartha's new youthful face remained hard and unresponsive, she did not seem to mind the chortling gnome in her lap.

"I just never believed a withered old crone like you could ever seduce the Nethering's first and only son."

Kartha finally responded, tossing the gnome off the horse like a sack of potatoes. Fainly yelped as he tumbled to the ground, cursing as he rolled into the grass alongside the small dirt road.

"It's true," Kartha said, turning to Bennik, ignoring the Archmage's threats as he got to his feet and chased after the two horses. "I fell in love with Stane when he came to my city, and he chose me to bear his messiah—our messiah."

Fainly muttered something under his breath as he huffed after them, his short legs tangled in his robes.

Kartha was deaf to the gnome, eyes still fixed on the awaiting storm. "I believed everything he said to me, because his power was plain to see. He brought wondrous gifts from around the world—strange totems given to him by the ancient elf tribes of Laustreal, mysterious writings from the sunken lands, and of course his book."

Bennik slowed his horse and lowered a hand to Fainly, easily lifting the little gnome up into his saddle. The Archmage brushed off his robes and grumbled some more, gesturing rudely toward Kartha with his hands before asking, "So that's where you got his writings."

"No. I would not lay my hands on that book until long after Gravern had defeated Stane and he was banished to the Abyss. I wouldn't be able to read its contents until many years after that. But Stane's time in Arkath is what made me his most ardent believer."

"And the messiah?" Bennik asked. He had heard Stane called a messiah, particularly by his Disciples, but he had not heard of such an offspring.

Kartha turned to Bennik, a sad smile on those deep green lips. "We tried—for nearly a year we tried. But his seed would not quicken within me. He said he had searched the world for a worthy mother of his child, and he knew me to be it—it was why he came to the city." She looked back to the storm. "We were destined.

"Stane became restless, leaving Arkath for weeks or months at a time. I suspected he was attempting to pump his messiah into another woman's womb, but as to that I cannot say. I was young and foolish, and he would always return with soothing words and passionate touches. Deep down, I felt I had to prove myself to him...if I couldn't bear him a child, what good was I to such a man?"

"Spare us the details," Fainly said. "I take it you never gave him what he wanted?"

Kartha hung her head when the first roll of thunder came, but none of them reacted, as if the storm was expected. Bennik and Fainly both watched the disguised witch, waiting for her to continue. Eventually, she looked back at them, her green eyes glistening with tears.

"In a way, I did. I convinced myself that my womb was not the problem, and if Stane had sought other mothers, the problem lay in his seed. So I went to my cousin, Niles, who had fondled me often as a girl, and I asked for his help right after Stane had left on one of his adventures. By the time he returned, I was swollen with a child." A tear rolled down her cheek, pooling in the perfect corner of her mouth.

"He knew, didn't he?" The acid had gone out of Fainly's voice. He looked away from her awkwardly, clearly not wanting to revel in her misery, but also not wanting to give her too much sympathy. "Did he kill the whelp?"

"I wish. It would have been the merciful thing to do. But when Stane first laid eyes on the swell of my stomach, he knew it was not his—it was not the messiah. So it was not long until the truth came out. Niles surprisingly suffered the least of Stane's wrath, receiving only a black eye, a broken hand, and a blow to his manhood that likely made him infertile.

"He didn't harm me—not physically at least—but he became cold, never touching me again. And it wasn't long until the Three Dooms came."

Bennik knew the apocalyptic weight the Three Dooms carried, but he—like any other common person in the world—had no idea what they were. They might as well have been the Three Terrible Interchangeable Things, since the years allowed any horrible event to lay claim to one of those Dooms.

As if reading his mind, Fainly asked, "Which three might that be?"

"The only ones," Kartha said, sniffing and wiping the wetness from her cheek with the back of her hand. "The plague came first, claiming my mother. The dragon came next, killing my father and two brothers. And then finally Stane's curse, what he had been working on in the shadows of Arkath, the one that would claim the city itself.

"The one I gave birth to."

Lightning crashed ahead, casting the world in bright flashes. Bennik had not even realized how dark it had gotten, so absorbed in Kartha's darker words. The thunder that followed was a weighty grumble, as if Eyen had was pulling himself from the grave Corvanna had tried to bury him in.

When the sky quieted, Fainly looked back at Kartha. "He cursed the child." It wasn't a question, but there was still room for doubt in the statement.

"I cursed the child. It was my foolishness that created a life that was certainly doomed. I loved Stane more than I thought any living thing could love another, and I would have done anything for him." Her voice finally broke slightly. "There was no line I wouldn't cross. Until I became a mother, I didn't know there were things in this world more important than my own happiness—that there were lines I would regret crossing."

When she began to sob, Bennik felt Fainly straighten, his bald head looking toward the storm. Both men allowed the mother to mourn as Bennik silently put the pieces together.

Kartha was leading them to break the curse that had brought down the First City.

They were going to kill her child.

Chapter Twenty-Three
RETURN TO JATH

In Layla's dream, Valix still had her head. The elf traced her fingers around the swirling tattoos along its scalp. Her hair was starting to roughly grow in, but it felt nice on Layla's fingertips, scratching tiny itches that she herself could never scratch.

As she stared into the woman's eyes, Layla knew it was a dream, but savored it nonetheless, knowing at any moment the ship might rock again and she would be thrown back into the cruel world that had separated her from what might have been her only true love.

It happened too quickly.

Valix's lips parted as if to speak, but the foggy world surrounding them shifted sickeningly and Layla felt herself lift into the air, weightless. Slowly, a bloody line separated Valix's head from her strained, tattooed neck, the skin peeling away like wisps of silk against a burning blade. The Disciple's lips turned icy blue, then a rotting violet, before blackening completely.

As Layla relived the beheading, the dream faded away, ever so slowly and far too fast. She floated into a cold reckoning.

The elf's body slammed to the damp floor, the waking world's creaks, shouts, and angry thunder drowning out any merciful splendor she may have found in sleep. Her body felt ragged, and she struggled to push herself up. The shackles around her wrist felt like they had just been pulled from a forge, but she didn't smell burning flesh, so she gently touched the black metal with her finger.

Nothing.

She felt nothing, as if she wasn't touching anything.

"They're forged from blackshards."

Layla struggled to raise her head enough to see who spoke. It was dark below deck, not even the windows provided enough light to see. *The storm,* Layla thought, hearing a roll of thunder as if in response. Her eyes slowly adjusted and she saw a figure seated on a nearby barrel.

"I wouldn't try any spells while wearing them," the figure warned, shifting enough in her seat for Layla to make out a womanly form. "You'll get quite a headache for your efforts and little else."

Layla had no reason to doubt the warning; even without anti-magic, she felt too weak and sick to focus on channeling anything. And she didn't feel the book's presence nearby—certainly her abductors had taken it.

"Who are you?" Layla wasn't sure why she asked; she didn't care. All she wanted was to go back to sleep, forever.

"Just a thief," the woman said, leaning forward into the faint light coming from the window. Layla could see she was a dark elf, her deep violet skin looking almost silver in the gloom. "Like you, Layla Abrigale."

"So you know my name but I can't know yours?"

"There are only a few that know my name." She stood up as the ship swayed once more, but the self-proclaimed thief had a cat's grace, barely seeming to notice the lurch that made Layla want to vomit. "But you may call me Grip."

"Guild scum." Layla felt a dull ache in her head and pressed two weak fingers to her temple. Grip seemed amused, as if she had caused it. She stepped silently toward Layla.

"I heard a story once, about a mage in Raventhal. Nasty piece of work, she was, but powerful. The good ones are always a little unstable." Grip knelt down on one knee, her presence like a heavy shadow falling over Layla. The elf could smell the distinct aroma of Westerran wine on her captor's breath. One of her eyes didn't look quite right. "Aren't they?"

Layla felt the ache in her head strengthen, a cramp forming in her stomach. "What are you doing?"

"Me?" Grip gave another scoff. "Not a thing. It's you that's letting your emotions take control. That pain you feel is magic, and you can't help but reach for it, can you? But those shackles will kill you before they let you touch it. You see, you remind me of her—the girl from Raventhal. I never met her, but in my line of work, learning about strangers—even those far away—has its value."

"What value am I to you?" Layla knew there was a game here, otherwise her head would have been removed as well. The thought rekindled the memory of Valix's head spiraling through the air and gently splashing into the sea, and her stomach finally had enough.

Grip kept still as a statue while the mage emptied her stomach onto the floor. The ship's rocking had steadied now, and the flash of lightning that lit the spoiled floorboards was weak and distant.

"That is still to be seen," Grip said, her voice gentler. She crossed her legs and returned to her seat now that the storm had apparently begun to pass. "There is much I still don't know about how you came by the book and became thrown in with the Disciples—quite an unsavory and unruly lot, if you ask me—but what I do know is you departed Andelor with Desmond Everton."

That name seemed to settle Layla's stomach, hardening her. In reality, it was probably the act of vomiting that truly relieved her nausea, but just hearing her tormentor's name spoken aloud made her emotional resolve tighten.

Grip must have noticed. "I won't pretend to know the exact nature of your relationship with the man, but he was the queen's personal mage. He was the one who chose you to succeed Klara after he killed her—oh, you didn't know about that? Regardless, you both went to Jath to retrieve that book, even though Knife warned it would be a fruitless quest. Yet, now we find you alone with the *Book of Stane*, taking it to Xe'dann with a Disciple."

Layla didn't answer. She slowly wiped her mouth with the back of her manacled hand and turned to face the dark elf.

Grip gave her an oddly friendly smile. "I can only suspect that Desmond died and you felt reluctant to return that news to the queen. You don't strike me as someone eager to engage in deception, which is what returning to Andelor alone might require. Also, I would guess that the woman Jaffron killed was important to you—important enough that you would join a fanatical religious order for her, one you have shown no interest in throughout your life."

Layla watched the woman accurately summarize the events that led her here with remarkable accuracy, wondering if it was some sort of witchcraft. *No*, Layla thought, remembering the few Guild agents she had seen operate in Andelor, *she relies on something much more cunning than magic.*

A sudden ray of light shone through the window, bathing Grip's dark skin and turning it a soft violet. "All this tells me that Desmond had you under a spell, and when it broke, he paid the price."

Layla tried desperately to keep her face hard, but the tears felt like grave worms, digging their way up through the dirt Layla had piled atop those horrid memories. She broke and began sobbing, turning away from Grip and hiding her face in the crook of her arm.

She didn't cry for Desmond's death—she had already convinced herself that he deserved to die for what he had done—she wept for everything that followed. While she believed she had fallen in love with Valix, the rational part of her mind knew that the circumstances of their meeting likely played a huge part in her feelings for the Disciple.

A deep sense of shame took root in her as she wept away the pent-up sorrow. She felt like she had given up control of her life after killing Desmond; not that Valix had manipulated her—at least Layla hoped that wasn't the case—but she couldn't deny her head wasn't in the right place to be making such drastic decisions; like running away from her duties as the queen's personal mage, or joining the Disciples of Stane on a whim.

She continued to cry, not caring that some Guild agent watched as she fell apart. But after a few mournful sobs, Layla felt the shame and guilt lessen. She had needed to cry, but it was done now, and she refused to let herself become a pitiful creature waiting to be saved again. Layla dried her eyes and turned around.

But Grip was gone.

"She's gone," Layla said, sitting up, unsure of who she was speaking to.

"Yes," Stane said, "but I am not."

Above deck, the sun was shining and the briny smell of the open sea was replaced by the wafting aromas from Caraby.

Grip felt her spirits lift as the port came into view. She had only been to Jath twice before, and to Caraby only once, but it was when she and Ransil had first embraced their affections for each other. She remembered clambering across those steepled rooftops with the halfling, spying on the Coperan lords who conspired to take the Vale throne before Sopheena won it by rights.

We saved the kingdom, she thought morosely, *and nobody would ever know. Just like no one would ever know of our true love for one another.*

That thought conjured up the images that Ransil had once put in her mind of them settling down in a cottage in the Acreage, while he ran a tavern and she did whatever a dark elf might do in halfling country.

Grip smiled sadly at the thought, but the visions of them prowling the rooftops and growing old in Westerra darkened when Jaffron's face appeared over the railing above her, his sinister smile reminding her that those days were dead and buried.

"How's our guest?"

The prisoner was not what she had been expecting, especially after Jaffron's accusations. Grip had known killers, and Layla Abrigale was no killer—you have to do more than kill to be a killer.

"Awake," Grip offered, turning to lean against the rail overlooking the sea. She focused on the sights of Jath instead of *Revery*'s crew scrambling about to prepare for docking. "I think your little bracelets will hold while she recovers from whatever it was that let her kill that dragon. But once she's rested..."

Grip didn't even know what the woman was fully capable of. She hadn't been lying when she told Lyla that her reputation preceded her. But what Grip witnessed two days ago was beyond anything she had ever seen or even heard of outside of drunken fable.

Jaffron's fine boots clacked loudly as he descended from the ship's helm—*clack, clack, clack*—and strode over to Grip—*clack, clack, clack*—so he could lean on the railing next to her, observing Caraby as the ship glided across the calm waters.

"We won't need them to hold much longer." Grip smelled Caimish wine on Jaffron's breath, which nearly conjured up childhood memories that she had banished long ago. Fortunately, she was too distracted by his words to let the ghosts fully materialize.

Grip kept her eyes steady on the horizon. "What do you need her for?"

Jaffron peered at her. She could see his devilish grin and captivating eyes out of the corner of hers, but she kept her own expression flat and her eyes distant.

"Who says I have need of some traitor witch?"

"Save it, Jaff. If she wasn't worth something to you, her head would be sinking with that Disciple's." She turned to look at him now, keeping her face earnest to contrast his disarming mask. "Just tell me the play."

His smile didn't change—*why are the slimiest men the most handsome?*—but his posture seemed to relax a bit, his shoulders slumping and his hips leaning against the rail. "That's complicated." He nodded toward Caraby as *Revery* eased into the harbor. "I should probably let them explain."

"Them?"

A dwarven sailor that reeked of piss and spoke like his tongue filled his entire mouth told Layla to cover her head with a sack. Not even caring what awaited her anymore, she did as she was bid, and the man gruffly led her out of her cage—which was actually not much different than her quarters on *Severynth*, except for the distinct lack of bedding.

Layla's clothes were in tatters, and she couldn't even be sure she was fully covered as she shuffled up the stairs. But as her shackles were continuously tugged by her swollen-tongued jailor, she couldn't make herself care if she died naked or clothed.

Just as long as she died sooner rather than later.

He led her to another set of stairs, and as she tripped on the first step and bashed her shin, she found herself wishing that she had been less nasty to the dark elf—she seemed to share a bit of sympathy with her, even if she had disappeared on her during her grief. There was the faintest hint of camaraderie there that made her think of Valix.

But thinking of Valix just made her heart break again and the urge to shove herself away from the dwarf and find the quickest rail to throw herself over was almost too tempting to resist. But something kept her in check—weariness, most likely. *Gods, am I weary,* she thought, as if she had forgotten—and eventually she felt the cool breeze on her skin. A parrot cawed in the distance, and the voice of men and women docking the ship surrounded her.

Suddenly, as the wind gently flowed through her hair, death didn't feel so urgent to Layla. But Jaffron's voice ruined the serene interlude almost immediately.

"Ah, our most esteemed guest. Dickie, take that rag off her head. Honestly..."

The dwarf grabbed a bit of her hair when pulling the bag off her head, but the pain it caused was diminished by the bright light that blinded her. She raised her hands against the burning sunlight, as if she had been in a cave for the past year.

Still blinded, Layla heard a different yet familiar voice.

"And get those shackles off her. I do hope you don't intend to treat all your passengers thusly—I may seek other means of transport."

"A necessary precaution," Jaffron said with annoyance in his voice. "She stays chained for now." Footsteps. Layla recoiled when he added, "For how long is up to her."

Layla still couldn't see, but she imagined the face of Valix's killer within a hand's span of her own, and a deep vengeful part of her wanted to test the shackles. She imagined setting her hands on fire and grabbing hold of the elf lord's pretty face—but in her mind it was Desmond's face, burning under her touch.

"You can do it," Stane whispered.

And that stayed her. She would die, and take others with her, but she would not be a puppet.

Never again.

Layla took a deep breath, savoring the open sea air, and slowly opened her eyes. As her vision adjusted to the bright sunlight, she could see the empty blue horizons of the Racivic Sea replaced by the loud, bustling port of Caraby. *No, not here,* she thought, not wanting to relive the hazy memories of the last time she was here. Desmond's wretched phantom fingers were already creeping up her thighs and she squirmed reflexively away from them.

"Welcome back to Jath, my lovely elf witch."

Layla's eyes went from the familiar steeped walls of Caraby's tiered cove to another familiar sight. *It can't be,* she thought, eyeing the figure with suspicion. The face was unmistakable, fine features accentuated with flawless makeup, framed by the short silver and deep green hair. But the body was very different—still of no discernable sex, but different nonetheless.

Most notably, the body was standing on two sturdy legs.

"Maze?"

A kind smile spread across their face and they bent over in a formal bow. Not only was Maze standing on two perfectly good legs, but the body that Layla had assumed was bloated and misshapen during their last encounter in The Wresting Tide was anything but. Tall and broad shouldered, Maze cut an imposing figure, but carried themselves with the grace of a queen.

"As I live and breathe," Maze said with a flourish of their hand, standing tall again. "You will excuse my little deception when last we met. But it was on account of your late accomplice." Stepping forward, the mirth left Maze's face. "I never trusted Desmond Everton."

A thousand questions raced through Layla's mind, but only one seemed to matter to her at the moment. "Did you know?"

"Yes," Maze said, taking Layla's hands in her own. They were soft hands, and Layla could smell a floral fragrance from them as Maze drew Layla's fingers to her lips. The kiss was so unexpected, Layla didn't resist—she was too weak to do much but stand there. "I knew what he was, and I knew he had you prisoner." Maze shook the shackles. "Get these off her now."

"Why…" Layla didn't know what she wanted to ask, and the sob caught in her throat prevented her from even doing so. As she began to cry, someone was fiddling with the shackles around her wrists.

"You had to free yourself," Maze said sternly, with no emotion. She let go of Layla's hands. "His power over you was drawn from the Shadow, I could feel it. Years old, it was, and dripping with cold hatred wrapped up in false love. Not even I could have dispelled that."

A great weight was lifted off Layla's shoulders as the black chains clattered to the floor.

"This is a mistake," Jaffron warned, in a voice that sounded far too unconcerned to be issuing any warnings. "I don't think you fully understand what this elf is capable of."

"Which means she is not one you want to remain an enemy of," Maze said, casting Jaffron an annoyed look. "Though you killed the woman who helped her escape the clutches of her abuser, so there's little hope we can keep her from putting an end to you eventually."

Jaffron scoffed. "The Disciple killed Sauthorn. How else would I be able to make sense of your precious visions if I didn't avenge him? Her existence was clouding—"

"Enough." Maze's voice quieted the entire ship, halting the work of making port. Jaffron's crew stopped scurrying about the deck and they all studied the tall individual that commanded their captain. "Meet us in the Tide once you're done here. You too, Grip." Maze's eyes fell back on a stunned Layla. "If you'll be good enough to come with me, I will answer all your questions."

Unlike Maze, The Wresting Tide was exactly how Layla remembered it. However, she had hoped to never see it again. Without Valix, every cursed memory of Jath that came to her mind was poisoned by Desmond's ghost.

As she sat down at the same table Maze had met her at before, an unbidden vision came to Layla of her and Desmond writhing around in the bed above. Her stomach heaved in response and she wanted to rid her body of the foulness, but she had thrown everything up back on the ship.

"Seasick?" Maze set a cup of wine down for her, but Layla couldn't even find the strength to lift her arms to drink it. She had never felt so physically exhausted.

"Why am I here?"

Maze let out a little laugh. "If I told you because a prophecy decreed it, would that suffice? No, I supposed it wouldn't. As to why you're in Jath, I will require Jaffron's presence to explain." Maze sat down, opening their short coat to reveal a frilly blue top. "Why you're here back in my establishment is so I can convince you to not kill Jaffron."

Layla felt a surge of fury awaken her limbs and she clenched a fist. "That monster took off Valix's head as if it were nothing..."

"Jaffron Casryk is a cruel, heartless, and vain bastard," Maze said with abundant calm. "But you have to understand—the Disciples of Stane have done far worse to his kind..."

His kind? Layla's rage was stilled by sudden confusion. "You mean high elves?"

"Prophets. There are not many left to this world, and the Disciples have taken to butchering those that they are able to root out. Your Valix kidnapped Sauthorn from his home in Velcarthe, brutally murdering his family in the process."

Even as the words slithered into her mind like poisonous vipers, she could still see the tattooed woman she loved, naked on their bed in *Severynth*'s hold. She remembered Valix's eyes perfectly—or so she thought—but in the memory they were orbs of gray fog.

Grip appeared then as if from nowhere and pulled up a chair, spinning it around so she could straddle the back of it as she joined them at the table.

Maze continued. "I won't paint Sauthorn as some sort of martyr. He was a fine man, but he used his visions for trivial—some might say greedy—pursuits.

And he lived a longer life than any of us were meant to. Still," Maze shook their head, looking down at something that wasn't there while taking a drawn-out sip of wine, "I would not wish his fate on anyone."

Layla was feeling lightheaded, and she forced herself to lift her weary arms enough to take a drink of her own wine. She couldn't shake the memories of Valix—the woman she knew and loved—standing naked with her on the Jathi plains, both of them splashed with Desmond's blood. And then she watched Desmond die again, but this time Valix tore off his flesh with long shadowy tendrils. The wine burned as it went down her throat.

"Bastard cost me my eye," Grip said, setting her empty cup on the table and wiping her lips with the back of her gloved hand. "I won't miss him, but I can't say I'm thrilled with his successor." Layla now noticed the dark elf's glass eye, which was darker than her other.

As if in response, the door to the Tide opened. Layla looked over her shoulder to see Valix's killer saunter in. The arrogance that Jaffron exuded made it nearly impossible for Layla to feel the slightest bit of sympathy for the man, despite Maze's words.

As she watched Jaffron approach their table, she couldn't stop picturing Valix's head spinning in the air. Her stomach lurched again, but she settled it with another sip of wine.

"You're next."

Layla stiffened, and turned back to Jaffron. The man wore his casual, condescending grin, but his lips didn't move when she heard the voice again.

"Next time it will be *your* head."

Stane, Layla realized.

It was then that she saw the book under Jaffron's arm; the man was carrying it as if it were just some high lord's ledger and not the rarest tome in the world.

"Honestly, Casryk," Maze said with uncharacteristic annoyance. "Your kin died for that book, the least you can do is conceal it while you prance about the busiest port in the world."

Jaffron casually dropped the item in question on the table, nearly upending all the cups of wine as it shook the table under its weight. "The chances that any of those miscreants out there care about a damn book are about the same as Grip here still being a maiden."

"Not all of us can be as chaste as you, Jaff." Grip leaned forward with her elbows on the table as Jaffron pulled up a chair. "Tell me: have you even tried it without having to pay?"

"Enough," Maze said, placing a hand on the book. "We have too much to discuss."

Layla visibly stiffened as Jaffron scooted his chair in between her and Grip. There was a vile fluttering in her chest with the realization that he was close enough for her to strangle. She pictured wrapping her hands around the pale neck beneath that fine coat collar, her fingers turning into groping black tendrils as they snaked around Jaffron's throat and tightened.

"Do it," Stane said again.

"But first thing's first," Maze said, giving Jaffron a smoldering gaze. "You will apologize to Lady Abrigale for your rashness in handling the Disciple situation."

Jaffron's casual harrumph in response strengthened Layla, fury replacing the weariness that had kept her so docile in the company of these fiends. She clenched her fists, her eyes fixed on the book. Stane's whispers continued.

"We have much to discuss," Maze said sternly. "Do not waste our time."

Jaffron planted both hands on the table and sighed. "My lady, I humbly ask for your forgiveness. I was blinded by revenge and haunted by the visions that I am now cursed with."

A sudden, unexpected chill in Layla's chest stilled her growing rage. Never would she have imagined such a man asking for her forgiveness. She would not give it, of course, but the shock caused her to unclench her fists ever so slightly.

It was Grip's turn to harrumph. "Wow. I almost believe that."

"You wouldn't know what it's like, bitch," Jaffron snapped, anger finally finding its way into his voice. "My sister was the one who was supposed to shoulder this, not me. Beatrim was born for prophecy, not me! But that Oather killed her!"

"Enough," Maze said with surprising calm. "We have treason to discuss, and time is short."

The single word drew all eyes and hushed Stane's whispers.

"I know each of you have sworn fealty to Queen Sopheena, in one way or another. But it seems fate has brought us together in order to thwart what I fear might be the undoing of the Joined Realms."

Grip moved to speak, but Maze held up a hand.

"I know Nipheena—sorry, Knife—has the Guild working to maintain order in Vale, but it is a great deception. Their intentions lie in Caim. They want this," Maze tapped the book, "so they can resurrect their father, Count Delucar, and give Noveth over to the vampires."

Layla noticed Grip's face change at the mention of that name, and the dark elf leaned forward. "Why would Sopheena want to give up her queendom for her father who she helped put down?"

Jaffron knocked on the table and motioned to Layla. "That's what we need her to help us find out."

"Me? Why would you expect me to help with this treason?"

"Well," Maze said, sliding the book toward Layla, "you were entrusted to find this; without it, you have nowhere to go—you can't return to Andelor. And there will be questions about your companion."

The chill returned to Layla's chest. She knew Maze was right. She had nowhere to go. Still, she was justifiably reluctant to join this band of conspirators.

Maze clearly saw the doubt on her face. "I have a feeling you will want to return to Vale, and by serving as our spy, you can."

"Why would I want to return to Vale?"

"Because Desmond is still alive," Jaffron said, casually taking a sip of wine.

The words were an icy dagger in Layla's stomach. She listened for Stane to tell her it was a lie, but there was only silence. As she watched Jaffron gently set his cup down, she looked into his eyes—the eyes that she had been avoiding since she watched him kill Valix. Those eyes looked as earnest as Layla could have imagined, given the circumstances.

Stane remained silent.

Layla stood up, her strength returned. "When do we leave?"

Chapter Twenty-Four
Uprooted

Quinn dreamed of Fallon.

Before the harpies came and the two of them were yanked from their comfortable lives in Sathford, Quinn believed Fallon Shaw to be a truly good person. But the Fallon dwelling in his mind now was driven by utter, impenetrable darkness. His last memories of her were drenched in fear, loathing, and shame.

Quinn's betrayal played out during his slumber, causing him to toss and turn in his bed, sweating, despite the night's chill.

"Embrace that anger," Naya had told Fallon while Quinn concealed himself in the mists. "Do not fight that hatred you feel. It is natural. Your father was killed, and it is in our nature to feel that rage. You must use it."

Fallon hung her head in the dream, but Quinn did not remember her feeling any shame as she nodded along to the priestess' instructions. The Xe'danni's grip on Fallon was absolute now, no matter what Quinn could say to his friend. Fallon was lost to him, and the only hope of saving her was by stealing her father's keyshard.

In the dream, Quinn crept through the Old Ways as if trudging through drying mud. His legs felt like they were weighed down with heavy chains, links of Shadow that tried desperately to keep him from his task. But he grit his teeth like any good valiant hero of the dreamlands would do and persevered.

In the dream, he didn't get the stone. Naya was there, looming like some malicious witch from a story, cackling as her huge spidery fingers wrapped themselves around the small green stone just before he could reach it.

He awoke with a start, forgetting where he was for a long panicked moment. But as his eyes fell on Ransil's empty bed, he remembered they were safe in Oakworth. But even as that realization dawned on him, an unmistakable and familiar coldness passed by him. He recoiled from that side of the bed, feeling an undeniable presence there.

As he held his breath, Quinn's eyes searched and found nothing. He sat there frozen, waiting to feel that chill again, but fortunately—or unfortunately—there was nothing.

A crash sounded behind his closed door, and then distant shouts. The obvious sounds of a struggle snapped him out of his trance and he rolled out of bed to slip into his robes, rushing over to the bedside table. As he opened the drawer, he froze again.

Fallon's keyshard was gone.

The sounds outside his door grew closer as Quinn stared in stupefied disbelief, and only when the door was violently thrown open did he spin around in time to see the dryad.

Like the ones he saw in the woods with Ransil, the feminine horror before him had bark-like skin. Her arms were shaped like curved swords, and her eyes were burning emeralds that narrowed on Quinn as she opened her thorny mouth to let out a feral cry.

Quinn scrambled back onto his bed, reaching for any power that might stay the monster that now reared back to leap on him. But before he got the chance, a spear came from the doorway behind the dryad and burst through her chest.

"Come on, boy!" The guard pulled the spear out of the dryad and kicked her lifeless body aside. "The keep is under attack!"

"You will regret not killing that little bastard," Naya hissed as the three figures cloaked in Shadow magic passed unseen through the hall. Around them, the baroness' guards were rushing about, escorting half-naked, sleepy bystanders away from the keep's invaders. "He is powerful."

"I'm not scared of some boy mage," Desmond said dismissively, looking over his shoulder to ensure Gage was close behind. "You feel it, don't you?"

Gage couldn't lie. The stone in his hand felt right, as if it had always been his. It was such a strange sensation, but since leaving Blakehurst it was the only time he truly felt like himself again.

"I told you," Desmond said with genuine kindness, "you're meant for this."

The trio hugged the wall as they made their way back toward Mawsurath, avoiding the terrified guards who did battle with the maddened dryads. There was a dark sense of mirth blooming within Gage's mind, thinking about how the frantic guards around him were fighting and dying to prevent the forces of nature that wanted only to kill the incarnate.

A new sense of purpose burned away his better judgment. The Gage who once spent his days hunting rabbits and his nights sneaking about Blakehurst with Robin would have felt sympathy for the people of Oakworth. He would feel dread as chaos erupted around him.

But now, he felt invigorated. He thought back to Anika's birthday, when he stole that stone. He knew now why she had craved it, why she had more or less begged him to steal it for her. When he touched that piece of Skythe, he only felt a tiny miserable echo of what he felt now.

The keyshard he held in his hand connected him to the world, gave him a place. That power made him feel worthy, and in that overwhelming sense of belonging, he found it much easier to take joy in the cruel whims of fate.

As if she could read his thoughts, Naya let out a low, breathy laugh. "If these fools only knew that the creatures they are fighting were on their side."

"Be thankful they don't," Desmond said morosely. "I'd rather not have to deal with them ourselves. Oakus has more devoted legions than Eyen, it would seem."

A dryad fell to the ground, dark—almost black—blood spilling from its wounds as a guard shouted and hurried by the hidden intruders. The darkness that hid them intensified as Fallon's keyshard began to pulse.

While Gage felt the power of Oakus filling him, he smiled, knowing he wouldn't need his dark companions much longer.

A drawn-out silence hung between the strange gathering in the Oakhold. Mawsurath's hulking body swayed, creaking like old roots being pulled slowly from the earth. But the elf that was held suspended within the creature just glared, her lips pulled back in a feral snarl.

It took Ransil a moment to realize that this was Quinn's companion—the incarnate of Oakus. When he did, he took a step forward, keeping his knives loose in his fingers.

"Fallon?"

The elf's fury faded slightly, as if her name held some power over the monstrosity she occupied. She eyed Ransil suspiciously, looking for a reason to charge forward.

"That's your name, right? Fallon Shaw?"

"I don't care what her name is," Kasia said. Ransil could see the Oather pivoting her back foot, ready to charge. "She needs to get out of this creature or die with it. That is her only choice."

Ransil ignored the woman, taking another step forward. "Quinn is here."

"I know he is!" Fallon—no, Mawsurath—stomped, shaking the ground violently, dropping dirt and larger debris on the gathered. "I can feel him! He took my father's stone. I've come to take back what's mine."

Those words stole Ransil's breath. Quinn was just a boy, and this thing—which was no longer his friend—would kill to get to the power in that keyshard. He tightened his grip on his knives, knowing that he couldn't let her pass. Remembering his own confrontation with Corvanna, Ransil didn't expect to survive a fight with an incarnate, not without Anika. But maybe he could buy the kid some time to escape.

As long as the fool doesn't bring the damn stone down here, Ransil thought, suddenly cursing himself for not thinking to alert the boy before rushing toward this doom.

"And you!" Mawsurath raised a massive arm to point over Ransil's head. The halfling looked over his shoulder to see Avrim stepping forward; the priest had a soft radiance around him. "Another minion of the Light...have you come to claim more heads?"

Avrim's face remained hard, but he looked at Ransil for some sort of explanation.

"Fallon Shaw. Mawsurath." Each name was a dreadful curse from Kasia, who looked like she would charge forward any moment. "I charge you with defying your Oath of Sorcery..."

"To the Abyss with your oaths!" Mawsurath stomped again as Fallon gnashed her teeth, her face twisted in unnatural rage.

"Watch out!"

Ransil glanced to his left, just in time to see Melaine darting towards Brace Cobbit. With a swift dive, she pushed him aside, narrowly avoiding a massive stone chunk, as big as the half-orc herself, that plummeted to where Brace had just been standing. Both bodies rolled into the dirt in a heap.

Kasia didn't yield. "With the authority of the Arcania and the Valiant Throne, I hereby sentence you to the custody of the Archmage. Or death, if you prefer."

Fallon's hateful scowl shifted into a sneer, Mawsurath's creaking limbs now sounding like breaking bones as the creature tensed. A sickly green aura began swirling around both of them as the elf raised Mawsurath's arm to point at Kasia.

Ransil barely had time to blink before an explosion of roots burst up from the ground around the Oather. They wrapped themselves around her throat and wrists like tentacles, causing Kasia to drop her sword. The dark glyphs on her armor faded almost instantly, and the green aura around the incarnate intensified.

"I prefer death," Fallon said, with a voice that Ransil knew was not truly hers. There was an ancient grudge in that voice, something primal that was channeling itself through these combined vessels. "All of your deaths. Your time is over. We should have listened to Stane."

Darrance slashed with his sword, hacking at the roots and vines that held Kasia. But for each one he cleaved through, three more burst from below to grapple the Oather again.

Ransil kept low as he moved forward to help, hearing his companions joining the fray. The dwarf Deina barreled ahead of the halfling, rushing toward the incarnate, the green aura now becoming a thick atmosphere of arcane energy. Avrim was close behind her, hefting his mace and shouting a prayer to the Light.

As Ransil reached Kasia, his knives already working at her snake-like bonds, he could hear the Oather grunting, trying to tell him something. He motioned for Darrance to steady his sweeping blade, then began cautiously cutting the roots around Kasia's neck.

Deina cursed loudly, but Ransil wouldn't risk looking—he could cut the Oather's throat if he wasn't careful. Avrim cried out in pain.

Finally, Kasia managed to say, "My...glyphs!"

Ransil understood immediately; the Oather's armor required its wearer to concentrate to function properly, and they would need its anti-magic to face such a terrible foe. As Darrance helped Ransil pull the appendages from Kasia's throat, they both looked toward Deina, who was hacking at Mawsurath's tree trunk legs with her axe.

Fallon screamed again with a disembodied voice, and swung a massive arm down to crush the dwarf. Fortunately, Deina leapt aside just in time, but the impact of the blow shook the Oakhold once more. Ransil felt a fist-sized stone smash into his brow, but he focused on cutting away the last of the vines that were strangling Kasia.

"Deina! Down!"

Ransil turned to see Melaine on her knee, taking careful aim with her bow. The arrow she had nocked had a burning tip, and next to her Brace was holding what looked like a ball of fire in one hand.

The half-orc unleashed the fiery missile and it struck true, thunking solidly into Mawsurath's shoulder—barely avoiding Fallon's head. The flames spread immediately, as if the incarnate was forged from bone-dry wood. Ransil noticed once the flames took hold the green aura surrounding Mawsurath began to recede slightly.

Whether it was the fire weakening the incarnate or Kasia's Oathmail, the halfling couldn't say, because as he turned back to Kasia, he saw the black glyphs on her armor taking shape again. Roots stopped bursting up from the ground to restrain her, and Darrance cut the last ones holding her wrists.

Fallon shrieked again as a small sun flashed in the chamber, blinding everyone, including Ransil. All he could hear was the thunk of Avrim's mace pounding uselessly against the incarnate. As his vision returned, Ransil saw another fiery arrow get deflected by more falling debris.

Darrance grabbed the Oather's forearm and pulled her to her feet, Kasia's sword now back in her hand. Fallon was screaming as Mawsurath's body seemed to shrink slightly, groping roots trying to smother the flames that threatened to consume it. Deina was back on her feet hacking at the incarnate's legs while Melaine fired another flaming arrow, which barely missed its mark, setting a wooden beam behind Mawsurath on fire.

"Now's our chance," Darrance said, moving to join Deina and Avrim.

As Ransil spun his knives to join the fight, he felt an unmistakable chill pass by him. The Oakhold was warm, even without the fire and smoke, but the halfling felt a crypt chill touch his arm, which gave him pause. He saw nothing in the empty space between him and where Brace and Melaine stood, but he felt a presence creep by which reminded him of the baron's bedchambers not so long ago.

"There's too much power," Kasia said, struggling to stay on her feet. Ransil turned away from the ghostly cold to see the Oather's glyphs start to fade slightly.

"More fire!" Melaine barked behind them.

Brace cursed through grit teeth. "I can't! It's the Oather! I can't light it!"

A flameless arrow buried itself uselessly into Mawsurath's wooden body. The incarnate didn't notice as it swept one of its arms in a wide arc to slam both Deina and Darrance into the wall. Avrim sidestepped it and began pounding on the limb to free them, to no avail.

Ransil was about to tell Kasia to forget about her armor, they had to help the others. But before he could, Kasia arched her back and dropped her sword. The glyphs on her armor faded again. Behind him, Ransil heard Brace curse, and the entire chamber was bathed in fire. The halfling turned to see a jet of flame bursting from Brace's hand, engulfing Mawsurath.

Fallon screamed wildly, sounding as if she were burning alive. Meanwhile, Brace let out his own wail of agony as the fire consumed his hand.

But in response, the green atmosphere around the incarnate became thick and foggy, with the sound of twisting and breaking bones intensifying. Ransil could just barely see Mawsurath's body growing again, groping roots smothering the flames. With horror, he noticed the fire had begun to engulf the wooden beams supporting the tunnel.

As Kasia fell to her knees, Ransil could see the hilt of a dagger jammed into a gap in her armor, just above her waist. That was when he noticed Dolly at his side, her face contorted with a rage he had never seen—a mother's rage.

"You monster!" The halfling was blind to the surrounding chaos, moving to look Kasia in the face. "Tell me where you sent my girls! Or I won't avoid pricking your guts next time!"

"Melaine! Look out!"

His heart both sinking and racing, Rasil turned from one peril to the next, now seeing Deina and Darrance pinned against a wall by the incarnate's massive arm while a whip-like appendage flew toward Brace and Melaine. Despite the dwarf's warning, neither had time to avoid it, and the grasping tendril knocked them both into the wall, shattering it and sending them into the adjoining tunnel.

"No!" Deina and Darrance both screamed as the fire continued to consume their surroundings. There was a crash behind Mawsurath and the ceiling gave out, bringing down another heavy load of stones and dirt.

"Through the gate, now! We have the stone!" Ransil couldn't tell who shouted that, but he ignored it and raced toward Brace and Melaine, hoping they survived being so violently slammed through solid wood and earth.

The ground shook, telling Ransil that Mawsurath was moving, but as he looked over his shoulder, he saw Deina and Darrance both scrambling in his direction, Deina's axe still lodged in Mawsurath's leg. Avrim limped behind, his leg looking twisted. The incarnate retreated into the fire as the tunnel began to cave in.

"Melaine!" Deina screamed as a chunk of ceiling nearly flattened her.

"There's no time, we need to go!" Darrance grabbed the dwarf and hefted her toward the stairs. Deina flailed wildly calling after the half-orc. Dolly had snapped out of her trance and began helping Avrim drag Kasia toward the exit.

Ransil spared Melaine and Brace a quick glance, but all he saw were the shadows of their two broken bodies, one of which was burning as the world above began to bury them.

"Melaine!"

Deina's anguished cries were slowly drowned out as the world collapsed in burnt roots and heavy dirt. Ransil scrambled over to help drag the Oather to safety, feeling wretched that two companions had perished while he had to help Dolly rescue the woman who kidnapped her children.

As they struggled to the stairs, he cast a glance at Dolly. She wore an expression of remorse or shame—likely both—but he found that he couldn't blame her. Avrim had torn the dagger out of Kasia's back, whispering a prayer as Light gathered in his hand over her wound.

"Where are my girls?" The malice in Dolly's voice was now replaced with desperation.

Kasia grunted as they dragged her up the stairs, struggling to get to her feet. As Avrim's healing surged through her, she managed to lift her arm to point toward the collapsing Oakhold. "I had Jak...take them down...to the tunnels..."

There was genuine sadness in the Oather's normally vacant eyes.

Ransil had to let Darrance and Avrim restrain Deina from digging her way toward Melaine with her bare hands while he cradled Dolly, carrying her up the stairs where they could properly mourn her daughters.

Gage tore the axe from the golem's leg, surprised by the weight of it. The dwarf had wielded it as if it were hollow, but now that he held the weapon, Gage could tell it was intentionally weighted to cause as much damage as possible.

She's strong, he thought, wondering if she had survived. It wasn't likely, the entire Oakhold was collapsing just as they passed through the gate. The way behind them was now forever closed as the decorated archway that once provided passage between the bowels of Oakworth and the Old Ways was burned and broken.

"It won't matter," Naya said, her eyes distant as she stared at its ruin. "I can feel the gates in this place, even from a distance; like a presence in my mind...a memory. And they are fading, one by one. Someone is closing them. I don't know how, but it's undeniable."

Desmond seemed unbothered. "Then we don't have time to dwell."

"I...need a moment." Fallon's voice was strained, and as Gage looked up at her, he was not surprised. Her skin looked charred from the flames, her hair mostly gone. There were fissures across her flesh, but between the broken skin he could see coarse growths.

Moss, Gage thought. *The creature is healing her.* The keyshard in his palm was reacting. He was no wizard, but he knew it was magic. The power of Oakus. And something darker...

Naya stepped toward the kneeling form of Mawsurath, reaching up with her remaining hand. "Here, my dear. Let me help you." Dark energy gathered between her fingers and the cracked skin of Fallon's cheek. The moss-like growth spread faster where the skin split, and her flesh began turning from black to an earthen brown. "Those Light-blind savages will pay for this, child."

The darkness Gage felt intensified as Naya channeled the Shadow, and he opened his hand to look into Fallon's stone. There was a voice on the edge of his hearing, but he couldn't make out the words.

"I can hear Ruke," Fallon said, her eyes closed, the pain receding from her voice. "The Purveyor of Light...she speaks to me through her stone." The elf reached a hand up to where the keyshard Desmond gave her was affixed to Mawsurath's chest.

Desmond, pacing impatiently, spun around at that, his tattered black robes whipping around like a bunch of snakes. "What did she say?"

Gage still couldn't make out the voice in his head, but he wondered if it was Ruke as well. He only knew the halfling priestess from stories, enough to know that she was inexorably tied to Oakus.

Fallon flicked her eyes open, casting Gage a cautious look. "Do you have my father's keyshard?" The elf's eyes shifted nervously toward Desmond.

Closing his fist, Gage gave Desmond a confused look. The voice became clearer in his head, and he took a step away from the ghoulish man.

"What did she say?" Desmond's voice was ice now, and there was a panicked look in his eyes. "Tell me. She is cunning."

That was when the words took root in Gage's mind.

"He is a Scion of Stane."

Something about those words awoke a terror in Gage, and he ensured he had a steady grip on the axe.

"I want my father's keyshard."

"Give her the stone," Naya commanded. She looked at Gage and then Desmond, but neither of them moved. "That is why we came here, no? What is this? She needs the stone if she is to become what she is meant to be."

Desmond stepped forward, putting his hands behind his back in what may have been a show of peace, but to Gage it looked threatening. "Ruke deceived me. She spoke to me as well, when I was..." His scarred brow furrowed, as if trying to recall something. "She is trapped in that keyshard, and will say anything to get out of it."

"He is the Scion, as I told your sister," the voice continued. "You must protect him, if you hope to break the cycle."

Whether or not he intended to kill, Gage felt compelled to move the keyshard—still clenched in his fist, hidden from his companions—toward the axe.

He remembered watching Anika forge Stormender by placing the shard he had given her to the knife their father had given her. The weapon meant something to his sister, but what did this axe mean to Gage? Regardless, he saw it forged in his mind, begging to be made.

Harvester. Every legendary weapon needed a name, and Gage couldn't think of one more fitting for the Harvest Lord's axe. Something about envisioning the weapon made him think of Robin and he became certain of his path.

While Desmond looked on with an expression of fearful resignation, Gage touched the keyshard to the axe and the tunnel exploded in a flash of gray-green magic. The underworld itself began to buckle, and Gage closed his eyes as unfamiliar and ancient powers coursed through him into the forging.

In that brief moment, Gage left the world, his consciousness hanging in a void beyond time. He opened his eyes to see a small woman with glowing green eyes, one of them twitching slightly.

"She will try to kill him."

It was the voice from before, warning him about Desmond.

"Ruke?"

"She needs to kill him, because Oakus commands it—it's the only way the gods can escape their bonds."

Gage didn't understand, but nodded as if he did. Whatever certainty he felt about forging Harvester was gone now, replaced by a strange emptiness that made him wonder if he had died by touching the keyshard to Deina's axe.

"Only you can kill the incarnate now," Ruke continued, her form starting to fade. "You are our only hope. Do not let the Shadow sway you…"

Gage opened his eyes. The axe had transformed; its double-blade now met with the green gem socketed in a twisted collection of roots. The handle was still smooth wood, but veins of moss sprouted along its length, and the axe's blades were now a deep metallic green. It radiated Oakus' power, and Gage felt a connection to the Old Ways and the network of roots above.

Looking up from the weapon, Gage saw a horrified look on Naya's face and one of surprise on Fallon's. Mawsurath seemed lifeless now, a kneeling treeman statue that served as some decorative casket for the elf who occupied it. Desmond's expression was unreadable; it was as if he was entirely bored by the revelation.

"What have you done?"

Gage looked back at Naya with a scowl, the memory of her manipulations now stronger than ever. She had used the Shadow against him back in Oakworth, and he had not realized it then. But now he knew who he was, and he could feel her tugging at his mind again, trying to sway him.

He gripped the axe tighter. "You can't control me."

"We aren't trying to control you, Gage," Fallon said, her voice still thick and dry from the healing. "The Light is trying to control you. I know you can hear Ruke too. Listen…"

"She's lying," Ruke said, her voice a roll of thunder in Gage's mind. "I wouldn't speak to an incarnate! They are abominations. Thieves of the old gods' power!"

"Stop!" Gage hefted the axe—which felt light as a feather to him now—and slammed it down. When the blade struck the shifting earth below his feet, a fissure split open. From that glowing emerald crevice, dozens of roots reached up to entangle Naya and Fallon, pulling them into the green oblivion.

As the women struggled against their bindings, Gage turned to Desmond, who still wore the same ghoulish look that revealed no emotion. "The Old Ways are collapsing, I can feel each gate falling."

Desmond nodded.

"Gage, please..." Fallon's voice was cut off as a root gripped her throat.

"Take me to Robin."

Mawsurath surged to life, breaking the roots holding him and Fallon down. Naya screamed as she was pulled into whatever void existed below the Old Ways. The incarnate charged toward Desmond, Fallon shouting something. Gage stepped forward and slashed with Harvester, the axe cleaved through the incarnate's arm and sent Mawsurath stumbling backward as more twisting vines grappled him.

"Kill him, Gage! Ruke told me...you're hearing the Shadow! Desmond must die! If you want to save your sister, kill him!" The sound of cracking bones began to drown out Fallon's voice as Mawsurath's limbs were crushed.

"Hurry," Desmond said, ignoring Fallon's cries. "We still have time to reach Raventhal."

Gage followed the scion, but neither of them spared a glance at the army of undead that shambled toward them from further down the tunnel.

As Harvester thrummed in his hand, Gage was able to quiet Ruke's voice in his mind, not convinced it truly was the Purveyor who spoke to him. It didn't matter to him now. All his thoughts were on Robin. With Harvester, they wouldn't have to run and hide. He wouldn't need Desmond either once he got to Sathford.

A smile came to Gage's lips. His purpose had never been so clear. He may be the Child of Shadow, but his destiny was his own.

Even though he couldn't hear it, Ruke giggled in his mind.

Chapter Twenty-Five

The Lost Daughter

"I told you all I knew of that girl," the old woman said, carefully separating beads by colors. Her wrinkled fingers worked deftly, placing one bead at a time in a tray with dozens of compartments. She seemed entirely unbothered by the presence of a Lightmother and nomarch in her meager home.

"Actually," Jamira said, swirling the tea around in the small cup, "you told me just enough. You're a clever woman, and you know the punishment for lying to a nomarch. But you can lie by telling the truth, if the wrong questions are asked."

The old woman carefully inspected a bead that could have been yellow or orange, depending on the angle under the faint light from the hearth. She decided on yellow and dropped it in the appropriate compartment. "Who am I to presume to do a nomarch's job for them?"

Jamira couldn't help but smirk. Despite the urgency of their situation, she couldn't help but like the old lady.

Taliah set her tea down. "It's so dark in here, Zanese. Do you mind if I light some candles?" The Lightmother gave the nomarch a knowing glance.

"Of course, of course."

As Taliah rose to cross the small room, Jamira took a moment to truly appreciate how some of her people lived. The cramped quarters contained everything a person needed to survive, but not necessarily enough to *live*. There was a bed crammed in next to the small table at which she currently sat, and the kitchen was little more than a short iron stove next to the hearth. A tub of gray, tepid water was probably used to bathe, wash dishes, and maybe even to brew tea.

Jamira set her teacup down at that thought. Despite Zanese's home having a certain charm, it struck the nomarch in a way that angered her, thinking of the massive pyramid where the majest and his loyalists lived in overbearing luxury.

Candlelight soon bathed the small home.

"There, that's better," Taliah said, taking her seat again next to Jamira. The nomarch noticed the Lightmother's hands working under the table, gathering Light in a silent prayer. "Now, do you mind if I ask you about Anika Lawson?"

"You mean Anika Voth?"

Taliah and Jamira shared a shocked look before turning back to Zanese, waiting for elaboration.

The old woman dropped a red bead in with the others and began slowly inspecting the next one. "The Voths were good folks, no matter what they may have done during the rebellion."

"Who were the Voths?" The name didn't sound familiar to Jamira, but she had trouble remembering all the noble family names aligned with the Trivestiture, and she was even worse with commoners.

"Simple folk, like me," Zanese said, still focused on her beads. "Kora Voth was a lovely woman, not meant for the hard labor she endured out in the fields. But when her husband, Aren, got his tongue cut out for slandering the majest at the time—but honestly, who didn't slander that sloth—he almost died from the fever. She had to work, even while carrying little Anika." The woman finally stopped inspecting her beads, giving Jamira a hard look. "It's honestly a miracle the child survived childbirth."

With sorrow in her eyes, Taliah also looked toward Jamira, and the nomarch suddenly felt like she was being held accountable for the whole situation. But it was during her father's time, and he was a much more ruthless nomarch than she.

"How do you know Anika is this child?" Jamira asked.

The old woman's face finally broke into an expression of surprise. "Well, she told me of course." She picked up another bead and returned to sorting as she added, "In a way, that is. She was a spitting image of Kora, with just enough of her father. But she awoke one night and startled me, and said the same thing Kora had said before they left." Zanese dropped two green beads with a clatter. "Over fifteen years ago, and I'll never forget those words..."

Taliah's hands stopped working and the Light began to fade. "What words?"

Zanese looked at them. "She needs a sibling, or else she's doomed." She went back to her beads before adding, "Of course Anika said '*I* need a sibling, or else *I'm* doomed,' which still gave me chills."

Jamira turned to Taliah, whose mouth hung agape. "What does that mean?"

The Lightmother rose swiftly. "Thank you, Zanese. May the Light continue guiding your days."

"Sun's almost up," Zanese said, still mindlessly sorting, "I'll tell it to guide away."

Jamira followed the Lightmother out of the small house into the dawn. When they were a few paces away, the nomarch grabbed Taliah's shoulder and spun her around. "What am I missing here?"

"She has a Key!"

Jamira scowled. "As in a Key of Transience? Who, Zanese?!"

"No," Taliah pointed toward the silhouette of Pyram in the distance. "Anika! The knife! I knew it was a Key. And that can only mean that she's the Child of Light!"

The Lightmother must have read the confusion on Jamira's face.

"All that talk about the siblings...there are theories within the Luminaura that the Child of Light and the Child of Shadow will continue battling one another—dying only to be reborn again—until the cycle can be broken. It's said that can only happen when they are somehow reborn as siblings..."

The notion sounded familiar to Jamira, but she was never one to spend much time dwelling on old prophecies and fanciful histories. "So do we even know if the Voth's had another child?"

"Does that matter?!" Taliah's voice broke and her eyes grew wide. "She's the Child of Light! And she's being manipulated into marrying the majest for his own political games."

Jamira knew she was right; Child of Light or not, they couldn't stand by while Lekan deceived Anika into solidifying his reign. Beyond the political ramifications that Jamira knew would surely bring war to Karrane, she wouldn't allow Anika to believe that she was the missing Drastil girl.

"We have to return to Pyram," Taliah said. "If I know the majest, he will try to arrange the wedding as soon as possible."

―――――◆〇◆―――――

Anika admired herself in the mirror; she never imagined herself looking so beautiful. It was almost like the face that stared back at her wasn't her own, but some dignified version of herself.

It's not me, Anika thought, smiling drunkenly at the reflection, *it's Kalany Drastil, soon to be Kalany Nafir, Royene of Pyram.*

Anika Lawson seemed a distant memory to her now, the naive tanner from Blakehurst believing she was some great champion from a legend. Though she still felt the pull of Stormender from its resting place behind her on the bedside table, even that longing had begun to feel weaker.

She took another sip of the wine Lekan had left her. It made her head swim. She had told him it was too early for wine. "But it's our wedding day, my love," he had said with that devilish grin. Kalany was easily swayed.

"You look divine," Stevra said, appearing from behind the girl who was once known as Anika. The halfling smoothed the dress around Kalany's hips. It was deep orange, like the morning sun that could be seen through the balcony doors. "A proper royene."

Kalany smiled and drained the rest of her wine. The room spun and she felt weightless, but not like last night. She handed the wine to Stevra and ran her hands down the front of the dress. As her vision steadied, she noticed the curves of her body accentuated by the gown; her breasts were pushed up, her exposed shoulders defined, and her hips just wide enough. The paintings of her mother in Drastil Manor came to her mind.

"Are you ready?" Stevra asked, smiling wide.

Kalany nodded. "Perhaps some more of that wine."

"Certainly," Stevra said, taking the empty cup to the nearby pitcher. "Though, I might suggest only half a cup this time. You'll want to have a clear head for the ceremony."

Will I? When Kalany turned away from the mirror, Anika's thoughts returned for a moment. *Will I want a clear head to promise my life to Lekan Nafir? It seems I may need some more wine...what am I even doing here?* But when she looked back at the mirror, Kalany smiled, ready to start her life anew.

There was a tapping at the door. Stevra set the pitcher and cup down to go answer. Kalany strode over to the wine, struggling to walk in the tight dress; she saw Elrin whispering something to Stevra, but when he saw her he gave Kalany an uncharacteristically charming smile.

"You look lovely, Lady Drastil."

Kalany nodded and took a sip. Now her shoulders began to feel numb, and she no longer felt any connection to Stormender. It should have concerned her, but she found it very freeing. "Thank you, Elrin. I wanted to ask..."

He stepped into the room, Stevra moving aside. "Yes?"

"Before the ceremony, may I visit the chapel?" She set the rest of her wine aside, suddenly remembering something when she thought of Stormender. "I wanted to pray in the glowery with Taliah last night, but I was told by the acolytes that she had departed the city."

Elrin gave that unnerving smile again—since she had been in the city, the man had given her nothing but scowls—but Kalany seemed to find it comforting. "Yes, I'm afraid she was pulled away on Luminaura business in Westerra."

Anika found that very curious, but Kalany just smiled.

"Besides, my lady, the majest awaits you. The ceremony will begin shortly."

Drunk on the wine and the awaiting romance of a splendid wedding, Kalany glided toward the door in a daze. She didn't bother looking behind her to see the vizier move to collect her knife from the bedside table, tucking it into his robes; Anika would have found that more curious as well, but Kalany would have found it perfectly acceptable.

Despite her drunkenness, Kalany managed to gasp when she entered the hall. The walls were lined with people, mostly dark Karranese folk dressed in vibrant oranges and yellows. Kalany had never seen so many refined lords and ladies, and all their faces were watching her. They wore kind expressions and many women gasped or even wept when Kalany appeared.

Anika may have been uncomfortable, but Kalany reveled in the attention, feeling as if she were in a dream. She nearly jumped when a small hand touched her arm, but smiled brightly when she turned to see Stevra.

"Normally," the halfling whispered, "your mother would present you." She offered up her open hand. "Hopefully you would allow me to escort you down to the majest's altar."

Her heart swelling, Kalany gladly took the woman's hand, and together they walked down the crowded hall toward the awaiting sunlight. The procession was accompanied by unseen musicians, the tinkling melody sounding like it was coming from several metallic stringed instruments hidden in the walls. The faces that Kalany saw on either side were all strangers, but they were happy.

Despite the surrounding joy, deep down, Anika felt a miserable sadness. None of this felt right—it was all a lie that she couldn't seem to convince herself to see. Kalany easily ignored the strange feeling. *It's just butterflies in your tummy,* she thought, suffocating Anika's misgivings with the intoxicating splendor surrounding her. *You're going to be the royene; act like it.*

They continued down the great stairs, and the crowds grew once they were outside. Each tier of the pyramid was lined with onlookers. On the upper terraces, the high lords and ladies waved colorful scarves in the morning breeze, and on the lower terraces the commoners were much rowdier, singing songs and shouting brazen things that Kalany couldn't quite make out.

The music continued echoing even outside, obviously through some sort of spell that bathed the whole city in song. Kalany spared a look over her shoulder as she reached the bottom of the stairs, seeing Elrin following close behind with his hands in his sleeves. The elf's smile would seem treacherous to Anika, but Kalany found it charming, and she just beamed back as Stevra guided her toward the lifts.

Once they were on the platform, Kalany stared at the smooth walls of the lift's shaft, hypnotized by small imperfections in the stone that passed them by. "Are weddings normally held beneath the city?" It was Anika's question, asked through Kalany's nearly numb lips.

Elrin cleared his throat.

"The majest wanted to honor your family," Stevra explained. "The Drastils made their fortune from the mines, and formed the first hewer's guild. Here in Karrane, we honor both legacies at a wedding. The Drastils helped with the founding of Pyram, so what better place to forge this glorious union."

It made perfect sense to Kalany.

"There will be a grand celebration on the High Terrace," Elrin added. "Our ceremonies are more intimate affairs, but once you are married before the altar, we shall return above to properly crown you royene for the whole city to see."

Kalany's breath quickened as they went further into the underworld, the enchantment of the day only increased with the vizier's description of the banquet that would follow her marriage. When the lift shuttered to a stop and the doors opened, she stepped eagerly into the chilly world below the city.

Goosebumps crawled up Kalany's exposed skin and a chill breeze snaked its way up her legs. *How is there a breeze down here?* But that was Anika's thoughts. *Just enjoy this,* Kalany responded, as a dull ache in her head started to blossom.

The world underneath Pyram was vast. Kalany did not realize they had ridden so far beneath the city, but they were so deep below the earth that there didn't seem to be a ceiling above. If there was, it was so high up that the light from the decorative lanterns lining the wide cobbled road couldn't find it in the darkness.

Between two flanking rows of orange-armored guards, Stevra led Kalany onward from the lift. The cobbled road ran straight through what looked like a city of its own, with buildings crammed together in the jagged alcoves of the hewn rock face. The soft echoing of the music from above accompanied the small wedding party as they made their way across a series of bridges.

There were still onlookers, though much fewer than on the pyramid. Many commoners and craftsmen gathered alongside the road, eager to get a glimpse as Kalany smiled and waved. *These will be my people,* she thought, *my subjects. I will be a good royene for them.* Anika struggled to swallow the sentiments, but it seemed like any time she tried to voice a thought, the headache would worsen.

Stevra must have noticed. "Are you well, my lady?" she whispered. Her voice carried in the fathomless depths.

"It is a day for celebration," Elrin offered from behind. "We all might drink a bit too much before the day is out, but such an occasion calls for indulgence."

Kalany didn't have a chance to respond; as they crossed a bridge that curved around a wide column, a pulsing blue light made her stop and gasp.

Down a short tunnel, Kalany could see her groom. Lekan stood bathed in a familiar glow—one that Anika recognized immediately as a foreboding portent, but Kalany merely found soothing and inviting. The majest stood in front of a ring of his royal guard, along with several exquisitely dressed lords and ladies that Kalany did not know.

But her eyes were drawn to the altar.

It was a massive chunk of blue stone, like a precious gem the size of a boulder. It jutted out of the earth if it had been violently forced out of the depths of the world, and it pulsated like a beating heart, casting the high chamber in a warm blue glow.

"What is that?" Kalany asked, finally voicing Anika's thoughts.

"A sign," Elrin said, stepping up next to her. "It was said that the Drastils were responsible for the First Hewing. Your mother devoted her life to the excavations down here. And upon your return, this appeared."

Kalany turned to the vizier, taken by the reverence in the man's voice. She had always suspected the majest's councilor to be disdainful of her and her presence, but his attitude today made her feel accepted—something that every part of her desired.

"It is a sign of your union and your purpose," Elrin continued. He turned to give Kalany an almost fatherly smile. "Where is your brother?"

What brother? Kalany thought, but the question went unanswered as her hazy thoughts began to drown under Anika's resurging thoughts. *Gage,* Anika remembered, as if the fact that she had a brother was some revelation she had been searching for.

Focusing her blurry vision, she drew back as Elrin's face shifted; it grew thicker, with a bearded square jaw replacing the elf's gaunt one. The vizier faded away and Bennik Lawson stared at his daughter with questioning eyes.

Anika struggled to speak as time seemed to stop. *Was this all a dream?* It would not be too hard for Anika to believe, with the wine and this grand wedding that seemed to be pulled from the pages of some Eastlund fable. Even more dream-like was her inability to speak, like her mouth was sewn closed, or her body was frozen in time leaving only her thoughts to persist.

Just when she thought she felt her lips respond to her commands, Bennik's face washed away and Elrin was looking at her; he was still smiling, but his head was slightly tilted, inquisitory.

"What did you say?"

Elrin's smile seemed to widen. "I said you look so much like your mother."

The word conjured up warring images in Anika's mind; the older version of herself that had haunted her from The Early Mule in Blakehurst mouthed a warning to her that she couldn't hear. That woman's visage then melted into Renay's, the only mother Anika had truly known. Her lovely red hair was disheveled and blood splattered her face, but her eyes were warm and loving.

Finally, Domina Mavala Drastil appeared, looking now like a complete stranger. Anika remembered the immediate sense of confusion that had washed over her when the artist listening to her description of her mother presented Mavala's face. It was a brief sensation then, but now it returned with a vengeance, threatening to break the morning's romantic spell.

The domina spoke, giving voice to Kalany's thoughts. "You are where you belong, Child; away from the pain and loss of a life that was never yours to begin with. Look around..."

Anika did, seeing frozen faces that adored her—worshiped her.

"...you can start again—take the life that you want, the one that you deserve."

Kalany smiled at Elrin as they both fell back into step with time, the procession sweeping them both toward the awaiting altar.

Gasping for breath as she struggled to keep up with Jamira, Taliah managed to complain once again. "The south lift would most likely have been free...we'd have been down there by now."

"It doesn't matter now, does it?" Jamira turned down the next flight of stairs. "Save your breath, woman. We don't have time to turn back...we're already halfway there."

Taliah nearly tripped over her skirts as she reached the next landing, only to have to descend a hundred more steps to the following landing. She took a moment to take a deep breath, losing sight of Jamira as the nomarch's quick strides took her out of the pool of brazier light.

The clacking sound of Jamira's armor suddenly ceased. "Come on! You know as well as I that if this wedding happens, there will be war! Catch your breath later!"

Biting her tongue against a thousand curses for the foolish majest she had once served—the one who had ordered her death—Taliah began the long descent once more. With each exhausting step, she reminded herself that the Shadow would take hold in this wonderful city if she did not protect it. The Light had chosen her as its champion, and she would not fail.

It would be a lie to say that there wasn't something else driving the Lightmother in this perilous ordeal, though. Even as Taliah convinced herself that her faith needed her, she also imagined the Child of Light seated atop the great pyramid as its new ruler.

Andelor can keep its Lighthold, Taliah thought, remembering the last time she had to supplicate before Archbeacon Vaughn. *Soon Pyram will be the new seat of the Luminaura*, she told herself, *and I will be the right hand to the Child of Light.*

It may have been a selfish thought, but at least it kept Taliah's legs moving.

The music began to fade as the two women neared the final flight of stairs, and the lights seemed to dim slightly.

Standing before the altar, Kalany was slightly sobered by the weight of the occasion. Her hands were in Lekan's, their eyes locked. The majest looked incredibly handsome in a soft, sun-yellow tunic with an orange embroidered pyramid on its breast, a wide neckline exposing his prominent collar bones. He smiled widely for her, displaying his bright teeth.

"We are gathered this morning," a man's voice began suddenly, "to join the great houses of Nafir and Drastil."

Kalany shifted her eyes toward the speaker. *Where did he come from?* Her walk to the altar had been anything but uneventful, but she was sure she would have noticed such a striking figure. He was a tall, pale-skinned man dressed in elaborate gray robes trimmed in silver rune work.

His eyes went from the gathered nobles in attendance to Kalany, and something in his gaze terrified her, so she looked back to her betrothed.

"It is with great honor and humbleness that I stand here," the man continued, his voice low but powerful, a slithering Xe'danni accent carrying it through the chamber, "a lowly priest of the Gloaming Word, allowed to lead this historic union."

A gray priest, Anika thought distantly. *Why would Lekan have a gray priest conducting the wedding when he kept a Luminaurian temple?*

Quiet, Kalany thought in return, growing frustrated with Anika's doubts and concerns. This was their wedding day; the start of a new life, just like Elrin had said.

"For those who do not know me, my name is Fahid Salak, former advisor for Mavala Drastil. When my church received word that our lost daughter had returned," he motioned to Kalany, "I begged our glorious majest to allow me to do the honor of crowning her as the new royene."

There was a sudden burst of cheers from the gathered, jolting Kalany. But Lekan gripped her hands tighter and leaned toward her.

"They cheer for you, my love. They worship you."

Kalany couldn't help but beam. But as the cries quieted, the altar began drawing her eyes. At first, she only stole the occasional glance at the massive blue stone during Fahid's ponderous ceremony. Yet with each of the gray priest's declarations came a cheer from the crowd and a pulse of light from the altar.

Soon, Kalany was staring at the altar and not Lekan. There were memories locked within that giant gem, but she wasn't entirely sure they were her own;

nostalgia gripped her in this otherwise foreign place, and Anika's thoughts began to suppress Kalany's.

No, Kalany begged, but now that Anika's eyes were lost in the blue swirls of the altar's depths, she realized that Kalany was just her drunken fancies—the hopes and desires that she had convinced herself of, but they were not truly her own.

As Anika once again lost herself in Eyen's swirling power, she began to feel trapped, just like the old god; imprisoned and unable to fly. Power gathered in Anika's hands, but when she felt Lekan squeeze them, it faded. She looked at him and she was Kalany again, intoxicated, trapped, and thrilled.

"Why is *he* here?!"

Jamira cast Taliah a scowl as she pulled the Lightmother back into the shadowy alcove. "Do not draw attention—you're supposed to be dead, remember?"

Taliah pulled the hood to cover more of her face as she motioned toward the ceremony. "The gray priest. Fahid was banished from the city nearly twenty years ago—he was part of some scheme, smuggling outlawed elixirs from Xe'dann into Noveth."

"I remember," Jamira said, waving a dismissive hand. "It was never proven. He's been in Truine since the fall of House Drastil—seems fitting he has returned now."

"Look at Anika..."

Jamira was looking at her, but now that Taliah pointed toward her, the nomarch narrowed her eyes, straining to see whatever it was that the Lightmother saw.

Now that she focused, Jamira could see that Anika looked...dazed. It was as if she had quaffed an entire wine cask; but it was too early in the morning for her to be so drunk. And from the little Jamira knew of the girl from Vale, Anika didn't strike her as someone that would drink herself under the table the morning of her wedding to a foreign dignitary.

Something was certainly amiss.

"They've poisoned her," Taliah whispered, stepping forward as if to enter the throng of people surrounding the altar. But Jamira caught her arm.

"Do not rush. We need to blend in—shoving our way through these people will bring down the guards immediately." Jamira shifted her gaze to the glowing blue stone; while Anika's demeanor was bothersome, she was more concerned with a massive keyshard jutting up out of the ground.

As they stepped forward together, both wearing hoods to conceal themselves amongst the well-dressed nobles, Jamira whispered to her companion. "The Light...can it clear her mind? Whatever is ailing her?"

Taliah nodded. "I have to lay hands on her to be sure."

Jamira was afraid of that. Unsure of how they would interject themselves into a royal wedding without causing a riot, she followed Taliah's lead toward the altar.

The gray priest's words were lost on Kalany as she stared into Lekan's eyes. In them she saw her future, free from pain and struggle. She would enjoy the luxuries of Pyram with a kind, gentle, and beautiful man and help him rule an entire realm.

There was so much certainty in those visions that they felt like memories rather than imaginations. And yet Kalany still felt the pull toward the altar, begging her to look into its depths again.

Fahid clapped his hands together, startling Kalany. "While I cannot imagine why anyone would object to such a prophetic union, I am inclined to allow the gathered a brief opportunity to state their case against the proceedings..."

"I certainly object," came a gruff voice. The crowd parted to reveal a Karranese man with long, tangled hair. He was dressed like a noble, but his clothes were ill-fitting, as if he had stolen them. He pointed at the bride. "This is not Kalany Drastil! She's an imposter!"

A wave of gasps shook the chamber, with several shouts to take the man's blasphemous tongue. But Lekan calmly let go of Kalany's hands so he could motion for the convened to quiet down.

"My friends, please," he said, flashing a smile as if it was all a big jest. "You all know our traditions. A marriage is a sacred pact, and it is only fitting that any possible grievances are laid bare before a knot is properly tied."

There were some mutterings of agreement.

"Please, step forward," Lekan said to the man, motioning him forward. "What is your name?"

"Shanith." The man came forward, looking a little abashed. He cast Kalany a look; she certainly didn't recognize the man.

"Shanith. Could you tell us how you are so certain our dear Kalany is not who she claims to be?" Lekan gave her a knowing grin, as if to say that he had cleverly trapped this man in some battle of wits.

"Because...I seen the girl die when she was a babe."

Another wave of gasps overtook the chamber as Lekan waved his arms to calm everyone down.

"How can that be?" Elrin stepped forward now, his hands clasped behind his back. "During the riots, Drastil Manor was locked down, and only Kalany's parents were found."

The man licked his lips nervously, looking at the vizier.

Kalany understood now. The only way someone could prove such a thing would be to implicate themselves as one of the rebels who had raided the Drastil estate. However, that didn't necessarily comfort her—why would someone confess to such a crime just to lie about her identity?

Shanith had no reply for Elrin.

"Well," Lekan spun from the man to the awaiting crowd, "it seems our friend was mistaken. Guards, perhaps you could escort him to the lower terraces so he may perhaps gather his wits?"

"Wait."

Everyone turned to Kalany, who stood slack-jawed—*why'd you say that?* she asked herself, but without Lekan's hands on hers, Anika's wits were recovering. She stepped toward the man, who was now flanked by two of the majest's guards.

"What did you see?"

The man stared at her feet, as if he could take back what he said if he did not meet her gaze.

Lekan reached for her. "Kalany..."

But Anika took another step toward the accuser, away from Lekan. "Tell me—you've already doomed yourself, why not say the rest?" She looked around, drawing confidence from somewhere, and turning back to give the man a hard look. "The floor is yours."

"Do not subject us to his lies," Elrin said; any kindness he had shown Kalany was now gone. He motioned for the guards to continue apprehending him.

But the guards were stayed by Anika's raised hand. "I will hear him."

"If I may," Fahid began, but before he finished, Anika swiftly dropped her hand and a strong gust of wind burst from the altar. The gray priest was knocked off his feet, as were Lekan and Elrin. The man, Shanith, kept his footing by holding on to the guards. The crowd gasped.

"Now," Anika demanded.

The man stared at her now, eyes wide. "I seen the babe's head bashed on the floor in the Drastil palace...stomped on by the rebels. I tried to save her...but I...I was just a boy. I was nearly trampled as well..."

"Take him away!" Elrin commanded, getting to his feet. "High Priest! Continue the ceremony."

Anika rounded on him, the confusion she felt was turning into a something more akin to anger. "No, wait."

"Kalany," Lekan began, struggling to his feet.

"My name," she said, without turning from the vizier, "is Anika Lawson." The low pulsing blue light from the altar intensified with her words. Kalany's thoughts were gone, as was whatever was suppressing Anika. She felt a hole inside of her now, and she knew exactly what caused it. "And I'll have my knife now."

The gasps in the crowd had slowly escalated to a rising panic, with many nobles backing out of the chamber while others shoved each other and argued over the accusations. Anika ignored it all, focusing only on the old elf who held her true father's heirloom.

In that moment, as she glared at the man that she now realized had been deceiving her—letting her believe she was someone she was not—she felt a deep shame. She couldn't even remember why she was here; her father had entrusted her with his legacy and she had squandered it. And for what? What was she chasing?

The moment passed, and Elrin was on his feet, his hand in his robes and Anika knew that he gripped Stormender. She called it to her, raising a hand to catch it.

But it didn't come.

The altar's blue light began to fade.

"Ka—Anika," Lekan said, kneeling now. He was holding his arm as if he had broken it. "Don't let this man's lies ruin our day."

She kept her eyes on the vizier. "Give me the knife."

Elrin drew the knife out, the keyshard glowing brilliantly and intensifying the altar again. The old elf smiled at her. "I don't know how you reforged a Key of Transience, girl, but I cannot in good conscience allow it to leave Pyram." He nodded toward the majest. "Let us finish the ceremony. Become the royene, and help unite the three cities of Karrane under one rule. Then, I will return the knife to you."

Anika called to the blade again, but something had severed her connection to it. She could feel Stormender through the altar, but the hole within her remained; it was the bond she had once felt with the knife, now out of reach.

"What have you done to me?" Even as she asked, Anika turned in either direction, looking for Stevra. She found the halfling toward the front of the audience, her head down in shame. *The wine,* Anika thought, heartbroken that the woman had betrayed her trust. A memory of the halfling smiling while pouring Anika a glass of wine thrust itself through her chest.

"We've given you a life," Elrin said, motioning to the gray priest, now back on his feet near the altar. "All you have to do is say the words."

"Are we too late for the objections?"

Two hooded figures strode out of the audience, mummers and gasps marking their passage. As they neared, Anika recognized both of them before they even lowered their hoods.

"You!" Lekan hissed. "You're supposed to be—and you!"

"Majest Lekan Nafir has ordered me to execute the Lightmother," Jamira announced loudly, rousing the audience once again. "The royal council has decided to trick all of you into believing the most powerful house in Pyram had suddenly been resurrected and joined itself to the High Terrace."

"Silence, traitor!" Lekan's voice became shrill. "Guards!"

Jamira drew her sword, ready to meet any guards that responded. None did; they were all watching Anika levitate as a concentrated cyclone whirled around her.

"Wait!" Taliah stepped toward Anika, raising her hands against the strong gusts. "Let me help!"

Anika took a deep breath, and as she exhaled, she slowly descended back to the ground, her gown still flapping wildly. The Lightmother reached up and gently laid her hands on either side of Anika's face. White light emitted where their flesh touched, and Anika closed her eyes against its brilliance. The Lightmother whispered a silent prayer.

With each word Taliah spoke, Anika felt the hole within her shrink smaller and smaller. But before it went away entirely, Anika heard Taliah gasp, the warmth of her touch gone.

"No!" Jamira shouted. The sounds of clashing steel followed as battle erupted.

Anika opened her eyes to see Taliah's shocked expression. Her face fell away as the woman dropped to her knees, and Anika saw Elrin's vile scowl, Stormender bloodied in his hands.

Instinctively, Anika reached for the knife—her connection wasn't restored, so she had to physically reach for it with her hand. But Elrin reacted, grabbing for Anika's throat and pushing her backward. Together they stumbled until Anika fell onto the altar. Out of the corner of her eye, she saw Lekan scramble away behind his guards.

Touching the altar sent a surge of power through Anika, but she couldn't focus enough to direct it. Relying purely on her strength, she struggled to pry Stormender from Elrin's grip.

"You foolish child!" Elrin growled, clenching his teeth as he tried to push the bloody knife into Anika's chest. "You could have made this easy!"

With both hands, she used all of her might to keep the blade away, struggling to focus on the flood of power that she absorbed from the altar. But the primal fear she felt in the face of imminent death made it impossible for her to comprehend everything that was happening.

Stormender was only inches away from her heart, the swirling winds she summoned doing little against the old elf's surprising strength. Her strength was failing, and she screamed, tears welling in her eyes as she saw the blade pierce her flesh to end her life.

With every ounce of strength she had remaining, she pushed Elrin away, and managed to move the knife. But that was when Fahid's face appeared behind the vizier, lending his weight and pushing the blade into her.

Anika gasped as she felt her father's knife go through her, biting into the altar itself. With wide eyes, she felt her arms go slack, pinned to the altar by her own knife.

Her vision began to blur as the world became a bright, pristine sky that swallowed her completely.

Chapter Twenty-Six

Converging Paths

They found Brood's body on the third night of their journey. Agents of the Guild used hidden paths along the Valeway, sticking close to the Bracing River. It was there that Crawl discovered the remains.

Knife looked over what was left of the halfling. It was obviously him; she had never seen a halfling man built so solidly. Also, one of his big ears remained, the one with the chunk missing from it. Most of the rest of the poor man had been torn apart by wolves or other vermin in the ravine.

"Where's Grip? I told her to keep an eye on Brood."

Knife looked to Crawl, who voiced her own curiosity. "If she didn't return to the conclave, she's either in trouble or dead as well." She ran her tongue along her split lip as she scowled at the halfling's rotting body. "You don't think she maybe...took the stone for herself?"

The notion didn't completely elude Knife, but she couldn't imagine what could possibly turn the dark elf from the Guild. Of all her agents, Grip was the only one in line to take over if something were to happen to Knife.

She shook her head. "I don't think they even found the stone." Knife hadn't expected to divulge that suspicion, but with everything that had happened in Vale recently—especially the reports from Oakworth—she had a strong sense that someone had gotten to Ruke's stone before them.

"There's tracks here," Crawl said, motioning to the muddy path that led toward the river. "Someone knelt there next to Brood, and then went east...halfling or gnome. Goblins don't walk that straight."

Knife saw as well, always impressed that Crawl's eyes were nearly as keen as an elf's in the dark. "Looks like they crossed the river. Maybe returning to Oakworth."

Crawl grunted in agreement. "I'll tend to the horses. We can make camp here."

"Find something to dig a grave," Knife said, giving Brood one last look. It wasn't sadness she felt for the halfling's demise. He was a fine agent, and had a certain charm to his brutishness, but she had a certain hope that Brood would be a way to lure Scratch or even Ruse back into her service. His passing made that prospect almost an impossibility now.

She sighed. Of all the problems she faced now, that was relatively minor. But still a loss. Her dwindling cadre of rogues did not bode well for the task that lay ahead.

Together, the women dug a crude grave along the riverbank and laid Brood to rest. Neither said a word or gave the man any formal rites. They built a fire atop the loose dirt and cooked a meager meal of bone broth to go with their stale bread. When Crawl produced her flask of bogwater, she finally asked what Knife had been silently wondering.

"What do you suppose happened to him?"

Knife stared into the fire, considering the possibilities. Brood wasn't the most graceful of her agents, but it was certainly unlikely that his death was a result of clumsiness or some simple accident. And the halfling tracks made her suspect that one of his kin had traveled with him. It could have been a killer, but why not roll the body into the river afterward?

"He was killed," Knife said, fairly certain. "But he wasn't alone. Whoever left him here had urgent business elsewhere." She thought about Scratch and Ruse. The former had children to worry about and the latter was anchored down in Blakehurst. Neither would leave their kin to rot like this.

Unless...

Knife motioned for Crawl to pass the bogwater, lifting her mask only slightly so she could drink the putrid stuff. As the fiery substance laced through her throat, Knife considered the most likely culprits who could get the jump on a guild agent in the open, and for some reason she kept picturing the smug gnome Archmage who had recently abandoned his tower.

She couldn't imagine why the man would want Brood dead, but if somehow Brood had gotten his little hands on Ruke's stone, Fainly Lopke was indeed someone who would have taken an interest. There was gossip that Fainly Lopke and Ruke Ebbers were once involved.

The scenario fit too perfectly in Knife's mind as she took another drink. She imagined Brood scrambling in the dark away from Oakworth, his sister or cousin following, a halfling fist gripping the shard of Oakus that contained Ruke's consciousness.

Knife swallowed as she pictured a shimmering portal opening up, and the Archmage stepping out to summon a shard of ice, skewering Brood up against the mound of dirt they found him on. A shadowy halfling rogue scampered away in fear along the river as Fainly bent down and grabbed Ruke's stone from Brood's limp, dead fingers.

"Magic," Knife said, her voice straining against the burning alcohol.

"What's that?"

Knife handed the bogwater back to Crawl. "Nothing." She lowered her mask and reclined back. "You take first watch, I'll only need an hour or two." As Knife closed her eyes, thoughts of the king and their son were as distant as Andelor as she began plotting Fainly Lopke's demise.

Behind the mask, Knife smiled, beginning to feel like her old self again.

Karlton Tolle was a heavyset man who had seen forty-six summers, each one much less eventful and stressful than this one had begun. Despite his bulk, the Lord Mayor strode with youthful grace down the towering hall that led to his council chambers.

On either side of the massive doors were a pair of guards, husband and wife on one side and two husbands on the other.

"Good afternoon, Everet and Charla," he said with a nod to his left, then turning to the two men on the right, "Brant and Horrace. I appreciate your punctuality."

All four guards nodded, tight smiles behind their helms.

The Lord Mayor of Sathford stepped closer to them. "I apologize for the urgency, but we have had dire news from Wickham. Charla, Horrace, I want you in there with me, the news will concern the watch as well. You can share the news with Everet and Horrace later."

Once more, all four guards nodded their understanding.

Karlton took a deep breath and ran his hands through his boyish, unkempt hair before motioning for the guards to open the heavy doors. Inside, the council chamber was lit by a great chandelier that hung from the high ceiling, dozens of fat candles burning above a round lacquered table.

A heavy silence hung among the gathered. Hope Kandalot wore her battle armor, blue enamel mail that gleamed under the candlelight. She had been pacing around the table, stopping at the opposite end as the Lord Mayor entered. Karlton gave her a nod of greeting, though he did not like the look on her face.

To the Lord Mayor, she was far from an attractive woman—especially with that mark on her face that she didn't even attempt to hide with her short hair—but the expression she seemed to always wear made her downright ugly.

"I apologize for the wait," Karlton said as his guards closed the doors behind him. He strode toward the head of the table.

"Nonsense," Gwynna Grale purred in her perfectly maintained Caimish accent. Despite spending the last two decades married to Lord Janthy of House Grale, Gwynna still sounded as if she had just left her high elf homeland on Caim; Karlton suspected it was a concentrated effort on the elf's part to maintain an air of exotic wonder in Janthy's rather dull homestead near the woods. "You gave us plenty of time to commiserate."

While the two mages from Raventhal that sat across the table from Lady Grale nodded in agreement, the warpriest glared from the elf back to Karlton.

"Perhaps we can begin," Hope said tightly, moving to take a seat well away from Gwynna.

"If this is about the cathedral," Karlton began, as he adjusted his doublet over his belly, "then it'll have to wait. I bring more urgent matters."

"As do we," High Mage Konrath announced. Master Audreese stared at the table blankly as if she were a statue, looking paler than usual.

"This doesn't concern the cathedral." Hope kept her eyes on the Lord Mayor. "You have a prisoner that I must take into the church's custody."

Karlton raised an eyebrow. "A heretic?"

Hope considered that without blinking. "Of sorts."

"If it's a prisoner, that can wait," Konrath said. "The spire has been breached from within and Fainly has abandoned the Arcania."

"Yes," Karlton said gravely, "and we have reports from Wickham. The rebels in Copera have been put down, and Malcolmry has gathered an army along the borders. Scouting parties have been sent along the Rathaway. Mayor Drover believes that Copera intends to take Rathen, giving them a foothold in Vale that we cannot allow."

"Sulm is a tyrant," Gwynna said dismissively. "He'll have another uprising before we finish this council."

"We cannot rely on that," Karlton said, feeling sudden disdain for her presence today. Janthy brought the elf back from Merithian in his youth, and the woman had been a plague on Sathford's affairs ever since—always demanding with the air of a queen, while acting aloof in the face of dire circumstances. If it wasn't for the link she provided to the Eldercrowns in Lefayra, Karlton would go as far as expelling her from their councils. "Rathen may have been a free city, but it is also Vale's strongest presence in the north."

"I appreciate the severity of Sulm's forces threatening Vale's peace," the High Mage interjected, "yet we have more urgent troubles at our door. Corvanna's invasion has shown us how important Raventhal Spire is to the city's defense."

Hope cleared her throat, but Konrath pretended not to notice.

"The spire is vulnerable and cut off from the Arcania. As this council knows, Fainly appointed me as his Chosen. Which means I should be acting as interim Archmage in his absence. But we have received word that the queen has appointed some upstart—a Xe'danni sorceress—who isn't even a sitting member of the High Sanctum!"

Karlton nodded, frowning. He could not believe the report from Andelor—*Light, burn all these accursed reports,* he thought. Queen Sopheena seemed intent on bucking every tradition that the people of Vale held dear.

It was already strange enough that Aberheim's heir chose an unknown elf maiden from Caim to be his successor when the plague struck him, but now the queendom had to contend with Oathers running about once more, the oldest Archmage in the Arcania's history disappearing, and Guild agents hiding in every shadow.

"While I do not agree with the queen's interference," Karlton said, lacing his fingers and resting his hands on his belly, "I don't know what can be done about the matter. Perhaps you should take the gate to the tower and see to it in person."

"I would if I could!" Karlton's neck tensed, veins visible against tight muscle. Despite his outburst, there was deeper restrained rage in his face.

His elven companion leaned forward then. "An Oather passed through the gate two days ago. Sir Vance Koren. He delivered a message from the new Archmage that no mages are to pass through the gates. We have essentially been barred from the Arcania. I suspect that Vera Mourgael intends to destroy the Old Ways..."

Karlton felt a chill in the air as Master Audreese allowed the words to linger. Each member of the council must have felt it too, as there was no reply for a long moment. Finally, Hope stepped forward.

"What purpose would that serve?"

"None," Konrath said angrily. "It's villainy, I say. The Xe'danni are known to worship Shadowlords, and this Vera woman most likely means to turn the Arcania into some foul temple and its mages into her personal cult."

While Konrath fumed, Audreese maintained a cool composure. Her voice was so quiet that Karlton had to lean forward to hear her. "Fear drives most foolish decisions. With Raventhal's recent invasions, I can only surmise the other towers have been dealing with similar occurrences. The legions of Oakus have been stirred."

"Which is precisely what brings me here," Gwynna interjected. "Now I know we have no shortage of problems facing us, but Rathen is leagues to the north, King Sulm even further, and the Arcania is Andelor's problem. House Grale is under siege by these foul forest fiends even as we speak!"

"It is my understanding that the attack was thwarted," Karlton said, giving the elf a sideways glance while he still leaned toward the mages. "My reports said that the old Vaughn temple was overrun by these dryads, but some band of heroes flushed them out before any true harm came to your homesteads."

Lady Gwynna raised her chin in pride. "Yes, Lord Grale shrewdly hired the Crestony Crew to prevent a full-blown assault, but two of those brave adventurers nearly died—one lost a hand to some rabid black cat."

"Brigands die every day." Hope's voice dripped with disdain. "It sounds like they bought you some time. Let us return to other matters."

"Certainly," Gwynna said, holding her gaze on the Lord Mayor. "How about we discuss Tomen Shaw's execution? Or perhaps the burning of his temple? Or must we ask the Archbeacon if we are allowed to broach such topics now that Vale's rule seems to be falling under the church?"

Hope made to rise from her chair, but Karlton leaned in their direction to defuse the rising tension. "Not even Queen Sopheena interferes with the church's affairs, Lady Grale, as you well know. The charges laid against the vicar were severe, and he paid the price. The temple burned by my permission."

The last was a lie. In truth, Karlton had been furious when he heard about Hope ordering her paladins to torch the temple, which had been one of Sathford's first structures before the city moved closer to the Bracing River. However, he was in no position to reprimand the church, especially when they had single-handedly repelled the monstrosity assailing the city.

Gwynna finally looked away from Karlton, inspecting her painted fingernails. "Yes, well you have permitted the Luminaura to cut us off from the Eldercrowns. Those recluses in the woods may seem uncouth to you and me, but the power they command over the lost lores is undeniable." Her eyes fluttered slightly toward the warpriest. "They would be quite useful allies in such trying times. But any hope we may have had in their aid died with the vicar."

It was true. Relations with the Lohkrest elves were strained to begin with, but now that one of their own—a high-standing priest, no less—was cut down in his own temple by the same religious order that shunned the traditional elven faiths...well, Karlton did not expect to receive an audience with any of the Eldercrowns for the rest of his life.

"We do not need the elves." Hope relaxed slightly in her chair, but her voice remained hard. "The Light protected Sathford against Corvanna, and it will do so again. My paladins already dealt with the dryads from Raventhal. Besides, who's to say the Eldercrowns aren't aligned with those foul woodland wretches? They are all infected with Oakus' madness."

"The elves of Lefayra are not mad."

The Lord Mayor turned toward Master Audreese, surprised to hear such icy disdain in the elf's normally detached voice.

"Those dryads that attacked the spire were driven by some primal need. It is not the first time we have seen monsters drawn to keyshards, but this was different. Just like how Corvanna used the worst parts of Eyen to gather that storm, someone has tapped into the raw, primal fury of Oakus and infected those closest to his power."

That brought a silent stillness over the council. Karlton eyed each member, considering how he would keep his city united with such divided interests. So many threats with just as many differing paths to meet them.

Konrath broke the silence. "It would seem to me that our most pressing matter is that of this new Archmage. Between her sudden appointment, Fainly's disappearance, and now breaking the Old Ways…I mean, does everyone here appreciate the severity of that?"

"Are mages averse to traveling like the rest of us?" Hope's voice had found its edge now. "I'd say it would be a boon if those wretched tunnels collapsed. Your towers wouldn't have been invaded if it weren't for them, correct? We have birds to send letters and horses to carry us about…I think we will live without those tunnels that give the Shadow another place to fester."

"You are wrong, warpriest." Audreese reverted to her normal voice, unimpressed with the outburst. "The Old Ways provide us more than just travel between the Arcania's towers—although that alone has saved the Joined Realms from more threats than we can count. We would never have won the Nether War without them. Beyond that, we have tapped into lost magic in those tunnels, powers that were denied to the world. We don't even know what else lies deeper."

"And I guess we'll never know," Hope said, with clear satisfaction.

"Is this Vera Mourgael one of your priests?" Konrath asked angrily. "This all seems to be working out in your church's favor, Hope."

"Enough," Karlton said, feeling the tension reaching a breaking point. He could tell that the Luminaura and the spire would most likely not cooperate in his plans, at least not with Hope here. It shouldn't have been a surprise to him, knowing how strained the relations between the Arcania and the Luminaura had gotten in Andelor.

He had to approach this delicately.

"Dame Kandalot," Karlton said, after taking a deep breath, "it is my understanding that your company had originally planned to pass through the city on your way to Rathen, to take it back."

Hope watched the Lord Mayor's drumming fingers before nodding stiffly. "That was before Corvanna nearly decimated your city."

Do you need worship at every turn, woman? The Lord Mayor inclined his head. "And I hope the cathedral is a worthy payment of that debt that we owe the Luminaura for your timely arrival. However, Rathen was not as fortunate, nor was Rathaway Priory. Will you personally be leading your forces north while the cathedral is built?"

A sour look passed over Hope's face as she held the Lord Mayor's gaze, but it was quickly replaced by an uncharacteristic smile. "It was my intent to share with the council that my paladins have quelled the trouble in Oakworth. Sir Darrance Moore has sent word that they will depart for Sathford this morning."

"That is excellent news," Lady Grale interjected. "I'm not sure what has gotten into these wretched dryads, but I am glad to hear they have been driven back into their underworld."

"I don't believe that is the case," Audreese began, but was silenced by a wave of Karlton's hand.

"We will get onto that in a moment," the Lord Mayor told the elf, turning back to Hope. "So, the church will set out north upon the paladins' return?"

Hope still wore that strange smile. "Absolutely, but I must take the prisoner with me. Otherwise, I may have to remain in the city to oversee his confession."

The other councilors looked amongst themselves, each of them wondering if they were missing something. Turning back to Hope, Karlton raised an eyebrow. "Who is this prisoner?"

———◆◯◆———

Gage emerged from the Old Ways through the Onyx Gate, unsure of how that was possible. Desmond had assured him that the gates had been sealed when Gage brought the Shadow through Raventhal, but that didn't seem to stop them from passing through again.

As he hefted his glowing green axe, Gage turned to see the scarred man appear through the dark mist of the portal. Desmond had promised him answers, but it seemed the man could only inspire more questions.

"Did we unseal it?"

Desmond turned to look at the gate. "Can you not feel it? It bends to your will." He turned back to Gage, the angry red lines crisscrossing his pale face seemed more noticeable down here. "You wished it to be sealed when we passed through; it sealed. You wished it unsealed now, and it obeyed."

While Gage had felt the familiar tingle of ancient power before stepping through the Onyx Gate, he also sensed the underworld shudder, as if he were draining some trapped power from the earthen walls.

"Can they follow us?"

Desmond motioned to several other archways in the chamber, each one framing solid stone walls. "Anyone that knows how to navigate the Old Ways can access Audreese's gates, or any of the gates in Fainly's other towers scattered across the Joined Realms." He motioned to the dark, churning air they had stepped through. "The Onyx Gate was crafted to train students how to enter the Old Ways and find their way back. It acts like a beacon."

Now Gage looked over his shoulder, seeing the polished black stones that rose nearly thirty feet over his head in a menacing arch. He had felt something guiding him back here, but he had secretly hoped it was some fairytale connection he and Robin shared. He suddenly found the sight of the Onyx Gate revolting.

He breathed deep, imagining who had laid those stones, creating the dark portal. Picturing dark robed mages like Desmond drawing on forbidden powers they didn't understand, Gage gripped his axe tighter.

Despite the dankness, the air in Raventhal Spire's undercroft around felt refreshing. it was cool and wet, not dry and oppressive like the atmosphere in the Old Ways. He waited there in front of the Onyx Gate, knowing that Ruke would speak to him again. When she didn't, he held the axe up to stare into the depths of its stone

Still, Ruke remained silent.

"Gage?"

Was he right? Was Ruke lying to me? Gage turned around to face Desmond. "What did Ruke say to you?"

Desmond just stared for a long moment, considering. Finally, his eyes dropped. "There's too many voices...they argue in my head, telling me one thing, and then..." He raised his skeletal fingers to his temples, stringy black hair falling forward as he tried to rub the pain away. "Ruke spoke to me after..."

"After what?" Gage felt something dreadful approaching, but he wasn't sure if it was something Desmond was going to say or something approaching through the gate. Regardless, he waited.

"After I killed the halfling."

Ransil, Gage thought. He clenched his teeth and tightened his grip on Harvester. He pictured Robin's master in the kitchen at The Early Mule, laughing heartily as he stirred a huge pot of stew. *No, Ransil was still at Oakworth, alive...*

Desmond looked up, his eyes distant. "I found them by the river...drawn to them by Ruke's stone. His name was Brood. I..." A tear rolled down Desmond's cheek, leaving a trail of wet ash. "Once I touched the stone, Ruke told me she needed me—and then she said she didn't!"

Gage recoiled as Desmond lunged, his eyes wild. He pulled his hair and took another step toward Gage. "She says one thing, and then something else! And then says it's Stane speaking with her voice! I need it to end! And I know I can't die—not truly—unless your sister kills me! It was all I heard as those demons stitched me back together, over and over again..."

Gage held Harvester up with two hands now, ready to swing the axe at Desmond if he took another step toward him.

But Desmond's shoulders slumped, his hands dropping to his sides. His eyes went distant again as he spoke with a voice that didn't sound like his own. "It is only in the malice of Light that you will find release..."

The words hammered in Gage's chest painfully, his heart stamping each sound into his memory so he knew he would never forget them. Something about those words held truth and power, as if they couldn't be questioned. They were Desmond's convictions given form.

The mage looked at him now, his eyes focused. "Ruke says she needs me for something, but I am ruined...whatever those monsters did to me...I cannot be here for any suitable reason. I don't deserve to be...not after the things I have done." Wet black streaks ran down his face. "Please, Gage. We have to find your sister."

Before Gage could respond—or even begin to grasp the depth of Desmond's plight—there was a bestial growl from the Onyx Gate. They both turned toward it, and the dread that Gage had felt before intensified. Something was coming.

We need more time, he thought, knowing they had to find Anika, decipher Ruke's strange messages, honor Desmond's request, and—most importantly to him presently—get back to Robin.

Suddenly, he raised Harvester above his head and brought it down hard, burying it into the floor. Desmond gasped and fell back. Stone blocks cracked and gave way to smoky green light, a rent in the spire's ground splintering from where Harvester had pierced it.

The Shadow clouded Gage's eyes as he watched slithering roots emerge from the cracked floor, emerald mist pouring out in waves as Oakus reluctantly granted his blessings. Like creaking serpents, those roots twined themselves between the black stones of the Onyx Gate, shattering the intricate magical wards that took centuries to create.

Gage felt a euphoric sense of closure as the portal crumbled, the ensorcelled stones screaming in agony as they were pulled down by unholy limbs. The mist that once separated Aetha from the mystical underworld parted to reveal solid earth, loosening as Gage's roots wormed their way toward him.

As the Onyx Gate fell, Gage pulled Harvester free, feeling the connection to Oakus break suddenly. The roots stopped groping, falling still as the emerald mist dissipated. The path to the Old Ways was closed, and Gage smiled at Desmond as he helped the mage to his feet.

Darkness gathered around the Child of Shadow and the Scion of Stane, hiding them from the paladins that strode through the halls of Raventhal Spire.

I'm coming, Robin, Gage thought, the half-elf's face forming in his mind, unburdened by grief of bitterness. He felt Harvester's weight slacken in his grip, as if it had become a part of him. *And we'll never have to hide again.*

Back in the spire's undercroft, amongst the broken black stones and half-grown roots, undead hands began to burst up from the shattered ground.

"You're sure it was him?"

Mirim tucked her chin and raised her brows, rolling her eyes up to Knife to give her a look that said "have I ever forgotten a face?"

Satisfied, Knife dropped the pouch of queens on the table, turning to Crawl. She leaned toward the woman to whisper, though in The Riverstone's loud common room, it was probably not needed. "If the Collectors have had him this long, they're keeping him in the pens."

"How you want to play it?" Crawl ran her tongue anxiously across her gruesome lips. It was clear she was ready to spill some blood, but Knife's own anxiety was quelled by her companion's eagerness.

The guildmaster took a calming breath behind her mask before responding, "I'll play it. You stay here. Take Mirim to a room. Toss her around if you like, but stay put until I get back."

Crawl glanced at Mirim across the table, who watched the thieves with coy eyes as she massaged her new coin purse seductively. "Just know I'm not cheap like those corner boys you visit in Andelor, Crawl."

Not smiling, Crawl looked back at Knife. "You sure you don't want backup?"

"Whatever happens, we're not cutting our way through the streets of Sathford. The best way you can back me up is by staying out of sight and keeping an eye on her—I don't know who else knows…"

Knife trailed off as she turned toward the doors of the common room. The commotion had slackened suddenly, and she could clearly see why.

A boy with dark wild hair strode in, a hunched figure in his wake. There was a sense of familiarity that made Knife get to her feet, trying to watch the dark figure that followed the boy, but her eyes were constantly drawn to—*is that a keyshard in that axe?*

"Mirim," the boy said, striding briskly to their table. "Where's Robin?"

Crawl was on her feet now. "Who's asking?"

The boy with the axe didn't take his eyes off the Jathi woman, his dark gaze boring into her. Knife could sense trouble.

"Where?"

Mirim tucked the coin purse into her skirts, looking toward Knife, clearly unsure how to respond. "You might want to ask her."

Knife looked to the boy's companion now, that pale face now revealed by their table's candlelight.

"Desmond?"

The mage looked up and then Knife was sure. *What in the Abyss was he doing here?! And what happened to his face?* She thought of her own scars, and felt a strange kinship with her sister's personal mage, despite not really caring for the arrogant prick.

Before she could ask, the boy turned to Knife. Crawl stepped around the table, but the guildmaster raised a hand to calm her.

"Do you know where he is?" the boy asked.

From behind her mask, Knife looked from Desmond to this wild-eyed boy who carried an enchanted axe. So many questions raced through her mind. All she could think to ask was, "Who are you?"

Desmond stepped into the shadows, away from the light of their table. He motioned for Knife to follow. Keeping her gaze on the boy, she obliged.

"I take it things went south in Jathi?"

Desmond kept his eyes on his companion. "You could say that. We couldn't find the book."

Knife motioned to the boy. "We? Where's Layla?"

A curious expression passed over the man's ruined face, but when he locked eyes on Knife it was gone. Now he wore a cocky smile. Just like that, the queen's pompous mage had returned. "She didn't make it. But I found something better than the book." He nodded toward his companion, who still glared at Knife, waiting for an answer. "Something the queen will want to know about."

"What does he want with Robin?"

The boy stepped forward then. It was unlikely he could hear them over the din of the common room, but when approached he answered her question.

"I want to tell him I'm sorry."

Knife narrowed her eyes. "What is he to you?"

"He's everything to me."

Knife felt the urge to laugh, but resisted. There was genuine caring in this boy's voice. Did her son take a lover in that backwater town? It was just too sweet for her at the moment, but her eyes couldn't help but return to the green keyshard in his axe. She didn't know for sure if it was Ruke's stone, but it seemed unlikely that fate would miss such a unique opportunity.

"We can take you to him." Knife crossed her arms. Her heart was racing, but she projected as much casualness as she could muster.

The boy shifted his eyes to Desmond, then back to her. "What is he to you?"

Knife didn't need Desmond to tell her just who this boy was; she could feel power hanging around him like a heavy shroud. Whatever he was, she would need to bind him to her. And she only knew one sure way to do that.

When Knife removed her mask, Crawl gasped and moved to block the guildmaster from the view of any patrons in the common room. The boy just stared at her with obvious recognition—the family resemblance was unmistakable, despite her scars—and she knew he was hers.

As Hope spun her tale of a heretic who owed a debt of service to the church, Karlton still couldn't understand why the matter of this prisoner was of such import. But he was already weary of talking about it. There were much bigger issues facing his city.

Let her have the damn thief, he thought.

Just as he was about to raise a hand, Konrath's gatemaster shot to her feet, knocking over her chair. The Lord Mayor's guards both reached for their swords, startled, but Karlton waved them back as the rest of the council stood up as well.

Lady Grale gasped. "What is it?"

"It's the Onyx Gate..." Master Audreese stared wide-eyed at the table, as if a horrendous beast was emerging from its smooth surface. Karlton had never seen her scared, and it more than unsettled him.

Konrath stepped toward the elf. "Has it been unsealed?"

"I wouldn't know...my wards—I wouldn't feel them unless..." Audreese turned to Konrath. The Lord Mayor saw terror in her eyes.

"No..." Konrath may have said more, but the doors were suddenly thrown open. From the hall came distant shouts and the echo of a horn.

Both guards had their swords drawn. "Lord Mayor, there's trouble at the spire!"

The High Mage spun around and raced out the doors. Master Audreese followed.

Karlton moved toward the guards. "What has happened?"

Everet looked panicked. "They said...one of the paladins said—there's undead in the streets, my lord."

"Undead?!" Visions conjured in Karlton's mind of dozens of putrid corpses shambling through his streets, causing chaos. It seemed impossible to believe.

He had heard horror stories of zombies in Guyen, but he—like most civilized people—credited those stories to those poor savages who fell under the thrall of sadistic warlocks.

Hope walked calmly but briskly toward the doors. "I will join the paladins. See that the city watch secures the streets and the bridges. If it is the undead, we need to contain them."

Karlton looked to his guards, nodding in agreement. "You heard the Lady Commander. See to it."

Lady Grale was also on her feet. "Lord Mayor, if I could have a moment?"

Karlton turned to the elf. "Now?!"

"I have something from the druid's circle." Gwynna motioned toward the door. "I wasn't sure if you would want to share it with the council."

Intrigued, Karlton turned to his guards. "See to the city watch. Report back when you have discerned the threat. Follow the warpriest's command." Seeing Everet giving the Lady Grale a cautious glance, the Lord Mayor added, "I will only be a moment, and then will return to my solar. Double the house guard if it eases your mind."

With that, the guards left them, and Karlton returned his attention to Lady Grale as the doors to the hall were closed again.

Gwynna reached into her billowing skirt and produced a lavish box. "I didn't share with the council that I met with the vicar's old order. I don't know how our holy guests would receive that news. However, the druids are my last connection with Lefayra since...well, since Hope snipped off Tomen's head."

Karlton's eyes were fixed on the box, curious why it was so urgent to require a private audience in the midst of an undead invasion.

Lady Grale stepped closer holding the box in her palm. It was intricately carved jade, with flowing leaves and vines across its surface. "It's a message from the Archdruid Wrenda."

Karlton frowned, hesitant to reach out for it. "What is it?"

"Just a token," she began, just as the lid to the box snapped open suddenly to reveal a fat, winged insect of vivid yellow and green. Before Karlton could even recoil from the grotesque bug, it took flight with a loud buzzing of its wings. It flew straight for the Lord Mayor's face. "...of the order's appreciation."

Karlton finally took a step back, waving his arms in front of his face to shield himself from the exotic pest. But it was too late; he felt the sharp sting on his neck. It felt like a hot dagger burying itself into his jowls.

Coldness gripped him almost immediately. He tried to cry out, but his mouth only hung open silently. *Venom,* he thought. Karlton was far from a survivalist, but he knew that he had been poisoned by something. He felt death creeping through his veins, locking up his joints.

"The Ranewood is full of such wonders," Lady Grale said, closing the box gently and setting it on the long table as Karlton fell to his knees, choking. "Of all the places in Laustreal, those lush forests are perhaps the most beautiful, and the most deadly for unwary visitors. The Braxel wasp is probably the least fearsome insect in those trees." Gwynna knelt down so the Lord Mayor could see her.

Karlton's vision was clear, despite the icy daggers shooting through his limbs, turning his body into a statue. He saw the Lady Grale's face twist into an expression of wicked ecstasy as she held out a hand for the colorful wasp to land on. The insect perched on the elf's perfect palm, staring up at the Lord Mayor mockingly.

"You see, Karlton, this little fellow's paralytic poison may eventually kill you, but a single drop of basilisk blood mixed with witchleaf will stop its effects. The other inhabitants of Ranewood are not so kind. Their venom would stop your heart immediately."

Karlton tried to ask her why, but still no words came. Breathing was becoming difficult, and his heart felt as if it were about to burst from his chest.

Gwynna's smile faded. "I can see that you want the antidote, and I do wish I could give it to you, for old time's sake. But the druids have spoken. You cannot be trusted any longer, not after Tomen. We suspect you had his daughter killed as well—no, don't bother denying. I know you wouldn't tell me if you had."

Gwynna waved her hand, and the wasp took flight again, disappearing. She stood up and adjusted her skirt. "Tomen Shaw was the only man who could have bridged the divide between the druids and the Luminaura, but you and Hope have chosen war." She picked up the box and looked down at Karlton as his vision finally started to fade. "I'm sorry you chose the wrong side, old friend. But I feel this is a small mercy I could offer you. When Wrenda's legions bring your city down, they will want to see the church's allies suffer."

Karlton didn't understand. His final thoughts wrestled with questions about Tomen's ties to the druids and what animosity hung between the Luminaura and the Order of Oakus. He was grateful to have a puzzle to solve as he fell to his side, his limbs rigid as he struggled for a few last breaths.

He would rather spend his last ragged breaths reaching for answers than focusing on the awaiting oblivion.

Hope raced down the stairs, thankful for the chaos in the streets. The jailors had been called to supplement the city watch as riots had broken out on the docks. Word of the spire's trouble had caused a surge of panic in Sathford, and Hope knew this would be her best chance to hide the king's bastard before Karlton realized what kind of prize his Collector's had snagged.

She grabbed a lantern from the jailor's table and strode quickly down to the boy's cell. Her breath caught in her throat as the weak light from the lantern lit the dark, windowless hall.

The cell was empty, its bars bent and twisted like branches on some strange iron tree. Blackened roots had burst up out of the ground, pushing through the old gray stones of the dungeon.

As she stared at the bizarre scene, Hope didn't notice the undead hand burst up from the loosened earth. By the time the rotten corpse had halfway dug itself out of the ground, Hope dropped the lantern and drew her sword. With the rage she felt burning inside of her, she wouldn't need the light.

Chapter Twenty-Seven

A Mother's Mercy

Bennik jammed his elven knife into the side of the rotting woman's skull. Her body crumpled lifelessly to the cobbled road, the living roots that were twining themselves into her long-dead limbs—snaking their way through leathery, putrid flesh—seemed to finally go still.

As he watched the dark, clotted blood drip from his blade, Bennik felt overcome with sadness—not horror, as he had expected. While Arkath was certainly a dreadful place infested with ominous shadows that did not yield to Fainly's conjured lights, its occupants did not inspire the same terror that the tales of them had.

While the dead woman bore no particular resemblance to Madison—her features had mostly rotted away at this point—Bennik couldn't help but see the reeve's likeness when he looked down at the withered face. He wanted nothing more in that moment than to flee this decayed, underground empire and ride for Mistbrook.

Maybe that was how this place claimed its legacy, by inspiring such futile dread in its visitors that they dropped their guard to become easy prey for the dead. Maybe they abandoned whatever quest they had embarked upon due to their minds convincing them that only doom lay below Arkath's surface.

Suddenly, the dead woman opened her sunken eyelids, revealing Madison's eyes. Dry, cracked lips parted to say, "This isn't right."

Bennik stumbled backward, dropping his knife.

"What's not right?" Fainly asked, casting Bennik a confused look before returning his gaze to Kartha.

"None of this is right…"

"Yes," Fainly said, making a motion with his hand so the orb of light floating in front of him intensified. When the shadows refused to yield, the gnome scowled. "I could have told you this place was not right. The dead are walking if you hadn't noticed."

Bennik got to his feet, keeping a watchful eye on the corpse that was still dead and still not Madison. He could hear the sounds of more shuffling feet in the distance.

Kartha turned away from them. "You know that's not what I mean. It's not right that this place should be so...peaceful."

Fainly chuckled as more shambling zombies stepped into the light, at least a dozen of them. The dead were dressed in colorful rags that may have once denoted them as high lords and ladies when Arkath had been at its peak, but now it made them look like morbid jesters dressed in motley.

"Your idea of peaceful conflicts greatly with my own." The Archmage brought his left hand around in a flourish and three small, swirling streaks of violet energy put holes in the heads of several of the walking dead. They crumpled to the ground, the vines commanding their limbs creaking and dying

While the gnome worked his magic to dispatch the other assailants, Bennik took another look around, still avoiding Madison-who-was-not-Madison's dead gaze. Fainly's light was soft white, but the glow that came off Kartha was an emerald haze that—combined with the invading roots—made the ruined city look like some verdant, poisoned wood elf kingdom.

Bennik had never been to the distant continent of Laustreal, but he imagined the rumored underground cities there looked much like this. Even though dwarves had carved Arkath into the mountains, the elven influence was clearly evident, from the knotting stonework of its pillars to the rigid awnings that swooped down from the darkness above.

It was said that Arkath was the first joint building effort between the dwarves and the early high elf sailors who were chased from Vaina, and it certainly showed.

Thunder boomed outside, its echo like a menacing groan that carried into the city a sense of urgency, making Bennik turn to his companions. "We should go, before more of them come."

"The gate is at the back of the city," Fainly said, dusting off his robes as the last of the shambling corpses was put to rest. "There's an old tower along the Wane Coast, older than the Arcania. It was there that I helped create the first gates, and there was one that led here."

"It's not right," Kartha repeated, turning to walk in the direction opposite the way Fainly had indicated. "This place should be swarming. The Arkathians were all cursed to wander these streets." She spun slowly around, looking for something hiding in the darkness. "Where are they?"

Her answer came in the form of the ground quaking, as if great serpents were tunneling beneath their feet. But Bennik knew it was the same roots that had taken control of the undead. He remembered the stories Madison had told them of Mistborok's troubles, and it all suddenly seemed to make sense to him.

The dryads, the zombies infested with serpentine roots, the empty ruined city...

Bennik imagined an army of undead, controlled by the primal fury of Oakus, clawing their way through the underworld. Like Eyen's storm, the power of the harvest god was taking form to fight against the incarnate or any other force that stood in its way.

Before he could give voice to his revelation, the ground exploded, spraying brick and dirt in all directions. Bennik dove to the ground, and he heard Fainly give a shocked cry while the earth continued to tremble. A cloud of dirt obscured his vision as Bennik rolled over onto his side.

"The incarnate has awakened," Kartha shouted, all previous doubt fleeing from her voice. "Oakus is retaliating, we need to move!"

Not needing the motivation, Bennik scrambled to his feet, shoving his knife into the sheath at his waist as he pulled out the bow Madison had given him and nocked an arrow. Firing at the enormous, twisted growth of living roots seemed useless, so he loosed at a zombie that blocked his path to Kartha. The arrow took off half the corpse's skull, sending it stumbling backward.

"I can't burn it," Fainly shouted, his voice strained. "There are wards in here blocking me!" The rest of what he wanted to say was cut off by the sound of a huge stone falling from above, crushing a row of buildings. The deafening crash made Bennik reach up to cover his ears as he ran between several undead Arkathians, their rotting arms extended by grasping roots.

"Save your magic!" Kartha shouted. "We'll be needing it soon."

Bennik followed her around a corner of buildings. The road ahead was ruined by the new powers that ruled in Arkath. They both turned to wait for the gnome, Bennik drawing his bow while Kartha bent to pick up a rusty, notched broadsword held by an armored skeleton (which was thankfully lifeless).

Bennik saw the gnome hobble into view, stumbling through the haze of dust kicked up by the mass of roots now serving as the underground city's central pillar. Bennik unleashed a missile at a gruesome corpse that lurched after Fainly. The undead Arkathian toppled back, its flailing arms cleaving a line of sight through the clouds.

It was then that Bennik could see the way they had come in—the great arched stairway leading into the city—had become a wall of slithering vines and claw-like branches, grasping for purchase on ruined buildings and decayed statues.

There's no way out, Bennik thought. He knew he was foolish to think they would have ever walked back out of Arkath. This was always meant to be a one-way journey.

"We'll have to climb," Kartha said with a grunt. Bennik spun around to see a zombie's head rolling toward him, its body crumpling to its knees near the green woman. She motioned to a set of broken stairs that wound their way up toward a stone bridge above.

Fainly scampered up the stairs as Bennik guarded their rear. While waiting for Kartha to boost the gnome across the first gap in the stairs, Bennik fired his last two arrows—both striking true—and then shouldered his bow as he lifted himself off the road. He could hear the horde shambling out of the settling dust, but he didn't look back, focusing on the climb that would take them out of reach.

They ascended the stairs in silence, stepping carefully and avoiding the edges where the railing had fallen away. Below, the city was slowly overtaken by what remained of Arkath's undead and the corrupted roots. The higher they got, the harder it was to see; Fainly's weakening light was enough to reveal their immediate path, but little else.

As they reached the dark heights of the city, Bennik felt a heavy emptiness above. It was as if there was an unnatural oblivion hanging over them, a consuming darkness that would entomb them here. *It's almost worse than Rathen,* Bennik thought. *Almost.*

Eventually, Fainly spoke. "We're going away from the gate, Kartha. We don't have time to visit your childhood home; this place is going to collapse."

"I know the way. We cannot let these roots take hold here." In response to her words, the creaking sounds of more corruption followed them below, the city further crumbling in their wake. "Their presence here will empower the incarnate. Like Corvanna's storm, this is Oakus fighting against the incarnate taking his power, but they have been deceived—the old gods only fight against themselves this way, playing Stane's game."

Bennik was too busy running across the bridge to make sense of her riddles, but he assumed she had come to a similar conclusion as he had regarding the undead and the dryads. If finding Fendra and stopping whatever this was would in any way help his children, then he would do whatever Kartha said, even if doing so would find him buried in this accursed kingdom forever.

The city continued crumbling around them, and Bennik had to grab Fainly so he didn't fall too far behind. The gnome loudly complained, but otherwise allowed himself to be carried like a limp sack of potatoes under the bigger man's arm.

"There!" Kartha pointed down a wide staircase that was once connected to the side of the bridge—now it hung far enough away to make Bennik grimace, thinking of how he would make that jump with a gnome in tow.

"I don't have much left." The Archmage's words were punctuated by each of Bennik's quick strides. "But I'll get us across there. Just don't drop me, Lawson!"

"I make no promises."

With a wave of his hand, Bennik felt his tired legs become nearly weightless. The ache in his shoulder from carrying Fainly went away, and he felt a sick sense of vertigo as his feet lost their grip on the ground.

"Grab hold!" Fainly's voice sounded anguished and exhausted.

Kartha turned just in time to grab Bennik's outstretched hand. As they soared across the emptiness below, Bennik braved a quick glance. In the dark, he saw the reaches of Fainly's conjured lights barely reflecting on a sea of pulsating roots. Twisted branches were slowly reaching up, dead bodies propped up by them, reaching skeletal hands toward the invaders.

Bennik closed his eyes against that living nightmare, and that was when he felt the weight return to his body. The three began falling, hitting the other side of the broken stairs in a bodily crash. Bennik felt sharp rocks cut his arms and legs. His ass took the brunt of the fall, collapsing his spine painfully. Bennik cradled the gnome, saving him from the worst of it, but Kartha went flailing down the remaining stairs in a spinning heap.

"We have to move," Fainly said; his voice was thick now, slurring slightly like he was drunk. Bennik knew the signs of a mage who had overexerted themselves. Unlike a warrior—who would outwardly show their fatigue with their body—a wizard exhausts their mind, which often presents as drunkenness.

As Bennik got painfully to his feet—barely able to straighten his aching back—he saw the need for urgency. The roots were wrapping themselves around the stairs, cracking the old stone. It wouldn't hold for long. Bennik pushed through the pain and hefted the gnome, stepping carefully down the crumbling steps to reach Kartha. The witch was already getting to her feet, bloody cuts marring her otherwise perfect emerald flesh.

The witch guided them toward a set of burning torches. Unnatural green fire cast a haunting pool of light near a huge archway at the bottom of the stairs. Fainly let out a gasp.

"The Arkhold."

Bennik knew little about the Arkhold, other than that it was once the primary seat of power in Noveth, before the first king of Eastlund defied the First Mothers and founded Menevere.

As they neared the high archway, Bennik could see the slithering roots climbing up its edges. The green glow from the torches gave them a supernatural, otherworldly quality, and there was a pungent scent of corruption in the dank air. Regardless, Bennik breathed it in as he followed Kartha into the darkness.

Fainly's lights still followed them, but they had begun flickering as they ran down the massive hall. "Put me down, Lawson. I can't concentrate anymore."

"It's through here," Kartha said as Bennik let the Archmage back to his feet. They turned a corner to face another massive hall, this one lined with more statues of the First Mothers. Time and corruption had eroded their features, but Bennik could still make out some of them.

Heather Falkry watched over their left. The wings of her helm had fallen away, but she looked no less majestic. Next to her was Abbitha Kahn with her two-handed mace raised above her head. Her bear's-head helm was smoothed down, making it look like she had a swollen skull. Across from them were the sisters Rayla and Victora Monteague, both wielding sword and shield. Rayla's cat helm was less worn by time than the others, but Victora's head had fallen off completely.

"The Hall of the Mothers." Despite their desperate situation, Fainly could not keep the wonder from his voice. "I've never been this far into Arkhold."

"Come," Kartha said, not waiting to admire the city's founders. She ran toward the closed doors at the end of the hall. As Fainly's light reached it, Bennik saw a set of monstrous gilded double doors barring their way. Kartha stopped before them.

Bennik heard an echoing moan from the hall behind them, and then another. The dead were coming for them. He looked at Kartha. "What are we waiting for?"

The witch didn't blink, staring at the time-worn doors. "I haven't been beyond these doors since the birth…"

Fainly pushed forward. "Can we revel in the majesty of your glorious return home on the other side of the doors?"

Kartha didn't respond.

As the moans behind them grew louder, Bennik threw his body against the door. Pain exploded from his shoulder as he hit solid stone—it was as if the doors weren't there at all and he had thrown himself against the wall.

Finally, the witch blinked. "Move." She stepped forward and placed a palm on an ornate circle where a door handle should have been. Flexing each finger in a precise rhythm, Kartha began activating the door's glyphs. Small lines of light coursed from her hand, creating a jagged pattern across the surface of the door. Then, something inside clicked.

Just as the sounds of shambling feet told Bennik that the horde of Arkathians had crossed the threshold behind them, the doors groaned inward, revealing another vaulted chamber.

Arkath's throne room was the subject of legend. But what Bennik saw now was a mausoleum, overrun by a poisonous growth like the one in the heart of the city, only this one gave off a sickly green aura—visible corruption. Behind him, he heard Kartha and Fainly working their magic to seal the doors, cutting off the sound of their pursuers.

However, as he studied the massive collection of roots that had burst through the center of the chamber, Bennik could tell they were anything but safe here.

"Mother...is that you?"

The voice sounded ethereal, echoing from the entire room, as if the stone floor beneath their feet spoke. The roots began to shift, creaking loudly as an opening appeared, revealing a figure bathed in emerald light.

"Fendra." Kartha moved in a daze, walking like a zombie herself as she approached her long-lost daughter. "Your voice...the curse?"

There was a horrid cackle as Fendra's body spasmed within her strange cocoon. "Oakus has assuaged me of it—for the first time in decades, I am not under Stane's malignant influence." She laughed again, which sounded eerily like sobbing.

Bennik stepped closer, still wary of the corrupted growth, but oddly confident that the entrapped lich meant them no harm.

"It only seems fitting that to rid myself of Father, I would be made the pawn of something else."

"Are you the incarnate?"

Fendra struggled to turn her serpentine face toward Fainly, her neck creaking like snapping twigs. Now that the Archmage's lights enveloped the lich, Bennik could see vines had wormed their way into her scaled flesh, throbbing like veins.

"I am his weapon against the incarnate," Fendra said, "poorly aimed and indiscriminate in its wrath. Through me, Oakus has commanded my legions through the Old Ways to seek out his usurper." She turned to Kartha. "You hide behind strange flesh, Mother, but I know you. Have you come to free me?"

Kartha reached up to put a hand on her daughter's cheek, the reptilian flesh nearly matching the shade of the witch's borrowed hand. "What has he done to you, child?"

"Of whom do you speak? The Blooming One? Or your beloved Stane?"

When Kartha didn't answer, Fendra raised her hands. Her arms were covered in more unhealed wounds from which came more pulsing roots that connected her to the horrible growth encasing her. "On his return from those old naga temples in Guyen, Father made me one of those monsters for your betrayal, and then Oakus made me a wrathful vegetable for your other betrayal."

Like Fainly, Bennik silently watched the mother and daughter, frozen in anticipation. He saw tears in Kartha's eyes and a look of sad loathing in Fendra's. The moaning outside the doors became more fervent.

Kartha finally let out a quivering sigh. "What are you now, child?"

The question seemed to stun Fendra, who just stared at her mother with those snake eyes. She licked her lips with a forked tongue before replying. "At the moment...I am nothing. I feel nothing." Her expression softened. "Someone else is channeling Oakus—not the incarnate." The lich closed her eyes, raising her hands to her temples. "The druids."

"The Order of Oakus?" There was a hint of fear in Fainly's voice. Why the Archmage would fear some druids in the woods, Bennik couldn't say.

The mother and daughter ignored the gnome, Kartha still caressing her daughter's cheek, sobbing now.

"You know what to do," Fendra said finally, pushing her mother's hand away. "You have to do it now, because once they release me," she smiled wickedly, "I won't let you do it. Now is the only chance."

"Fendra..."

"Do it!" The plant material surrounding Fendra rose and fell with the lich's voice. The throne room rocked, raining dust and debris down on them. "For a thousand years you have cursed me and this place; it is the least you can do, Mother."

The last word dripped venom, and Fendra lowered herself toward Kartha. She pulled her arms inward, snapping the roots that had infested her body. Grabbing her lavish, tattered robes, she tore them away, baring scaled breasts.

"Release me and the rest of the Arkathians from this bondage, and I'll forgive you," Fendra wept. "Now!"

Bennik's heart stopped as he watched Kartha's face twist in agony. The witch raised her sword with both hands, aiming it downward toward her daughter's heart. The undead choir outside reached a crescendo as Kartha screamed and drove the sword into her only child's chest.

The curse of Arkath was broken with a screech and an explosion of blades of emerald light bursting from Fendra's wound. The lich arched her back as the corrupted roots holding her prisoner began to wither away, shriveling and turning to ash. Outside the doors, the undead moans had turned to shrieks.

That's when the city began to fall apart.

Kartha dropped to her knees, leaving Bennik and Fainly to drag her away from her daughter's remains. They got her to her feet just as a giant chunk of rock smashed the lich's body and rolled to flatten them. Together, they raced to the back of the throne room, following Kartha the Cursed as she led them toward their only escape.

"I want Mother."

Jak rubbed his eyes, trying to maintain his calm. The girls had become an unbearable burden since they reached Stelmont, but he knew his life depended on their wellbeing.

If he ever wanted to become an Oather, he would have to carry out his duty.

"I told you, your mother's probably in Andelor. Which is where we're going once I get enough coin. Until then, remember—you two are my half-sisters, which means your mother is *our* mother, right?"

Kadie scrunched up her face and went back to playing with her doll. Her sister, Sadie, happily chewed on an apple, staring at Jak with vacant eyes. Ignoring the girl's unsettling gaze, he stood up, dreading another day in the field on Gordon's farm. But High Mage Stacy was right: he couldn't reveal who he was. Kasia Strallow's squire escorting two halfling children would invite unwanted scrutiny.

The last thing Jak wanted was to jeopardize his master's trust in him. His brother, Roy, had died in her service, and he would not further soil his family's name by being the second Warner to fail as a squire.

"Just stay here," he told the girls, kicking his blankets back onto his bed. "I'll have some food brought up."

Jak left the room, closing the door behind him. A human girl not much younger than him walked by, offering him a shy smile. She wore gray robes like the rest of the mages at the Vestige. With the Arcania so nearby—drawing away more accomplished wizards—it seemed to Jak that the Vestige specialized in bumpkins who had dreams of sorcery.

He nodded kindly to the girl, but didn't return the smile. Once upon a time, he would stiffen at the mere thought of a pretty girl looking at him. But after Dame Strallow had taken him to bed, he couldn't imagine being with any other woman. Just like the proud knights in the stories his father used to read to him, Jak was meant to devote himself purely to his sword and his lady.

Even if his lady frightened him.

"Warner."

Jak spun around to see Sir Paul Stone, the Vestige's lone Oather, striding toward him. He was a middle-aged man who tucked his portly belly in a strained sword belt. His armor looked a size too small, but he wore his normal proud expression.

"Sir."

Paul looked over his cloaked shoulder to make sure the gray-robed girl had disappeared down the stairs before he leaned toward Jak. "The other two you arrived with—the beast and the burned man, not the wee ones—friends of yours?"

Jak shook his head nervously.

It wasn't a lie. When the chamber that he and the girls were hiding in caught fire in the Oakhold, it was the half-orc woman who had saved them, dragging them into the Old Ways, but that didn't necessarily make her a friend.

Jak didn't remember much from the journey—there was lots of shouting from him and crying from the girls—but it ended with them stumbling through a gate in the bowels of the Vestige here in Stelmont.

The man—Brand or Brant, if Jak recalled—looked as good as dead, burned black by the fires that had engulfed the Oakhold. The monstrous woman hadn't looked much better, her clothes mostly burnt away. But Master Stacy had them both taken to the Light's Mercy chapel on the hill overlooking town. That was the last Jak had seen of the two strangers.

Paul reached into a pouch next to his sword and drew out a small, jagged red rock. A keyshard. It glimmered in the faint sunlight streaming in from the high window.

"The man had this." Paul closed his fist around it. "You said Kasia was looking for something in Blakehurst? Think it was those two? Trying to escape the Arcania through the gateways?"

In truth, Jak didn't even know what their purpose in Blakehurst had been. All he knew is that he had been devastated when, in Oakworth, Kasia had told him that he would not be returning to his home—where he might see and comfort his father after Roy's passing—but would instead be babysitting a couple of snot-nosed halfling girls.

"Hide them somewhere in the keep," his master had told him, uncharacteristically lacking any discernible plan. "I need some leverage on their mother. If I'm not back to collect you in two days, take them to Andelor."

It was by sheer luck that Jak had stumbled across the hidden library underneath the baron's keep, a perfect place to hide the little ones for a couple days. He hadn't expected the place to catch fire when those wretched dryads invaded.

Now, having seen the red keyshard, the conflagration underground made sense to Jak. The man must have been a rogue sorcerer and the brutish woman his bodyguard.

"I don't know what Kasia was looking for," Jak said now. "She didn't share her plans with me—I just followed her orders."

Paul nodded at that, clearly not wanting to press the matter of his Lady Commander's activities. "Wouldn't hurt to lock the man up, should he survive. With all that trouble in Oakworth...and the timing of them spilling through the gates just as the new Archmage ordered them to be dismantled...all very suspicious if you ask me."

Jak didn't know what Paul was talking about. "New Archmage?" *Was that why High Mage Stacy wouldn't allow me to take the gate back to Andelor?* Traveling between the towers wasn't exactly a common way to get around Noveth, but he had assumed—given his role as the Lady Commander's squire—that he would be allowed to use the gates.

Paul's eyes were distant now, ignoring the question as he considered something. "We may need the shackles." He nodded in agreement with himself, rubbing a gloved hand over his bald head before motioning for Jak to follow him.

Not having much time to argue or explain that he needed to get to Gordon's field, he followed Paul down the stairs.

The Vestige was once a mighty tower, reduced to little more than a turret during the Nether War. While an effort to rebuild it had begun nearly a hundred years ago, it was never completed, and the tower now stood only a few stories above ground and a few below.

Jak and Paul swiftly reached the first level of the undercroft, neither of them speaking as they passed students giving them curious looks. They turned down a tight hallway lit by the occasional arcane lantern, casting soft aquamarine pools of light at each doorway. They passed two and entered the third, where Jak and the halflings had arrived in this dump.

While Jak had only been to three different towers in Noveth, one of them being the Arcania, he still found it curious that the Vestige only had two gates—one leading to the eponymous towers in Andelor and another leading to Raventhal Spire in Sathford.

They found High Mage Stacy Augustine in front of the gateway to the Arcania.

"It's done," she said, not turning to them. She was alone in the small room, the hood of her red cloak drawn up to cover a head of curly red hair and a pudgy face that had reminded Jak of a wild boar. "That bitch has done it."

"Done what?"

She turned now to address Paul. "The gate's closed. The bitch has really done it." Stacy flicked her deep-set eyes toward Jak. "Looks like you may just be the last one to travel through the Old Ways, kid."

Despite the circumstances, being called *kid* rankled Jak. He was a man grown, and squire to one of the most powerful women in the Joined Realms. But he knew better than to pick a fight with a witch.

"We have cause to believe that the others who came through may have nefarious intentions," Paul informed her. "Still have the shackles down here?"

Stacy puffed out her cheeks and crossed her thick arms under her breasts. She cocked a head to the cabinet behind her, the only real furnishing in the room. "Will you be needing one of the cells in the dungeon? We still have a couple of the cultists locked up...tried every spell I know, yet they still won't give up this Combustress woman."

"Let 'em stew," Paul said as he moved toward the cabinet. "Even if this bastard survives, I'm hoping to make quick work of him." He held up the keyshard and summoned a small flame. "I haven't had a proper burning since the last time I bent you over in the—"

"*Not* in front of the kid, Sir Stone."

"Right," Paul said with a chuckle, opening the cabinet. There was a clatter of metal as he sifted through the contents. "You sure these still work?"

As the High Mage consulted with the Oather, Jak felt a sudden compulsion to turn toward the gates. The one to the Arcania was certainly dead—a cold, damn stone wall inside an elegant archway, its glyphs no longer burning with magical energy. However, the other gate—the one he had passed through—was certainly not dead.

Framed by a similar archway with still-burning glyphs of magical blue fire, the hazy mists of the gate seemed to come alive as Jak stared into it. It felt as if his gaze had awoken it. Taking a step forward, he focused his eyes on something in those undulating curtains of sorcerous energy.

There was a figure—no, three figures—coming toward him. As his eyes adjusted to the gloom within the gate, he could tell it was more than three figures. It was an entire army; a legion of shadows coming from the beyond. He tried to scream, but his mouth dried up and his throat tightened. Sudden horror had seized his body and his mind, and he could only watch as whatever it was came through the gate.

"I only need one," Paul's voice said, from some other dimension. "He's just a burnt man; this is really just for show."

It was then the waving curtains of the gate were torn away and a familiar man tumbled out. Jak barely dove out of the way as Bennik Lawson tumbled to the floor, bloody and barely conscious. He had been gripping a knife in one hand and a bloodied bag tightly in the other, both of which spilled to the floor as he went limp.

"Who's there?!" Despite his shock, Jak couldn't help but notice that Paul's voice was surprisingly shrill.

Jak wanted to identify the man, but before he could think how to explain, another figure spilled out of the gate. *Is that a dryad?* And then another.

The third figure caused Jak, Paul, and Stacy all to gasp simultaneously.

The former Archmage of the Arcania fell atop the others in a heap, his small body rolling off the larger two, landing heap near Paul's feet.

Silence hung in the chamber as the three conscious people stared at the new arrivals. The gate they had fallen through slowly stilled, the magic coursing through the flowing glyphs fading.

"On second thought, I will need more than one," Paul said, turning to take out three more sets of black shackles, forged with the same Sutheki ore as Oather armor to negate magical abilities.

Jak couldn't hide his shock. "What do you mean? That's the Archmage!"

"Was the Archmage," Paul said calmly. "Besides, look." He pointed to the ground.

Next to Bennik Lawson's limp hand, Jak saw a pile of bright red keyshards spilling from a bloodied bag.

Chapter Twenty-Eight

Appointments & Ambushes

Before the company began their trek to Sathford, Avrim retreated to the Temple of the Lightborn for a brief moment of solitude. The temple's acolytes and Mother Agathene were tending to the wounded in the keep, leaving Avrim alone with his thoughts, which were darker than they had ever been while in a sanctuary.

Even within the temple's stone walls, Avrim could hear the commotion outside. It made it hard for him to find the inner focus he needed for what lay ahead, but he tried keeping his eyes closed and his mind fixed on the only power he could rely on.

He sighed and opened his eyes.

It was no good; he would find no relief, not even here. And he felt guilty for confining himself here while there was so much to be done.

Darrance had commanded the Luminaura forces to prepare to return immediately, concerned that the incarnate meant to lay siege to Sathford from behind Raventhal's weakened defenses. But there were hundreds of dryad corpses to clean up, and still the dead and wounded to tend to.

Avrim gave the candles on the altar one last glance—remembering the raging fires that had consumed Melaine in the Oakhold—and turned to leave. But he was startled to see the baroness blocking his path.

"Your ladyship, my apologies..."

Vivian Caffery raised her hand to silence him. She looked weary. With her hair disheveled and lack of sleep weighing down her eyes, the woman had aged almost a decade since Avrim had last seen her during his judgment.

"There is no need for apologies," she said in a whisper, her eyes moving between him and the dozen burning candles atop the altar. Stepping down the aisle between the pews, she approached Avrim, her expression unreadable. "Not after everything you've done."

What I've done, Avrim thought, *or what I failed to do?* But he just lowered his head, not sure how to respond.

"I wanted to come see you after that unfortunate display, but I needed to be with my children...after such a...well. I'm glad to have caught you before you ride to your next heroic quest." She waited until he looked up into her eyes. "I must ask you something."

Avrim swallowed, trying not to think of her late husband's face or of his own fists smashing into it. "Anything, my lady."

"How did you do it?"

While he suspected she referred to her children, he waited for her to specify.

"My children should be dead—after what that monster did to them." She glanced at the temple's plain stone walls, the blue hanging banners with the brilliant white Brightstar emblazoned on either side of the chapel. "I don't profess to be a deeply religious person, but I know what the Light is capable of."

Feeling a knot in his stomach, Avrim dreaded the words he knew were coming. Like the certainty of mortality, he knew he would have to face the realization that had been lurking—unspoken—since that fateful night when he encountered the Child of Light.

"What you did—no one should have been able to do that."

Again, Avrim had no reply. But he didn't shy away from her gaze.

"I held my tongue during the hearing—in front of the Oather—because I did not think you belonged in the Arcania's custody. I did not speak of my own concerns about what happened in Lenora's room. I vouched for you, Brother, on House Caffery's reputation; so please...repay me with your honesty."

Avrim nodded, his eyes finally breaking away from hers. "The truth is, I do not know how I saved your children. Or why I beat your husband." He looked up into her eyes again. "I had just killed a man—a dwarf, down in the baron's hidden library. It was the Xe'danni's man...I suspect a member of the Shrouded."

"Then he was a villain," Vivian said, her expression remarkably calm in the face of a murder confession, one committed in her own home. "Surely there was cause."

"There wasn't," Avrim said, more angrily than he intended. "We had him unarmed and outnumbered...we could have delivered him to your dungeons. Or tied him up, knocked him unconscious. Instead I caved in his skull, because—because," he looked *through* her now, into that familiar bright void that beckoned him, "the Light decreed it."

"Just as it decreed that my children be spared?"

Even though he hadn't thought of it that way, he nodded in agreement, immediately convinced.

"Then, Brother, please," she reached out to take his hand in her own, placing her other hand gently over his. "Heed the Light. At all costs. For whatever reason, it has chosen you."

For what?

Avrim found Ransil Osbury and his young Raventhal companion in the keep's courtyard, tending to a couple of mules that looked to be their mounts for the journey to Sathford.

"Brother," the halfling said, giving him a curt nod. "I'm terribly sorry about your companion—Melaine, was her name?"

Just hearing her name made Avrim wince, immediately conjuring recent memories of him trying to drag Deina out of the baron's crumbling library as the flames licked at them hungrily.

He nodded to Ransil, tightening his lips in a show of genuine grief. "And your nieces—how tragic. I understand they were below as well?"

Ransil's kind face twisted, then his eyes darted to his left. Avrim turned to see a familiar figure limping toward the stables. Dame Kasia Strallow looked half-dead as she dragged herself and her breastplate toward the stableman tending to her mount.

"Between you and me, Brother, I'll believe they're dead when I see their remains." He flicked his eyes back to the priest before adding, "I'll let my cousin grieve instead of giving her false hope, but I would find it passing strange if Kasia weren't hiding something."

Avrim wasn't sure what he was getting at, but he nodded in any case. "How is your cousin?"

"The baroness has taken her in," Ransil said, turning to inspect his mule's saddlebags. "I don't blame Dolly for what she did, but attacking an Oather like that in a noble keep—well, she'd normally be strung up immediately. We're fortunate Oakworth is under a new ladyship, if you ask me."

"Indeed," Avrim said, considering how his own fate would have played out in the hands of the former Baron of Oakworth. "May the Light be with her during this time of grief."

Ransil snapped his fingers. "Speaking of which, that paladin who claimed Vivian's daughter was the Child of Light—he was looking for you. Was headed to the bathhouse last I saw him."

Avrim looked from Ransil to his young wizard companion who offered him only a confused, boyish shrug. With a nod, he let them about their business as he made for the barracks. Despite the pressing circumstances, he walked slowly, dreading an encounter with the paladin.

As he passed by a group of acolytes in dark green cloaks, he gave them a nod of greeting that wasn't returned. From their dark hoods, the archers watched him warily, keeping a considerable distance as they rounded the corner toward the courtyard. It seemed his reputation had preceded him.

He approached the bathhouse as a squire was making his exit, carrying pieces of armor and clothing covered in ash—Darrance's. The boy gave Avrim a terrified look before scampering away, leaving the door open for the priest. Steam obscured the view through the door, but Avrim stepped in, welcoming the oppressive warmth.

"I said don't come back without some—oh, Brother Kaust."

As his eyes adjusted to the thick air, Avrim saw a softly candlelit room packed with several tubs that looked like little more than oversized cauldrons. Two of the baths were heated by burning charcoal, and only one of them was occupied.

Darrance Moore reclined against the edge of his bath, his muscular arms draped casually over the side. The perfect blonde hair that Avrim had seen in Caffery's great hall was now matted with sweat, plastered over his handsome face.

Avrim felt a strange affection for the man, and found himself suddenly uncomfortable, wanting to turn back around and leave. But this man was his superior—First Paladin of the Luminaura and commander of the Light's army, a position that Avrim himself would covet at night when sleep evaded him—so he dared not disrespect him.

"Sir," he managed, realizing he was staring vacantly at the naked man.

"Call me Darrance here," he said kindly without the hint of a smile. "Disrobe. Join me. Wash the filth of the baron's Shadow lair from yourself."

His stomach tightened. "I'm fine, sir—Darrance. I need to prepare for our return to Sathford."

"That is what I wanted to speak to you about." The paladin reached into the steaming water with a cupped hand and splashed his face. "But if you'd rather stand there and sweat in your armor while we confer, so be it."

Avrim did.

"By now, you've probably heard about your temple."

With everything that had happened, Avrim found himself occasionally forgetting about the vicar's execution. Even walking here, he had assumed the paladin would want to speak to him about the incarnate; it wasn't until the topic was broached now that the knowledge took the wind out of him all over again.

"Apostasy is a high charge."

Darrance nodded, splashing bathwater on his shoulders now. "That it is. Dame Kandalot swung the blade herself, so I was not present to hear the specifics of the charge. But from what I have gathered about you…I don't suspect you were in league with the Order of Oakus?"

The druids? "What does the Order have to do with it?"

The paladin cocked an eyebrow. "The vicar's daughter—she's in league with the druids. Their sect has been a pain in the church's side since even before the Nether War. Surely you were aware of Tomen's ties?"

Of course Avrim knew about Tomen's daughter, and the vicar's own history with the Order of Oakus, but the man was devoted to the Light. Shaking his head now, Avrim refused to believe otherwise. "He was a man of the Light, I would swear by it. Any judgment of my own character should be likewise made of his—he was the man that trained me and swore me into the church."

Darrance considered that silently, his piercing blue eyes taking full measure of Avrim. Finally, he began to rise out of the bath. Avrim's eyes wandered, and he couldn't help but notice the paladin was built like no other man he had ever seen, hung like a Sutheki, if rumors could be believed. He averted his gaze, his mouth dry and suddenly tasing of bile.

Stepping out of the bath, Darrance stood before Avrim, as if awaiting defiance. The priest gave none, knowing that despite everything, Darrance would—in one way or another—control his fate.

The paladin pushed the damp hair from his brow. "Before coming to Oakworth, we held council with High Mage Konrath; the elf serving under him informed Hope that the Light should not be used to combat the incarnate's legions."

That sounded absurd to Avrim, but he let Darrance continue.

"Drawing on both Shadow and Light, these monstrosities will feed off one or the other. Upsetting the balance of either will inevitably empower those in service to an incarnate." His expression stern and unchanging, Darrance raised a calm finger to lay on Avrim's chest, tapping the steel plates that protected him. "It could be said that whatever you did to that little girl—the Light you fed into her—may have caused this…may have caused the death of Hope's dear cousin, Brace Cobbit."

Avrim felt the familiar rage building within him, just like when killed that dwarf, or almost strangled Mother Agathene to death. He tried to quell it, but could already feel his fist clenching. Everywhere he turned was another accusation, and the baroness' words about embracing the Light only weakened his resistance to the divine wrath brewing within him.

The hint of a smile touched Darrance's lips. "However, I think there are so many pressing matters currently, it may slip my mind to share that with the High Warpriest."

There was a hanging threat there. "What do you want of me?"

The look that passed over the paladin's face—and his continued nudeness—made Avrim suddenly suspect that the man had certain intimate arrangements in mind. But then the man turned to walk past Avrim, toward a shelf of towels.

"I want you to serve as Sathford's beacon—the new cathedral will need leadership. And I feel your proven piety is just what the city needs."

The request—no, not request, decree—blindsided Avrim. Since he had walked into these sweltering confines, he had been accused of scheming with the druids and the incarnates, and now he was being given one of the highest honors in the Luminaura.

While his mind raced, considering his options, he quickly came to the conclusion that he really had no options beyond leaving the church (and probably dying in the process) or accepting Darrance's offer (knowing full well he would be in the man's pocket).

"You better get ready, Beacon," Darrance said, putting his leg up on a bench so he could dry himself with the towel in a way that made Avrim even more uncomfortable. "We have a long ride back to Sathford, and your flock will need your reassurance that you will be more true to the Light than their late vicar."

Avrim just stared into the vacant bathwater, watching the filth that Darrance had washed from his body and regretting not joining the man when he had the chance.

The march from Oakworth to Sathford would normally take most of the day, but the procession of Luminaura soldiers—a mix of acolytes, paladins, and a faithful local militia of Oakworth residents rallied by the Light's valor against the frenzied dryads—moved at a healthy trot.

Ransil and Quinn struggled to keep pace on their small ponies, but the halfling didn't mind. He rode in silence, his eyes never straying too far from the Oather. The rest of the company—with the exception of Avrim and Deina, who rode to either side of them—were whipped into a frenzy, many occasionally shouting loud prayers while others sang battle hymns.

While he hoped there wasn't a battle ahead, Ransil had to admit that he felt a good deal of comfort traveling alongside such an emboldened company.

"The Shadow comes for Sathford," Darrance had decreed before the departure, as his legions gathered outside the town's gates. He had made a show of announcing Avrim as the new beacon, adding more fervor to the clamor; it was then that Ransil realized just how notorious the priest had become since their first visit to Oakworth.

Darrance had put on his helm and drawn his sword as he steered his horse in a circle. "So we must make haste! The darkness doesn't sleep and neither shall we! We cross the river before nightfall, and ensure the Light defends Sathford and the rest of Vale from whatever evils the Abyss spits out!"

Driven by the First Paladin's words, the company reached the Valeway quicker than Ransil could have imagined.

It was then that the fighting began.

The first attack came after the acolytes reported an overturned wagon on the Valeway, about a mile north from where the short road to Oakworth connected. There were no bodies, but clear signs of retreat into the adjoining woods. As the company came to a halt to investigate, they were assaulted from either side.

As roots burst out of the ground—some gripping corpses, others ending in snapping mouths that dripped venom—Darrance called out, "Meet them with steel! Do not channel the Light! Save your strength for the real foes!"

Even in the erupting chaos, Ransil knew that the warning went deeper. Something Quinn had told him about what had been written about incarnates. As embodiments of the old gods' primal powers, the incarnates fed off such magic.

"True arcane magic is different," Quinn had explained, when Ransil had told him of the events in the Oakhold. "Channeled magic calls upon the connection to the old gods, but arcane magic—wielded by a studied mage—is created from those threads. That is why Brace's keyshard erupted—it was fighting fire with fire."

Being no mage, Ransil had little use for the advice, but he pocketed it like he did most things he heard (or overheard). What he lacked in practiced knowledge he made up for with a remarkable memory.

The armored paladins made short work of the savage plant life blocking the Valeway, their disciplined formations holding off the worst of the attack while the acolytes provided ranged support. Quinn conjured bright yellow flames to burn away a knot of roots shaped like an ogre crawling out of the loosened earth while Ransil wielded his two knives, slashing at anything that got too close.

The armored Luminaurians remained ahorse during the battle, but Ransil and Quinn had climbed off their skittish ponies; the terrified beasts fled immediately back down the Valeway. As Ransil rolled away from a whipping vine, he caught sight of Deina, Avrim's dwarven bodyguard, launching herself into battle with an axe and shield borrowed from Vivian Caffery's armory. The priest himself swung his mace nearby, smashing the skull of a lurching corpse.

As the dust of the ambush settled, Darrance called out to the newly appointed Chaplain Jenore, the late Brace Cobbit's replacement. "Take seven scouts north on either side of the road, the rest will take the rear. Don't let anything come out of those woods!"

Ransil thought *woods* was a generous term for the sporadic collection of trees to the north, but after his time in the Hollowood and encountering those dryads in the outskirts of Buckley Woods, he would be happy to be as far away from a forest as possible.

Before Jenore could lead her acolytes away, there was a clamor on the Valeway. The paladins reassembled in a tight formation, those mounted taking position on either side of the wrecked wagon while those on foot closed ranks in the middle of the road.

"Hail the Light!"

Darrance rode forward to meet the approaching company, which Ransil could barely make out through the bodies of armored holy knights. It looked to be a rabble of assorted travelers, mostly human—a small wagon pulled by two burly, identical brutes, both bloodied with mops of disheveled brown hair plastered to their brows, with several well-dressed merchants excitedly saluting the paladins. They immediately began shouting at Darrance.

Ransil moved forward so he could better hear their report.

"—they've taken the city!"

Darrance checked his horse as he reached them. "Who has?"

One of the merchants—an older woman clutching her ripped dress—stepped forward as she pointed north. "The dead! Those witches brought them from the Abyss—brought them to avenge their order!"

A mounted paladin near Ransil took off her helm, revealing short red hair framing a pinched face. "What order?"

"The Order of Oakus! You killed one o' their kin, it's said! The old vicar."

Ransil's cunning eyes couldn't miss the glare that Darrance cast in his direction. The halfling turned to see Avrim staring back at the paladin, and he couldn't tell if the priest's expression was one of fear or fury. But as the mounted Luminaurians broke into a full charge up the Valeway, he didn't have time to concern himself with it. Several paladins gave Ransil, Quinn, Avrim, and Deina a place on their saddles as the rest of the company raced to Sathford, no longer caring about any ambushes.

Watching the thinning trees to the east, Ransil thought he saw figures moving. Whether they were dryads or druids—or both—didn't seem to matter anymore. He knew the incarnate would be waiting for them, and the thought of fighting it without Anika made it feel like he was riding to his death.

Of the many deaths he had ridden towards, this one felt much more certain.

Chapter Twenty-Nine

Bridal Gifts

Once again, time yielded to Anika. The searing pain in her shoulder paused with the rest of the world's passing, and she fell into the beyond, momentarily abandoning the chaos of her wedding.

She couldn't see the two robed men pinning her to the altar, their faces frozen in menacing snarls. Nor could she feel the deep connection with Taliah as the Lightmother called upon the Light to blind the majest's forces and protect Jamira from harm. Not even Stormender, biting into her shoulder—cleaving through flesh, bone, muscle—could pierce the veil that fell over the world.

Anika Lawson left it all behind and ventured into oblivion.

Much like the visions she had in Oakworth when her brother stood ready to slay their mother, she hung weightless in a plane far from her own. Ruke's words from those previous visions came back to her.

"You know…you are the Child of Light, and you will already know all I tell you—deep down."

Deep down.

The words were gravity, suddenly pulling her through the nothingness. She didn't scream—she knew where she was going.

"You will already know all I tell you," Ruke said again, the echoing phrase repeated in her mind as visions of her flight from Oakworth to Pyram whipped by in reverse.

"But you must remember."

On command, Anika tried to remember. The vision of her flight paused then, and she hung suspended in midair overlooking a peaceful stretch of land—the Acreage. She had never been to the halfling lands, but they looked exactly as Ransil had described them to her: rolling hills overlooking tucked-away farms, quaint cottages made for smaller folk with smoke billowing out of their chimneys.

The simplicity and quaintness of the landscape was in such contrast to the luxurious and exotic sights of Pyram that Anika wished for nothing more than to descend and craft a life among the halflings. But she had no control here—all she could do was watch and wait and yearn for escape.

A sudden pull sent the world rushing by again, and Anika realized she wasn't flying to Pyram again—she was being pulled back to Oakworth, toward her battle with Corvanna. Recalling her flight in vivid detail, now, she dreaded what lay ahead, but knew she could not escape the past.

The Harvest Breeze stood like a mausoleum, waiting to show Anika the rotting remains of her grief. She had no choice but to enter, if only to move the misery along. Her mother's body still lay in a pool of blood on the floor of the empty room—the dresser, bed, and table had been replaced by writhing roots cloaked in shadows.

The pale, lifeless orbs in Renay's sunken eye sockets shifted and fell on Anika. Her blood-speckled lips parted.

"He needed us."

She spoke Anika's thoughts.

"We tried to do what was right. But the Shadow has taken him, and there is no right anymore..."

Footsteps behind her made Anika whirl around to see Matty, black roots wrapped around his bruised neck.

"You didn't kill us."

The words, and the realization that came with them, were a knife in Anika's chest—it was the heart of why she had run away. She wasn't running from her family or her destiny, but the guilt associated with both. Deep down, Matty's sacrifice was a throbbing scar reminding her of how little she understood her purpose as the Child of Light. She fled from this place that gave her that wound, and applied the majest of Pyram as a poultice to soothe the lingering pain.

Despite the revelation, the vision was unrelenting. The phantom Renay rose from her place of unrest, dead eyes still holding a motherly gaze on Anika.

"He still needs us."

Anika thought of Gage, and the mere memory of her brother distorted the world around her. The room in The Harvest Breeze melted away, turning into a cloud of smoke. She was outside now, in a city consumed in flames. Her instincts told her she was seeing the present.

Gage stepped through the smoke, the hood of his dark cloak drawn over his wild hair. He passed by Anika, unseen, a glowing axe held with both hands. *Harvester*, she thought, not knowing why. There was a definite connection with the weapon—not as potent as Stormender, but it was there.

Sounds of battle raged and chaos flooded the streets—*is this Andelor?* Anika wondered, now unsure if she was seeing some possible future—and her brother brought his axe down, decapitating a shadowed figure.

Anika gasped, "Gage!"

Her brother turned, looking at her. No, looking *through* her.

"Come on! Through the alley!"

Anika spun to see Robin race through her ethereal presence. As shocked as she was to see her brother kill someone, feeling Robin pass through her filled her with icy realization. Whether seeing Gage triggered some sort of connection between the Child of Light and the Child of Shadow, or Robin coincidently passing through the spot she occupied, Anika couldn't say.

All she knew, without a shadow of a doubt, was that Robin had killed her mother.

That knowledge came with bittersweet relief, knowing now that Gage had not murdered his mother—maybe the Shadow hadn't taken him completely. But it also awakened a new kind of malice within Anika—the kind that required violence to adequately sate.

As Robin passed through her, the rage subsided, quickly replaced by fear when she saw what apparently chased her brother and his accomplice. Two bandits—a lithe woman in a ghostly mask and a hooded, hulking brute of indiscernible gender—hurried after Gage and Robin, the masked woman slashing at several zombies, twirling knives in each hand.

Assassins, Anika thought, unsure why they would be hunting her brother, but feeling a certainty she dare not question.

"Not him," a voice said.

The vision began to fade.

"No!" Anika tried to focus, needing to know who the two rogues were—she needed to warn Gage, to help him. Now that she knew he hadn't killed their mother, unbearable grief made her physically ill. Her heart ached, shooting throbbing pains through her shoulder.

It was then that she realized the world beckoned her—time was pulling her back, slowly resuming its flow, dragging her along with it. She felt Stormender rammed into her shoulder once more, the source of the agony, energy from the altar coursing its way through the knife's blade.

Anika was no wizard, but even in the throes of visceral pain, she could tell what flowed into her body was the purest form of magic.

She opened her eyes to see the cruel faces of Elrin and Fahid mouthing unheard threats at her through gnashed teeth. There was only hatred and lust in their eyes—they hated her for having the power they so coveted. Gritting her teeth, she closed her eyes again, trying to hold onto the vision of Gage.

"Not him."

Renay's voice stopped time again, easing the pain immediately. Anika opened her eyes to see she was in The Harvest Breeze. Matty stood in the shadows like a statue, wheezing through his crushed windpipe. Renay stood before her—no, not Renay, her other mother.

The woman who was certainly not Mavala Drastil stared at Anika with ghostly pale eyes. Blood spattered her dead lips, but Anika still thought she was beautiful.

"Gage doesn't need us," the woman said, still with Renay's voice. "He's not ready. Not him."

She thought of her father then, the only other person she knew of who would need her now. But even the thought felt foolish—he didn't need her, she needed him. Picturing her father's face in this timeless place pulled her elsewhere. The inn's room blurred as if Anika were spinning in fog, and a familiar cackle sent a shiver down her spine.

"Rake him again, Skraw!" Corvanna's laughter echoed from the grave.

A city of ash rose up around her, burned stone walls with no roofs, charred headstones in a massive cemetery that was a once-mighty city. *Rathen*, she knew without knowing. *This was Corvanna's queendom before she came for me.*

Corvanna, perched on a balcony, spread her blue feathered wings and exhaled as thousands of harpies took flight behind her. She was framed by the storm that Anika had ended, sickening shades of putrid greens and moldering grays as far as she could see.

"I killed you," she tried to say, but her words held no weight here in the past.

A scream pulled her view from the towering demigod, and she saw her father chained to the floor. His bare torso was shredded, torn flesh hanging in tatters as a harpy slashed his face with her talons, spraying blood across the ruined rug.

"No!" Again, a shroud of oblivion kept Anika's voice from interrupting the past. All she could do was watch the wretched harpy torture her father as Corvanna cackled above them in murderous glee.

"He needed you." The voice in her head was Corvanna's, mocking her with a vile laugh. "And you left him to find a more suitable family."

Blood sprayed again and her father wailed in agony—agony she had left him to.

"No," she said again, weaker, a war of emotions choking her. "I needed to know...where I came from."

Bennik suddenly paused his grotesque writhing, his eyes settling on her firmly while the harpy continued shredding his flesh. "You've always known."

Before she could reply, blackness consumed the scene and she was back in The Harvest Breeze. Her birth mother stood before her in place of Renay, and Matty's face had darkened and changed shape, his throat still a sickening purple color. He moved his mouth, but no words came out.

My true father was mute, she thought, not knowing how she knew that, but she had given up questioning the hidden knowledge lurking deep in her mind that had just now begun to reveal itself.

The pain in her shoulder returned as the silent man continued mouthing something to her, his eyes like pale, vacant orbs.

Whatever the man said was lost on her, because all she could think about was her actual father being tortured by those harpies. She could have flown to him instead of chasing her own past in Pyram. Visions of her passionate nights with Lekan flashed her mind like poisoned daggers, injecting agonizing guilt through her body.

But again, the pain became a real throbbing near her heart, where Stormender held her pinned to the altar.

The world rushed back faster now, time righting itself as the chaos of her wedding resumed with a sound like a roll of thunder in reverse.

"Make her submit!" Elrin was screaming in her face, his eyes wild as the veins in his neck tightened.

"It's not working," the gray priest behind him hissed, his own face twisted in rage. "Something's happening...with the altar."

The altar.

Time stopped again, Fahid's mouth frozen around that word.

Altar.

"You know about the altar."

There was a new voice in her head. *The first voice,* she thought. That eerie sense of familiarity that would sometimes confuse the present with distant memories overcame her as the world grayed and faded away.

Oblivion again.

"They are my altars."

It was a man's voice, inviting and dangerous. She knew it was the voice of Stane, but she had no way of knowing how she could be so certain. *It was the Light,* she thought. *I am the Child of Light...the Light knows.*

"Yes," Stane said, "you are cursed with all this knowledge. But I can help you silence it—the tedious bits. No one wants to know all, trust me. It makes living seem redundant. Best to leave some of it a mystery."

The darkness began to yield, revealing a figure bathed in a soft glow. Stane stepped toward her. He was a handsome man, with skin only a little lighter than her own and thick, dark hair pushed back in a lazy tangle that made him look like some Caimish prince stepping out of an old painting.

"You are much lovelier than the last Child." Stane brandished a smile that set loose a reluctant swarm of butterflies in Anika's stomach. In another time and place, she was stabbed, her own blade pinning her to her wedding altar by two scheming men, but in this unknown place she almost felt like blushing despite herself. "Though, that one had a beard."

Anika had no response. She was completely unprepared for a dialogue with a demigod.

No one truly knew who Stane was, but most legends spoke of him as the first man ever born, created by powers older than the old gods or Light and Shadow. Whatever was true about him, Stane was a constant presence throughout the ages. And now he stood before Anika, waiting for her to acknowledge him.

She spoke without words, her thoughts echoing in this place. "What do you want?"

"I want the same thing you want," he said, motioning to the darkness surrounding them. "Freedom."

She remembered flying—the feeling of being completely unchained, free from confusion, concern, and grief. Looking at Stane gave her that same sensation, and she tried to look away from him, but couldn't.

"You seek freedom from whatever is expected of the Child of Light and I seek freedom from the Abyss." He motioned again to the lifeless emptiness surrounding them. "For thousands of years, I've been trapped in Mural's domain, waiting for one of the Children to break this damn cycle."

Ruke's words returned to Anika— *"The only way to break the cycle of Light versus Shadow is to kill the deceiver"*—as if the halfling whispered them to her once more.

"You want me to kill you?"

Stane laughed. "You're welcome to try. But no, that is not my desire."

"Ruke said that is the only way."

Stane stepped closer, the dark surroundings taking form slowly. The infinite blackness shifted, turning to smoke. "Ruke says what she believes." Stane's voice changed slightly, as if emotion had begun to creep in at the mention of the halfling priestess. Behind him, the forms of six distinct figures took shape—*mages*, Anika realized—pacing the shadows that now became vast hallways lit with sorcerous blue sconces. "Even if she lies, I cannot fault her for that. Belief is a powerful thing...it has the power to create gods."

The final word breathed life to the materializing scene. Blackness receded and the dim magical glow suddenly became radiant—if she had her physical eyes, it would have been blinding—lighting a scene that felt like a hazy memory.

"In ancient Ghulta," Stane told her, "we forged the first altars. The one that brought you here was either the two-hundred and twenty-eighth or ninth, depending on if you consider the one that Corsa destroyed when Eyen took that maiden to bed...love corrupts all."

Anika barely made out the words, her thoughts lost to the visions of Ghulta. The legendary empire was depicted in so many different ways that she never knew how to imagine how it actually may have looked. Now that she saw its fabled architecture, she could safely say that all attempts to capture its splendor were in vain. It was indescribable.

While the mages—with their elegant robes, armor, and weaponry—strode through the high archway connecting two cavernous chambers, Anika was whisked through the vaulted ceilings of the Ghultan keep. Stane's voice followed her as she took a grand tour of the ancient structure, but she only half-listened.

She twisted through decorative rafters carved with sculptures of dragons, demons, and manticores, reminded of the splendor she had experienced when first seeing the high halls of Pyram. But this place was even more wondrous.

"The Ghultans spent thousands of years building up their empire," Stane told her from afar. She began to descend, following the group of mages. "It only took one year for me to destroy it."

"You devil, Stane!"

The mage spoke Ghultan, but Anika could somehow understand it perfectly, which was almost as perplexing as to how she knew what the Ghultan language even sounded like.

Loud footsteps drew Anika's eyes down the hall, where she saw him walking toward the mages.

Stane.

For the legends that preceded him, he seemed an altogether disappointing figure. Known as a shapeshifting trickster, he could take many forms, but Anika felt a deep certainty that this was his true self. With his pale Caimish flesh and long, greasy black hair, he had the look of a commoner: unremarkable face, broad brow, a strange gait to his walk. His attire, however, was quite remarkable. He wore a lush, purple sable cloak draped over flared steel pauldrons on his shoulders enameled in deep violet.

He smiled as he neared the mages. "Devils don't keep gods for company."

Several of the mages laughed. One of them—a tall, pale elf wearing a blue-gray cloak—stepped toward Stane and embraced him. "We're not gods here, friend." The mage pulled back and put his hands on Stane's shoulders. "We're equals."

"Nonsense, Eyen," Stane said with a smirk. "The Six Saviors were always meant for more than I could aspire to. I am just a mere servant."

"Servant or no," a big man with bushy red hair said, stepping forward, "those Netherlords would have seen through our plans if it weren't for you, Stane. Your cunning has won the day again."

Stane gave the man a gracious smile. "Thank you, Oakus. I'm happy I could help."

What is this? Anika wondered, feeling that strange sense of familiarity to this scene. She felt a revelation here, but she was too perplexed by this bizarre scene that felt more like a stage show than someone's memory.

The vision of Stane turned to her then, the other mages suddenly frozen. "It's your memory, Anika. The Light has seen all."

A blur of visions whipped through her mind then—wars, weddings, births, deaths—a million scenes that felt like memories, but there was no way she could have so many.

"Stop!"

They did. Ghulta had fallen away and now Stane was all she saw.

Laughing, Stane said, "Not ready for that one, I see. Well, the truth can be quite painful." He reached up a hand then. His finger was extended, pointing at her as he slowly brought it down to her chest. "Let me show you."

When his finger touched her, she was thrust back into the real world—the real, agonizing pain of her knife impaled in her shoulder replacing Stane's touch. She opened her eyes to see Elrin and Fahid, still screaming their wordless rage while the fathoms fell to absolute chaos behind them. Anika squeezed her eyes shut again, hoping to go away again.

Through the blinding ache of Stormender in her shoulder, Anika could still hear Stane. "You know what I say is true...the Light reveals. I can show you."

She opened her eyes, seeing Elrin and Fahid cursing her, trying to kill her.

"I can show you what they did. All you have to do is ask."

Ruke's face appeared in her mind then, shouting some wordless warning, but the pain in her shoulder pushed the halfling away. Anika couldn't focus on a single thought; between the knife, the altar, and the pestering voice of a demigod, she was overwhelmed.

"That is uncertainty that consumes you, Child. I can free you."

Yes, she thought desperately.

"Say it."

Gage's face appeared in her mind, bloody tears streaming down his cheeks as he screamed for her to help him. Shadowy fingers stretched around her brother's face, pulling him into darkness.

"As a sign of faith—you have to say it, Anika."

"Yes!"

The knowing came like the cool breeze of a shade in summer, banishing the unrelenting misery that fed into her from the altar. She no longer felt the knife; it was like a part of her, almost comforting. All the attendees of her wedding—including the men attacking her—were still statues, giving her a reprieve to consider Stane's offering.

The scenes playing through her mind were horrible, but now she knew the truth.

Now she was ready.

Jamira merely blinked, and in that time the world shifted.

One moment she was fending off the majest's guards as the gray priest and Elrin tried to gut Anika. Taliah had fallen to the ground, blood pouring from the wound in her back. Jamira had closed her eyes against a spray of blood as she wounded a guard—careful to avoid killing if she could—and that was all the time Anika needed to upend the chaos.

A powerful gust of wind knocked the nomarch backward, her armor clattering loudly against the hard ground. Screams rang throughout the small chamber as bodies were thrown heavily against the wall. Jamira rolled to her knee, squinting against the rocks and dirt that blew from the direction of the altar.

When the gust finally died down, Jamira could see Anika through the hazy atmosphere, floating above a funnel of wind that gathered below her. The hilt of a knife jutted out from her shoulder, just above her heart, blood staining her beautiful gown. Her eyes were small orbs of radiance, bathing the chamber in white light.

"Arise, citizens of Pyram." Anika's voice was calm thunder; the expression on her face was carved of stone. "You are called upon to judge these men."

Jamira got to her feet, still shielding her eyes from Anika's gaze and the dry earth being kicked up by the wind. She could see gray robes flapping wildly as Fahid was lifted into the air. His limbs were stretched out as if he were bound by tightened rope.

"A witch!" The priest shook his head wildly, struggling against the magic that restrained him. "She's a witch! Guards!" Nobody moved.

Elrin was brought up similarly, but the vizier didn't resist. The old elf had a bizarre look of satisfied resignation on his face.

Still hanging in the air, Anika motioned to her prisoners. "These men have conspired with your majest to lure me into a political marriage so they could retain their power. Using an artist to fool me into believing I was a long-lost daughter of the last domina, and then poisoning me to suppress my powers, they orchestrated this wedding to fool you all into going to war against the chamberlords."

There were gasps and shouts demanding proof of these accusations.

"It's true," Jamira said, stepping forward. "They lied to her, telling her she was Kalany Drastil, daughter to Mavala." Looking into Anika's eyes, despite their radiance, Jamira added, "She is not a dominess. Her parents were commoners from my nome. Her name is Anika Voth, daughter to Aren and Kora Voth."

As if the names were some sort of counterspell, the winds immediately died and both men fell to the floor, each of them grunting in pain. Anika dropped lithely to her feet, landing gracefully. When she looked at Jamira, the nomarch could see the girl's eyes had returned to normal. There was sadness in them.

"I remember…"

Anika's gaze drifted from Jamira to something that wasn't in the chamber with them. Her hand mindlessly went to the knife in her shoulder and she tore it out, spraying blood across the glowing altar, which seemed to pulsate quicker as the blood splattered on it.

"I remember Deerun and the assassin who chased us." Anika reached a hand up to her wound, Light gathering as she pressed her palm against the bloody ruin of her dress. "Her name was Lukahna Strail, and she was the Child of Shadow that chose my brother—thinking she was saving the world." When she lowered her hand, the wound in her shoulder was completely healed.

Other wedding guests began to rise, cautiously watching the bride as she stood up and walked over to the lifeless body of the Lightmother. Jamira gripped her sword as Fahid and Elrin both moaned and began struggling to their feet—she would not let them escape their judgment.

"I was just a baby," Anika continued, her voice distant and fading slightly. She knelt over Taliah, her hand glowing again with the same healing power as she placed it on the Lightmother's fatal injury. "But I remember the Shadow leaving her body…taking root in my new mother. I still remember…"

The Lightmother's body jerked to life as she took a desperate breath. The guests who hadn't already fled gasped along with Taliah, but Jamira just asked, "How?"

Anika looked up, a strange smile on her lips.

"Because I am the Child of Light."

There were even more gasps as Anika helped Taliah to her feet. Jamira moved to help her, but Anika stood upright suddenly, turning her head toward the tunnel that led back into the fathoms.

"Gage."

Before the nomarch could ask what that meant, Anika led Taliah into Jamira's arms and said, "I have to go."

Without another word, the wind gathered and blew Anika from the chamber. The light from the altar went out, leaving the chamber in darkness. By the time the hewers came with lanterns, Jamira saw what she had already known.

Fahid and Elrin were gone.

Chapter Thirty
Unearthed

Naya fell through her worst nightmares

She had heard thousands of versions of what the Abyss might be like, and as the indescribable horrific visions assaulted her, she knew that's where she had been pulled into.

Between the unrelenting scenes of violent mutilations and perverse acts of sexual deviance, Naya found a moment to gather her panicked thoughts. Her body was thrashing wildly as she still fell into nothingness, but she managed to slow her breathing and focus with the logical side of her mind—the side that was able to distinguish between the corrupting presence of Light and the chaotic nature of Shadow.

Neither power was here. This was a void of silent, existential dread.

Naya had always believed the High Shroud's teaching that the Abyss was the ultimate sanctuary for Shadow. But as she continued spinning through the landscape of terrifying brutality, she realized that it was all a lie.

If this truly was the Abyss, it was not what the Shadow promised; it was a place for the murdered, the unsatisfied, the desperate. Memories belonging to the damned took root in her as if they were always a part of her.

In one memory she was wreathed in flames, drawing in a breath to scream in agony as her flesh cracked under the unbelievable heat. The smell of burning meat filled her nostrils, giving her a momentary sense of morbid comfort before she shrieked in preparation for the pain.

But it never came. The vision left as quickly as it came, and now she was tied to a glowing stone altar. She could feel a man thrusting himself inside her as she laughed and screamed in artificial ecstasy. Whoever she was in this memory was unsatisfied as the next man took his turn, blood running down her thighs.

Yet she craved more, praying to some power trapped within the altar to feel something...anything.

Naya blinked away the foreign memory, but in this hellscape there was no escape from her mind—a mind that was no longer her own.

The countless ghosts that held dominion here took turns showing Naya glimpses of their eternal sufferings, begging for their unrequited loves or unresolved purposes to be fulfilled. She took on their miseries, one by one, until they became a blur of torments attempting to suffocate her.

After what could have been a moment, a day, or a century, she felt the hands, pulling her from the Abyss.

"No," she said, her voice a choked sob. "Not yet."

Despite the misery that consumed her here, Naya felt like she couldn't leave until she had seen some resolution—echoes of the ghosts who had invaded her mind. But she had no choice. The hands drew her out.

"What good is she to us? There's no way she's the incarnate."

"That remains to be seen, Sharell."

The voices were distant, faint. To Naya, they were just ghosts looking to fill her mortal vessel with more heartache. But the visions ceased. A warmth had replaced the coldness of the Abyss, and slowly the voices became more real. There was a soft, rhythmic chanting that gave the bickering voices a celestial quality.

"We don't have time for this. We have lost Arkath, and it seems Gwynna has taken matters into her own hands."

The chanting continued its ponderous melody.

"Wait—she's waking."

Naya's eyes fluttered open to see soft green light replace the nothingness of the Abyss. Emerald mists hung over her, framing the faces of three women: a wood elf, a gnome, and a human. The wood elf wore an elegant headdress—*an Eldercrown*, Naya thought hazily—and the human and gnome were clearly druids, their decorative hoods pulled back to reveal hair tied back in gnarled headbands.

Naya blinked as the women watched her warily. "Where am I?" Looking around, she saw there was a ring of hooded figures swaying—the source of the haunting chant that seemed oblivious to her presence.

"Never mind that," the human said, rising from her knees. She was a broad woman with pale, blemished skin. Her face would have been lovely if she had not been scowling, and the belly that hung out of her leathers gave her an oafish demeanor. "Who are you? You're no incarnate—would you knock it off over there! It didn't work, we just plucked some Xe'danni rat from the Harvester's seed sack."

The chanting ceased.

"Sharell." The gnome's voice was soft and musical, but it clearly held power over the gathered. Voices responding to Sharell's outburst ceased immediately, awaiting the gnome's next words. "I think you should take the initiates to the Janthy's estate, to prepare for the siege."

The woman named Sharell gave the gnome a hard look. Even in Naya's semi-lucid state, she could tell there was animosity hanging between the two. Despite that, the human grunted and turned away, her cloak billowing in her wake.

"Get dressed, you hags," she said to the gathered, consisting of about five women and two men, one of whom was the thinnest dwarf that Naya had ever seen. They gathered their gnarled staves and followed Sharell out of the misty glade. The heavy druid trudged away like a scolded youth, shoulders slumped and arms swaying dramatically.

"Wrenda."

Naya turned to the wood elf, a woman who appeared as young as the Child of Light but regarded the gnome with wizened eyes.

"The Shadow clings to this one."

The gnome nodded, looking back to Naya. "Yes, I suspect she is Shrouded. But would she save us the time and confess it so we can discuss more pressing matters?"

Naya felt a chill as she looked from the elf to the gnome named Wrenda. The Eldercrown could feel the Shadow on her, but Naya could barely lift her head from the ground in her current state—she would be unable to magic her way out of this predicament.

"I will," Naya said, with more confidence than she felt.

"Good," Wrenda said, standing up. She had tanned skin and wavy brown hair adorned with thin branches. A decorative club hung from her waist, along with dozens of pouches that likely contained herbs and remedies. "In times like these, I believe the Shrouded to be our fiercest allies."

"Is that why I'm here?" Naya struggled to roll to her side, propping herself up with an elbow. Dried leaves crunched below her. Looking around, she saw an unnatural wall of trees encircling them beyond the mists. Now that she could focus slightly, she felt undeniable power coming from the Eldercrown.

We are in between, Naya thought. She knew the wood elves had the power to shift their place in the world between Aetha and the Nethering, creating a temporary void. *That was how they reached me.*

"You are here," the elf said, also rising to her feet, "because I called upon the keyshard stolen from the Eldercrowns last year—one that was supposed to be with the incarnate. So," she crossed her arms over the emerald silk vest that did little to conceal her chest, "perhaps you can tell us why you're here."

Naya stared at the woman's face, feeling a sense of familiarity that she couldn't quite explain. *I know her.* But Naya had never stepped foot in Lefayra; she may have thought little of the wood elves, but she knew better than to cross them, and she had never imagined them to be overly welcoming of a Xe'danni Shadow priestess trespassing in their domain.

Wrenda broke the silence. She stepped forward and motioned to the elf. "Cethany has traced last year's keyshard thefts in the north back to a small-time band of ruffians known as the Bluedridge Boys." The gnome chuckled at that. "Aptly named, considering all the members were women."

Naya knew the name. While the Guild was the most established criminal organization in the Joined Realms, they refused to deal with the Shrouded—a principle that Naya still found idiotic—so the Shadow priests were left to fence with even more unsavory ruffians. The Boys had smuggled a stash of red keyshards out of Wickham on their way into Vale and sold even more green shards to Naya before making their way toward the coast.

"We all know the keyshard black market is nothing new," Wrenda continued, "but with the incarnate from Rathen..." She looked to Cethany.

"It's no coincidence," the elf said. "I know Father Damien in Wickham was behind the harpies. The question is: was he following church orders?"

Wreda shook her head. "Even if the Luminaura wanted to wake the old gods—for what reason I couldn't even begin to conjure—doing so would be far too brazen, even for a Vaughn." The gnome turned toward the elf. "And what good would an incarnate serve them?"

"A show of force!" Cethany motioned beyond the arcane trees that surrounded them. "Look at Sathford! The Lord Mayor commissioned a blooming cathedral for them after the harpies were chased off!"

Wrenda raised a hand. "You've made your case—let us focus on the present."

Naya managed to sit up. "You want the incarnate to strike at Sathford, and you want me to help you control it."

Both women looked at her with tightened expressions, but it was the Eldercrown who spoke.

"I know what you are and you know what I am. The only way you could be here is if you had a hand in calling the incarnate." She waved a hand and the vision of the trees rippled, turning to smoke that dissipated to reveal an elegant royal chamber.

Ignoring the sudden return to reality, Naya narrowed her eyes. "I made it," she said, her confidence returning now that she understood these two needed her. "I am Mawsurath's mother."

The gnome scoffed. "A fitting name I suppose." She stepped away toward a nearby table, pouring herself a glass of wine. "Well then, where is your child?"

Something occurred to Naya then. "You're the Archdruid of the Order of Oakus."

Wrenda took a sip of the dark Caimish wine, such a deep red it looked black. "And you are the High Shroud's puppet. What of it?"

Naya smiled.

Fallon sat down on the writhing ground, not finding any comfort in her resignation. The crumbled remains of the Onyx Gate seemed to be a fitting headstone for her grave.

"I'm sorry, Father." Her voice had a godlike quality down here, echoing with ancient power, its commanding sound countering the sadness in her heart.

Behind her, Mawsurath stood like what it truly was—an empty suit of armor. Its once glowing emerald eyes were dull chunks of jade stone. Once Fallon had felt a kinship with the incarnate, something joining them on this quest for vengeance. But now, she felt a coldness between them, and she did not want to share her tomb with it.

As she began to stand to move away from the ruined gate, she felt something replace that coldness.

"Fallon."

She spun around to look at Mawsurath, even though she knew who the voice belonged to. The incarnate looked at her with those dead eyes, still as a statue.

"I'm with your order, outside Sathford. In Janthy Grale's keep."

After jerking her head in all directions for some sign of Naya's presence, she realized the voice was in her head. "How?"

"We can explain later. Right now, you have to get out of there before the Old Ways collapse—you'll be trapped."

Fallon looked at her lifeless companion again. "How? I can't feel Mawsurath anymore. That axe...I think Gage killed him."

There was silence. "Naya?"

"Listen carefully, Fallon. You are the incarnate. I made you believe that it was Mawsurath, but the incarnate is a gathering of power...and you were the missing piece of that power. Mawsurath is a vessel, and only you can possess it."

Fallon stared at Mawsurath, feeling the ground beneath her quake again. There were distant shrieks—creatures and plants enthralled by the rage trapped in the Old Ways—and time was running out. She felt hot tears welling up, and her thoughts returned to the chapel where her father's headless body lay, forever bleeding.

"The Luminaura wants you trapped down there, Fallon. They could not stand against you if you were to escape. The Child of Shadow deceived us because he is afraid of the Light...we must show him that together, we can bring down the church."

Fallon's eyes narrowed, and Mawsurath's eyes began to glow green in response.

"They spit upon your father's grave," Naya continued, her voice like jagged claws raking Fallon's mind. "Before the ashes of his chapel cooled, they began constructing their cathedral. It is up to you to destroy it before they seal your father's legacy under their palace of deceit."

Even though Fallon could tell the woman was manipulating her, it didn't matter. She spoke true, and the words restored her bond with Mawsurath. The incarnate groaned as it rose on its feet, the limb that was wounded by Gage's axe was regrowing, tightening under layers of living tree bark.

As Mawsurath's chest opened up, Fallon stepped inside and she felt more power coursing through her body than ever before. She expected to hear Ruke's voice again, but it was only Naya once more.

"Follow them."

"Who?" But Fallon heard the loosening dirt then. She turned toward the sound, Mawsurath's head following her gaze. Hunched figures dug their way through the earthen passages as the world continued to shake. Debris fell in waves, creating new crevices for the lumbering army to continue their climb upwards.

"The Arkathians," Naya said, wonder and elation carrying her words. "It seems fate brought us together, Fallon. Your order was able to commune with Oakus, channeling his rage into the forces lurking in the Old Ways between here and Laustreal—the dryads, their panthers, even the roots themselves, all of them have flocked to your banner."

Fallon felt a surge of energy from Mawsurath, as if he had heard Naya's words as well and was enlivened by them. It was infectious, and she was ready for whatever awaited her above.

"How do I get out of here?"

Naya didn't respond. Stones fell from above, knocking loose more remains of the Onyx Gate. Fallon raised Mawsurath's arm to shield herself from the falling earth. "Naya?!"

"Cethany said she will send a sign."

Cethany?! Fallon couldn't understand why the Eldercrown who had been the one originally responsible for enrolling her in Raventhal would be involved in this communion. But before she could even form a question, a circle of earth at her feet began to swirl with misty green magic. The rocks and dirt began to take shape, forming an image that nearly broke Fallon.

Tomen Shaw smiled at his daughter, his face sculpted perfectly as if from her memories of his younger days. It was a hollow image, that Fallon could literally see through—just dirt held together by elder magicks—but she nearly wept seeing him alive again.

The vicar motioned for Fallon to follow him as another chunk of the Onyx Gate toppled against Mawsurath's sturdy frame. As the undead continued their slow crawling toward Aetha's surface, the incarnate of Oakus began its own ascent.

Naya collapsed into the luxurious bed, more exhausted than she ever imagined. After her fall through the Abyss and the exertion the druids just put her through, she feared she might not actually physically survive.

But she had to.

Determination kept her awake, even though all her body wanted was sweet oblivion.

"That shouldn't have been possible," Naya managed to say.

Wrenda scoffed. As she sat on the bed next to Naya, she removed her headband and shook her dark green hair out; it framed her child-like face like a thorny bush. "A lot of things shouldn't be possible these days. But the world is changing."

"Yes," Cethany said, removing her headdress. "For better or worse, the balance is shifting. Soon, the Eldercrowns will have no choice but to leave their precious havens and join the war."

Naya's vision slowly began to fade, despite her efforts to remain conscious. She had so many questions for an Eldercrown, especially one who had revolted against the wood elf court. "What war?"

The world began to spin away.

"The final war."

Chapter Thirty-One

ROOT & STEM

Gage held Robin's hand tightly, thinking only of his safety as they navigated the heaving bodies that began to flood the alleyways. Desmond followed them as if in a daze, his eyes distant ever since Gage had closed the Onyx Gate. But there was little time for Gage to dwell on it.

Sathford was in absolute chaos.

As if thousands of undead crawling up from the streets wasn't enough, it seemed every ruffian had decided to take vengeance against the Tolle Collectors. Magic occasionally lit the night sky.

"They've reached Raventhal." Desmond sounded detached, as if bored with the revelation. "They must have breached the Old Ways somehow."

"The city gates will be overrun," Knife's companion shouted over the mage, grunting as she drew her shortsword from the belly of a maniacal half-orc who had chased them into the alley. "We have to try for the bridge."

"No," Knife said from behind her mask, pulling her son—and Gage in tow—around a corner as two guards came bellowing down the end of the alley. "Something's happened in Castle Tolle. If there's panic here, it'll certainly send most of the nobles to the docks. Sathler Bridge will be worse."

"Yeah, something happened," the bigger woman replied. "The fucking dead have invaded, or haven't you noticed?" As if in response, a skeletal arm entwined with roots burst up from the grown, grasping for the woman's leg.

"Crawl!" But Knife's warning was too late. The arm latched onto the rogue's ankle, causing her to sprawl across the cobbled ground, her sword clattering away. Just then, the guards in pursuit rounded the corner to meet them.

"There's the assassin!"

Gage finally let go of Robin so he could grip his axe in both hands, stepping toward the guards as Harvester began to glow. Knife's hand shot out to stop him, her eyes wide behind her mask, fixed on the weapon. She nodded toward the guards. "Don't let them see."

Gage let one hand drop from Harvester and the glow faded. Robin took his free hand again, his fingers soft and calming.

"I'll be your assassin," Crawl snarled, producing a broad knife from her belt to sever the undead arm grasping her leg. The cobblestones heaved as the rest of the dead thing continued pulling itself out of its grave. "Take it and go."

"Surrender and face your judgment," one of the guards insisted. "There's no escape!"

Desmond stepped forward, assuming an authoritative posture. "Stand down, Collectors. I am Desmond Everton, First Mage to Queen Sopheena of the Valiant Keep. These individuals are under my protection."

The guards looked at each other, then back to the mage. One of them loosened their grip on their sword and raised their shield, the Tolle Bridge emblem gleaming under the burning brazier nearby.

"We don't care if you're the queen's bleedin' husband," the Collector said. "The Lord Mayor is dead, and that there is the assassin." The guard raised his sword and pointed toward Robin.

Gage looked from the sword to his mother's killer. A brief doubt blossomed within him. It had taken Gage facing an incarnate to bridge the divide between himself and Robin after his mother's death, and suddenly he was left questioning if Robin was indeed the person he knew back in Blakehurst.

But Robin tightened his grip on Gage's hand as he looked into his eyes. He shook his head. "I didn't."

Gage knew it was the truth, and turned back to the guard, determination renewed.

"Don't try to deny it," the guard said as he stepped forward. He brought his sword down on the decaying invader that had pulled its torso up from the stones. The sword easily cut the thing in half, ending its struggle. "Dame Kandalot saw you in the Lord Mayor's council chambers, then found your cell empty."

"The warpriest," Robin whispered. Gage saw Knife's head snap toward the half-elf. Robin turned his shocked face toward her. "She knows who I am. S-she knows about you."

"You come with us, wizard," the guard continued. "It ain't safe out here. You can shelter at Castle Tolle until the steward figures out what to do with you. The rest of you are under arrest. Throw down your arms."

Crawl spun around to her feet, gracefully stepping on her fallen sword's blade and kicking it up into her hand. "Come and get them."

The guards both moved to oblige, the rear one taking a horn from their belt and sounding a shrill alarm. "We've found the assassin!"

"Come on," Knife said, pushing Robin and Gage behind her toward a tight alley leading back into the chaos. "Crawl, let's go."

The bigger woman looked over her shoulder, her mask lowered to reveal a pair of maimed lips twisted in a kind of snarl. "My boy's already dead. Go. I'll hold them off." She turned back and shouted. "I killed your fat Lord Mayor! Just like I'll gut both of you!"

The last Gage saw of the woman was her dodging under a wide slash while she thrust her sword up under the first guard's helmet.

"Where can we go?" Robin asked as Knife led them down another side alley. They all ducked behind a stack of crates as two more guards rushed toward the source of the alarm.

"The undead are everywhere," Gage said. Not only could they all see gaping holes in the ground where corpses had dug their way to the surface, but Gage *felt* their presence. Power emanated from Harvester in waves, more than before. He felt the husks spreading out, encircling the city, and something much larger approaching.

Knife stopped them at the end of the alley opening up to the merchant quarter that was the site of a huge battle between the city guards, the invading undead, and frenzied looters who were trying to rob the merchant carts that were abandoned in the chaos.

"Something doesn't want you to leave this city," Desmond said, drawing all their eyes to Gage. "We have to go back to Raventhal."

"Raventhal?!" Gage moved toward him, speaking low so the others wouldn't hear him over the fighting in the streets. "I destroyed the gate."

Desmond gave him the faintest hint of a smile. "There are more gates."

Ransil rolled away from a huge half-orc zombie. It had several of the halfling's knives buried in what remained of its rotting flesh, but it was unbothered by them, still lumbering after its prey. A shambling dwarf corpse in scraps of noble attire followed close behind.

The paladins were busy defending the bridge, leaving Ransil, Avrim, and Deina to fight their way toward the merchant quarter where they were told most of the guards had convened.

"Back to the tomb with ye!" Deina bellowed, burying an axe into the undead dwarf's skull. It collapsed, pulling the weapon from Deina's hand. She growled as a taller decaying invader fell atop her.

"No!" A flash of blinding light followed Avrim's cry and Ransil turned in time to see whatever was attacking Deina had turned to a cloud of ash. The halfling spared the priest a quick glance and was startled to see Avrim's eyes had turned into two narrowed suns—the man looked like divine judgment made flesh.

"We have to go." Terror punctuated each of Quinn's words. "Look." He motioned toward Raventhal looming over the madness of the merchant quarter. Ransil could see roots crawling up its squat towers, pulling winged statues down. Bright blue blasts of arcane fire burned some of the roots away, but more came from below, just like the undead.

The boy looked back at Ransil. "I have to save my spells to help defend the tower, but we have to go through the market—it's the fastest way. Can you get me through?"

Behind him, Ransil heard the undead half-orc lunging only to collapse as Deina let out a triumphant grunt. The halfling flung one of his few remaining knives at another zombie lurching out of the ruined road behind Quinn as Deina stepped toward the mage.

"If them roots mean the bitch that killed Melaine is at your tower, I'll get ye there."

"We all will," Avrim added, his eyes still aflame.

"Not you."

Ransil turned to see the First Paladin remove his gleaming blue helm, his sword black with foul blood. Darrance stepped toward Avrim, motioning to Sathler Bridge behind him.

"The nobles are watching across the way." Darrance had to shout over the distant fighting, but spoke as if only Avrim could hear. "They need to see you—their new beacon—holding the bridge against this unholy assault." Bathed in the light from Avrim's eyes, Ransil could see desperate fear on Darrance's face.

The confrontation was interrupted by a massive root bursting up from the cobbled road, showering both men in dirt and stone. Ransil recoiled and heard Quinn shout something, his voice lost to the sound of hurried footsteps. The boy had made a break for Raventhal alone.

Ransil saw Avrim's bodyguard charge after the boy, abandoning the priest. *Grief has claimed her,* he thought, never having known a dwarf who would forsake such a debt. Regardless, he rolled to his feet and followed. He cast a brief glance over his shoulder to see Avrim swing his mace, creating an arch of bladed light that cleaved through the massive plant.

That man is possessed, Ransil thought, feeling a strange mix of dread and hope at the thought of Avrim possibly following them to Raventhal. As he glanced above Sathford's rooftops at the roots ensnaring the spire, Ransil knew that they would need the help of whatever possessed Avrim Kaust.

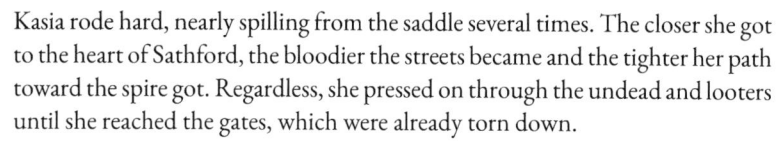

Kasia rode hard, nearly spilling from the saddle several times. The closer she got to the heart of Sathford, the bloodier the streets became and the tighter her path toward the spire got. Regardless, she pressed on through the undead and looters until she reached the gates, which were already torn down.

Too late, she thought, the wound in her back—despite being healed—ached as her horse leapt over the broken gates and landed roughly. Kasia ignored the pain and dismounted, letting her horse flee from the terror that spilled from the spire's entrance. She drew her sword and activated her armor, knowing it would do little good against the invaders.

But if she was lucky, the incarnate would be somewhere inside. As if in response to her thoughts, more magic exploded in the sky. The lack of reaction from her enchantments told her that the Raventhal mages—whoever survived—were the source. The battle was not lost yet.

There were bodies of several initiates on the stairs, torn apart and partially eaten by the ravenous dead that seemed to be pulled toward the academy. Kasia kicked their mutilated bodies clear of her path and moved into the main vestibule. Crossing the threshold, she felt no connection between her Oathmail and the glyphs that were supposed to protect the spire.

Damn you, Dolly! The halfling's smirking face flashed in Kasia's mind, and she felt the cruel dagger again. *I could have stopped the incarnate back in Oakworth if it wasn't for your pathetic meddling.* Raventhal's wards would take years to restore, but she couldn't worry about that now. She pressed on through a cloud of smoke.

Inside, the foyer was partially barricaded by a flight of stairs that had been knocked down. Several pairs of undead arms reached for the Oather from underneath the ruins. Kasia made quick work of ending their struggle, her sword plunging between the fallen stones.

A few small fires burned where braziers had been knocked over, burning the few carpets that adorned Raventhal's cold stone floors. Through the smoke, she could see several shapes in the distance—mages, their robes ornate.

"Name yourself, trespasser."

Kasia lowered her sword as the big man emerged from the smoke, his hands clenched in two volcanic fists of burning magic. "It's me, Hoon. Strallow."

High Mage Konrath released the energy, but his fists remained clenched. He wore a sleeveless robe, exposing arms corded with tightened muscles. Behind him, his elven gatekeeper held a long staff tipped with a large red keyshard.

Konrath stepped past the Oather to observe the courtyard. "What are you doing here, Kasia?" He turned back toward her. "I thought you were in Blakehurst."

"Thought you might be glad to see me." She motioned to the ruined foyer. "There hasn't been an Oather here since that one you killed."

"Not now," Audreese said. "You can help the initiates upstairs, Dame Strallow. They are holding off those roots, but we need to stay down here to watch the gates."

"The gates?"

Konrath joined them. "Whatever is causing this, it's coming from the Old Ways. Since that Xe'danni witch was appointed Archmage, the gates have been closing, but something is still using them somehow."

Kasia turned toward the stairs. "The incarnate. I saw it in Oakworth. It'll be coming soon."

As if in response, the entire tower shook, knocking Kasia and the mages to the ground. The stone floor split and more roots burst up, each one carrying several moaning corpses. Thundering footsteps shook the still quaking spire.

From the ground, Kasia could feel immense power through her Oathmail; it was beyond anything she could possibly contain. Struggling to her feet, she beheld Mawsurath up close.

The monster Kasia had seen under Oakworth paled in comparison to what the incarnate had evolved into. The elf carried within the treeman's chest was burned and furious, her eyes glowing with mystical green energy. Mawsurath itself was reinforced with additional layers of its wooden armor, knotted over with writhing vines and branches. It filled the foyer as it fully emerged from below.

"Fallon!"

The elf inside the incarnate turned to High Mage Hoon, but—despite the familiarity in Konrath's eyes—it was not him who called to her. Kasia turned and saw several figures now standing in the entryway, still managing to be shocked despite the circumstances.

The queen's mage, Desmond Everton, stood covered in gruesome scars. The man had always seemed like a ghoul to Kasia, but now he certainly looked the part. Beside him was an even stranger figure. Knife looked out of place standing there in plain view, a short, curved blade in each hand. A young half-elf—likely one of her recruits—stood behind the woman.

But it was the final figure who managed to hold Kasia's attention despite the incarnate standing before her. The axe that figure held radiated a power that Kasia never felt possible.

Like fractured whispers finally forming words she could hear, the Oather felt the presence of a Key of Transience.

"You want this place pulled down as much as I do," the incarnate growled at Desmond, a voice echoing from the earth itself. "Just like the Luminaura, it only exists to control."

"Don't listen to Ruke," Desmond said, cautiously stepping closer, raising his hands to stay the mages who had begun to prepare their spells behind Mawsurath. "She tried to deceive me as well, telling me that I must die to prevent his coming, but it is *him* using us...manipulating us with Ruke's voice."

He pulled at his robes, shrugging out of them to reveal his milky, ruined body. He stood before the incarnate, naked but for a filthy rag around his waist. The scars that riddled his body made even Kasia's stomach heave, and she had witnessed some of the worst violence the world offered.

"This is what Stane does, Fallon," Desmond continued, motioning to his body. "I was given power...*for me and for me alone*, she said...to make me his scion."

Kasia felt the rumbling ground steady itself then, the creaking vines growing still as the elf inside the incarnate watched Desmond warily. The Oather loosened the grip on her sword, waiting for an opening.

Desmond motioned behind him to the Eastlund boy with the axe. "He can destroy you with one swing of that axe, Fallon—Mawsurath is doomed, no matter what you do. Do not help Stane usher in his next scion." He hung his head, speaking to the gaping chasm that was the foyer floor. "I would not wish that fate on anyone."

Silence fell over the strange gathering, and the fighting outside was punctuated by groaning roots that still gripped the outside of the spire. Kasia shifted on the balls of her feet, careful not to let any creak of her armor give her away.

"Desmond..."

The voice no longer echoed from below, and Kasia knew this was the only moment she had. She launched herself toward the incarnate, her blade poised to pierce the druid's exposed neck. But before she took her third step forward, something heavy smashed against her, slamming her to the wall and knocking her unconscious.

The tower shook, knocking Gage to a knee. He felt Robin let go of his shoulder as a piece of the entryway fell, crashing between them. The incarnate bellowed its challenge in response to the Oather's attack, but it was drowned out by the voice in Gage's head.

"You must kill it, Gage!"

It was Ruke—or Stane, speaking with Ruke's voice, if Desmond was right—her face appearing in his mind. Something about the way she looked at him made him doubtful of Desmond's warnings.

"It has to be you. You hold the Key, and only a Key can seal it away and free me!"

The last part was what strengthened Gage's resolve. There was always a selfish need at the core of any request, even when it came to ancient prophecies and powers he didn't understand. The old halfling was stuck, and she needed him to help her out of it.

The Shadow wanted Gage to kill Anika. Desmond wanted Gage to help him die. Ruke wanted Gage to free her from the stone. Stane wanted Gage to play some game that no one in history had truly figured out.

None of them cared what Gage wanted. He watched Robin climb over the debris separating them. It felt like everything was trying to keep them apart.

Gage got to his feet, holding Harvester. He saw the battle within Raventhal as if it were happening in a sluggish dream, each moment drawn out so he could observe it all carefully.

The incarnate was roaring like some caged beast, Fallon's eyes possessed by powers as old as the world itself. Behind her, a muscled mage with long, silver-streaked hair conjured fire, while an elven mage near him spun a fiery staff at a dryad emerging from the broken floor.

Desmond remained where he was, unbothered by the turn of events, but Gage could feel Shadow magic gathering around the man. It looked as if he were about to attack the woman he had called friend, the woman he had just tried to reason with. Gage tightened his grip on Harvester, feeling connected to the energy Desmond channeled.

What do you really want? Gage asked Desmond through the Shadow. He had followed Desmond on the promise of understanding his purpose, but Gage felt even more lost than when they first met.

As the mages behind Mawsurath unleashed their magic, bathing the incarnate in arcane fire, Gage could feel a sudden wave of sorrow from Desmond.

Redemption, Desmond said, as he unleashed his gathered Shadow magic. Black tendrils emerged from the dark recesses of the foyer, grasping the two mages defending their tower and pulling them into the depths. Time resumed its normal flow, and the burning incarnate slammed its fists down, destroying the floor and dropping them all into the undercroft below.

"Quinn, wait!"

Ransil struggled to keep up with the boy, the cramp in his side reminding him to eat less breakfast the next time he stumbled into a siege. Deina struggled for breath behind him, clearly not enjoying the chase any more than the halfling.

The main Raventhal tower ahead seemed ready to collapse, the roots that climbed up its exterior withstanding the magical assault from above as they crept higher toward the parapets where robed figures could be seen hurling their spells. Quinn rushed heedlessly toward the entrance, dodging the slow zombies that continued to climb up from below.

A sudden gust of wind nearly knocked Ransil over, but Deina braced herself behind him.

"Watch yerself!"

Ransil didn't have time to worry about the wind as several familiar figures leapt up from one of the many chasms in the floor. These dryads may have been different from the ones Ransil had encountered outside of Oakworth, but they glared at him with the same furious, emerald eyes. And the same primal, wrathful voice pierced his thoughts.

"This is Mawsurath's domain now! Die for the Blooming One's chosen!"

Ransil didn't have time to react as roots burst up from behind him, grappling him and Deina as the dryads advanced. He just gritted his teeth and closed his eyes as one of the dryads raised its bladed arm to end the halfling's life.

Then the wind returned, this time stronger. As if the cool gust was poisonous to the roots, they loosened and hissed like dying snakes, releasing Ransil and Deina, who were both forced into a forward roll from the strength of the wind. Landing roughly on his arm, Ransil could barely open his eyes due to the pain. But through the cyclone, he could see a figure descending.

"Anika!"

The dryads hissed and surged forward against the strong currents of air, but Anika, dressed in what looked like a Karranese gown, stepped heedlessly toward them. A blue disk spun in Anika's raised palm, and with a flick of her wrist it flew toward the charging foes. Each of the dryads were decapitated in a spray of dark green blood, and the blue disk came flying back toward Anika, who caught it. Ransil could now see it was the knife she had forged in the baron's keep—the weapon that slew Corvanna.

"Are you alright, Ransil?"

He realized he was staring, and he blinked away the settling dust as he got to his feet. "Am *I* alright?! I was worried you might have—I mean...where have you been, Anika?"

Something passed over her face then, and she swayed on her feet, dropping to a knee. Deina rushed over to steady her. "Careful, lass. I reckon you're spent after that display."

"No," Anika said weakly, looking toward Ransil. "Gage is here, I saw him."

Ransil looked across Raventhal's courtyard, seeing nothing except the undead closing in. He could hear creaking from the gaping crevice below, and he knew more dryads were coming. "Where?"

"It's hard to explain." She got back to her feet.

"Explain later," Deina grunted. "That boy wizard just scampered into that tower...which looks ready to collapse."

Ransil looked at Anika, ready to tell her to wait here, but she was already moving toward the tower.

"Gage is in there. Robin, too?"

Robin?! Ransil forgot about the pain and broke into a sprint for the door, Anika and Deina following closely. But before they could make it to the entryway's stairs, nearly a dozen figures emerged from the broken floor within. Undead wizards, freshly wrapped in corrupted roots.

"I can't..." Anika began, breathless. "The incarnate's below."

Ransil spun his knives, as Deina charged forward, unsure they could handle that many by themselves. His dread was short-lived, as a pillar of blinding light turned the figures into clouds of ash. Ransil turned to see Avrim at the courtyard entrance, an army of undead behind him. The priest was covered in dark blood and his eyes were still two radiant orbs.

"Go! I'll hold them off!"

Ransil didn't argue, turning to join Anika and Deina on their hasty descent into the crumbling tower.

"Robin!" Gage's left arm felt broken from the fall, but his right still held Harvester, and the power that came from it dulled the pain. "Where are you?"

He could hear the incarnate digging itself out of the rubble, and Desmond groaned nearby, looking bruised but otherwise unharmed.

"Robin!"

"I'm here."

Gage looked up and saw the half-elf helping Knife dislodge herself from a tangle of roots. On the broken floor nearby, he saw the elven mage laying still and the human mage hung impaled on a spiked root, his burning hands dispelled.

Relieved that Robin was alright, Gage turned back toward Fallon, whose eyes had returned to normal.

"You can still hear her," Gage said, limping toward the looming golem, but looking only into the druid's eyes. "Ruke."

Fallon shook her head. "No. Naya. She sent me here to destroy the Light. To avenge my father."

"To do her dirty work," Gage corrected, spitting. "Just like she tried to get me to kill my own mother, and then my sister." He motioned to Desmond who had finally gotten to his feet. "Just like Ruke tried to make him lure my sister into killing him, and then convinced me to trap you in the Old Ways."

He saw Fallon turn toward Desmond and her hard expression slackened. Suddenly, she looked like a lost child.

"They're just using us, Fallon." *No,* the voice in Gage's head pleaded, *this is the only way! You have to believe me.* "Because we have the power, and they don't. But they don't get to decide how we use it; we do."

Fallon lowered her eyes, and Gage knew that she understood him. They were connected through Oakus. He could pacify the incarnate and undo this foolish prophecy that had wrecked his family.

"High Mage Hoon!"

A shrill voice called from above, pulling their attention.

"Quinn!?" Fallon's voice cracked with emotion.

Gage looked up and saw a young boy in tattered yellow robes. He was levitating, his body radiating a glowing aura of blue magic. He stopped in front of the impaled High Mage, looking down on Fallon with an accusatory stare.

"What have you done?!"

Anger flared from Harvester, and Gage looked toward Fallon to see her sad, lost face twist into a furious scowl. "You took my father's stone! I trusted you, and you betrayed me!" Mawsurath stomped, and roots began to emerge from the rubble.

"We need to go."

Knife's voice was barely a whisper, but somehow Gage heard it perfectly as if he were next to her. He whipped his head around and shouted to Robin, "Go! I'll handle this. Then, I'll find you."

Robin made to protest, but Knife nearly shoved him through a gap in the wall.

A familiar voice shouted, "Don't you take him!"

Gage looked up through the gaping hole in the floor above. Ransil Osbury's face peered down, glaring at the masked woman. Gage saw Robin hesitate, but Knife pulled him into the darkness. Ransil flipped down, his hands grasping the edge of the broken floor so he could swing down and fling himself in pursuit.

He shouted, "Protect Quinn, Deina!"

Gage saw the dwarf from Oakworth glare down at him then, her eyes fixed on Harvester. But his own eyes were on the figure who floated down on a gust of intense wind that knocked the boy mage out of the air.

"You!" Fallon's voice was a thunderous growl, causing the spire to shudder once more. "The cowardly Light has sent its child to answer for killing my father!"

No, Gage thought, but the word wouldn't come to his lips. Ruke was screaming in his mind, disorienting him. *The incarnate must die!* Gage shook his head, trying to let go of Harvester. *I can reach her, Ruke! Let me handle this!*

Gage heard Mawsurath let out another roar as he fell back, unable to deal with the voices in his head. Through Harvester, he could sense everything that he couldn't see—Anika descending on the incarnate, Stormender poised to strike, while Robin disappeared into the Old Ways with Knife—the power of Oakus connecting him with Fallon, Desmond, and the breached paths leading to the world below.

Feeling intense, dark power surging through him, coming from the weapon he held, Gage knew what he had to do—but something wouldn't let him. He visualized letting go of the axe—the thing that connected him to all of these competing pressures—but his fingers wouldn't loosen their grip. Time slowed as he thought of Robin again, facing the wretched Old Ways without him, and the dark presence yielded to Gage's own desires finally.

With all of his strength, Gage let go of Harvester. Immediately, he felt the Shadow cleanse him, purging all the other voices from his mind.

Fallon's piercing shriek brought him back to reality. Anika collapsed onto the ruined stones near Gage. Dressed like some princess that had just lost a battle with a dragon, she had never looked more beautiful to Gage, and he was filled with a sudden shame for every ill thought he ever had toward her.

The incarnate fell back, Stormender thrust hilt-deep into Fallon's chest. Beams of emerald light shone from the wound, as if a green sun tried desperately to escape from within the druid's flesh. Mawsurath flailed as the light grew brighter, its bulk of twisting vines withering away slowly. While he watched the incarnate die, Gage heard a familiar voice in his mind.

"You're next," Naya told him. His eyes went to Harvester, laying discarded nearby. It wasn't Stane or Ruke or Oakus toying with him. It was the Shadow that still connected him with the priestess. "She will kill you next. The malice of Light has awoken in her, and it has claimed two incarnates."

The sudden inexplicable fear those words inspired within Gage darkened his mind. Even though he knew the Shadow's presence bloomed within him, he had no means to fight it. He allowed the panic to take hold, and he scrambled to his feet, thinking only of escaping his sister's wrath and finding Robin.

In his haste, he didn't see the diminutive figure emerge from darkness behind the smoldering remains of the incarnate, a faint green light pulsating from one of its eyes.

Ransil had run out of knives, throwing his last one into the eye of a dryad who still chased after him. But he was focused on the two figures scrambling ahead of him, dispatching most of the awaiting foes for him.

"Robin, stop!"

The boy didn't listen, and Ransil was running out of breath to shout. The twisting halls of Raventhal's undercroft were foreign to him, but fortunately, the invaders had made short work of most of the walls. Ransil was gaining on Knife now, his small stature making it easier to navigate the chaotic structure that the spire had become.

Finally, they came to a series of archways—the gateways. Only one remained active, its glyphs still alive with a violet energy; the others were cold stone now. Having heard that the new Archmage was dispelling any passage to the Old Ways, Ransil knew that the portal would lead them to the Arcania itself.

"Wait, please!" Ransil stopped, gasping for breath. He would not catch them before they entered, and his only hope was to try using reason. "You'll die, Robin!"

The half-elf spun around, one step away from entering the portal. He looked to Knife, and then to the halfling. "I'm sorry, Ransil. I need to go home."

Ransil glared at Knife. "You know what they'll do to him! How can you lead your own son to his death?!"

The woman's eyes betrayed no emotion. "The Guild is in debt to you, Osbury. Do not squander that." She removed her mask, still not giving Ransil any clue to her feelings on the matter. "And you have my personal thanks for keeping my son safe."

What was once a suspicion of Ransil's was now confirmed, but he looked back toward Robin. "She's going to get you killed, Robin. You can't believe—"

His next words were lost in a painful choke as he felt cold steel in his back. Looking up over his shoulder he saw Gage with blackened eyes and a cruel smile. Despite the vile shroud that had fallen over that familiar face, Ransil felt something like sorrow staring into the boy's dead eyes.

"I'm sorry, Ransil," Gage said through that wicked smile. "I could have stopped this, but Anika had to get the Light involved."

Ransil fell to his knees as he felt blood pooling within his leather vest, life leaving him slowly. He watched Gage join Robin, taking the half-elf by the hand and stepping through the shimmering portal. Knife waited behind. She put her mask back on and stepped toward Ransil, reaching into her pouch.

"I owe you a debt," she said, placing a vial of pinkish liquid on the stone next to him. "Drink it slow. But pull that dagger out first so the wound can heal. Should keep you breathing until that priest of yours gets here." Before she stepped through the portal, she turned to look at him through those narrow slits in her mask. "Come see me when you're better. I'll keep the boys safe until then." She disappeared through the ensorcelled passage.

Begrudgingly, Ransil grabbed the potion in a clenched fist and watched her disappear into the arcane gate. A moment later, a root burst through the archway, shattering the enchantments and closing the gate forever.

A sudden memory came to him then, of Robin rolling out a fresh dough with him in The Early Mule. He wept alone with one of his own knives in his back.

Chapter Thirty-Two

What Remains

Desmond knelt over the remains of the incarnate of Oakus, which consisted of little more than ash and moldering plants covering Fallon's burned body. The druid took a shallow breath as Desmond placed a shaking hand on her shoulder.

She opened her eyes, the faintest hint of a smile on her bloodied lips.

"I should have listened to you, Desmond."

He shook his head with a long sigh. "We both listened too often to voices other than our own." He looked up, imagining a night so long ago when Fallon had visited his quarters above, before that fateful meeting with Fainly Lopke. "Be thankful, Fallon, that you resisted the Shadow as much as you did."

Fallon coughed weakly, but as it persisted, Desmond realized she was laughing.

"It was the Light," she said. "It was always the Light."

He didn't know what to say, but it didn't matter. Her eyelids fluttered closed as the waning green light from her wound faded.

"Fallon..."

Desmond looked over his shoulder to see the boy mage stepping closer to the druid's body, altogether ignoring the naked scion of Stane that knelt near her. He couldn't help but notice the Arcanian mark—High Mage Konrath Hoon's crystal necklace—dangling from the boy's clenched fist.

Would Konrath truly entrust the spire to a child?!

"Watch yourself, boy," a gruff voice said from behind. "That there's the bastard that killed this girl's mate." The boy didn't seem to hear, sitting down carefully on the rubble next to Fallon's lifeless body.

Desmond stood, spinning slowly around to see an armored dwarf woman holding Harvester in both hands. By her feet, the Child of Light lay unconscious.

"A misunderstanding," Desmond said, secretly hoping that the woman would bury that axe in his skull—maybe that would set him free...he honestly didn't know anymore.

"Ain't it always," the dwarf said through clenched teeth. With Harvester held out in front of her, she looked ready to grant Desmond his unspoken wish. "Yer the scion of Stane, ain't ye? Killed that boy Matty...and..." Her lips quivered slightly. "Got me Melaine killed as well."

"It wasn't him."

They both turned toward the voice, a small, shadowed figure obscured by clouds of smoke from the smoldering remains of Mawsurath. The figure stepped forward, revealing herself to be a halfling woman in simple green robes. One of her eyes twitched as she regarded Desmond sadly.

"It was Stane," Ruke said.

"It was you," Desmond replied without anger, only knowledge. "It was your voice that told me only the Child of Light could set me free."

"Because she can," Ruke replied. "She is the only one who can stop Stane."

Deina spat. "Who are ye, then? The next scion?"

Ruke regarded the dwarf with a sardonic smirk. "The first, actually. Desmond here was the last." She turned back to him. "But the most powerful."

Finally, hatred flared within Desmond, knowing now that this was the being responsible for his fate. He gathered Shadow into his hands, ready to strike.

"You know you can't kill me," Ruke said, her gaze not faltering, despite her twitching eye.

He knew, but he also knew he could cause her excruciating pain. Yet, as the Shadow crept up his limbs, snaking its way into his mind, he could see Gage's face. With blackened eyes, the Child of Shadow urged him to unleash what brewed inside of him. Something about Gage's smile stayed him, and Desmond felt the Shadow recede.

"We have much to discuss," Ruke said, as Desmond's hands went limp, dismissing their summoned power. She stepped over the rubble carefully, nodding toward Anika. "The Child of Light will awaken soon, and it's best we not be here."

"Who says ye can go?" Deina asked. She motioned toward the boy mage who stared vacantly at Fallon's body. "That there's the High Mage now apparently, and you be in his tower."

"We are hunted," Ruke said, not looking up from her feet as she navigated the ruins of the undercroft, "by forces that you will not want descending upon you. Trust me, good dwarf, it is best we depart before the dust settles."

Desmond's eyes fell on Fallon one last time, thinking about the vengeance that she did not live to see.

"There is one thing we must do."

Hope felt the Light fading, her vision starting to blur. She limped down the alley toward the source of the alarms, hoping that the boy was found. Whatever happened to Sathford, she could not return to the Archbeacon without the leverage that the boy provided.

A wave of pain from her side sent her reeling again. Catching herself on the corner of a wall, the warpriest looked down at the huge dryad scythe that had hooked through her stomach, piercing her blue armor. The wound still gushed blood, but she had exhausted any healing the Light had allowed her this day.

Hope could crawl toward Sathler Bridge, where her paladins were. There she would find plenty of healing; that would be the sensible thing to do.

Instead, gritting her teeth, she limped forward, determined to survive long enough to see this through. She had always imagined she would die fighting the scourge of the undead—the first Archbeacon decreed that it was the Light's destiny to rid the world of the poison of undeath. Hope felt satisfaction in that much, but it was anger that drove her—anger that for everything the Luminaura had accomplished, everything hinged on the whims of that pesky elf queen.

"Is that her?"

Such a whimsical voice sounded completely alien to Hope in the throes of madness that had gripped Sathford. She found herself frozen by it, unable to push on. Turning, an even more bizarre sight greeted her.

A naked undead man stood before her, riddled with scars and—those eyes…he wasn't undead at all. But he was easily the most ghoulish man Hope had ever seen.

"She looks dead already."

Hope looked at the speaker, a rather plain halfling woman in vibrant green robes. The woman's eye twitched as she regarded Hope. "I'd say your friend has had her vengeance. Let us go."

"No," the man said, stepping forward. Hope felt her stomach heave, and not because it had been pierced by a heathen's sharpened arm; the man stepping toward her was Shadowfiend. Black tendrils crawled up those sinewy arms, snakes seeking their prey. "I can still feel Fallon's desire…the High Warpriest must suffer…"

Hope did indeed suffer and then died miserably in a filthy alley, alongside the undead wretches she so despised.

Several days later, Anika woke up, her body aching more than it had when she woke up in Karrane, which seemed like forever ago. Her vision was cloudy, as was her memory, but she remembered the last thing she had felt—rescuing Gage from the next incarnate, then collapsing from the insurmountable power that had carried her back to Vale—and she found the strength to turn her head, forcing her eyes to focus on her surroundings.

All she saw was Ransil Osbury looking dead to the world, sprawled on a big chair. The halfling's head hung over the side of the human-sized seat, his mouth hanging open as he snored loudly. There was a huge pot of stew on the floor between them, as well as a stack of books—it looked as if the little man had made a home at her bedside.

"He hasn't left," a voice whispered from the other side of her bed. Anika turned to see an unfamiliar elf woman in dark robes sitting in a chair similar to Ransil's. "You have a true guardian, there. Your other companions are below, helping restore order to the spire, but this one insisted on keeping watch over you. That is loyalty."

As touching as that was, it made Anika feel horrible, knowing that Ransil was probably worried she would disappear again. "I don't deserve such loyalty." She tried to rise, but couldn't even find the strength to roll over.

"You need more time," the elf said. "But you will be safe here. The priest you travel with is to be the beacon of the new cathedral, and the boy Ransil saved is our new High Mage here at Raventhal. With such allies, you will have the time and protection needed to recover."

The elf stood up, pacing over to a nearby window to open the curtain, letting sunlight in. "I have a feeling there will be need of you soon, so we need to ensure you are fully recovered."

Anika tried to take comfort in that, but she still felt a gaping hole within herself. She had foolishly fled to Karrane to find her family, only to realize she had abandoned her true family. While in Pyram, she had thought that hole could be filled by the Key—Stormender—but it only covered the hole, shielding her from the emptiness.

That hollow place was where her family belonged.

"Where is my brother?"

The elf returned to her bedside. "He fled through the gates. Your friend, Ransil, tried to stop him, but nearly died. I believe he is in Andelor with the Guild, but the Archmage is not answering our communications with the Arcania. Once the tower is restored, we will send an envoy—perhaps I will go personally."

"And who are you?"

"Audreese," the elf said. "I was once the Gatemaster here at Raventhal Spire, but now that the Old Ways have been sealed, it seems I must find a new way to serve."

Feeling exhausted, Anika relaxed back on the soft pillow, looking up into the dark recesses of the room's high ceiling. She thought of all the books she read in Pyram's archives, about her purpose. *A new way to serve.* The words continued echoing in her mind as she began to let weariness take her.

"Perhaps," Anika said, looking back toward Ransil, thinking of how she had failed him, "you can teach me."

"Teach you? You're the Child of Light, Anika. What could I teach you?"

She looked back toward Audreese. "You can teach me how to be the Child of Light."

Audreese stared out the window, considering that. "I will do what I can."

Anika closed her eyes. "That's all any of us can do."

She fell into a calm, empty sleep. In the absence of dreams, she heard Stane's voice.

"When you are ready, Anika, you will know how to repay me for the gifts I have given you." His soft laughter drew her deeper into a welcoming oblivion.

"Your father will be so proud..."

EPILOGUE

THE KINDLED ONE

The mines that ran under New Hold were still young, especially to the dwarves, who were known to dig deeper than they should; it was in their blood. A young mine was a promise of gold or precious jewels—possibly even keyshards—awaiting for a bold miner to unearth them.

Zakrin was that miner; he just knew it.

Wiping the sweat from his brow, he looked back at his crew. Nebby still threw her pickaxe as if it were weightless, a smile on her grimy face, while the brothers, Aerik and Jarn, alternated their own picks on the same boulder, forming a massive crack along its face.

It was all music to Zakrin's ears.

"Water," he called, tossing his own pickaxe aside so he could make his way back to their packs. He ran his calloused fingers through his massive beard, feeling rough pieces of earth throughout the coarse hairs. The hammering didn't stop. "Now! I won't have ye dying on me before we can reach another vein."

The brothers stopped their work, but Nebby's—*crack*—steady strikes—*crack*—persisted. *Women*, he thought amusingly, *wear themselves out in the mines, but can't be bothered to do so in me bed.*

"We headin' back soon?" Aerik was one of the few bald dwarves in New Hold, a result of a lost bet. A bald head in dwarven society could either mark you as foolish or bold; Aerik was both. "I don't mean to return empty-handed again."

Crack. Crack. Crack. Nebby's work continued.

"Eh," Jarn spat, his own hair fiery red and down to his prominent waist. "This ain't Farhelm, brother. Most we could hope for this far south is some iron. Suppose we might find a few gems, if we be lucky."

Zakrin took a long pull on his waterskin, refusing to get into it again with Jarn. The man was as pessimistic as a halfling in a cookpot, and Zakrin would not bicker with him again about the potential the Founders saw in Vale. Zakrin believed positive outcomes required positive thinking, and he saw the groaning that Jarn was prone to as a useless trait.

"Regardless, we dig," Zakrin said. It brooked no argument between the brothers, who just drank their water in silence—except for Nebby's *crack, crack, crack.*

Aerik seemed concerned, staring at his own waterskin rather than drinking it, his eyes growing distant.

"You still nervous?" Zakrin asked him between gulps of water, each of their heavy breathing now slowing. "Worried the Cleavers won't approve of our operation?"

Aerik didn't look up, but snapped out of his gaze and took a drink before answering. "To the Abyss with the Cleavers. The baron owns them—well, did, before he up and died."

It was true. Baron Caffery had made a deal with the most prominent family of miners in New Hold, through their matriarch, Dureen Cleaver. In turn, most of the tunnels had been turned over to their joint operation. Currently, Zakrin's crew were defying the Founders' Accords by mining without the proper permits.

Zakrin nodded. "With Caffery dead, and those damn cultists prowling about, now's the time to strike." As the youngest son to one of the most lowly families in New Hold, Zakrin was determined to use the opportunity all this recent chaos had provided. "We find a vein here, connect it from one of your uncle's mines and claim it as his, and that'll open the floodgates."

Crack. Crack. Crack.

Both brothers nodded in agreement, tossing back their heads to gulp down the rest of their water.

They were gathering up their tools as they finished their drinks when Nebby's hammering ceased, the final *crack* followed by the sound of metal clattering uselessly onto stone. The three dwarves made their way back into the tunnel.

Zakrin was first around the final turn in the passage, seeing Nebby standing with her back to them, her shoulders slumped. They couldn't see around her, but Zakrin found that he couldn't move. Fear, or something akin to it, kept him in place.

"Nebby?"

The woman didn't respond. Zakrin cautiously stepped forward to peer around her, and gasped at what he saw.

There was a gaping hole where Nebby had been digging, as if a chunk of the earth had just fallen away to reveal a chamber beyond. Within that chamber, Zakrin saw a soft red glow coming off a chunk of rock. The source of the glow was what made him gasp—dozens, no it must be hundreds of fiery red keyshards were embedded in a charred stone which was much bigger than him; and he was big for a dwarf.

"Myretha's child," Aerik said in reverence. "What is it?"

Zakrin couldn't help but smile like a boy about to stoke his first forge. "That's our fortune, friends."

"No."

The voice echoed from behind them, and Zakrin spun to face their foe, tearing the axe off his back. But the tunnel behind them was empty, the soft red glow from their discovery transforming it into a fiery underworld.

"That is your doom, friends."

Nebby was the first to scream as the precious treasure they uncovered released a wave of fire hotter than any forge imaginable. The inferno wrapped around the dwarves and slithered its way down their hidden tunnel, consuming Zakrin and his crew in a fiery, painful death.

The Combustress waited for the heat to die down. Even though she knew it wouldn't harm her or her followers, she respected Wick too much to intrude on his holy work. As wonderful smoke enveloped her, she breathed deep, lowering her crimson hood to reveal a bald head wrapped in burn scars.

"How did you know, Combustress?"

She smiled, looking down to the young half-orc girl in tattered red robes. "I didn't, young kindler. Wick did. I just listen to him."

The girl seemed more confused by the answer, but as the other cultists knelt down, raising their burnt hands toward their master, she bowed her head and joined them.

The cultists began to cough as the smoke from Wick's altar choked them, filling them with noxious fumes. But the Combustress breathed deep, the keyshard around her neck glowing a furious red as it allowed her to consume Wick's offering.

Once the coughing stopped, the old man who claimed to be Branton Pembrook's heir rose, lowering his hood to reveal a mane of gray hair. "Shall we loosen the keyshards now?"

The Combustress regarded the altar, knowing it wasn't time—she had not yet figured out how to control it. "No. Bury it and collapse these tunnels. Do not let anyone find it." She turned to a dwarf cultist who had also lowered her hood. "You did well to alert us of this, Dureen."

The woman nodded, looking at the smoldering dwarf corpses. "Clan Cleaver serves the Cult of the Combustress. Forever." She bent over to grab a handful of ashes, rubbing them through her thick auburn hair. "May the Kindled One know who serve him before his flames ignite the world."

"Before his flames ignite the world," the rest of the cultists chanted as they began their work of sealing the altar.

The Combustress felt something then, the slightest of pulls. Before the rocks were stacked high enough to hide the altar from her view, she swore she felt something pulling her west toward the Wane Coast. She had felt the pull of keyshards before, but this was something more. This felt...

Godlike.

About the Author

Brady J. Sadler is a drummer, board game designer, and occasional author. He lives in Indiana with his wife, two children, and usually one too many cats. In addition to working on books in The Malice of Light series, he is still tinkering with tabletop games, both playing and designing.
You can keep up with him at www.bradyjsadler.com.

Made in the USA
Columbia, SC
26 June 2024

3daee231-f99e-44c3-9c9c-fe1bf48c7a07R01